Praise for Karen Whiddon

"Original and exciting, the constant tension—
both dangerous and sexual—
will keep readers on the edge of their seats."
—*RT Book Reviews* on *The Wolf Prince*

"*The Lost Wolf's Destiny* is action-packed
with a lot of twists and turns that lead
the reader on an amazing ride."
—*Fresh Fiction*

"I would recommend *The Wolf Whisperer* for
anyone who is looking for a fast, fun read about
werewolves. The story is well written
and absorbing."
—*Goodreads*

Praise for Bonnie Vanak

"*Phantom Wolf* is constantly entertaining and
remarkably fascinating."
—*CataRomance Reviews*

"*Phantom Wolf* starts with a blast and keeps
exploding throughout the book."
—*Fresh Fiction*

"The tale's constant action is a perfect foil for
the sexual tension between Matt and Sienna.
Vanak's descriptions sparkle—as do her
colorful descriptions of the evil forces
chasing the couple."
—*RT Book Reviews* on *The Covert Wolf*

KAREN WHIDDON

started weaving fanciful tales for her younger brothers at the age of eleven. Amid the Catskill Mountains of New York, then the Rocky Mountains of Colorado, she fueled her imagination with the natural beauty that surrounded her. Karen now lives in north Texas, where she shares her life with her very own hero of a husband and three doting dogs. Also an entrepreneur, she divides her time between the business she started and writing. You can email Karen at kwhiddon1@aol.com or write to her at P.O. Box 820807, Fort Worth, TX 76182. Fans of her writing can also check out her website, www.karenwhiddon.com.

KAREN WHIDDON
AND
BONNIE VANAK

The Wolf Siren

and

Demon Wolf

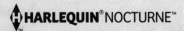
HARLEQUIN® NOCTURNE™

Recycling programs
for this product may
not exist in your area.

ISBN-13: 978-0-373-60637-5

THE WOLF SIREN AND DEMON WOLF

Copyright © 2014 by Harlequin Books S.A.

The publisher acknowledges the copyright holders
of the individual works as follows:

THE WOLF SIREN
Copyright © 2014 by Karen Whiddon

DEMON WOLF
Copyright © 2014 by Bonnie Vanak

Printed in U.S.A.

HARLEQUIN®
™ www.Harlequin.com

CONTENTS

THE WOLF SIREN

Karen Whiddon

To Patricia Ann Corcoran, 5-2-35 to 9-27-13.

You were many things in the 78 years you lived in this world, but to me you were first and foremost my mother. I will always miss you.

Chapter 1

"You look…" The tall, dark-haired man stared, his silver gaze intense. "A thousand times better than the last time I saw you."

Clutching the door handle and peering out through the six-inch crack, Lilly Gideon tried hard not to tremble. Belatedly, she realized she never should have opened the door. But then, she hadn't known this man had been coming up the sidewalk.

Or had she? Something, some inner restlessness, had given her the urge to step out onto the front porch. Surely, she hadn't been going to meet this stranger who talked as if he knew her. He had a confident air of masculine authority and the sheer strength of his muscular body overwhelmed her.

She struggled to speak, to summon up some sort of relatively normal response. She was safe, she told herself over and over like a mantra, ignoring the shiver of dread working its way up her spine. Finally safe. Her brother, Lucas, his wife, Blythe, and her daughter, Hailey, were in the kitchen and would come running at the slightest sound. All she had to do was call. But staring at the handsome stranger, still she couldn't seem to force words past her closed-up throat.

"Lilly?" he asked, the deep dustiness of his voice striking a chord inside her, as if her soul recognized him. "It's me, Kane McGraw. Don't you remember me?"

Pushing away the panic, she struggled to simply breathe. The chiseled planes of his rugged face did seem achingly familiar, but with her tangled confusion of memories, she didn't know if this was a good thing or bad. He wore his dark hair short, spiky, a bit longer than military style, which added to his self-confident appearance. Once again, she found him intimidating.

Despite her best effort to appear brave, she let her hand creep up to her throat and dredged up words. "I... no. I don't remember you."

Her twin brother, Lucas, must have had a second sense, too. Something that told him she needed him right now. "Lilly?" he called, appearing in the arched opening that led to the foyer. "Are you all right?"

Relief flooding her, she turned her panicked gaze toward him, imploring silently for help.

"What's wrong?" Lucas strode toward her, putting himself in front of her even as he yanked the door all the way open.

"Kane?" Despite hearing the joy in her brother's voice, Lilly stepped back, taking refuge in the small space between the door and the wall. She hated the way terror still consumed her, but for now she didn't yet have the strength to overcome it. Maybe someday, but not just yet. She only hoped that with time...

"Lucas!" The two men gave each other the quick shoulder hug used by men.

"That was fast," Lucas said, the sun making his brown hair appear blond. He glanced at Lilly, and then back at their visitor, grinning. Lilly envied her brother's carefree attitude. Newly married and in love, his clear blue eyes radiated happiness. She kept hoping some of it would rub off on her. So far, she hadn't been so blessed.

Kane laughed, a throaty chuckle, drawing her attention. "As soon as you told me what you needed, I dropped everything. My vacation days were piling up unused anyway. I think the Society of Pack Protectors was shocked that I wanted to take them."

Though the deep rumble of this stranger's voice chased away the chill inside her, she kept herself utterly still, hoping she wouldn't draw any attention to herself. Of course, her brother noticed immediately.

"Lilly?" Lucas held out his hand, waiting until she'd slipped her fingers into his before continuing. "Don't you remember Kane? He helped us rescue you."

The reassuring sincerity in Lucas's expression calmed her enough to enable her to look at the other man. "I'm sorry," she murmured. "My memories from that time are all blurry."

Kane's smoky gaze held hers. "That's understandable. You've been through a lot."

She nodded, although fifteen years of torture, clinging to the edge of life, had been more than a lot. She was damaged, broken in more ways than one. Though she was eager to purge that time from her memory and heal herself so she could stride with confidence into the world, first she had to shake the paralyzing terror that dogged her every move.

Before she could run, she needed to walk. Before she could walk, she'd have to manage a crawl.

"Come on in," Lucas said, pulling Lilly toward him so he could fully open the door. She yanked her hand free, fighting the awful tide of panic rising in her throat. Though she wanted to flee, to tear down the hall toward her room, where she could close herself in and feel safe, she kept herself still, legs rooted in the carpet. She hated her fear and used this to find the strength to stand her ground. Her hands were clenched into fists, but despite that, she managed to lift her head and study Lucas's friend.

"Welcome," she said, trying to remember how to sound warm.

At her greeting, he smiled. Not just any smile, but a devastating curve of the mouth that heated her and inexplicably sent her pulse racing. Before, she'd thought him good-looking, in a muscular, dangerous sort of way. But now, feeling the pull of his grin, she realized he was more than that. He was beautiful, like a dark angel who'd recently tumbled from heaven.

She shivered. She'd had enough of angels and prophets, thank you very much.

"Blythe will be happy to see you." Lucas strode toward the kitchen, calling his wife's name as he went. Blythe met him halfway, her long blond hair pulled into a neat braid. As she moved toward them, she appeared to dance on her bare feet. Her bright green eyes lit up when she saw Kane.

Lilly watched, as detached as if she were separated from the others by a thick sheet of glass. Blythe, hugged Kane as if he was a long-lost brother, then her daughter, Hailey, squealed with delight as she threw herself at the tall man's legs.

Once the greetings and hugs were finished and things quieted down, Lucas led the way into the kitchen. He waited until everyone else had disappeared inside before returning to retrieve Lilly, who still stood frozen, unable to make herself move.

"Are you coming?" he asked, the concern in his voice making her feel guilty.

Rather than answer, she shook her head, sending her long hair whipping around her. Wrapping her arms around herself, even though the movement gave her no comfort, she swallowed. "I'm not feeling well," she told him. "I'm going to go lie down."

His expression sharpened, letting her know he didn't entirely buy the lie. But then, as she'd known he would, he nodded. "I'll bring you something to eat later then, okay?"

Angry—both at herself for lacking the courage to join them and, unreasonably, at him for cutting her so much slack—she nodded. Then, without another word, she spun on her heel and marched away to her room.

Once there, she didn't dissolve into tears and throw herself on her bed. She supposed that would have been progress, at least. Instead, she went to the small desk she'd placed in front of the window, and took a seat, gazing outside and marveling once again at how green everything was here. As she'd learned to do while trapped in a dank, basement cell, she let her mind separate from her body. She wondered if she'd ever stop wanting to curl up and die.

Following Lucas and Blythe into the kitchen, Kane fought the urge to turn back and go after Lilly. His wolf had once again reared his wild head the instant he'd inhaled Lilly's fragile and feminine scent. On the long drive from Texas to Seattle, he'd thought about this reaction, which had stunned him the first time he'd seen her, half-dead in a concrete cell. Then, he'd wondered if it had been a fluke. Now he knew it hadn't. The question was, what was he going to do about it?

Though she no longer looked like a broken rag-doll, Lilly was still clearly damaged. Kane would have to be careful, especially since he'd just agreed to act as her full-time bodyguard.

"Does she know why I'm here?" Kane asked, taking a seat at the oak-planked, country-style table and accepting the beer Blythe brought him.

"Just a minute." Lucas cast a warning look at Hailey, which Blythe picked up on.

"Hailey, why don't we watch one of your DVDs," Blythe said, taking her daughter's hand and leading her from the kitchen.

Kane sipped on his beer. Lucas waited until the sound of the television came on before speaking. "No. Despite therapy once a week, she spends most of her time in a state close to terrified anxiety. I thought it better if she didn't know." He got up, crossed to the fridge and snagged his own beer.

"About any of it?"

Lucas's troubled expression gave Kane his answer. "I've been trying to shield her as best I can. She isn't aware of the break-in attempt. I had Blythe and Hailey take her out for ice cream when the police came to make their report."

"And you're confident they weren't after Hailey?"

"Yes." Lucas clenched his jaw. "They broke in through Lilly's window. This might have been a coincidence, except they never left her room. They tore it apart like they were looking for something."

"You also said someone tried to abduct her?"

"Yes. Someone tried to grab her when she and Blythe were leaving therapy, but Blythe pretty much convinced her that the guy was trying to rob them."

"How sure are you that he wasn't?"

Dragging his hand across his chin, Lucas nodded. "First off, he didn't try and get their purses. Second, he left Blythe alone. The SOB went right for Lilly."

Kane nodded. Both he and Lucas had dealt with the crazy cult members who'd belonged to Sanctuary, Jacob Gideon's pseudo-religious organization. They'd worked together, along with The Society of Pack Protectors, to take them down. In the process, they'd not only rescued Blythe and her daughter, Hailey, but they'd saved Lilly, Lucas's sister, whom he'd believed had been murdered fifteen years earlier.

"Most of the cultists are locked up," Kane mused. "Though we've been made aware of a few others who weren't there the day the raid went down."

"You know how determined those bastards are." Lucas didn't bother to hide his bitterness. "My sister suffered for years because of them."

"I think I should take her out of here," Kane said. "And quickly."

Lucas stared at him in shock. Of course, Kane had known getting Lucas to accept his plan wasn't going to be easy.

"Hear me out."

After a moment, Lucas finally nodded. His guarded expression made it clear he wasn't happy with the idea. "Go on."

"You want me to keep her safe." Kane leaned forward. "I can do that. I'm good at my job. But…"

The word hung in the air. Lucas took a long drink of his beer, waiting for his friend to finish the statement.

"She needs to go into hiding."

"You really think you can protect her better away from here?" The low pitch of Lucas's voice told Kane he recognized the truth, whether or not he liked it.

"Don't you?"

Grimacing, Lucas gave a reluctant nod. "Where are you planning to take her?"

"I think it's actually better if you don't know."

"Then she's not going anywhere." Lucas's emphatic answer came without hesitation. "I lost her once before. I won't do so again."

This Kane could understand. He nodded. "Fine. I want to take her to my hometown. Leaning Tree, New York."

From Lucas's frown, it was clear he'd never heard of it. This was one of the reasons Kane had chosen the small town. "Is it Pack?"

"Mostly. It's pretty remote, tucked away in the rolling Catskill Mountains. My entire family lives there—parents, siblings, aunts and uncles, cousins." He shrugged. "I haven't been home in a few years. My parents own a resort—actually, it's an old-fashioned motor court. With separate cabins. They're pretty secluded and there's only one road in and out. I'm thinking Lilly and I will stay there."

Lucas narrowed his eyes. "You've got this all planned out, don't you?"

"Yes." Kane smiled and then rolled his shoulders, trying to release some of the knots he'd incurred on the long drive northwest. "I'm damn good at what I do. That's why you called me, isn't it?"

Instead of answering, Lucas pushed to his feet. He strode to the doorway and peered out into the den, his expression softening noticeably. "Blythe, could you come here for a minute? I need to get your opinion."

Instantly, Blythe appeared, sweeping her silky, brownish-blond hair away from her face.

"Kane wants to take Lilly away," Lucas said. "He feels he can keep her safer if he does."

Blythe's bright green gaze locked on her husband's as they linked hands. She and Lucas appeared to communicate silently. Watching them, Kane pushed away a sharp stab of envy. Not everyone in the Pack was fortunate enough to find their mate like their wild cousins. Human Shape-shifters only mated once. Kane had been privileged to be present when Lucas and Blythe had realized they were meant for each other. Witnessing this had only increased Kane's intense and private hunger to join with a mate of his own someday.

"How do you feel about that?" Blythe finally asked, a soft frown of worry creasing her smooth brow. Kane noted she didn't ask whether Lucas felt Lilly would be safer somewhere else. She knew her husband well and understood how tightly Lucas wanted to hold on to the sister he'd believed to be dead fifteen years gone. Kane got this, too, but he knew what he wanted to do was ultimately the best way to keep Lilly safe.

Hands linked, Lucas and Blythe turned to face Kane. "Do you promise to keep us in the loop? We want frequent updates, texts and pictures, all of it, you know," Blythe said.

"As much as I can," Kane answered. "As long as it doesn't compromise Lilly's safety."

Still Lucas hadn't spoken. Kane waited, arms crossed. He needed to be sure he had Lucas's 100-percent approval or his plan was a no-go.

Finally, Lucas gave a slow nod. "Fine. Let me get her and we'll tell her now. When do you want to leave?"

"As soon as possible."

Lucas jerked his chin and turned. Blythe's hand on his arm stopped him. "Let me fetch her," she said softly. "You and Kane need to present a united front in this."

Though Lucas nodded, Kane saw Blythe's comment perplexed him. Clearly he hadn't considered the possibility that his sister wouldn't go along with his plans.

A moment later, Blythe returned. Behind her came Lilly, a quiet wraith of a woman, strands of her long, honey-blond hair drifting around her shoulders as she moved. She slipped into the room, the graceful way she seemed to glide making Kane think of a dancer.

"You want me to what?" she said, as soon as Lucas finished explaining to her. Her bright blue eyes appeared to glow in her delicate oval face. "That makes no sense. Why would you think I'd want to take a trip with a man I barely remember?"

That stung, though Kane kept the same pleasant expression he always wore when around her. Since the first time he'd seen Lilly, emaciated and filthy, huddled in a heap of rags in a dark and dank cell, she'd haunted his every thought.

Lucas exchanged a glance with Blythe and Kane knew they were deciding whether or not to tell her the truth. While this wasn't his call, at least not yet, he felt he had to make his position known. "I'm not going to lie," he warned the other man, his arms still crossed. "I don't see a reason to."

"Lie?" Frowning, Lilly looked from Kane to Lucas and back again. "What are you talking about? Is there something you're not telling me?"

Judging from Lucas's clenched jaw, he wasn't happy.

Yet when he spoke, his tone was soft and soothing. "We think a few of the doctors from Sanctuary are still at large."

Suddenly, Lilly's entire demeanor changed. Kane watched as all the animation disappeared from her face and she…shut down. That was the only way he could describe it. All the light simply vanished from her eyes.

"And you think they're going to try and take me back." Not even a question, she delivered the statement in a flat, emotionally dead voice.

Kane found himself aching to reach out and comfort her, but of course he couldn't.

Having no such compunction, Blythe wrapped Lilly in her arms. "It's okay," she murmured. "We've got your back."

Lilly stood like a statue, neither returning nor rejecting the embrace. Finally, she stepped away from Blythe and faced her brother. "Why didn't you tell me?"

"We didn't want to stress you. You've already been through so much." Lucas's voice broke as he tried to explain. Lilly continued to wait, her gaze unblinking, while Lucas struggled to find the right words to express his concern without completely terrifying her. A difficult task.

Finally, Kane took pity on him. "Your brother is worried about you. Rightly so. That's why he asked me to come help. I promise, you'll be safe with me," he said, the certainty in his tone meant to let her know she needn't be anxious.

"Will I?" Just like that, with one sweep of her eyes through impossibly long lashes, she let him know she'd rather stay. "No offense, but I think I'd rather take my chances here, with my brother and his family."

Lucas shook his head, his gaze full of pain and regret. "That's not an option, Lilly. Much as I'd like it to be."

Lilly glanced from her brother to his new bride, and then toward the living room where a newly healed five-year-old watched television. Kane saw the moment the realization came to her. Both hurt and understanding flashed across her fragile features before she gave a wooden nod.

"I understand," she said, her flat tone letting them know she'd retreated to that place inside herself that made her feel safe. "When do you need me to be ready?"

Steeling himself, Kane glanced at his watch. "How about in one hour?"

Ignoring the instant protests by both Lucas and Blythe—their voices merging together as they insisted Kane stay for dinner or better yet, the night—Lilly jerked her chin in a simple nod and glided out of the room.

Kane waited until she was gone before lifting his hand. "Enough."

Just like that, they fell silent. "I'm leaving tonight. She's getting ready. The sooner we get out of town, the better. I don't want whoever is watching her to get a make on me or my vehicle."

Blythe frowned. "You think they're watching the house?"

Careful to appear casual, Kane gave a nonchalant shrug. "It's possible. One thing I've learned over the years is to always expect the worst."

Though Lucas nodded, agreeing with him, Blythe's frown deepened. "If that's the case, when they see you leaving with her, they're going to follow."

"I've already considered that." Fishing in his back-pack, he pulled out a plastic bag containing one of the wigs he'd purchased before leaving Texas. "Have her put this on. The color and style are similar to yours. Also, it'd help if you lend her one of your outfits. Something you wear often, that might be easily recognizable as yours."

Accepting the wig, she finally graced him with a small smile. "You think you can make them believe Lilly is me."

Again he shrugged. "People generally see what they want to see. They'll have no reason to think otherwise. But to make certain, I'd like you to put on this." Again he dug in his bag, bringing out a second wig. "This is as close as I could get to her hairstyle."

Taking this wig, too, Blythe laughed, the musical sound making both Lucas and Kane smile. "You really have thought of everything."

Still smiling at his wife, Lucas clapped him on the shoulder. "I told you he's good."

Before Blythe could respond, Lilly appeared in the doorway. "I'm ready," she said quietly, holding a small overnight bag. Though she wore a determined look, she couldn't manage to banish the trepidation in her eyes.

"Is that all you're bringing?" Blythe crossed to her and took her arm. "Would you like me to help you pack a few more things?"

"No." Lilly's gaze found Kane's. He felt a connection sizzling along his nerve endings. "I don't need much," she said.

He nodded. "And if she needs more, I can always buy something for her. Now," he continued, his tone brisk. "The two of you go in the bathroom and change clothes and put on the wigs I got you."

"What?" Lilly appeared thoroughly confused. "I don't—"

Blythe took her arm, steering her in the right direction. "I'll explain while we're changing."

After the two women had gone, Kane turned to find Lucas eyeing him. "Don't worry. I'll take good care of her," Kane said.

"You'd better." Lucas's harsh tone spoke of deep emotion. "I don't want to lose her again."

"You won't." Kane uttered the two words fiercely. They both knew he'd given an oath. Nothing would happen to Lilly Gideon while on his watch.

When the two women reappeared, he eyed them critically. Up close, he could tell that the wigs were cheaply made, but even through binoculars they'd do the trick. Blythe's clothing hung on Lilly's too-thin frame, but again, the disguise should serve its purpose.

"Are you ready?" Kane asked Lilly, holding out his hand.

Though she nodded, she stepped back rather than touch him. Which was okay, for now. Eventually, he hoped she'd trust him enough to welcome his touch.

And more, his inner voice whispered. He banished the thought as soon as it occurred to him. Life was messy enough without unnecessary complications.

Lilly waited until they were on the highway before speaking. "More than anything," she said, sounding softer than she would have liked, "I wish I could be like everyone else."

"Really?" A smile curved Kane's hard slash of a mouth. "How's that?"

She shrugged, hurriedly glancing away from him. "Normal." Hesitating the space of a heartbeat, she resolutely continued. "Sane. I'm not, you know."

Though he had to realize she was, in all fairness, trying to warn him, Kane didn't appear concerned. His chiseled features still radiated masculine confidence, as if there was no problem she could throw his way that he couldn't handle. "Don't be so hard on yourself. You've been through a lot. You're stronger than you think. Not too many women could have survived an ordeal like that."

Rote words, the kind of meaningless phrases her therapist was fond of throwing around. The anger surging through Lilly startled and surprised her. "You don't even know me." Her even tone gave no hint of the resentment simmering just below the surface. She'd learned the hard way how to impose an icy self-control, to pretend a confidence she didn't feel.

Even now, having finally gained both her freedom and her brother, she felt as if she walked under the shadow of her father's madness. He'd hurt and abused her, all in the name of love. After fifteen years of living as his captive, trying to hang on to the rapidly diminishing spark that made up her inner self, she no longer knew how to interact with others. Especially not men. Most particularly men like Kane, the kind that embodied all that was male.

"You'll be fine," he said, smiling, looking like some dark angel who ought to frighten her, but instead intrigued her way too much.

"Don't," she ordered, the catch in her voice contradicting its sharpness. "Don't patronize me."

"I wasn't," he said firmly. "Believe me, Lilly Gideon. That's the last thing I want to do with you."

She didn't dare ask him what the first was. Though she knew he didn't do it on purpose, the underlying sensuality in his husky voice made her shiver. If that was, in fact, what sensuality sounded like. She, who knew everything about how to endure torture and experiments and pain, knew absolutely nothing about a healthy relationship between a man and a woman. The closeness she'd experienced with her brother and his wife had been her first experience in fifteen years with anything remotely resembling love.

If that's what it was. With the ground constantly shifting under her feet, she didn't feel certain about anything. After all, she'd just begun to feel comfortable around her new-found family, and now she was being sent away with a man she barely knew.

"For your own safety," Kane said, making her start and wonder if she'd said what was in her head. She hoped not.

"Did I…?" she asked, waving her hand to indicate what she meant.

"Speak your thoughts aloud? No." He shook his head. "But you didn't have to. Believe me, Lucas loves you. He only wants to keep you safe."

"I understand." Again, she thought she sounded cool and confident, the opposite of how she felt. Everything about this man made her feel unsettled. Even the throaty rasp of his voice danced along her nerve endings like a silk edged sword soaked in fire.

How did one respond to that?

"What's in this for you?" she asked, more to distract herself than any real curiosity.

Instead of answering, he laughed. While she stared at him with a weird mixture of annoyance and trepidation. "Not everyone is completely self-serving. Some of us do things because it's the right thing to do."

She wanted to ask him to explain this cryptic message, but wasn't sure how. Instead, she turned and pretended an interest in the passing scenery.

He didn't speak again, which should have relieved her. Instead, her discomfort grew, making her fight the urge to squirm in her seat. Finally, she gave in and glanced at him. "Where are we going?"

"Someplace safe." Though he barely looked at her, one corner of his mouth lifted to take the sting off his words.

"How far away?" Again she had to quell her own uneasy restlessness. She hated—no, *despised*—this weakness within her. She'd felt unsafe for so long she'd begun to wonder if she even knew how to be strong. Even with her brother, she'd found herself jumping at the slightest sound and battling the urge to crawl into her bed and take refuge under the covers.

"Across the country. It'll take us four days to get there, if we travel easy."

Again she nodded, keeping her face expressionless while she wondered what the hell was wrong with her, that she could don a mask of normalcy while inside she struggled with a maelstrom of conflicting emotions.

"And then what?"

He cocked one eyebrow, looking devilish and dangerous and a thousand other things that all made her want to wrench open her door and leap from the vehicle. Only the knowledge that she'd promised her brother—sworn to Lucas that she'd let Kane keep her safe—made her stay in the car.

"Once we arrive at our destination, we'll work on beginning to teach you to protect yourself."

Even trying to understand his cryptic pronouncements fatigued her. In fact, weariness slammed her with a force nearly as strong as one of her father's blows. Too exhausted to fight any longer, she relaxed and gave in to it, closing her eyes and willing herself to fall asleep.

Chapter 2

Kane nearly grinned as Lilly closed her eyes and pretended sleep, as if by doing so she could shut him out.
Whether she liked it or not, and she'd made it quite clear
she did not, they were going to be spending a lot of time
together.

The first few miles were awkward, as Kane had suspected they'd be. He drove in silence, giving her the space
he knew she needed, trying not to let her scent make him
dizzy. Her breathing slowed and evened, and he realized
she truly had dropped off to slumber. Oddly enough, he
felt honored. The fact that she could do so meant she
trusted him, even on a subconscious level.

Either that or, in her years of captivity, she'd learned
to take her rest when she could.

Though he couldn't get a read on her inner wolf, his
own beast had gone into an adrenaline-fueled high alert.
Kane couldn't figure out why, unless it was reacting to

Lilly's unusual aura. The visible aura was the way all Shape-shifters identified their own kind. Most were a subtle glow of color, pleasing to the eye.

Not Lilly's. Hers pulsed a violent purple, so dark it appeared black. Such an unnatural color, the Pack doctors had said, could mean madness or even…death. None of them had seen anything like it.

Naturally, this worried Lucas and Blythe. Now that Kane had seen it, he understood their concern. He hoped with time he could help Lilly regain her confidence and perhaps bring her fractured inner wolf some kind of healing.

She dozed for a little over an hour, giving him time to work on relaxing, as well. It surprised him, this antsy restless feeling. In his work for the Protectors, he'd been in lots of dangerous situations. He and his wolf had always been in accord—none of the warring between the two halves of himself, as he'd heard happened with others.

But now, when there was no apparent danger, at least at this exact moment, his inner beast couldn't be calmed.

Finally, Lilly stirred. Stretching, she smiled sleepily and opened her eyes. When she speared him with her bright blue gaze, the catch in his heart nearly made him recoil. What the hell?

An instant later, when Lilly realized where she was and who she was with, her smile vanished. Turning away, she resumed staring straight ahead, her entire body stiff and tense.

He put on a CD of old-school country music classics, believing that even the most die-hard introvert couldn't sit quietly through Johnny Cash, Loretta Lynn, and Dolly Parton.

Eventually, even though she never looked directly at him, she began tapping her foot, proving him right.

Good. An outward sign she was finally relaxing.

Again she glanced sideways at him, and then looked away without speaking. He didn't ask her if she had a question or needed something. Not yet. Since it would be a long drive cross-country from Seattle to upstate New York, he had the luxury of taking things slow.

Her stomach rumbled, causing her to flush red.

"Are you hungry?" he asked quietly.

"I could eat," she admitted, careful to keep her eyes firmly fixed on the passing terrain. "What did you have in mind?"

An image flashed before him. He saw himself, as vividly as if it were happening, slanting his lips over hers, plundering her mouth with his tongue.

Swallowing hard, he blinked to dispel the picture. "How about a burger?" he managed. "I'm sure we can find a fast-food place."

She made a noncommittal sound that he chose to take as agreement. He stifled the urge to smile. After speaking to Lucas and agreeing to help, Kane hadn't been sure what to expect. While he knew Lilly was emotionally and physically fragile, he hadn't realized he'd have to continually fight the urge to pull her into his arms and swear to her he'd give his life to keep her safe.

This was a given, even though she didn't realize it yet. Maybe she never would. None of that mattered. She was his to protect, no matter the cost. As a Pack Protector, recruited at an early age, he always took his duties seriously. Even in his real job as a veterinarian, he considered himself dedicated. His clients and their pets— his patients—loved him for it. They'd even understood when he'd taken a leave of absence from the veterinary clinic to help Lucas protect Lilly.

"How often do you shape-shift?" Though she asked the question casually, the intent way she fixed her sky-blue eyes on him told Kane it was important.

Since he knew she wanted him to think it wasn't, he lifted one shoulder in a shrug. "As often as I can. How about you?"

"I'm the opposite. I'd be happiest if I could figure out a way to never shift again."

He'd expected this. Lucas had mentioned that Lilly had issues with shape-shifting. After what she'd been through, Kane could well imagine.

"There." She pointed at a sign for a well-known fast-food restaurant. Obliging her, he took the next exit and parked close to the entrance.

Her question pleased him. It showed a bit of natural curiosity, a spark of life, a quality he'd feared he'd have to help Lilly completely rebuild.

After they'd both eaten and freshened up, they got back on the road. Kane had barely driven thirty miles before Lilly fell asleep again. Eyeing her, he couldn't resist a smile.

She slept well for several hours. A good, clean rest, he thought. She didn't appear to suffer from nightmares or even dreams. Apparently she had no bad associations from riding in a car.

He drove until dusk, then a bit farther. His neck hurt, his hands were stiff from gripping the wheel and he needed to stretch his legs. In the passenger seat, Lilly had begun to stir, blinking sleepily and looking around her with the barely awake curiosity of the truly innocent.

"Where are we?" she finally asked, her voice rusty.

"Nearly to Billings, Montana. We're going to stop in a little bit."

"Okay."

Relief flooded him, though he was careful not to show it. Driving so long with only his own thoughts had made him wonder how she would do in a hotel room alone with him. He'd calculated they'd need to stop three times and they'd have to share a room each time. No way was he letting her out of his sight, not even to sleep. While he'd make sure they'd have separate beds, she'd be spending the darkest part of the night with a virtual stranger. Apparently, she wasn't concerned, which was much better than he'd expected. He nearly smiled at her. Only the notion that it would probably scare her kept his face expressionless.

With classic country music wailing away in the background, they continued on. He pulled off I-90 in Billings, figuring ten hours on the road was enough for the first day. Truth be told, since Lilly had slept for several hours, he could have gone farther, but having recently made the trip from Texas to Seattle, all that driving had begun to catch up with him and he needed to rest.

After stopping in the office and paying for one night, he returned to the car holding the plastic key card. They drove around to the back side of the building, looking for Room 149. Parking in front, he glanced again at Lilly and then killed the car engine. The exterior of the hotel appeared a bit shabby, but hopefully the rooms would be clean. He slid his key into the sensor and opened the door. Lilly drifted along behind him like a ghost.

Kane turned on the lights, inhaling the slightly musty scent, and looked around. Two beds, check. Worn carpet that had seen better days. But a working window air conditioner. The bathroom was large and had obviously been redone. There were four white towels, a bit thin but clean and serviceable. Exactly what he expected to find for thirty-nine dollars a night.

"After you," he told Lilly, gesturing toward the bathroom. "I don't know about you, but a hot shower would feel really good right now."

Though she dipped her chin to acknowledge him, she didn't comment. Instead, carrying her overnight bag, she brushed past him and closed the bathroom door behind her. A moment later, he heard the shower start. When he did, something that had been clenched inside of him relaxed. Odd, but he hadn't even realized he'd been so tense.

He took to roaming the room, stopping occasionally at the single window and peering out through the middle of the closed curtains. Not that he expected to see anything—he was 100 percent certain they hadn't been followed—but old habits were hard to break. Plus, during his twice-yearly stints working for the Protectors, he'd come to appreciate the value of being overly vigilant.

The shower cut off, drawing his attention to the closed bathroom door. Though he knew it might be a bit of a cliché, he was a man and couldn't help but picture her reaching for a towel, her pale and creamy skin glistening with water.

A few minutes later, she emerged, a towel piled high on her head. Her long legs were bare under a soft black T-shirt that skimmed her knees. She barely glanced at him, claiming the bed farthest from the door. He watched her pull the ugly, patterned bedspread down and fold it neatly, before she slid under the worn sheets.

"Here," he said, tossing the television remote on the bed near her. "I'll just be a few minutes."

Still keeping her profile averted, she ignored him.

Since he could well understand her nerves, he moved past her, careful to act as if everything was perfectly ordinary. He hoped she'd be able to relax once he closed himself in the bathroom. Maybe find something banal on television to help lull herself back to sleep.

The hot, as close to scalding as he could stand, shower improved his mood 100 percent. He dried off, dressing in loose gym shorts and an old T-shirt even though he preferred to sleep naked. After brushing his teeth, he opened the door, listening for the sound of the TV. Instead, only silence greeted him. Not completely unsurprised, he saw she hadn't turned it on. Instead, she lay curled into a ball, her long lashes fanning the curve of her cheek. She didn't move as he quietly approached her, though he could tell from the uneven rise and fall of her chest that she only pretended sleep. Even so, she was still the most beautiful thing he'd ever seen.

Then, while he stood drinking in the sight of her, she began trembling. A horrible, violent shivering, reminding him where she'd been and what a man looming over her bed most likely meant to her.

Horrified, he stepped back. His inner wolf snarled, evidently unsettled by the sudden, sharp ache just below his heart. Moving carefully, he crossed over to his own bed and pulled back the covers. A quick glance over his shoulder at her revealed her shaking hadn't abated in the slightest. Poor Lilly was clearly terrified.

His chest tight, he considered his options. Deciding, he snagged his car keys from the dresser. "Be right back," he murmured, even though he knew she wouldn't acknowledge his words.

Unlocking his car, he reached into the backseat and retrieved his battered guitar case. While he was out there, he did a quick scope of the parking lot, reassured by the emptiness of the well-lit area. Even the highway seemed quiet. Not a lot of activity on I-90 near Billings at night.

Back inside the room, he bolted the door behind him. Lilly continued to lie in the same position, her slender body still wracked by shudders. Cursing under his breath, he sat down on the edge of his bed and fumbled with the latches on his case, careful not to look too long at her.

Once he had the old acoustic guitar out, he considered. He needed something soothing, not the rollicking bluesy-country music he generally favored. His entire family played one instrument or another. One of the first things he'd learned on the guitar was the old Beatles song "Let It Be." Perfect.

She gave a reflexive jerk of her shoulders when he strummed the first chord. Ignoring this, he continued softly playing, singing the words in his low voice. While he sang, his wolf tried to sense hers. So far, even though such a thing was common among Shape-shifters, he hadn't been able to do this with her, not even the most minute fraction of contact. Kane couldn't understand why her wolf seemed to be locked away most of the time, though he guessed this was the result of the torture and experiments she'd suffered while locked away in the basement of Sanctuary. He had hopes that eventually, with the passage of time, she'd be able to return to a semblance of normalcy.

So he continued to play music for her, and for her wolf. He'd learned music not only calmed the savage beast, but provided a soothing balm to troubled souls.

Gradually, her trembling appeared to lessen. Encouraged, he began another song. This time the old Bob Dylan tune "Blowing in the Wind." Though several artists had done covers of this song, in Kane's head he always heard Bob Dylan's gravelly voice. Kane knew all the words to this one, too, and he sang with his heart, quietly paying homage to a beautiful woman who should never have had to endure what she had.

Midway through this second song, Lilly opened her eyes. She turned her head and, after a moment of silent scrutiny, she pushed up on one elbow to watch him.

Progress. He barely managed to suppress an encouraging smile. Instead, pretending not to notice, he launched into some old Judy Collins, refusing to reflect on how every soothing song he could think of was from four or five decades ago. What could he say? He'd always liked oldies.

Once the last notes of the music died away, he placed the guitar on the chair next to his bed. "Good night," he told her, inclining his head in a sort of salute before reaching up and quickly extinguishing the light.

As he lay in the darkness, his heart inexplicably pounding in his chest, with his wolf wanting to howl mournfully, he listened. The faint sounds of the nearby interstate were muted, and the rest of the motel was quiet. But these things barely registered in his consciousness, because he attuned every fiber of his being to hearing her.

At first, there was nothing, as if she was frozen in place. But then Lilly must have accepted the need to sleep or resigned herself to the inevitable. He heard the slight rustle of her sheets as she tried to make herself comfortable, the soft sigh that escaped her lips. And finally, her breathing slowed, became even and deep.

The tightness eased in his chest. She'd fallen asleep. Why he should feel as if he'd accomplished a victory, he couldn't say. This drive would take four long days, with three overnight stops. They'd made it through the first. He could only hope the next two would be easier for her.

Eventually, he drifted into a restless slumber of his own.

Lilly came awake sometime in the dark of the night. As was her habit, she held herself utterly still while she gathered her bearings. The even breathing of the man in the bed next to her told her he was out, safely locked in the throes of REM sleep.

Kane. He looked like a fallen angel, or at least how she'd always pictured them when her father had ranted. Maybe not Lucifer, but one of the others caught in the fallout. She thought this because she detected no malice in those amazing silver eyes of his.

Everything about him affected her. Her experience outside of Sanctuary was too small for her to know why. She couldn't understand her reaction toward him. Lucas had told her she could trust him, and she took what her twin brother told her as gospel. But the effect Kane had on her wasn't like fear. He exerted some kind of magnetic pull on her, the way a candle attracts a moth. She wasn't sure what it was exactly. An odd combination of trepidation and fascination, maybe. The latter worried her.

Of course, it seemed as if everything made her anxious these days—ever since gaining her freedom, something she'd once hoped for but had given up on. Now she wished for normalcy, to understand how to interact with others without the crippling sense of trepidation. Lucas had said she needed to be patient, to give it time.

But she couldn't lie, not to herself. She suspected that the fear would always be with her. Even in Lucas's home, she couldn't control her immediate reaction if someone inadvertently startled her. The first few times that she'd dropped into a feral crouch and bared her teeth had been humiliating, to say the least. She'd just begun to try to train herself to relax when Kane had shown up and she'd learned she'd have to travel.

Among the many things she was working on was trying to blur her memory of the years of her captivity. Sometimes, she held out hope that she could be successful, but then the dreams would come and she'd wake panicked, believing herself to be still shackled to a bed, a helpless prisoner while nameless people shoved needles into her or hooked her up to machines that brought nothing but pain.

At such times, she'd learned the trick of leaving her body, a sort of disassociation that allowed her to travel far, far away. It was this ability, she now knew, that had enabled her to hang on to the last shreds of her sanity.

Had this been a good thing? Often, she found herself wondering. She certainly hadn't expected life after captivity to be so painful. Sometimes she thought life might have been easier if she was mindless and drooling.

Pushing aside her dark thoughts, she wondered what the followers of Jacob Gideon and his church of Sanctuary found so valuable about her that would make them continue to hunt her. As far as she knew, none of the multitude of experiments they'd performed on her had been even remotely successful.

The man in the bed next to her, Kane, made a sound, low in his throat. More like a growl than a snore, even though she knew he was still deeply asleep. She wondered if he knew she sensed his wolf and how much such a thing terrified her. The only other wolf she'd ever been able to be aware of was her twin brother's. And even that had been before the man who'd called himself their father had discovered that they were abominations.

His music… She smiled to herself in the darkness. She'd never heard anything like it—or hadn't in at least fifteen years. The *thing* inside her, the abomination, had actually gone quiet for once.

Should she tell Kane this? Or would doing so somehow give him a weapon to use against her?

Trust, no matter what her brother said, had to be earned. As of yet, she trusted no one. Least of all herself. Unable to sleep, she lay awake waiting for sunrise, listening for any sounds that might mean danger had found her.

Once the sky began to lighten and Kane began to stir, she sat up, pushed back the sheets and padded to the bathroom, where she brushed her teeth and got dressed. When she returned, Kane sat on the edge of his bed with the television on. Some sort of daybreak news show played.

"Mornin'," he drawled, the kindness of his smile making her feel warm all over. Struck speechless, she could only dip her chin in a nod.

He didn't seem to notice. "My turn." Pushing off from the bed, he headed for the bathroom, closing the door behind him.

With nothing to do but wait, Lilly sat down to watch the television. A commercial about laundry detergent wrapped up, and then the perky woman anchor appeared, her hot-pink suit matching her bright voice.

"Breaking news," she exclaimed. "Police in Maine have rescued two women who have been held captive for twelve years. This is eerily similar to the case in Ohio, where two girls were abducted as teens and held for ten years."

Lilly froze. There were others like her? As the women's photos appeared on the screen, first the older ones from Missing posters showing them as teens, and then shots of them as they emerged from the house that had been their prison, she wrapped her arms around her waist and her eyes filled with tears. She knew these women, not personally but in spirit. In their sad gazes, the tightness around their mouths, and the way they walked, shoulders rounded as if they expected a blow, she recognized herself.

She barely heard Kane emerge from the bathroom. Engrossed in the story, she didn't look up. Nor did she make a move to wipe away the tears streaming down her face.

"What's wrong?" He sounded alarmed. When she didn't respond, he dropped down onto the bed next to her and put his arm around her shoulders. "Lilly?"

Gathering her shredded composure, and überconscious of his arm, she gestured at the TV, where they were wrapping up the segment. Then she whispered, "Those women were held captive for twelve years. And they mentioned there were others, held somewhere else for ten."

"Yes." He hugged her. She wasn't sure whether to stiffen, push him away or simply accept the comfort he offered. In the end, she stayed where she was.

"You're not alone," he continued.

Enough of this wallowing in emotion. "They told me that in therapy." Pushing to her feet, she swiped the back of her hand across her wet face. "Are you about ready to go?"

Watching her carefully, he nodded.

"Give me just a minute." And she hurried to the bathroom, where she blew her nose, splashed some cold water on her face and shook her head at her image in the mirror.

They ran through a drive-through and grabbed breakfast sandwiches and coffee. In a few minutes they were back on I-90, heading east. Something about the motion of the car made her sleepy, and she accepted this as a gift.

When she opened her eyes again, she saw several hours had passed. They stopped for lunch and this time when they got back on the road, she felt jittery and wide-awake.

Noticing this, Kane turned down the radio. Stomach sinking, Lilly glanced sideways at him. He was going to ask questions. She recognized the signs.

"You know, I'll never forget when we found you," Kane said. "All those years, with both you and Lucas believing the other one dead."

She nodded. Lucas was the only one with whom she'd spoken honestly. As twins, their emotions usually were mirror images of each other's. But Kane had been kind to her and he was her brother's friend. Trying like hell to calm her jangled nerves, she took a deep breath and braced herself for his curiosity.

"Seeing my brother was the highlight of my life," she told him honestly. "At first, I thought I was dreaming. I'd carried the knowledge of his death for so many years."

"What was it like?" Kane asked, his casual tone not fooling her one bit. "You don't have to talk about it if you don't want to, but I can't imagine.... It must have been pretty awful."

"Awful doesn't begin to describe it." She gave a rueful smile, settling back in her seat and folding her hands in her lap. This, discussing her captivity, was something she'd actually grown accustomed to. After all, she'd been dutifully attending therapy sessions twice a week ever since she'd gotten out of the hospital. And before that, she'd had to tell her story numerous times to the police, the FBI and the media.

She had gotten quite adept at giving details without revealing any of her inner turmoil.

Glancing at the large man behind the steering wheel,

she launched into the standard, memorized description she'd given so many times before.

"You saw where he kept me," she said, grimacing. "Dark, cold, isolated. Exactly where demons should be kept, according to him. Sometimes I was left alone for days at a time. They fed me just enough to keep me alive. I craved water more than food, maybe because that was doled out sporadically. I had a large bucket to use as my bathroom. It was rarely emptied and stank, but after a while I didn't even notice the smell."

Rote stuff. She'd said it a hundred times in exactly the same way. Usually, it was enough. She raised her eyes to find him watching her. The observant look in his narrowed gaze told her for him, it wasn't. Somehow, he knew.

Such a look… The sharpness of it might have stripped another woman naked. But Lilly had been through much worse. Though the slightly guilty pang she felt inside surprised her. She didn't care what he thought. Or she shouldn't. It was all so puzzling.

Confusion exhausted her. Instead of continuing, she closed her eyes and tried to pretend he wasn't making her remember, making her hurt. In fact, she tried to act as if he didn't exist.

"Are you okay?" The gentle tone in his whiskey voice made her insides quiver.

"Yes." Short answer, total untruth. Keeping her eyes closed, she averted her profile, hoping he'd take the hint.

"If you don't want to discuss it, that's fine," he said. "But don't feed me all that bullshit you rehearsed for the press. I saw the interviews. I read the news magazine reports. If I could find one right now, it'd probably show you parroting the same exact thing you said then. Why is that?"

Was that *anger* vibrating under his words? She took a moment, mulling over the fact that she felt no fear, instead a sort of baffled curiosity.

She understood what he was saying, even if it made absolutely no sense. Kane barely knew her. Why did he want so badly to know the inner her? She'd shared that with no one, including her own twin brother. Though she suspected Lucas had a good idea, not only since they were so much alike, but because he too had briefly suffered at the hands of their father.

At her lack of response, he gave a slow shake of his head. "If you don't want to talk about it, all you have to do is say so."

Clenching her teeth, she swallowed. "I. Don't. Want. To. Talk. About. It."

"Fine." His jaw appeared as tight as hers. "Let me know if you need anything." And before she could even consider replying, he turned up the radio and began singing along to the music, some country-western song about something called a redneck.

Mystified, she turned away and faced the window. She decided to practice her deep breathing, something her last therapist claimed would help calm her but which hadn't worked so far. To her complete amazement, with Kane singing happily in the background, this time she felt tranquility washing over her. But it had nothing to do with her breaths and everything to do with Kane's deep, melodic voice. The night before, she'd thought it was the guitar, but she realized now she'd been wrong. The instrument was only part of it. The rest was him. Something about the way he sang reached deep inside her, into her bones and her blood.

Chapter 3

Foolishness. Or so Lilly quickly told herself. That didn't stop her from enjoying the respite from the constant buzz of trepidation that usually swirled inside her, mingling with the fear. Abstractly, she knew she wasn't supposed to be so uneasy, but the queasy feeling that there was danger all around her persisted. She didn't know how to stop it. Therapy was supposed to help, but it hadn't.

In fact, she could count on the fingers of one hand the moments of calm since she'd been freed from captivity. Last night and right now—this was huge. Allowing herself a small smile while making sure Kane couldn't see, she sighed. She closed her eyes and let herself slide into sleep.

She'd slept a little, and then they'd stopped for lunch and stretched their legs, and gotten right back on the road. They didn't talk much, which to her surprise felt comfortable.

That night, they stopped in Sioux Falls, South Dakota. When he pulled into the small motel's parking lot, asking her to wait in the car while he got them a room, anticipation filled her rather than dread. Because later, surely he'd sing. Stunned, she realized she craved this, the same way she'd once craved water.

After checking into their room, which oddly bore a close resemblance to the previous one, Kane suggested they walk across the parking lot to the small, brightly lit café.

"Okay." She didn't even have to consider her answer. The fast-food they'd consumed hours ago for lunch had long since been digested and she felt hollow. Which meant she was hungry. Not a new sensation by any means, but her body had once been accustomed to being starved. Allowing herself to want food, to actually anticipate the flavor on her taste buds, was yet another thing that should have brought her happiness, but instead stressed her out. She couldn't shake the certainty of believing if she allowed herself to enjoy one thing—anything—it would be promptly taken away from her. Conditioning, her shrink had said. Whatever it was, it was a part of her that she now hated.

He stayed close to her side as they crossed the well-lit motel lot into the café. The place was bright and crowded, and the scent of hamburgers cooking made her mouth water.

"Heaven," she breathed, before realizing what she'd done and immediately trying to shut the instant of pleasure down.

"Don't," he said quietly, as if he understood. And then, shocking her, he took her hand. When he closed his large fingers firmly around hers, she struggled against a sharp stab of panic.

"I…" Tugging, she stopped when she saw the kindness in his eyes. "Sorry."

"Don't apologize." Instead of releasing her, he continued to hold on to her hand while they waited for the hostess to gather menus. As they followed the woman to their booth, Lilly wondered when Kane planned to let her go.

He released her when they reached their seats, sliding into the booth on the side facing the door. Studying him, she thought he appeared relaxed. Which was good, as that would mean they weren't in any immediate danger.

She wished she could relax, as well.

"Are you always so jumpy?"

As if to underscore his comment, she started at his words. "Yes," she answered, refusing to sugarcoat it. "As I'm sure you noticed, I'm pretty messed up."

"That's understandable." No censure, only compassion in that wonderful, rich voice of his. He opened his menu, to her relief. "What are you in the mood for?"

"A burger," she blurted, her mouth starting to water, "and fries."

He nodded. "Sounds good. I'll have the same."

With a start, she realized the waitress stood nearby, ready to take their orders. Lilly'd been too lost in her thoughts to notice.

"And two milkshakes," Kane continued, handing the menus back.

"What flavor?" the waitress asked.

Kane's silver eyes met Lilly's, causing a spark to flare low in her belly. "Are you a chocolate or vanilla person?"

"Do you have banana?" she blurted, forcing herself to meet the waitress's gaze.

"Yep."

"I'd like that."

"We'll take two," Kane seconded, grinning so broadly Lilly wondered if she'd made some sort of public mistake.

Once the waitress moved away, Kane reached across the table and lightly touched her cheek, pretending not to notice when she flinched. "You know what you want," he said, his tone vibrating with praise. "I like that."

To her befuddled amazement, she felt her face heat at the compliment. "Thanks."

When their food arrived along with the milkshakes, huge burgers next to a mound of crispy fries that looked every bit as good as they smelled, she froze. After shooting Kane a quick glance, she snatched hers up and sank her teeth into it. The flavor exploded in her mouth, making her hum with pleasure.

Half the thing was gone before she realized it. Glancing at Kane, she saw he watched her while he ate his own, much more slowly. Sheepishly, she put her burger down and made herself take some of her fries.

"You look like you're enjoying that," he said, smiling.

"I am." Careful not to talk with her mouth full, she took a long drink of her shake, almost purring out loud at the sweet banana deliciousness as it slid down her throat.

He laughed, a sound of genuine pleasure. "I take it you like your milkshake, too."

She nodded, swallowing one last sip before answering. "This is great." Looking up, she met his laughing gaze. With a sense of shock, she realized Kane was damn near beautiful when he smiled. The thought made her full stomach hurt. Careful to look away, she tried to think of something else.

As seemed to be his wont, Kane came to the rescue. "Didn't Lucas feed you back there in Seattle?"

"He did." She tried to think of a diplomatic way to explain. Since there was none, she went ahead and told the truth. "Food is another one of my…neuroses. I have a lot. Too many to count, actually." Her lame attempt at a joke fell flat. Once again, she felt her face color.

When he didn't respond, she glanced up at him. He appeared to be engrossed in devouring the remains of his meal. With a feeling of relief, she did the same.

After they'd finished, Lilly declined dessert, even though the apple pie the waitress mentioned made her mouth water again. Amusement flickering in his eyes, Kane asked for the check. As they got up to leave, she half expected him to reach for her hand again. When he didn't, she marveled at her feeling of disappointment.

Still, full and sated, she noticed an unusual lightness in her steps as they walked side by side to the motel.

Back in the room, as soon as he closed the door, the familiar uneasiness swept over her. She knew she should try to fight it. After all, they'd spent two days driving in the car together. Intellectually, she knew he meant her no harm, but some kind of rationality based on past experience made terror grab her by the throat and refuse to let go. Paralyzed, she tried to regain control, to push back the dizziness, to slow her rapid heartbeat.

Deep breathing, deep breathing. She would be strong. She *was* strong. Purposefully avoiding looking at the bed, where she longed to crawl under the covers and curl into a protective ball, she headed for the bathroom and a hot shower.

When she emerged, instead of sitting on the edge of the bed waiting for her, Kane had stretched out, still fully dressed, and fallen asleep. Padding over on her bare feet, she studied his strong profile. Even asleep, she saw the inherent strength in his hawklike features. Emboldened, she let her gaze travel over the rest of him, his impossibly long, black lashes, high cheekbones, and firm yet sensual lips. An unfamiliar warmth began inside her. He really was dangerously beautiful. Tendrils of his thick dark hair curled on his tanned forehead, and his broad shoulders and muscular arms made him look virile in his T-shirt. Even his bare arm silky with hairs and his long fingered hands fascinated her. The same way one would marvel at a great work of art, she told herself. Nothing more.

Sleep had muted the air of isolation she'd sensed in him and identified with, making him appear unexpectedly vulnerable. If not for the power she sensed coiled within him, making his aura pulse with potent masculinity, that is.

Aching to touch the heat emanating from his flesh, she cleared her throat instead. Oddly enough, she felt more at risk now than she did when he was awake with his quiet confidence filling the room.

At the sound, he opened his eyes. His silver gaze locked on hers, making her catch her breath.

"All done?" he asked, sitting up. Momentarily struck dumb, she nodded.

"Great." Pushing himself off the bed, he smiled at her. "I'll only be a minute or two. Go ahead and sleep if you want."

An instant of panic clawed at her. Unreasonable, but still… "Will you," she began, trying to bring the words up a suddenly tight throat. "Will you play and sing again tonight?"

He went so still she wondered if she'd offended him. But his expression appeared neutral when he looked her way. "Do you want me to?"

Nodding, she glanced down, aware she'd begun twisting her hands together. "I would like that," she managed.

"Then I will." His easy tone made her think he hadn't noticed her uneasiness. But then she was coming to realize he pretended not to notice a lot of her weirdness in order to put her at ease.

"But first, I want a shower." Turning, he headed toward the bathroom.

"Thank you," she said, right when he closed the door behind him. She wasn't sure he'd heard her, but at least she'd tried.

Carefully she removed the bedspread, folding it neatly at the end of the bed. Then, peeling back the sheets, she slipped in between them, trying to lie on her back, propped up with a pillow, or on her side, stretched out like normal people. In the end, she gave up and curled up into her usual, comforting ball and lay inflexible and rigid.

She'd give anything to have the ability to drift off to sleep. Just close her eyes, and let herself get carried away to the land of dreams. Instead, she lay absolutely still, her heartbeat fast, her mind racing.

Though she'd tried to school herself against it, she stiffened the instant the door opened. Keeping her eyes closed, she felt his presence fill the room. Damn it. No reason for fear, no reason at all. But helpless against instinct, she couldn't stop the dread from filling her. A few minutes later, the familiar shivers started. Clenching her jaw, she tried to keep her teeth from chattering.

"It's okay," he said, his deep voice calm and sure. "I'll get my guitar. Just a minute." She heard the sound of him unlocking the dead bolt, then the door opened and closed as he went outside.

Her jaw began to ache as she waited.

After what seemed like an eternity, but in reality was probably only a moment, he returned. Eyes still closed, she held herself rigid, hating that she felt so tense. She listened as he moved around the room, heard the click of the fasteners as he opened his guitar case, the rustle and creak of the bed next to her as he settled on it. She could barely contain her impatience.

And then finally, he strummed the guitar. As the soft notes filled the room, she loosened her iron grip on herself, letting them pull some of the tension from her. When he sang, his husky voice low and sensual, and just exactly right, she heaved a great sigh, willing herself to become unknotted.

One song ended—she wasn't even sure of the words— and he began another. As the music filled her, releasing her from the iron grip of her damaged psyche, she smiled. Muttering a slurred thank-you, she let herself fall toward the blessed oblivion of sleep.

Kane kept playing, long after he'd watched Lilly fall into slumber. Though exhaustion made him unsteady, he knew he had to keep playing or he might do something he'd regret. Like touch her.

Hell, the aching need to lay a hand on her had only intensified the longer he was around her. Only the certain knowledge of how badly such a thing would freak her out kept him from giving in to the craving. He'd been surprised as hell when she'd let him hold her hand earlier. And pleased, more than he should have been.

Four songs in, as the last notes died away, he made himself stop. Moving slowly, his body uncomfortable and aching, he returned the guitar to its case. He then went to bed, hoping he could get to sleep. He had another full day of driving tomorrow.

When he opened his eyes again, the grayish light told him dawn had nearly arrived. He sat up, glancing over at Lilly, who still slept. Heading toward the shower, he braced himself for yet another long day of driving. South Bend, Indiana, here we come.

Though this was only their second morning together, Kane considered it odd the way he and Lilly seemed to have developed a routine. In less than forty-five minutes, they were on the road, both having showered and dressed. After running through a drive-through for breakfast, they hit the highway. Once again, Lilly was silent, so he again located a country-music radio station and turned up the volume.

Several hours later, fueled by two large coffees, he debated trying again to engage her in conversation. She was a quiet little thing, though her slender, wild beauty lit up the interior of his car. He knew she had no idea of her impact on him, though everything about her fascinated him, from the apricot cream of her soft skin to the long lashes framing her clear blue eyes. He struggled against the temptation to taste her lush mouth, to tangle his fingers in her careless tumble of thick, honey-gold hair.

Even the first time he'd seen her, emaciated and filthy, huddled on a cold stone floor with nothing but rags to keep her warm, he'd seen the light of her beauty shining through her damaged exterior. For the first time in his life, he'd wanted to kill another human being, to find the one who had done this to her and wrap his fingers around his throat.

Since he couldn't, he'd managed to hold himself in check. The bastard, one Jacob Gideon, a prominent religious leader of a church called Sanctuary, had been arrested. The worst part of it was that Lilly'd believed Jacob to be her father. It'd turned out Jacob had killed her parents back when she and Lucas had been infants.

Shaking off his thoughts, he focused on the road. When she finally spoke, he nearly missed it.

"What's your story?" Her soft-voiced question had

him hurrying to turn down the radio. "How'd you get into the bodyguard business?"

He couldn't help but smile at her description. "I'm actually a veterinarian. I work at a veterinary clinic in Fort Worth. I also work for The Society of Pack Protectors."

To his amazement, she smiled back, making an ember smolder inside him. "Lucas told me about the Protectors. They…you helped free me and the others from Sanctuary. He said you're sworn to keep safe others of our kind. Shape-shifters."

Since he knew she'd believed her and her brother to be freaks of nature and hadn't realized there were others, her calm acceptance now made him make a mental note to call Lucas and thank him for teaching his sister so much in such a short period of time. At least she knew some of her heritage.

"Exactly. The Protectors recruited me when I was still in high school. They paid a full scholarship to Texas A&M University and then to the veterinary program. In exchange, I have to work for them a few times a year. It's similar to the military reserves here in the United States."

"And you just finished up working undercover at Sanctuary." She glanced sideways at him. "Since you're an animal doctor, then how are you able to do this for Lucas?"

"And you," he added softly. "I took a leave of absence, the same way I always do when I go work for the Protectors."

She nodded and turned to look out the window.

By the time they made South Bend, he had to force himself to stay awake. Aware of the danger, he took the first exit with a motel sign and pulled in and parked in front of the dingy window with the red, neon vacancy sign.

Half turning in his seat, he dragged his hand through his hair. "I'm sorry, but I'm beat."

She nodded without looking at him.

"Wait here." Getting out, he went inside the office and procured them a room.

Which turned out to be yet another carbon copy of the previous two.

Dropping his gear on the floor, he didn't even have the energy to hit the shower. "You go ahead," he told her, lying back on to the bed and closing his eyes. "I'll take mine in the morning."

That was his last conscious thought before sleep claimed him.

Overnight bag still in hand, Lilly stood and watched as Kane dropped off into a deep sleep. She felt a flare of panic that he hadn't even brought his guitar case inside.

She shook her head at her own weakness and took her bag with her into the bathroom. She made the water piping hot, and took her time, trying to summon up the courage to let Kane sleep undisturbed. The poor man obviously needed his rest. He'd been driving for a solid three days, and since she didn't know how to drive she couldn't even spell him.

But though she knew her thoughts were selfish, she couldn't help but wonder what kind of a night she'd have, alone with him in a small hotel room, without even his music to soothe her. Telling herself to stop thinking of herself, she toweled off and put on her soft sleep T-shirt.

When she emerged into the room, Kane's deep, even breaths told her he was still deeply asleep. She moved quietly, went through her familiar routine of folding the bedspread and slipped into the still tucked sheets. Only once she had, she realized she'd forgotten to put out the light. On her way to do so, she once again found herself entranced by Kane. A sudden image of what it would feel like to slide into his bed next to him, wrapping herself around him, made her gasp in shock and confusion.

What the... Staggering back, she managed to click off the light and hightail it back to her own bed.

Once there, she curled up in her familiar ball, but couldn't relax enough to get comfortable. Again she briefly considered waking Kane up and asking him to sing to her, but she hadn't the heart. So far, he'd been nothing but accommodating to her. She couldn't be such a selfish person to keep such a man from his well-deserved rest.

If she didn't manage to get to sleep tonight, she always had the car during the drive tomorrow. He'd promised it would be their last day of driving. And then they'd be... Grimacing, she realized she didn't even know their destination. She told herself she needed to be more proactive, to take charge of her own destiny, or at least try.

And with that thought, somehow she must have fallen asleep, because when she next opened her eyes, it was morning. Kane's bed was empty. Sitting up, she heard the sound of a shower going and smiled.

She'd done it. Gone to sleep alone in a room with a strange man, who wasn't really a stranger anymore. Still... Baby steps, as her therapist had been fond of saying.

He gave her a curious look when he emerged from his shower, his dark hair still damp. She smiled at him, which appeared to shock him, since he froze, though he didn't speak as she continued past him. Her smile held, even as she disappeared into the still-steamy bathroom.

When she came out, dressed and ready, he'd taken a seat in the chair by the door. "I've already loaded the car and turned in the key."

Though she wondered at the impersonal tone to his voice, she simply nodded.

As usual, they got breakfast on the road. She waited until they'd both finished eating their egg sandwiches, turning the questions she wanted to ask around and around in her mind. For the past two days, she'd been wanting to ask, but hadn't summoned the energy or the nerve. Finally, with her usual lack of finesse, she just blurted out the first one. "Where are we going?"

Kane's smile told her he approved of her curiosity. "Leaning Tree, New York. It's upstate, in the Catskill mountains. My entire family lives there."

"Your family?" She hadn't anticipated having to meet anyone else. Somehow she'd thought Kane was taking her to some sort of remote safe house where she'd live alone with him until it was safe to return home.

"Yep. Both my parents, two brothers and a sister, along with their respective spouses and a bunch of nieces and nephews." He said this so cheerfully she could tell he expected her to greet this news with enthusiasm.

Damned if she didn't hate to let him down. But she had no choice—she could barely master her own emotions yet, never mind try to summon up fake ones.

"Are we…" Licking her lips nervously, she tried to sound upbeat. "Are we going to be living with them?" Which would be close to a nightmare as far as she was concerned.

"Sort of." Then, apparently noticing her crestfallen expression, he reached over and lightly squeezed her shoulder. "Don't worry, you'll still have your privacy."

Though she didn't see how, she didn't pursue the questions any further. In fact, she wished she'd never asked. Now that she knew, her anxiety had rocketed sky-high.

She couldn't imagine what Kane's family, his no-doubt

nice, normal family, would make of her, so clearly damaged and one short step away from crazy.

"Are you sure you want to impose on them?" she hesitantly asked. "Maybe we should find alternative lodging."

He laughed. "They'd never forgive me if I did that. I haven't been home in three years or more. Work got crazy and somehow I never made it. I owe them a nice long visit."

Crud. Settling back in her seat, she swallowed the huge lump in her throat and tried again to concentrate on her breathing.

"Hey." His voice softened. "My father owns a motel. It's actually more of an old-fashioned motor court. There are separate cabins. I've asked to use the most remote one. It's on the other side of a meadow and small lake. I promise, you won't be crowded in with anyone."

She nodded, wishing she could quiet the roiling turmoil inside her. Squaring her shoulders, she tried to reach inside her, to that dark, violent and often empty space, hoping she might find strength. Once or twice, she actually had, but that was years ago. Lucas and Blythe had talked often about their inner wolves, but Lilly was pretty sure hers had gone mad a long time ago. One thing she knew for sure, she could no longer touch her inner beast. Her father had believed this meant she'd conquered the demon he claimed lived inside her.

She knew better. The demon waited, crazed and hungry, ready to devour her the instant she gave it a chance.

"I've never seen anything like your aura," he said. "Just now it went from black to gray, then swirls of purple started exploding, like fireworks. It's unreal."

Yet one more thing different about her. Sometimes she couldn't help but believe Jacob Gideon had been right. She wasn't normal, nor would she ever be. A few times she had actually considered the possibility she might be better off dead.

"My aura?" Again she said the first thing that came to mind. "I can't see it, though Lucas told me it was… special. Can everyone see their own?"

From his crestfallen expression, he seemed to realize he'd hurt her. "I meant no offense. I'm sorry."

Lifting her shoulder in a casual shrug cost her more than he'd ever know. "None taken." She swallowed, steeling herself to meet his gaze. "Please, I'd really like to know. Can you see your own aura?"

"No." He held her gaze for a second, and then turned his attention back to the road. "We can only see each others'. Oh, every now and then, if I'm walking by a mirror, I might catch a glimpse of the light surrounding me, but when I look full-on, it's gone."

Frustrated, she nodded. "That's what I thought." Once again, she glanced his way. "Yours looks a lot like Lucas's. I figured mine looked more like Blythe's. I'm guessing it doesn't."

A shadow crossed his face. Though she hadn't exactly asked a question, she'd been hoping for confirmation. Blythe's aura was gorgeous, bright and golden, exactly like her. In the short time Lilly had gotten to know her, she'd come to see the woman her twin brother loved with all his heart was beautiful both inside and out.

From the way everyone reacted to Lilly's aura, she guessed now her own must be dark and twisted, full of holes and ugly mashes of color, like the ones inside her head.

Just like that, her faintly hopeful mood evaporated, and a crushing sense of doom settled down on her. Since these feelings frequently descended on her for no rhyme or reason, she knew there was no way to dissipate the blackness of her mood. She had to ride it out.

Turning her head away from Kane, she closed her eyes and waited for him to turn up the radio. When he didn't, she reached out and did it herself.

Kane saw the first billboard when they were still thirty miles out from Leaning Tree. "Wolf Hollow Motor Court Resort, only thirty miles to paradise!" the sign proclaimed, along with a picture of a wild wolf howling at a full moon. Years ago, Kane's father had decided to adopt an advertising strategy of using six billboards, five miles apart. Since the slogans never changed, Kane could recite all six of them from memory, even though he hadn't been home in three years.

Lilly stirred in her seat, opening her eyes and leaning forward. "Do you feel that?" she asked, her low voice thrumming with emotion.

Kane went absolutely still, using both his human senses and his wolf. "No," he finally said, regretful. "What was it?"

She settled back in her seat, shaking her head. "A feeling…intuition…I don't know. Never mind. It was probably just my imagination."

But he could tell it hadn't been, not to her. Absurdly, he felt as if he'd let her down. "You've been asleep awhile. We're almost there."

Now she looked at him full-on, her blue eyes clear and wide-awake. "We made it here without any trouble."

"Yes." Entranced, he wondered if it was possible to drown in her gaze.

"No one followed us or tried to intercept us. I think it's possible my brother was worried for nothing."

Glad of the distraction, he dragged his gaze away from

hers and flashed a grim smile. "No. All this means is we got away without them realizing it. Once they know you're gone, they'll be searching all over for you."

Her vivid gaze didn't waver. "Do you think they'll find me?"

"Not yet." At the stark fear flashing across her features, he almost swore, though at the last minute he bit back the words. "Bad choice of words. I don't think they'll find us. Not here."

"That's not what you said." Cocking her head, she made a face, evidently downplaying her own fear. "But you think eventually they'll track us down?"

He bit back a curse at his own carelessness. "It's possible. Look, anything can happen. You know that. But it won't be for a while, I promise. It'll give us time to prepare."

"Prepare how?"

Another billboard flashed into view. This time the wolf faced north, the direction they were heading.

Kane ignored it. "Lilly, in the time you spend with me, I'm going to teach you how to be strong, how to defend yourself. By the time we're done in Leaning Tree, you should be prepared to take on any comer."

Chapter 4

He'd surprised her, Kane realized. Her eyes widened and she opened her mouth, though no sound came out. He'd wondered how she'd react. Now, he was about to find out. What she said next stunned him.

"Good." Her lush lips twisted in a semblance of a smile. "I don't ever want to be a victim again. I'd like that. Very much."

They were approaching another sign. "Look," he urged, pointing. "My father's idea of a brilliant marketing plan."

She read out loud as they drove past. "Wolf Hollow? Is he—" she waved her hand vaguely "—like us?"

Kane appreciated the way she now lumped herself in with him and other Shifters. Lucas had told him that at first she'd been so terrified of being associated with her own kind, she'd tried to deny their existence.

Apparently, in the month she'd lived with her brother,

Lucas had managed to convince her that she wasn't a monster. Good.

"Yes." He smiled at her, hoping to take away some of the sting. "Both my parents are Shape-shifters. Most of the town is Pack."

A tiny frown creased her forehead. "Seriously? There are that many of us?"

He wasn't surprised Lucas hadn't fully educated her. In her situation, it made no sense to deluge her with too much information. He decided to keep things light. He'd give her more info later, when she was ready for it.

"Yes, there are millions of us, scattered all over the world. We exist alongside humans, living the same sort of lives they do. We also organize ourselves into Packs, but on a much broader scale than our wild brethren. Similar to the government, we have a national Pack, state Packs and local city and county ones."

She nodded, clearly unimpressed. "I suppose that's a good thing."

Unable to suppress a grin, he nodded. "It is." He liked this about her, this faint edge of prickliness. Much better than the reclusive shell of a woman he'd half expected. After what she'd been through, he considered any signs of a fighting spirit a good thing.

When he'd seen her reaction to the news story about the other women who'd been held captive, he'd seen sorrow, but not righteous rage. Quite honestly, he would have preferred the second.

Still, she'd come a long way. And he planned to be around to help her go the distance.

They pulled into Leaning Tree as the sun was beginning to set. The time of the gloaming, he'd heard it described once. The place looked just the way it always did in his mind; not much had changed since he'd lived there as a child. Huge leafy oaks and maples spread their thick green branches over the buildings on Main Street, shops and restaurants and a small Dutch Reform church that had been built in the early 1700s and had been lovingly restored.

Unlike downtown areas of most small towns, in Leaning Tree, cars still filled the parking lots and pedestrians strolled on well-lit sidewalks. Outdoor cafés did a bustling business—they passed full tables under umbrellas with tiny white lights. The scene could have been a postcard or the cover of a travel brochure. In fact, he thought it probably was.

"It's beautiful," Lilly breathed. Her eyes glowed as she took in her first glimpse of the place where she'd be living for the next few months.

He couldn't help himself; he grinned. After the flat, Texas landscape with its sparse trees, Leaning Tree looked like heaven.

"My family's motel is on the other side of town," he told her. "Part of it borders on New York State forest preserve land."

And just like that, she shut down. He grimaced, aware that the mention of his family had made her nervous again.

In fact, once they'd driven through downtown and taken the turnoff, following more strategically placed signs to Wolf Hollow Motor Court, she withdrew even further.

Refusing to acknowledge her tension, he knew the only thing he could do was express his own anticipation at seeing his family again. But how? As a man unaccustomed to sharing his feelings, he wasn't sure what to say.

In the end, he decided to go with the truth.

"Every time I come for a visit, my mother goes on a

baking binge," he confided. "She's a great cook, and I can't wait to see what she's made. Her apple pie melts in your mouth and no one can make chocolate chip cookies the way she does."

When Lilly turned to look at him, a reluctant gleam of interest flickered in her eyes. "Cookies?"

He nodded. "And pies, cakes and whatever else she feels like making. We usually have a huge family dinner. Since I haven't been home in several years, I imagine she's gone crazy with the cooking."

At least Lilly'd stopped twisting her hands in her lap. "What's your father like?"

"He's like a big, gruff bear." He smiled to take the sting off his words. "But a kindhearted bear."

"I see." Though she nodded, he could tell she had no idea what he meant.

"My sister and my brothers and their spouses will probably be there for a welcome-home dinner," he told her, aware it would be better if she were prepared for a crowd. "They can be a bit…boisterous."

She swallowed hard. "Do they have children?"

"Yes. I have three nephews and two nieces. They range in age from four to twelve."

Her smile seemed less wobbly. "I like children."

"Good." The road changed from pavement to gravel. "Here we are. Right around this bend."

They pulled up in front of the main house, a low-slung, stone-and-wood creation with lots of glass that his parents had designed and built over thirty years before. As he coasted to a stop and killed the ignition, the door opened and his family began to spill from inside.

As they surrounded the car, Lilly made a low sound. Seeing the terrified look in her eyes, he squeezed her shoulder before opening his door and climbing out. "I'll fend them off and then we'll introduce you, okay?"

He didn't hear her answer in the chorus of glad cries that followed as he was engulfed by family. His mama wrapped her plump arms around him, squeezing happily while raining kisses on his cheeks. She still smelled the same, like gardenias. She wore her long, gray hair in the same neat braid.

His brothers chimed in, thumping him on the back in glad "guy hugs." His dad, a bald giant of a man, stood back, watching with a happy grin as he waited for his turn. Kane had nearly made his way over to him when his sister, just emerging from inside, squealed and launched herself at him, hugging and laughing and babbling happy words of welcome.

Meanwhile, all the kids swarmed around, playing and yelling and doing the hundred loud and endearing and annoying things small children do. Finally, Kane's father tired of waiting and moved toward him, enveloping him in a bear hug. The scent of pipe tobacco and spearmint tickled Kane's nose. Home. Finally, he was home.

Turning, he took note of his guest. Through all this, Lilly sat quietly in the car, not moving, as if by being still, she hoped not to draw attention to herself. He could only imagine what she thought of the uncontrolled chaos outside the car.

Clearing his throat loudly, Kane gestured for silence. His family ignored him, too caught up in the joy of seeing him. Next he tried clapping his hands and asking them to calm down. Again, this had no result.

Finally, he put his fingers in his mouth and whistled as loudly and ear-piercingly as he could.

Everyone went silent.

"Thank you," he said, pitching his voice so that everyone could hear him. "As I mentioned to Mom and Dad, I have a guest with me. She's been through a lot."

Jostling each other to get a look at the passenger side of the car, some of them starting talking. Kane glared at the offending teenagers, and they instantly stopped. "As I was saying, Lilly Gideon is here with me. She's not used to the organized craziness of our family, so I need to ask you to give her a little bit of space. Can you do that?"

He thought his serious tone must have registered, because the younger family members looked at their feet. Of course his parents, siblings and their spouses all nodded solemnly.

"Thank you." He felt all eyes on his back as she crossed to the passenger side of his car and opened the door.

Lilly's wide blue eyes stared up at him.

"It's okay," he said, and held out his hand. "I won't let anything happen to you. You're safe with me."

She barely hesitated before sliding her fingers into his.

Helping her out of the car as if she was royalty, he kept his body close to her side as they turned to face his assembled family.

"These heathens," he said fondly. "Belong to me. Lilly, meet the McGraws."

As she bravely attempted a smile, he watched in gratified amusement while his normally boisterous family mumbled subdued hellos.

Then, Lilly lifted her chin and murmured hello back.

The instant she spoke, his family's tenuous grip on propriety shattered. Chattering all at once, the female members, young and old alike, surrounded Lilly, touching, patting, smoothing back her hair. Kane held on to her hand, and felt her suddenly go rigid. Still, he didn't interfere—he wouldn't unless she asked him. She'd have to get used to his family sooner or later. Might as well jump in the deep end and learn how to swim.

Of course, the gentle pressure of his fingers on hers let her knew he'd always be her life preserver. Always.

While the women made a fuss over Lilly, the masculine contingent regarded Kane with a mixture of awe and disbelief.

"She's beautiful," his brother Kyle said, cuffing him on the arm.

"Damn." His other brother Kris breathed, barely taking his gray eyes off Lilly. "How'd you rate a woman like that?"

Kane's father chuckled, rubbing his shiny bald head. "Boys, he already told you he brought her here to keep her safe. He's her bodyguard, nothing more."

As one, both of Kane's younger brothers turned to look at their father, disbelief plain on their rugged faces. "You're telling me you believe him?" they asked in unison.

The elder McGraw shrugged. "Guess we'll just have to wait and see."

Before Kane could respond, Lilly squeezed his hand, hard, letting him know she'd reached her limit of endurance.

Without hesitation, he turned away from his father and brothers and gently began moving his mother, sister, sisters-in-law and cousins aside. "Come on ladies, give her a little space. We've been driving for four long days and she's exhausted. Let me take her to our cabin so she can rest up."

Lilly shot him a grateful look before her long lashes swept down to hide her eyes.

"But you'll still be coming tonight for dinner, won't you?" his mother asked, self-consciously patting her long gray braid. Kane gave a reassuring nod. If he knew her, and he did, she'd spent the past ten hours cooking. His mouth watered at the thought.

"Here you go, son." His dad tossed him a set of keys. "I had cabin nine made ready for you, just like you requested."

Catching the keys, Kane grinned his thanks, then shepherded Lilly back into the car. Once he'd closed the door behind her, he crossed to the driver's side. "See you later," he said, lifting his hand in a wave.

Once he closed the door, cutting off the noise outside, he started the engine. "You all right?"

"Yes." The wobbly answer told him she wasn't, not exactly, but he knew she'd be fine.

"They mean well," he told her.

"I know," she said, her slight smile curving her lips surprising him. "And even though they're Shifters, they don't bite."

A joke? Was she making a joke? Just in case she was, he grinned back at her.

"Where are we going?" she asked.

"Our cabin. It's the most isolated one, and also the most difficult to get to. There's only one way in, at least by road."

The gravel road crunched under their tires as they passed the first four rental cabins. Made of wood and surrounded by towering trees, these were clustered around a parklike garden, complete with wild rose bushes in vivid colors, a vine-covered arbor and a wood-and-metal bench. A stone wolf statue occupied a place of honor in the middle, as if it had been meant to be a shrine of sorts. At one time in his family's long history of owning this land, Kane supposed it had been.

"That's beautiful," she breathed. He couldn't tell if she

meant the garden or the statue or both. Either way, though the land and the place glowed with earthen beauty, none of it could hold a candle to her.

"Yes," he answered, his heart full. The road curved ahead of them, steadily climbing through the untamed forest. The next four wooden cabins sat in a semi-circle to the right, situated around a small, spring-fed lake. A doe and two fawns looked up at their approach and vanished into the woods.

At the sight, Kane's inner wolf snarled, reminding him that soon they'd go hunting. Maybe even tonight after the big meal if they followed tradition. He'd have to make sure Lilly knew and offer her the choice to join them or retreat to their cabin.

"I've counted eight," she said, leaning forward to peer into the forest. "How many are there?"

"Nine. Ours is my favorite. It sits up at the top of a rise in the land, with a pretty good view of the entire acreage." Not to mention it was pretty damn near impossible to approach the cabin from any direction without being seen.

A slight frown creased her brow. "Exactly how isolated is it?"

"Not too far." They climbed in earnest now. "We're almost there."

One more curve in the road, and the cabin came into view. Unlike the others, this was made of stone. Two giant oak trees sheltered it. "This one is older than the others," he told her. "Originally, this was where my ancestors lived."

Though she nodded, he didn't tell her the significance of this. His entire family spoke of the power lingering in the ancient stones. In addition to being easily defensible, Kane had the vague hope that cabin nine might help Lilly heal.

They crested the hill, parking next to the covered porch. He killed the engine, pocketed the keys and climbed out. He'd made it halfway around the car, meaning to open her door, but she beat him to it. She unfolded her long and shapely legs and climbed out of his low-slung car. Stretching, she cocked her head and studied the house.

"I feel it again."

He understood what she meant. "It's a ley line. The strength of the earth, made manifest."

A shadow crossed her pretty face. "Are you sure you don't mean demons?"

Cursing the man who'd caused her to think something so natural was evil, he shook his head. "No. It's good energy. Beneficial. Since our kind has such close ties to the earth and the sky and moon, we appreciate and honor such places of power."

Holding utterly still, she considered his words. "Places? Are there more than one?"

"Yes." Relaxing again, he took her arm and steered her up on the porch. "I've been lucky enough to feel several of them."

Unlocking the door of the cabin, he flicked on the light switch. "After you. This will be our home for the next several weeks."

Gliding past him, she inspected the interior, from the weathered wood of the old plank floors to the cast-iron stove. The windows were double-paned and new, and over the years, different parts of the cabin had been updated. The most recent renovation had been to the bathroom.

He watched as she walked all around, wondering if she could sense the history trapped inside the old stone walls. Sometimes, late at night, he almost felt the ghosts of times long gone drifting up from the rocks.

Finally, she looked up and met his gaze. A reluctant smile hovered at the edge of her lush mouth. "Very nice." She swallowed, her cheeks turning pink. "But there's only one bed."

"I know." He indicated the couch. "That makes into a bed. I'll bunk there."

Relief palpable, she nodded.

He glanced at his watch. "We have about an hour until they'll expect us back at the main house for dinner. Do you want to freshen up or take a nap or..."

"What are you going to do?"

"I'm not sure." If he'd been alone, he'd already have turned and headed back to the house to be with his family. But since he knew this would be rough enough on her as it was, he wouldn't ask that of her. Nor would he leave her alone. Until the missing Sanctuary members were arrested, he didn't plan to let Lilly Gideon out of his sight.

"I think I'd like to take a walk," she said, surprising him. "After so long in the car, my legs could use a bit of a hike."

"Sounds like a plan." Crossing to the door, he held it open. "After you."

She didn't move. "If you don't mind, I'd like to be alone."

Compassion warred with common sense. "I'm sorry, but right now that's not a good idea."

He expected her to argue. Or maybe just challenge his statement. Instead, she dipped her chin in a sort of resigned acceptance and moved past him. He fought the urge to take her arm, and only the knowledge that she wouldn't have made it so long if she wasn't a fighter, kept him from demanding she try harder for what she wanted.

"How about I stay a bit behind you?" he offered. "Give you some space without leaving you completely alone?"

All the light had faded from her eyes, leaving them as dark as a storm. "Suit yourself."

So he did. Since she hadn't indicated a preference, he remained right by her side. Unspeaking, yet close enough to touch.

They'd barely gone a quarter mile when she stopped and rounded on him. "I understand you take this guarding me thing seriously," she began, "but I barely know you."

"You will," he said softly. "And, yes, I do take keeping you safe very seriously."

Her expressive face revealed a combination of frustration and determination. "I'm used to being alone. Even when I was staying with Lucas and Blythe, they were kind enough to give me some space."

"No worries. You'll have your liberty again, once those last three Sanctuary people are caught. Until then, I'm afraid you're going to have to put up with me. I'll be keeping you very, very close."

Jerking her head in a stiff nod, she turned and walked briskly away. He almost laughed, well aware of what she was trying to do. She didn't realize his long stride would enable him to effortlessly catch up to her without him having to run. If he wanted to, that is. He'd offered to give her as much space as he could, and that's what he intended to do. At least for right now.

So he dropped back, keeping his distance, and tried to ignore the enticing sway of her hips as he followed behind.

Lilly fumed, hating the way that once again, she had absolutely no control over her life. Even though she couldn't help but admire Kane's steadfast determination and his attempt to give her a small modicum of privacy, his refusal to let her walk alone angered and frustrated her.

Of course it didn't help her mood that she'd be paralyzed with terror if he actually did set her loose.

So she strode off, her fast pace practically daring him to keep up. A few offhand glances over her shoulder revealed he didn't seem to be having any trouble. She walked and walked, at first thinking she'd go until the path ended. Eventually she realized the trails apparently crisscrossed the woods for miles. Defeated yet again, she spun around and motored on past him, refusing to look at him even though she knew she was acting childish. After all, none of this was his fault.

Back at the cabin, she found herself still jumpy and out of sorts. She'd thought a good hike through the woods might soothe her—nature often did. But instead, she'd been ever conscious of the large man walking behind her, ready to rush to her side at the slightest threat and defend her. Her conflicted emotions about this didn't do anything to help improve her state of mind.

Part of her liked the way having him near made her feel protected. But part of her hated the necessity. She liked that he'd said he'd teach her to protect herself. As soon as they were settled in, she'd demand he make good on that promise.

Meanwhile, there was the dinner with his family to get through.

She didn't know why she felt so nervous about everything. The jangling rawness angered her, made her wish she could be a different person. After all, these were just regular people. They weren't going to shackle her to a machine and send volts of electricity coursing through her system. Having dinner with Kane's family shouldn't matter—a simple meal would be minor compared to the numerous atrocities she'd suffered at the hands of her father's minions in her fifteen years of captivity.

Thinking this helped. She squared her shoulders, dragged a brush through the tangle of her long hair and headed out into the living area where Kane waited.

He gave her a long look, and then offered his arm. "Are you ready?"

Forcing herself to move forward, she hesitated, just short of touching him. "Are we walking?"

"We can." His cheerful smile struck a chord of warmth inside her. "Though we might need a flashlight to make it back. There are no streetlights here, just cabin lights."

She frowned, trying to decide.

"Or we can drive," he added. "Whichever is easiest on you."

"Let's walk." More time to get herself psyched. "I don't mind a flashlight later." And she took his arm, the warmth of his skin sending a flush of warmth into her hand.

The woods were beautiful, a leafy canopy through which slashes of sky teased the eye. The gravel crunched under their feet as they made their way back toward the main house.

They'd just rounded the last turn, passing by the first four cabins, when a childish shout rang out. Kane shot her a rueful smile. "We've been spotted."

She couldn't help but tense. Her unease must have communicated itself to him through her hand.

"It's okay," he said. "They're only children."

The words had barely left his mouth when they were surrounded by kids of all ages and sizes.

"Uncle Kane!" They attached themselves to Kane, full

of a joyous exuberance that made Lilly smile. One of the little girls, seeing the smile, shyly tugged on Lilly's shirt.

"Hi, I'm Candace," she said. "I'm five. Are you Uncle Kane's girlfriend?"

"Um, no." Despite herself, Lilly blushed. "We're just friends."

"You're a girl. If you're friends, then you must be his girlfriend."

Grinning, Kane ruffled Candace's mop of red hair. "It's hard to argue with logic like that," he said, winking at her. Seeing that, some of the tightness eased off Lilly's chest. Just some, but at least now she could breathe.

With children dancing around them as if they were some sort of pied pipers, they reached the main house. A knot settled low in Lilly's stomach. She had zero practice with any kind of social situations. After all, the only interactions she'd had in the past fifteen years had been with her captor and the doctors who'd tortured her in the name of Sanctuary.

She felt as if she was about to take a blind leap off a cliff. Which she knew was foolish—this was only dinner, after all—but she couldn't help herself.

"It's going to be okay," Kane murmured, his breath tickling her ear. "I promise."

And then he pulled open the door and they went inside.

Her first impression was the chaos and the noise. A blur of activity—people and food and music—so much the swirl of energy overwhelmed her. She took a step back, forgetting Kane still had her hand engulfed in his.

"Come on." Smiling in reassurance, he tugged her into the middle of the maelstrom. As she tried to hold back the rising tide of fear, the creature inside her raised its bruised and battered head and curled its lip in the beginnings of a snarl.

The beast. *Her* beast. No. Not now. Fear changed to horror, to panic, to terror. She froze as the thing within her stretched, flexing its claws, making a garbled, sorrowful song low in its battered throat.

All around her, in the middle of the noise, people began looking around, sniffing the air, as if they somehow sensed the struggle being waged inside her. Maybe they did, perhaps this was a Shifter thing, but she knew whatever the creature inside her might be, it wasn't the same as theirs.

If she had her way, her beast would never again see the light of day. She'd vowed this, no matter the cost. She had to save the rest of the world from its awful vengeance, even if she had to die trying.

Kane turned to look at her, at the same time tightening his grip on her fingers. Something must have shown in her face. Using his body to block her from their sight, he shepherded her away from the others.

Chapter 5

"Come with me." The deep rumble of his voice sent a shudder through her. She felt as if he'd tossed her an invisible lifeline. Grateful, she went where he led, ashamed of the way she clung to him, yet unable to do more than that.

Inside her, the creature still stirred, wary now.

He took her down a long, narrow hallway and into a small room that had apparently once been a bedroom but had been converted to a craft room/storage space/office. Once inside, he kicked the door closed behind him.

"Are you all right?" Cupping her face with his other hand, he tilted her chin up, making her look at him.

Cautiously, she took a deep breath. She'd been lying to everyone, including her twin brother, and she knew she couldn't be truthful now, to Kane. She had no choice. He'd never understand. Whatever had been done to her had made her different than the rest of them. No one

could help her deal with this. She had only herself and
hoped to tap into some inner strength that so far had been
conspicuously absent.

"I think so," she managed, the answer to his question
coming a heartbeat too late.

Hand warm under her chin, he studied her, his silver
eyes missing nothing. Her entire body flushed. Slowly,
moving her head, she gave him no choice but to let her
go. Though their fingers were still linked, she backed
away, putting just enough space between them so she
could once again breathe.

"Are you going to tell me what that was?" he asked.

For a second, she considered feigning ignorance, but
since it appeared that everyone in the room had sensed
her internal battle, or some aspect of it, she knew this
would be futile. "I'd rather not. At least not right now."

Eyes narrowing, he nodded. "Are you going to be all
right to rejoin my family?"

For now, her beast had gone quiet again. She didn't
know what had set the monster off; whatever triggered it
seemed to follow no pattern that Lilly could see.

"I think so." She tried for a smile, partially succeeding.

"Good." Opening the door, he led her back down the
hallway toward the kitchen.

The organized chaos stilled the moment they reappeared. Kane broke the awkward silence by sniffing and
grinning as he made a broad gesture toward the pots
simmering on the stove. "Something sure smells good.
What's cooking?"

Just like that, everyone went back to what they'd been
doing. Bemused, no longer terrified of them, though she
wasn't sure why, Lilly let Kane tug her along by the hand,
while he joked and teased his family.

"Go ahead and get seated," the elder Mrs. McGraw

ordered, already bustling from the kitchen to the dining room, carrying steaming bowls of food. She wore a brightly colored apron and her plump hands were adorned with rings, one on every finger.

Judging from the scents wafting from the bowls, she'd made some kind of roast, along with vegetables, and homemade bread. Lilly's mouth began to water.

Everyone seemed to rush at once to take their seats at a long table. Lilly stopped counting at twelve chairs, amazed as she realized there was another table set up for the kids.

"Here you go." Kane pulled out a chair for her. Once she'd taken her seat, he dropped into the one next to her. Someone to his left good-naturedly jostled him, almost causing him to knock over his water glass. He saved it with another grin.

Once everyone had taken a seat, they began passing around the bowls. Lilly had never seen so much food in her life. Amazed, she accepted one bowl after another, spooning a little on to her plate, afraid she might offend Kane's mother if she didn't sample everything.

Watching, she noticed no one started eating. Apparently they were waiting until everyone had gotten everything. She waited, as well, even though she felt hollow from hunger.

Finally, Kane's father stood and tapped on his glass with his knife. He flashed a friendly smile at her before glancing around the table. "Today, in honor of Kane's guest, I'd like to say a little prayer."

At his words, everyone bowed their heads. Confused, Lilly glanced at Kane, only to realize he too had closed his eyes and dropped his chin.

Unnerved, she also bowed her head, though she kept

her eyes open so she could watch Kane through her lashes.

"Higher power, we thank thee for your blessings. This food, our company, the love we have for one another and, finally, our good health. In your name, we salute the earth, the sun, the stars and the moon."

The moon? She frowned, thinking of the kind of prayers Jacob Gideon and his followers had prayed with such fervor. They'd invoked a lot of retribution and hell-fire, and nothing about thankfulness or love. Then and there, she decided Sanctuary and Kane's family didn't share the same God.

Once the prayer was finished, everyone dug in. Bowls were continually passed as people took seconds, even thirds. Lilly tried, but she couldn't even finish every-thing on her plate.

"Wonderful meal," Mr. McGraw boomed, patting his ample stomach. "Leave the dishes, hon. Me and the boys will get them."

Once again, Lilly could scarcely believe her ears. In the world where she'd been raised, Sanctuary, all the men had treated the women as little more than serfs. And that had been in the best-case scenario. Once more she was forcibly reminded that the rest of the world wasn't like Sanctuary.

As the men pushed back from the table and began gathering the dishes, Kane touched her shoulder. "You'll be all right? I shouldn't be gone more than a minute or two."

Slowly, she nodded. He grabbed her plate and his, and moved to the other side of the table, picking up silver-ware. Lilly noted some of the other women pretending not to watch her. She offered Kane's mother a tentative smile, relieved when the older woman smiled back, genuine laugh lines creasing her light blue eyes.

With the background noise of silverware and plates clattering in the kitchen, chatter flowed easily among the women. Lilly didn't participate, but she listened, marveling at the feminine camaraderie. A swift stab of yearning filled her. The closest she'd ever come to having a friend had been one of the female doctors at Sanctuary, who'd exploited Lilly's loneliness. Dr. Silva had pretended friendship in order to make it easier for her to perform experiments on Lilly.

The first time Lilly had begged her to stop, her so-called friend had ignored her and tightened the screws instead.

Since that day, Lilly no longer believed in friendship.

But the camaraderie among these women, who were joined by blood or by marriage, felt different. None of them appeared to have anything to gain, no private agenda as they joked and laughed, teased and commiserated. Lilly made a note to watch them while she was here, and see who tried to exploit whom.

The men returned a few minutes later. They too seemed in high spirits, jostling one another, bumping shoulders and fists. Kane seemed slightly embarrassed, side-stepping when his two brothers tried to get him in a headlock. His gaze locked on hers, sitting so quietly, as if he knew she thought herself a weed among blooming flowers.

"You're beautiful, you know," he murmured, holding out his hand to help her up.

Shocked, she couldn't respond. As her face heated, she gripped his fingers and allowed him to help her up.

A loud whistle made everyone go silent as they turned their attention to where the elder McGraw stood at the head of the table. "After such a fine meal," he began, bestowing a grin on his wife, "I can think of nothing better than all of us heading to the woods to shift. It's been a long time since Kane was home for a family hunt."

At his words, a subtle change occurred in the atmosphere. While Lilly stared blankly, several of the others' auras changed, going from light to dark and back again. An invisible energy charged the room, like the low thrum of electricity just before a lightning strike.

Shift. He wanted them all to become their wolf selves.

The thing inside Lilly reacted violently. Taking her by surprise, the monster tried to break out, using claws and teeth and some sort of dark magic. Caught by the figurative throat, Lilly fought back. Because of the battle inside herself, she stood stock still. Though she bared her teeth, she made no sound.

The room grew quiet as the others somehow sensed her inner struggle.

"Lilly?" Kane's voice, strong and steady, gave her strength. Blindly, she held out her other hand, asking him to grip it. When he did, she clung to him like a lifeline. She'd fought this battle before and almost always won. The few times she hadn't, she couldn't bear to think about. Though these had been during her captivity at Sanctuary and induced with drugs, the end result had been bloodshed and terror.

Never, ever, would she willingly allow her beast out again. Especially not now, surrounded by these good, innocent people.

"Come on." Kane pulled Lilly away from the others, hustling her toward the front door. Though his father called him, he only shouted a quick apology and an order that no one follow them.

Once he had her outside, he let go of her hands and

pulled her close, wrapping his strong arms around her as if he could will away the monster.

Even as the thought occurred to her, she felt the beast falter in the middle of its onslaught. Taking advantage, she forced the thing back into a mental cage, slamming imaginary iron bars down.

Only then, was she able to relax her guard, and allow herself to sag in relief.

As she began to take note of her surroundings, she realized with some shock that Kane still held her. And she had no desire to push him away.

He felt...good. Warm and muscular and safe. As she had when he'd played his guitar, she felt the awful weight she carried 24/7 momentarily slip away from her shoulders.

Even as she let herself enjoy the temporary peace, she began gathering strength to push him away. Because she knew if she let him become involved with even the smallest aspect of what snarled and paced inside her, she'd risk him becoming infected with it, too.

Later, after Kane had gotten her into the cabin and made her drink some hot tea, Lilly claimed she wanted to sleep, even though the sun hadn't yet set. Before he could even respond, she fled to her room without meeting his gaze.

Once she'd closed the bedroom door, leaving him alone in the living room, he eyed his guitar case and debated playing a few notes. But the last night on the way here, he'd been so proud of Lilly when he'd realized he'd fallen asleep and she hadn't woken him to ask him to play.

She'd overcome her fears. Damned if he'd give her back the crutch she'd managed to kick to the curb.

He wanted his family, but wasn't up to the endless

questions he knew they'd have. They'd decided to post-
pone the family hunt, and he'd had to promise them he'd
participate as soon as things improved. By things, he
meant Lilly. Truth be told, he had no idea when that
might be.

His wolf grieved at the missed opportunity to change.
For half a second, he entertained the idea of shifting and
hunting solo. Only the thought of his family's disappointment and Lilly's shock dissuaded him. Instead, he left and
walked the woods, taking care to always keep the cabin
in his sight. Walking was like meditation for him. He'd
tried to empty his mind, refusing to dwell on anything
beyond the sound of his feet hitting the ground and the
crackle of the leaves underneath.

By the time the darkness was complete, he must have
walked several miles, picking his way over rocks and
sticks, guided only by moonlight and sheer luck. Despite
this, his unease and concern was no better than it had
been when he'd begun.

Finally, he returned to the cabin. Two handcrafted
rocking chairs sat to the left of the front door. He took
one, staring out into the dark woods, listening as the
sounds of the nocturnal creatures, which had grown silent at his passing, began again.

Something had happened earlier. Though they hadn't
discussed it, he knew his entire family had sensed it.
Something to do with her inner wolf, though he wasn't
sure he could call the animal he'd sensed inside Lilly a
wolf, exactly.

But what the hell else could it be? Despite rumors or
myths to the contrary, he'd never heard of any other kind
of Shape-shifter. Not bear or leopard or lion. As far as
he knew, there'd never been a documented instance of
such a thing.

And even if there had been, this wasn't possible. Not with Lilly. Kane knew her twin brother, Lucas, pretty well. He'd seen the other man shift, had been nose to nose with his wolf. Lilly's brother's beast had been perfectly normal.

Which meant something had been done to her, some poison injected or worse, during the experiments performed on her while she'd been her so-called father's prisoner.

Kane wanted to put his fist through the wall. He hated that Lilly had been suffering alone. He'd sensed her strength, her iron will and fierce resolve as she'd battled the misshapen thing that had once been a wolf. Was this fixable? Curable? He'd have to put a call in to the Protectors and have them ask the Healer.

He also needed to talk to Lucas to find out what the other man knew about his sister's wolf. He hadn't thought to ask if Lilly had shifted at all since getting out of the hospital, making the obviously erroneous assumption that of course she had. It had been several months, after all. Most Shifters couldn't go that long without changing into their wolf form. Those who tried were often known to become mad.

A chill ran through him. Not Lilly. He'd vowed to protect her from whatever dangers might threaten her. Even though he hadn't known one of those would come from within her, he didn't care. His oath remained unchanged. He would help her. No matter what the cost.

Pushing up from the chair, he walked a short distance away from the cabin before turning on his cell phone and locating Lucas's phone number, the one that went to the disposable phone they'd purchased for this purpose. Since it was three hours earlier in Seattle, he knew Lilly's brother would still be up.

"What's wrong?" Lucas asked upon hearing Kane's greeting. "Has something happened to Lilly?"

"No, nothing like that," Kane hurried to reassure the other man. "I was calling because I had a question. Has Lilly shape-shifted that you know of since she got out of the hospital?"

Lucas took time to consider the question. "Now that you mention it, no. I asked her if she wanted to a couple of times, but she said she wasn't well enough. Why?"

"It might be nothing…"

"No." Lucas wasn't having any of that. "If you're taking the time to call me, it's something. What happened?"

"I'm not sure. We had dinner with my family tonight, and several times over the course of the evening, she clearly struggled with her inner beast. Everyone noticed it."

"So?" Lucas sounded incredulous. "That's not unusual, you know that. Lots of inexperienced Shifters fight that same battle. It takes time and ease of practice before they can control it."

"I know. But that's not it. Have you ever seen her wolf?"

"I told you, not recently. In fact, the last time we shifted together was over fifteen years ago."

Briefly, Kane closed his eyes. "That's what I was afraid of. I don't know what they did to her while she was a captive, but something's happened to her wolf."

"What do you mean?"

"I'm not sure. You've noticed her aura. I think that's tied in with her beast."

Lucas cursed, low and furious. "I'd like to wrap my hands around Jacob's throat for what he did to her."

"Me, too."

"What are you going to do?"

Dragging his hand through his hair, Kane exhaled. "I don't know yet. Right now, I'm going to stick with my original plan. Teach her self-defense, instruct her in firearm use and keep an eye on things."

"Promise me you'll keep me posted."

Kane promised and ended the call. Then, heart inexplicably heavy, he went inside to try to get some sleep.

He woke just before sunrise and made coffee, carrying a cup outside to sit and watch the sun come up. He'd barely taken a couple of sips when the door opened and Lilly emerged, cradling her own steaming mug in her hands. Her disheveled hair tumbled over her shoulders, looking as though she'd just gotten out of bed. He felt a sudden urge to bury his hands in it, to see if the silken strands were as soft as they looked. Surprised, he shook his head, belatedly realizing she'd think he was warning her away.

"Good morning." She flashed an uncertain smile, already taking a half step back. "Do you mind company?"

"Mornin'." Patting the arm of the chair next to him, he smiled back. "I'd love some company."

Her gaze clung to his, before she nodded and lowered herself into the other rocker. For a moment, birdsong was the only sound as they each drank their coffee.

Someone rounded the corner, heading their way on foot. Kane stiffened, then saw that it was his sister, Kathy, her thick brown hair in a braid like their mother's, carrying a covered dish. This meant his mother had cooked something and sent Kathy to deliver it. His mouth began to water. He hadn't even realized he was hungry until right that instant.

Beside him, Lilly pushed to her feet. "I'm going inside," she said, her voice distant, her hands trembling.

He pretended not to notice. "Would you mind bringing me another cup of coffee?" He held up his mug, an excuse to get her to come back out.

Staring at him, her blue eyes wide, she finally took his cup and jerked her head in a nod.

"You might wait a second," he continued, ignoring her agitation. "My sister might want coffee, too. If she does, I'll get it."

She wanted to run, he could tell. Her face had the look of a startled doe caught in the headlights.

"Don't be afraid," he told her softly, holding her gaze. "She doesn't bite."

She blanched. "I'll go now," she said, rushing inside.

Lilly barely pulled the front door closed. A sudden image of a wolf, powerful jaws open, flashed through her mind. She blinked, breathing hard. She actually had to catch her breath. Automatic footsteps carried her into the kitchen and toward the coffeepot, where she inhaled the calming scent of Seattle's most popular coffee. Her brother had packed several bags for her to take with her, telling her just because she was traveling to the other side of the country, didn't mean she had to give up good coffee.

Lucas. If she tried really hard, she could remember the time before. Before their father had learned they were Shifters, before something so natural and beautiful had been made to seem ugly and evil. Closing her eyes, she attempted to remember his wolf. She thought she could see it, a vague gray shape in her mind's eye. But years of conditioning, years of being told what she'd seen was hideous and repugnant, dimmed her memory.

Opening her eyes, she filled Kane's mug, then her own. She rummaged in the cabinet, located one more cup and filled it, too. She found a tray, a plastic container of powdered cream, and some little packets of sugar and artificial sweetener. Lastly, she added a couple of plastic spoons. Then, squaring her shoulders, she turned and walked back outside, determined to face her foolish fears with her head held high.

Kathy looked up and smiled, genuine pleasure lighting her eyes, a lighter gray than Kane's, just like Kris and Kyle. "I brought over breakfast," she said, her smile widening as she spotted the tray and the three mugs full of steaming coffee.

"Coffee!" Drawing out the word and sounding ecstatic, Kathy set her covered dish down on the table. "Thank you, thank you, thank you."

"I take it you haven't had your morning caffeine fix?" Kane drawled, grinning at his sister as she waited, looking about to pounce, while Lilly placed the tray on the table next to her dish.

"I've been cutting down on caffeine." Grimacing, Kathy waved away the coffee as Lilly tried to hand her a cup. "Eliminating it, actually." She sighed. "And I won't have any now. I haven't had real coffee in two weeks. I've been drinking decaf."

"Decaf? Why even bother?"

She blushed. "I'm pregnant."

Kane whooped, hugging her. Watching, Lilly noted the siblings had nearly identical smiles.

When Kathy pulled away, she was still grinning. "But you can't tell anyone. Tom and I want to wait to announce it until after the first trimester."

"Understood." Glancing at Lilly, he gestured at his sister. "I'm going to go make some decaf. Will you be all right out here?"

Slowly, Lilly nodded. Kane disappeared inside the cabin.

An awkward silence fell now that the two women were alone.

"Congratulations on the baby," Lilly finally managed, pleased at how even her voice sounded.

"Thanks!" Kathy's gaze seemed friendly. "So how are you feeling this morning?"

Lilly blinked. She might be a tad bit socially awkward, but the question confused her. "Fine."

"I'm glad." Leaning forward, Kathy continued, her tone earnest. "We were all pretty worried last night. Kane never mentioned you being sick, but since it's clear you are, we're all willing to help any way we can."

Somehow, Lilly's reaction to their inner wolves anticipating a change had registered as illness. Which, if she thought about it, in a way it was. "Thanks," she replied, hoping that would be the end of it.

Instead, Kathy touched her arm. "If you don't mind me asking, what's wrong with you, exactly? Is it a terminal thing or something minor?"

Kane's arrival saved Lilly from answering. He handed Kathy a cup of decaf, lowering himself into his chair and snagging his own mug from the table. He took a long, deep drink before looking up. "What'd I miss?"

Kathy squirmed. "I was just asking Lilly about her health."

Frowning, he gave her a long look before glancing at Lilly. "Her health?"

Pretending a sudden interest in her mug, Kathy blushed. "After what happened at dinner…you know."

Kane's frown deepened. "Kath, I know you mean well, but—"

"It's all right." Eager to smooth things over, Lilly interrupted. "She's just curious. If I were in her place, I'd wonder too."

Though Kane's gaze sharpened, he simply nodded.

Meanwhile, Kathy leaned forward, her eyes sparkling with curiosity. "Are you going to tell me?"

Slowly, Lilly nodded. She'd have to choose her words carefully since she had no doubt Kathy wouldn't waste any time repeating what she learned to all the others.

"I'm recuperating," she finally said. "You may have seen my story on the news. I'm the woman who was rescued in Texas after being held captive for fifteen years by a religious cult called Sanctuary."

Eyes wide, Kathy looked to Kane for confirmation. When he nodded, she jumped to her feet and threw her arms around Lilly, hugging her close. "I'm so sorry," she murmured.

To her surprise, Lilly's eyes filled with tears. She stood frozen in place, unable to move, even when Kane's sister released her and stepped away, murmuring what sounded like a cross between an apology and a desire to hear more.

"Are you all right?"

Lilly nodded. "I am. Now."

"Oh, my gosh. How awful it must have been to go through that." Again, Kathy appeared to be on the verge of rushing her for another hug. In fact, Kane's grip on his sister's arm might be the only thing that prevented her from doing so.

Fighting an overwhelming urge to flee, Lilly forced herself to stay put, legs rooted in place. "It was," she said softly.

Glancing from Kane to Lilly, Kathy opened her mouth to ask more questions. "Did you—"

"Not now," Kane said, his voice firm as he took his sister's elbow and turned her back in the direction from which she'd come.

"But…"

"Congratulations on your news," Kane said smoothly, effectively cutting her off before she could begin asking more questions. "Now please, go on back to the house. And I'll have to ask you to keep what you know about Lilly under your hat for now. There are still a few of those Sanctuary people on the loose looking for her."

Finally, Kathy nodded. "Of course," she said, her gray gaze landing softly on Lilly. "If there's anything I can do…"

"We'll let you know," Kane finished. "See you later."

Lilly watched in silence until the other woman disappeared around the bend in the road.

"Does your entire family think I'm ill?" she asked, not entirely sure why she found the thought so upsetting.

Head cocked, Kane drank his coffee before replying. "Their inner wolves could tell something's wrong. When you started battling your beast, ours knew and reacted."

Horrified, Lilly swallowed. To disguise her shock, she reached for her own mug and drank, grimacing at the taste of cold coffee. "Can they… Can they *see* the thing inside me?" she asked, her voice quivering.

"No. No one can. Not until you actually change."

At this, she was able to release a breath she hadn't even known she'd been holding. "Good," she managed. "What's on the agenda for today?"

His smile took her breath away. "Nothing. Rest up, regain your strength and get used to the place. Tomorrow, if you feel up to it, we'll take a drive and go into town. But as far as today goes, enjoy doing nothing."

Though she nodded and tried to look pleased, she felt even more uneasy. Kane couldn't fathom how much of the past fifteen years of her life had been spent locked up in a concrete cell or chained to some machine in the lab at Sanctuary. Doing nothing was the absolute worst he could wish on her.

"I'm assuming you plan on being around?" she asked, mindful of his refusal to let her out of his sight for very long.

If anything, his smile widened. "Of course."

"I'm going for another hike," she told him, almost defiant. "Exercise helps me think."

Without waiting for an answer, she started off down the road, once again heading in the opposite direction of the main house. Despite the beauty of the forest, the massive trees blocked too much of the sky. She felt uneasy here, hemmed in by nature, trapped. Though she hadn't been allowed out much at Sanctuary, every so often Jacob Gideon had recognized her need for sunshine and fresh air. In the old days, her handlers had shackled her to keep her from running. She would have, too, especially believing Lucas dead.

The last few times, they had to wheel her in a chair, she'd grown so weak. Still, she'd relished the open landscape, the sky so huge she could pretend to change into a mockingbird and fly away from her private hell. She'd never forgotten that the mockingbird was the Texas state bird. It made sense, because they knew how to adapt.

Conscious of the big man shadowing her, she looked around. Here, not only were the birds different but she seldom saw them. There were no large grassy areas, no expanse of bright blue sky for them to fly into. The weight of the tree canopy felt heavy, as if made of glass. Or so she told herself, aware her finding fault with such beauty made little sense.

But it did, to her. Because the real reason she felt uneasy in the green New York forest was because the monster inside her loved it.

Chapter 6

Kane liked the determined way Lilly strode through the woods. She reminded him of some warrior princess, her long legs eating up the ground with an athletic and graceful movement, her straight blond hair streaming behind her. He found her desire to walk interesting, as if she thought she could outpace whatever demons haunted her.

By the time she left Leaning Tree and him, he hoped she would have managed to completely vanquish them.

Ignoring the sharp pang he felt at the thought, he trod after her. As he inhaled the pine scent of the woods, he realized how much he'd missed his childhood home. He wondered if Lilly found it as beautiful as he did, wishing she felt comfortable enough with him to walk by his side.

Someday. His chest constricted. He needed to give her time. And also, he needed to remember that in the end, once all the loose ends had been tied up and Lilly was free to live her life, he'd have to let her go.

Finally, she appeared to have worked off her anger or whatever it was that drove her to push herself so hard. Stopping, she put her hands on her legs and bent over, trying to catch her breath. As he drew close to her, he made sure to stop several feet away, allowing her the distance she wanted.

"So." Straightening, she rocked back gracefully on her heels. "What's next?"

"Would you like to go into town this afternoon?" he asked, keeping his tone gentle. The stark misery in her gaze made him want to pull her close. Since he doubted she even knew he could see the emotions she so valiantly battled, he didn't.

"What for?"

A casual shrug. "I thought you might want to see a bit of the area. Plus, there's an Irish pub where the corned beef is a once-in-a-lifetime experience. I've been craving it every since I knew we were coming back here."

Even saying the words made his mouth water. Corned beef. His particular Achilles' heel. In fact, nearly every Shifter he knew couldn't resist the temptation of red meat perfectly prepared. Judging from the way Lilly had reacted to that hamburger while they'd been on the road, he figured she was just like all the rest of them.

"Do they have anything else?" she asked, scrunching up her face like a child tasting a lemon. "I'm not normally a big fan of beef."

Not a fan? He let that pass, pretty sure that she hadn't been out in the real world long enough to even know what she liked. "Sure they do. There's shepherd's pie, some lamb stew, all kinds of excellent dishes."

"Do they have fish?"

"Of course."

"I could eat that. I don't eat a lot of red meat. Even when I was younger, I knew it wasn't good for you."

He nearly rolled his eyes. Those were words he hadn't ever heard another Shifter say. "You ate a burger on the way here. And seemed to enjoy it, from what I could tell."

"I did." Expression abashed, she nodded. "I allow myself something like that every couple of months. Beef's really not healthy for you, you know."

This he couldn't let pass. "Maybe not for humans, but we're different. We need our red meat."

"I'll stick with fish."

He cracked another smile. "Okay."

Arms crossed, she continued to eye him, looking impossibly gorgeous, with her mane of blond hair and bright blue eyes. "I thought you wanted to keep me hidden?"

Now he let his smile become laughter. "First off, Leaning Tree is a small town. Everyone already knows you're here, I'm sure. They just don't know who you are or why you're with us, and we'll keep it that way. Second, I grew up here. Most everyone in town is Pack, and even if your true identity is somehow found out, I can promise you we look after our own."

From the way she looked at him, he could tell she didn't understand. The entire concept was foreign to her. Of course it was. From the time she was fifteen years old, she'd never had anyone else looking after her or even caring about her. Her twin brother had believed she was dead. Meanwhile, her own father had betrayed her, mistreated her and tortured her. He'd actually hired doctors to perform experiments on her while teaching her she was possessed by demons. Kane figured it couldn't get much worse than that.

"If it'll make you feel better," he told her, "you can

put your hair in a ponytail and wear a baseball cap and dark glasses."

Expression solemn, she considered his words for a moment, and then nodded. "I think that'd be best."

So he found her a Yankees ball cap and borrowed one of his sister's many pairs of dark sunglasses that Kathy always left lying around. Handing them to Lilly, he waited while she took them into the bathroom so she could see how she looked once she'd donned her disguise. In that respect, he supposed she wasn't much different than any other woman.

When she emerged a minute or two later, he grinned. With her long hair in a jaunty ponytail, the ball cap pulled low, and the oversized dark glasses perched on the end of her delicate nose, she looked like some Hollywood starlet trying too hard to avoid the paparazzi.

"You know you'd look much less conspicuous if you ditched the hat and glasses," he pointed out.

"I like them."

Of course she did. Lilly didn't do well in one-on-one situations. She thought the hat and sunglasses would help her hide. Who knew, maybe she was right.

"Come on." He held out his hand without thinking. Peering at him over the sunglasses, her gaze traveled from his face to his outstretched arm and then back again. When she finally slipped her small fingers into his, warmth flooded him.

Maybe, she had begun to trust him. If so, this was sooner than he'd expected.

His Corvette navigated the familiar winding roads effortlessly. He pointed out the stream he and his brothers had often fished in during the summer as kids, the corner store where they'd all ridden their bikes to buy candy after school and then the elementary school itself.

The two-story brick building looked as new as it had the year it'd been built, when he'd been in the third grade. Prior to that, he'd had a long bus ride to a school in the next town over.

Lilly listened to him ramble, her expression bemused as she craned her neck trying to see everything the instant he pointed it out. She seemed more at ease than he'd seen her, so he continued to share his hometown with her.

Finally, they turned another tree-lined corner and reached the outskirts of town. Here, old Victorian houses had been lovingly restored. These soon gave way to funky little art galleries, restaurants with sidewalk cafés, the old grocers with one of the best meat markets within fifty miles and various other shops and establishments, most of which looked exactly the same as they had when Kane was a child. Apparently, nothing ever changed in Leaning Tree.

"We have some great restaurants here, too," he told her. "Sue's Catfish Hut, Papa's Pasta, Joe's Coffee Shop, plus Dublin's."

She nodded. "I'm getting hungry."

The normally bustling downtown area looked sleepy in the midday sun.

"It's beautiful," Lilly breathed. "Like something out of one of those books Blythe reads."

Since Blythe was partial to reading romances, Kane took this as a compliment.

"Here it is." They pulled up in front of the storefront that had been made to look like an ancient Celtic church. "We're in between the lunch and dinner crowds," he said, pleased. "I'm sure there's still the odd tourist, but our timing is perfect. Dublin's won't be crowded."

"If you say so." Though she still sounded less than

happy, she couldn't hide the interested excitement in her voice.

He parked in the small lot to the side of the pub. "Here we go."

The dimly lit interior felt familiar and welcoming. Despite her desire for independence, Lilly stayed close to him as he walked the creaky old wooden floors and headed for the long mahogany bar.

Shawn Ferguson looked up from the beer glass he was polishing, his shock of red hair looking as unruly as ever. His frown turned to a grin of delight. "Well, I'll be. If it's not Kane McGraw, finally deigning to show his face here in town."

The two men clasped arms, slapping each other's backs.

"Give me a break, Shawn. I just got home."

Shawn's bright green gaze had already slid past Kane, the laugh lines around his eyes deepening as he gazed at Lilly. "And you've already found the prettiest tourist in town, I see." Grabbing her hand, he made a show of bending as he kissed the back of it.

Kane fought the urge to growl low in his throat. "Lilly's no tourist. I brought her home with me. She and I are staying at Wolf Hollow. Together."

Immediately, the other man's entire demeanor changed. He released Lilly's hand as though it were a live coal. "I'm sorry, McGraw. I didn't know she was your—"

"It's okay." Kane cut him off before he could say *mate*. The last thing he needed was something else to frighten Lilly. She was as skittish as a newborn fawn that'd found itself alone in a wolf's den. "We came to eat. I've been craving your corned beef and cabbage ever since I got here."

At his words, Shawn's worried expression smoothed

out. "It's your lucky day," he drawled. "I just happen to have a bit left over from the lunch rush. I'm still cooking the one for tonight's dinner crowd."

"I'll take it." Kane climbed onto one of the bar stools, indicating that Lilly should do the same. "And a pint of Guinness."

Shawn grinned. "Coming right up." He looked at Lilly, this time the twinkle in his eyes a bit more constrained. "And what would you like, pretty lady?"

Swallowing, she squared her shoulders and lifted her gaze to meet his. "I'd like fish, if you have it. Rainbow Trout? And a glass of iced tea."

"You got it." Hurrying behind the bar, Shawn got Kane's Guinness and hurried into the kitchen to place their orders and fetch Lilly's tea.

Once he'd gone, Lilly turned and faced Kane, her blue gaze direct. "What was he about to call me?"

He pretended not to know what she meant. "When? I didn't hear him say anything."

Biting her lip, she shook her head. Shawn hurried back into the room, bearing her drink and a plate of something else.

"Fried pickles!" Shawn crowed, placing them on the bar. "On the house."

Lilly wrinkled her nose.

"Try one," Shawn urged. "I promise, they're good."

Lilly reached for the plate with the same tentative, two-fingered grip one might use for a bug. She snagged a fried pickle and brought it to her nose to check out the scent. Kane wondered if she realized this was a wolf thing since wolves used their sense of smell more than any other. He decided not to mention it. Instead, he watched as Lilly screwed up her courage and popped the fried pickle into her mouth.

Kane found himself captivated as she slowly chewed.

"It's good," she said, sounding shocked as a tentative smile hovered on the edge of her lush mouth.

"Told you!" Shawn grinned and high-fived Kane.

Lilly ate a couple more pickles before excusing herself to go to the bathroom.

The instant she disappeared around the corner, Shawn's smile vanished. "Kane, you should know that Anabel Lee thinks you've come back for her."

"Anabel Lee?" Kane nearly groaned. "Why would she think that? I haven't seen or talked to her since before I left for college."

"That doesn't surprise me." Shawn grimaced. "Her husband was killed in Afghanistan six months ago. Ever since then, she's been lost. And now she seems to have fixated on you. She was in here just last night, talking about how you'd come back for her. She said now that you're in town, she expects to have an announcement soon."

Kane narrowed his eyes. "How'd she know I was back?"

"Probably the same way we all do. You know how it is. News travels fast in a small town. And Debi does like to talk."

Debi was his brother Kris's wife. She'd always enjoyed the gossip.

"Still, what the heck is the deal with Anabel?" Kane dragged his hand through his hair. "You mentioned a husband. Surely she's had some sort of life in the eighteen years since high school."

Shawn nodded. "From all appearances, she and David were happily married. They were together five years before his tank hit an IUD and killed him. They never had kids. She was pretty broken up about losing him. Folks say she never quite got right in the head."

"I'm sorry for her loss, but I don't understand what any of this has to do with me."

"Who knows?" Turning away, Shawn grabbed a bar glass and began polishing it. "But for whatever reason, she's apparently convinced herself that you're her true mate. Maybe it's her way of dealing with her grief, I don't know. I can tell you, though, she's not going to take too well to your showing up with another woman. This Lilly, she seems delicate."

Both men glanced toward the bathroom.

"What's your point?" Kane finally asked. "I don't really care what Anabel thinks. While I feel bad that she lost her husband, hell, I don't even know her anymore. But I do want to keep things as quiet as possible for Lilly."

"My advice—let Anabel down gently. But in order to keep her away from you, you're going to need to publicly claim Lilly as yours." Shawn leaned in, his expression earnest. "Not only so word gets back to Anabel, but to keep all the single guys in town from beating a path to your doorstep."

Stunned, Kane looked at his old friend. "I hardly think that's necessary."

"What's necessary?" Lilly asked, her unexpected appearance nearly making Kane jump.

"Nothing," Kane answered, shooting Shawn a quelling look. "What's keeping our food?"

Taking the hint, the other man hurried off to check with the kitchen. A moment later, he returned, carrying two steaming plates.

Grateful, Kane smiled his thanks before leaning forward to breathe in the aromatic smell.

"This looks wonderful." Lilly sounded appreciative as she did the same with her perfectly cooked rainbow trout.

Shawn flashed them a smile before discreetly stepping back to the other side of the bar so they could eat.

When they'd finished, Kane paid the check, telling Shawn he'd see him around. He then turned to Lilly, reached out and lightly touched her shoulder. "How about we take a stroll around the downtown square?"

Again, Lilly seemed to draw back inside herself. "Why?"

He helped her down from the bar stool. If he kept his hand on her skin a little longer than necessary, he told himself he had a valid reason.

"First off, to show you the town." He slid his hand down her arm and took her hand. This time, she curled her fingers trustingly around his without hesitation. "Second, I want you to see other Shifters, so you can see how at home everyone is in their bodies."

When she turned to look at him, her gaze had gone flat. "Trying to undo my conditioning?"

Surprised, he frowned. He could have hemmed and hawed, but he believed in honesty whenever possible. "Yes. You never know. It might help you."

"Been there, done that. You forget, I was going to therapy while I was in Seattle. They took me to some church full of Shape-shifters." She shuddered. "It was creepy. Reminded me of Sanctuary, even though they could change into wolves."

Kane wanted to find that therapist and wring his or her neck for their stupidity. "I hope Lucas didn't waste a lot of money on that shrink," he said instead. "Sounds like an idiot."

This at least coaxed a reluctant smile. She nodded.

"He was. And yes, Lucas realized it. He switched me to a woman after that. She was a little better."

They'd made it to the parking lot. He stopped, enjoying the feel of her hand in his and aware he should give her a choice. "Do you want to see the rest of downtown? Or would you rather go back to Wolf Hollow?"

She gave him a long considering look before slipping her sunglasses back over her eyes. "We can take a short walk."

The flush of happiness he felt seemed way out of place. Or did it? He'd been charged with protecting her. He'd always planned to help her become physically stronger. If he could do so for her internally, as well, so much the better. It was nothing more than that.

As they turned, he kept her hand tucked into his, unwilling to release her just yet. Hand in hand they strolled, and hounds help him but he took pleasure in the knowledge that they looked like any other couple, out for an afternoon walk around the town. He felt…content. Maybe even happy, at least the most he had in a long time. Intellectually, he knew he and Lilly would never have any sort of future together, and he wasn't deceiving himself about that. He was her bodyguard, soon to be teacher, and his goal was to make her a stronger, more centered woman who could finally accept her dual nature as something good. Once the Protectors caught up with the last stragglers from Sanctuary, he hoped Lilly could go forward with confidence and the knowledge she had a right to a long, happy life.

Other people glanced at them, but took no real notice. It had been so long since Kane had been to Leaning Tree, he wasn't surprised he didn't see anyone he knew. Truth be told, he was actually glad. He didn't want his afternoon with Lilly to be interrupted.

Lilly continued to look at everything with a sort of interested delight. She constantly studied various groups of people, a slight frown creasing her creamy skin. "So all of these people are Shifters?"

He grinned. "Most of them. Do you see the auras?"

Lowering her sunglasses, she turned in a slow three-hundred-and-sixty-degree turn. "Yes," she said, her voice rising in excitement. "I do."

"Good. And the ones who have no auras, those are most likely humans. Or—" he hesitated, and then decided he might as well go all in "—they might be vampires."

After a startled second, she laughed. "Good one."

"I'm serious."

She shook her head, a smile still playing around her mouth. "Even if vampires did exist, it's broad daylight. And sunny."

"That's a myth," he began.

"Like vampires aren't?"

Kane laughed out loud, enjoying the verbal sparring. "You have to think of it this way. If Shape-shifters—aka werewolves—are real, then why not vampires?"

Her expression stilled and grew serious. "You're not kidding, are you?"

"Nope."

Silence while she pondered this. He gave her time, aware how much broader her world had just become.

They continued walking, stopping in front of store windows, lingering a while at the stained-glass shop. Still holding hands, which astounded him. With anyone else, he would have considered this too long for the kind of relationship they had. They weren't lovers, after all.

Lovers. The second the thought occurred to him, he had a mental image of her under him, naked and welcoming.

Damn. The flash of instant desire nearly had him pulling his hand away from hers. Nearly. He glanced at her, to see if he'd somehow communicated his need. Apparently not. With her fingers still intertwined with his, she appeared to be gazing across the square at the little curio shop, lost in her own thoughts.

"Vampires," she mused. Relieved that she hadn't noticed his insanity, he nodded.

"Yep."

They reached the park with its paved walking trails and a freshly painted white gazebo, surrounded by vibrant blooming rose bushes.

"How pretty," she said, smiling up at him.

"Yeah, it's a popular spot for weddings and photographers."

She nodded. "I imagine." Then, as they started back the way they'd come, she took a deep breath and squeezed his hand once, causing him to look at her.

"What else is there?" she asked, sounding slightly breathless. "I mean how much of the stories are real? Werewolves, vampires… Are there fairies and elves and zombies, too?"

Somehow he managed to keep a straight face. "I've never seen or heard of such a thing as a zombie."

"Really?" Peeking at him over her large sunglasses, she said, "Though I noticed you didn't say anything about fairies or elves."

He shrugged. "What can I say? The world is much more diverse than most people know."

For whatever reason, learning this appeared to energize her rather than add to her fear. Amusement flickered in her eyes, her expression animated and more alive than he'd ever seen her.

"I think I'd like to investigate this further."

He smiled back at her, aching with the need to kiss her. To distract himself, he glanced at his watch. "We should probably head back. I think you've had enough excitement for one day."

Her smile faded, causing him a pang of regret. "Since you're interested in learning, I'll rustle up some books for you to read."

True to his word, when they reached Wolf Hollow, he made a quick stop at his parents' house, running inside and snagging a few of the many books on Shifter history. Handing them to her, he drove the rest of the way to their cabin, unable to keep from smiling at the way she excitedly started paging through them.

They spent the rest of the afternoon reading. Lilly curled up in the big armchair by the window, while Kane took the couch.

Though he tried, he couldn't get lost in his story like he usually did. Lilly's presence proved too distracting.

But Lilly didn't seem to have any problem tuning him out. She dove into the books, beaming with an almost childish delight. Fascinated, he watched her, careful to appear engrossed in his own book whenever she looked up.

Lilly couldn't believe the wealth of knowledge now at her fingertips. For the short time she'd been in high school fifteen years ago, she'd loved history. The fact that these books were an appealing combination of myth and truth made her that much more eager to read them.

Doing her best to ignore Kane's continual perusal, she even managed to forget about that as she got lost in the words.

Deep into reading about vampires, a sound from outside had her lifting her head. Two big men, boisterous and happy. Their deep voices had a similar lilt and cadence. Kyle and Kris, Kane's two brothers. She could hear them before they even reached the porch.

Lifting his head from the book he'd been reading, Kane cocked his head. He heard them, too. She hoped he'd intercept them outside. Instead, he carefully marked his page and closed the book, placing it on the coffee table.

"It's about time they came for a visit," he said, smiling broadly.

Though she nodded, she couldn't help but consider taking her books and retreating into the bedroom. Once again she wished she could be stronger, confident. Not worrying about meeting men who, if they were anything like Kane, were kindhearted and honest. Good men.

The instant their boots clomped on the porch, Kane yanked open the door, not even waiting for the knock. "Hey," he said, thumping one and then the other on the back. Since men seemed to do this all the time, she guessed it didn't bother them, which was good. She would have thought it would hurt.

"Hey, yourself." Kyle's gaze, a darker gray than Kane's, drifted to Lilly. "How are you?" he asked, politely holding out his hand for her to shake.

Swallowing, she squared her shoulders and stepped forward. There was nothing left for her to do but take it.

When she did, he pulled her in for a quick bear hug. "None of this handshaking stuff for me," he said, laughing. 'We're all family here."

The instant Kyle released her, Kris mimicked him. She couldn't help but notice they both smelled the same, like pine trees and the outdoors.

Greetings finished, they turned in unison to look at

Kane. "We're going hunting after dark," Kyle said. "We thought you might want to join us."

For a second, Lilly thought she saw Kane's face morph into that of a wolf. She blinked, and it was gone. Which meant she must have imagined it, since he hadn't started shape-shifting or anything.

"I do," he said, and then glanced at Lilly. "I thought you could hang out with Sharon and Debi while we're gone."

"Kind of like a girls' night in." Kris beamed. "I have to tell you, our wives are so excited. They've rented some chick flick for you all to watch and Sharon's making some of her famous margaritas."

Put like that, there was no way she could refuse. Slowly she nodded, hoping her smile was enthusiastic enough.

"What about Tom?" Kane asked. Tom, Lilly remembered, was his sister Kathy's husband. "Is he going with us? I know Kathy loves those girls' nights."

"Nope. They drove up to Albany for the weekend. Going baby furniture shopping or something."

Kane nodded. "What about Dad?"

Kyle's smile faded. "He's not feeling well. Mom took him to the doctor this afternoon. They haven't gotten back yet."

"You sound worried." Kane glanced from one brother to the other. "What's wrong with him?"

"I don't know. You know how Dad is. He keeps saying he's fine. Mom said he was a bit dizzy." Kris waved his large hand. "I'm sure Doctor Miller will get him all fixed up."

Kane nodded, though he didn't seem convinced.

"So you're in?" Kris scratched his head.

"What time?"

"Debi will pick Lilly up at seven," Kyle said. "They'll be at my house. I figured us guys would hit the woods right at sundown."

Lilly's stomach clenched. She had to force herself to concentrate on breathing normally so she wouldn't hyperventilate. She had three hours. Plenty of time to get ready.

"Sounds good." After another round of back slapping, Kane's brothers left.

Neither Lilly or Kane spoke as they stood, side by side, listening as the sound of the two men's voices faded.

Finally, Kane cleared his throat. "Are you okay with this?"

Taking a deep breath, she nodded and tried again to smile. "It sounds like fun. As long as I don't do anything…wrong."

"You'll be fine." He cocked his head, his silver gaze darkening. "Just don't let them play twenty questions with you."

"What do you mean?"

"Debi loves to gossip. I imagine she and Sharon will try to pry as much information out of you as they can. Don't feel you have to share anything you don't want to."

Again she nodded. "I've read about these kinds of get-togethers. I guess it's high time I actually experienced one, even if it scares me to death."

For a second, he looked puzzled. Then, as his handsome face cleared, he slung his arm around her shoulder and pulled her close for a hug. Just touching him, no matter how briefly, made her feel better.

"How long will you be gone?" she asked. Then, embarrassed, she shook her head. "What I meant to ask is how long will this girls' night last?"

"Probably three or four hours, I'd guess. You've got the

movie, plus snacks and drinks. If I know Debi, there'll be lots of good food."

Again she swallowed, trying to ignore the flutter of panic in her belly. "What should I wear?"

At this, he chuckled. "Wear whatever you want. I imagine everyone will want to be comfortable. You can wear jeans or shorts with a T-shirt."

Though she felt as if her feet were rooted to the floor, she managed to walk a few steps away. "And you'll be in the woods with your brothers? Hunting?"

"Yep. Changing. Hunting as wolves." The way he flashed his teeth in a quick smile reminded her of a wild animal. "It's been way too long for me. I really need this."

At the thought, she shuddered. She couldn't help herself.

Kane's gaze sharpened. He'd seen. Thankfully, he didn't comment. Heaven help her, but she thought he might really understand. She didn't know if she should feel warm and fuzzy about that, or afraid.

Chapter 7

For the next several hours, Lilly tried on different outfits from her limited wardrobe, paced in front of the full-length mirror, and tried to rehearse possible conversations inside her head. She'd probably speak as little as possible, but she also wanted to be prepared. She knew the other women were extremely curious about what her life had been like as a captive for fifteen years and needed to find a polite way to say "none of your business."

Other than that, she supposed she'd survive. That didn't prevent her stomach from twisting in a knot, though.

Exactly two hours and thirty-five minutes later, she stepped into the living room, as ready as she was ever going to be. Kane sat on the couch, reading. He looked up, his gaze traveling over her, the warm glow of his approval making her feel hot. "You look…perfect."

Attempting a smile, she finally gave up and settled for a nod. "I wish I wasn't so nervous."

Pushing himself up in a fluid motion, he crossed the room to her. She stood frozen as he loomed over her. Heart in her throat, she stared up at him, wondering. One side of his mouth curved in a smile as he reached out and casually fingered a tendril of her hair. She sucked in her breath, heat pooling in her lower body. Her heart pounded and she wondered if he would hug her or…something. Instead, he simply smoothed her hair away from her face. The gesture felt more intimate than a kiss, making her feel even more exposed and naked.

And more. She burned.

Shocked, she jerked away, hand to her throat, breathing fast. He didn't speak, or come after her. He just let her go.

Which was good. Wasn't it?

Rattled and confused, she pushed past him to the front door. As she stumbled outside, she inhaled fresh air, her mind whirling.

What exactly had just happened?

The sound of car tires on gravel interrupted her attempt to think things through. A bright red convertible, top down, pulled up. Debi, her mop of curly black hair secured by a colorful, paisley scarf, waved. "Are you ready?"

Glancing back at the cabin, Lilly nodded. She reached for the car handle and turned one more time. Relief flooded her as Kane appeared in the doorway, lifting his hand in a wave. She waved back and then got in the car.

Debi grinned at her and gunned the motor, making the tires spin and kick up dirt and rock. She cranked up the radio as they barreled down the narrow road, taking the turns as effortlessly as Kane's car had while Lilly gripped the door handle and tried not to look worried.

To her surprise, they'd barely turned from the gravel

road onto the paved main one, before Debi hung a quick right. "We all live on part of the family land," she explained, correctly interpreting Lilly's silent question. "You could have actually walked here if you'd cut through the woods, but I was afraid you'd get lost since you're not familiar."

Debi's rapid-fire way of talking made Lilly's head ache, even though the other woman's tone was friendly.

They pulled up in front of a beautiful stone and wood A-frame house. Two other vehicles, a white minivan and a four-door sedan, were parked in the drive.

"Sharon's already here," Debi told her, killing the engine and jumping out of the car. She raced across the drive toward the house, moving gracefully despite her platform heels.

Lilly glanced at her own flip-flops and shrugged. She climbed from the car and hurried after the other woman, who'd already disappeared inside. The front door stood wide open and the sounds of music and laughter drifted out.

Hesitating, Lilly smoothed her shirt down and took a deep breath. She placed one foot after the other, making her way toward the kitchen.

The instant she went around the corner, Debi looked up, beaming, and motioned her forward. "You know Sharon. She makes the best margaritas."

On cue, Sharon reached for a pitcher and, her long, perfectly manicured nails gleaming, poured some into a blue-rimmed margarita glass. "Here you go."

Accepting the drink, Lilly took a sip. To her surprise, it tasted good. "I like this," she marveled, realizing too late she should have tried to keep the shock out of her voice.

Both Debi and Sharon laughed. "Of course you do!"

Sharon's long, red curls bounced as she moved. The freckles that covered her pale skin looked as if they'd been painted on, a kind of natural adornment. Next to the two vibrant women, Lilly felt mousy, with her straight, dirty-blond hair and ordinary figure. But they took her in to their circle as if she was just like them, and made her feel welcome and at home.

The next couple of hours passed before Lilly realized it. They talked and joked and watched a long, mushy movie that she didn't entirely understand, but which made the other two women cry. She lost track of how many of the delicious margaritas she had, but it didn't seem to matter as she didn't feel any different.

At least, until she got up from the couch to go to the bathroom and the entire room tilted crazily. "Oh, gosh!" she said, and then giggled. Which so wasn't like her, but she didn't seem to care.

Debi and Sharon giggled with her. "Careful, honey. There's more tequila in that drink than you realize."

Lilly nodded, but that only made the spinning worse. She stumbled into the small powder room and closed the door. When she caught sight of herself in the mirror, she stared. Her pupils looked dark and unfocused and why on earth was she smiling that goofy smile?

She moved too quickly and the room spun. She began to feel queasy and had the uneasy feeling she might get sick.

Gripping the door frame to steady herself, she squared her shoulders and took a deep breath. When she made it back to the den where the movie credits were just now rolling, she went over to Debi and lightly touched her arm. "I need to go home."

Debi peered at her, squinting as if her eyesight had become impaired. "I thought you were staying the night?"

Pushing back the stab of panic, Lilly shook her head, which turned out to be a mistake. "No. I don't…feel well."

The other woman stared at her with a mixture of fascination and horror. "Are you about to get sick?"

"I don't know." Lilly concentrated on a single spot on the wall, willing everything to stay still. "But it's likely. And if you don't mind, I'd rather do that in my own cabin."

Debi and Sharon exchanged glances. "Neither one of us is in any shape to drive."

"That's fine," Lilly hurried to say. "Earlier you said I could have walked here. If you'd just point me in the right direction, that's what I'll do."

"I don't think it's a good idea for you to go stumbling around in the woods," Sharon put in drily. "Why don't you stay a while longer, have some water or coffee, and see how you feel?"

But a sense of urgency had taken hold and wouldn't let go. Lilly had to fight the urge to run for the door and rush out of there. "Really, I'll be fine."

She must have sounded convincing or, more likely, the others were equally impaired because Debi finally shrugged. "Fine. I'll walk outside with you and show you which way to go. As long as you stay headed that direction, you'll end up back at your cabin."

Lilly thought she did a convincing job of walking a straight line as she followed Debi outside. Sharon hadn't protested, too occupied with mixing up one final batch of margaritas. Lilly imagined the two of them would pass out on the sofa before the night was over.

Once they reached the driveway, Debi marched around to the back of the house. She pointed to a star shining through the upper tree branches. "Follow that star and you'll be fine."

"Thanks."

"I'd go with you," Debi offered half-heartedly. "But these shoes weren't made for tromping around in the woods. At least you don't have to worry about wild animals. They tend to leave our kind alone."

Our kind? Lilly guessed she meant Shifters. She started forward, keeping the star in her sight. One wave and Debi turned around and went back into the house, leaving Lilly alone.

She could do this. Slipping into the woods, Lilly breathed in the scents of pine and oak and earth and felt her head clearing. Moving carefully as her eyes adjusted to the darkness, she felt a thousand times better. Even better, the alcohol appeared to have put the monster inside her into some kind of stupor.

Since she didn't have a watch, she had no way of knowing how much time had passed, but after walking a while, always keeping that dang star in view, she thought she should have come across some part of Wolf Hollow. Instead she came to a small stream, managed to cross it and continued on, hoping she didn't end up lost.

A while later, she had to admit defeat. Stopping next to the massive trunk of an ancient oak, she pondered her next move. Should she stay put and wait for the sun to come up or continue on and hope for the best?

The sound of a wolf howl made her freeze. It was close. Really close.

Since Kane and his brothers were out here somewhere, hunting in their wolf shapes, she hoped it had come from one of them rather than a wild animal. But then she realized she didn't even know if they'd recognize her while they were wolves. She knew pathetically little about her own kind and what she'd managed to learn before being taken prisoner, she'd been forcibly made to forget. While she knew what she'd been taught—that they were demons out to take souls—was nonsense, she couldn't shake her terror.

Heart pounding, she felt around on the tree, wishing she could find a branch so she could pull herself up.

Something screamed—the shrill death cry of a small animal. Lilly froze, horrified.

At that instant, the thing inside her made a break for freedom.

Defenses down, Lilly reacted a second too late. Alcohol had dulled her senses. She slammed her mental barrier down, but the beast had already begun reshaping her body. Painfully.

As she fell to all fours, she let out a cry of pain, an awful cross between a howl and a snarl. Dimly, she realized her clothes were tearing as her bones elongated. With her last human thought, she hoped none of the others found her. She'd learned the last time how deadly her monster was to anyone or anything that dared approach it.

Kane. As she pushed herself off the leaf-strewn forest floor, noting the blood among the pieces of human clothing, she squashed the awful urge to use the last remnants of her human voice to call him to her.

But she couldn't. Not only did she know she couldn't bear him to see the horrible beast she was inside, but she would be dangerous to him. Not only to him, but to any male shifter.

Long ago, in the midst of the too-horrible-to-think-of experiments, the doctors of Sanctuary had performed on her, she'd listened and learned they wanted eventually to mate her and get her with child. A super-beast, they'd called it. They'd wanted to create an army of demons eventually.

At that moment she'd vowed to do whatever was necessary to prevent that from happening. Even as they'd injected her with hormones, used specially formulated pheromones to make her irresistible to Louis, the other poor soul they'd captured, planning to put them together and perpetuate the most unholy indignity of all.

And then he'd died. Poor Louis had been tortured and experimented on as much as she. They'd said too much testosterone and steroids had made his heart give out. Jacob Gideon, the man who'd called himself her father, had not been pleased.

As she moved forward, keeping to the shadows to better hide her misshapen form, she realized with a start that her thoughts were still logical, clearly human. Not the mishmash of furious rage she'd come to associate with her other self.

Strange. Emboldened by this, she moved forward, using her powerful nose to track the presence of Kane and his brothers. Though her beast's natural instinct was to seek them out, Lilly had enough self-control to push in the opposite direction. She would hunt, for the first time in nature since she'd been fifteen, and then make her way back to the cabin so she could regain her human form.

Hopefully, no one would be any the wiser.

A small rabbit was foolish enough to cross her path. When it saw her, rather than running, it froze. She made short work of killing it, feasting on the fresh meat. Then, leaving only the fur and a few small bones, she lifted her snout and scented the wind, searching for the unique scent of mankind.

Wolf Kane skidded to a stop, causing his brother Kris to crash into him. He snarled a quick warning, but barely spared either of his siblings a glance. Below him lay the fresh remains of a recent kill. And the scent of something else, a Shifter perhaps, but no scent he recognized.

Kyle growled low in his throat, making the same connection. No one in town was foolish enough to hunt on the McGraw family land without an invitation. Since he and his brothers had made their plans way in advance for this night, he knew no one local would have come here.

Then who?

The scent, decidedly female, made his wolf self go into high alert. His brothers, even though they'd already found their mates, whined. The scent made them uncomfortable rather than aroused. Which meant the scent only affected him.

A sneaking suspicion made him freeze. Lilly? He discounted the idea. She was with Sharon and Debi.

Another female Shifter. Remembering what Shawn had said about Anabel Lee, he snarled. Spinning on his paws, he took off for the place where they'd left their clothing. Once he'd changed back to human form, he'd get to the bottom of this.

His brothers were close on his heels as they raced for the protected clearing where they'd first shifted into their wolf shapes.

Not only was her sense of smell forty times better, but her animal self had eyes that could see much better in the dark. She managed to locate the cabin, even though not a single light was burning. Padding up as close as she dared, she lowered her belly to the ground and tried to force the beast to let her have her human shape again.

Of course, monster that it was, it resisted.

Keeping her breathing deep and even, Lilly employed the techniques she'd been taught. Despite having learned them at the hateful hands of the doctors of Sanctuary, they were effective. In a few moments, her body began to contort and twist. She found this part extremely painful, but eventually she was herself again. Naked, sore and aroused, which she always seemed to be for some reason.

At least no one was around to witness her humiliation. Not like the old days at Sanctuary.

Tiredly, she pushed to her feet and padded up on the porch, hoping Kane hadn't locked the door. Luck was actually on her side, and the knob turned easily.

Once inside, she headed straight for the shower. Under the hot water, she shampooed her hair and soaped every inch of her skin, and then repeated it all for good measure.

When she'd finished, she toweled off, found a clean T-shirt and panties, and climbed up on the bed, not even bothering to turn on the light. Closing her eyes, she let herself slide off to sleep.

Once he'd become human again, Kane grabbed his clothing and got dressed. Behind him, both of his brothers were doing the same.

"What the hell was that?" Kyle came up beside him, frowning. "I didn't recognize the scent."

Teeth clenched, Kane managed to shrug. "I don't know. Are you familiar with every local Shifter's scent?"

"Pretty much," Kris joined them. "At least any of the ones who'd be running on our land. This one wasn't local."

"A tourist?" Kyle scratched his head. "That'd be kind of weird. They'd know to check in with the town Pack, who'd give them directions to the safe common area for changing."

"I'm betting this wasn't a tourist," Kane said, already

striding off toward Wolf Hollow. "I have a pretty good idea who it might have been."

As his brothers hurried after him, their sharp intake of breath told him they'd realized who he meant.

"Lilly?" Kyle jogged up next to Kane. "Do you think she's finally over her issues with shifting?"

"I don't know," Kane said.

"She's supposed to be with Sharon and Debi," Kris put in. "So I doubt that was her."

Cutting across the swath of forest that led to Kris and Debi's house, Kane slowed to a jog when the stone building came into view, halting before he reached the sidewalk. Kyle did the same, but Kris strode past them, heading for the front door.

Exchanging a quick look, Kane and Kyle followed.

Once inside, the blaring television was the only sound. The half-empty tequila bottle, a glass pitcher and three matching margarita glasses bore testament to the party the women had enjoyed earlier.

None of the women was anywhere in sight. Of course, Kane glanced at the wall clock, it was nearly 1:00 a.m.

Kris reappeared. "Debi's asleep in our bed and Sharon has the guest room. I can't find Lilly, though."

"Wake Debi up," Kane demanded. "I need to know what happened to Lilly."

Though Kris didn't look too happy at the prospect, he went to get his wife.

A few minutes later, a bleary-eyed Debi appeared in the kitchen. Swaying, her eyes bloodshot, clearly still inebriated, she peered at Kane and Kyle with her brow furrowed in confusion. "What's going on?"

"Where's Lilly?"

Looking down, she shuffled her feet uneasily. Her

unruly dark hair fell over her face. "She wasn't feeling well, so she went home."

"Did you drive her?" Kane asked, even though he suspected he already knew the answer.

Debi bit her lip as she met his gaze. "No. I think she drank too much. We all did. And by the time she decided she wanted to leave, there was no way I was going to risk driving her."

Furious, Kane glared at her. "She's not used to alcohol. Come on, Debi. You and Sharon were supposed to look after her. Instead, you let her go wandering around the woods drunk in the dark."

At his words, Debi paled, looking as if she was going to be violently ill. "She…she didn't make it home?"

"We haven't checked there yet," Kris hurried to reassure his wife, after shooting Kane a furious look. "I don't know why you're getting all worked up. For all we know, she could be in bed asleep."

"She'd better be," Kane snarled, spinning on his heel and heading for the door.

After the briefest hesitation, his brothers followed.

Cutting through the woods in the direction of the cabin, Kane cursed when he nearly stumbled over Lilly's torn and shredded clothing. He stopped, picking up the scraps of cloth, noting the blood.

Kyle winced. "Damn. That must have been some painful change."

Again Kane cursed. "She'd better not be hurt."

"I'm sure she's all right." Kris touched his arm. "You need to calm down."

Moving swiftly, barely keeping his violence contained, Kane knocked his brother's arm away. He gathered up the remainder of Lilly's clothes and took off running.

When he reached the cabin, the first thing he noticed

was the complete absence of light. His heart stuttered in his chest as he took the porch steps all at once. He burst through the front door, belatedly realizing it was unlocked, and flicked on a lamp.

Ignoring Kyle's urging to slow down, he headed for Lilly's bedroom. The door was closed, but that meant nothing since she'd left it that way. Taking a deep breath, he turned the knob and pushed it open. And froze. Lilly slept, her head pillowed on her hand, long hair streaming out alongside her, oblivious to all the ruckus.

Kyle and Kris came up behind him, peering over his shoulder.

"Whew," Kris whispered, clearly relieved.

Kane moved them back, carefully shutting the door and motioning them back outside.

"See," Kris said, the instant they were back out under the stars. "You were worried for nothing."

"I'm still worried," Kane told him, his jaw clenched so tightly it hurt. He held up the torn and bloody clothing. "I have to find out what happened to her."

"Let her rest, bro." Kyle peered at him, his expression concerned. "You can talk to her in the morning."

Taking a deep gulp of air, Kane tried like hell to retrieve his earlier sense of well-being and calm. He couldn't shake the notion that he'd failed Lilly. By leaving her in the company of his brothers' wives, he'd left her unprotected. The fact that Debi had foolishly let Lilly go alone into the forest proved this.

"You can go home now," he said, aware he sounded brusque but beyond caring. "I'll see you guys in the morning."

Though Kyle still looked worried, he nodded. After a moment, Kris did, too.

"See ya," they chimed in unison, trying to sound normal and not entirely succeeding. Lifting his hand in a wave, Kane watched them until the darkness swallowed them up. They didn't know how to take his extreme behavior, but there was no way in hell that he could explain the entire reason to them. They understood the bare bones, but Lilly's story was hers to tell or not.

Returning to the house, he found himself back in the bedroom, as if compelled. Lilly still slept soundly, her chest rising and falling with each breath. He stood in the doorway and watched her, aching, still clutching her ruined things.

Then, gathering up every ounce of his willpower, he forced himself to back out of the room, and shut the door.

Lilly woke, her head aching. Heck, her entire body felt as if it had been stretched on some sort of medieval torture rack. Stretched. She sat up in bed, too quickly, making the room spin and nausea rise in her throat.

Last night, she'd let the beast inside her free. Her monster had, however briefly, won.

Stunned and sickened, she gagged. She'd drank too much, for starters. She should have known better, especially since she hadn't ever had alcohol. Sipping mixed drinks wasn't an activity the people of Sanctuary had been prone to. In fact, she remembered the kids in high school talking about getting drunk, as though it was fun. This had been before her father had put her under lock and key.

Though Debi and Sharon had seemed to enjoy it, Lilly knew it wasn't something she'd try again. Ever.

Pushing herself off the bed, she grabbed the edge of the door to steady herself, and took a deep breath. She staggered into the bathroom, her head pounding, wishing she could get rid of the awful taste in her mouth.

Turning on the shower, she peeled off her T-shirt and stepped under the hot spray.

When she emerged from the bathroom, not feeling a whole lot better, her heart sank as she realized Kane waited for her, his expression once again turned to stone.

Did he know? Had the scent she'd left behind in the woods alerted him to the fact that when she shapeshifted, she wasn't a wolf, but something else entirely? Something much, much worse?

Some of the panic that had flared inside her must have communicated itself to him. As she stared, waiting for him to speak, his expression softened.

"Come here," he said, his voice quiet as he held out his hand. "I want you to tell me about last night."

Still, she stood frozen, unable to make herself move. She'd learn to lie, and well, in her time at Sanctuary, but this was different. Kane didn't want to cut her up inside just to find out what made her tick. He asked out of concern rather than a desire to hurt.

She took a deep breath. Unable to shake the notion if she took his hand, he'd somehow be able to discern everything from her touch, she moved past him without touching him.

Taking a seat on the couch and demurely crossing her legs, her heartbeat skipping fast, she hoped like hell she appeared calm and composed. Slowly, she dragged her gaze up to meet his. "I had too much to drink last night. I wasn't feeling well, so I walked back here."

Truth, so far.

Kane didn't respond. Arms crossed, he waited. Though he still seemed remote, he didn't appear threatening. Of course, ever since she'd met him, Kane had been nothing but kind to her.

"And?" he finally prompted, letting her know he was aware she had more to tell.

"My...beast—" she struggled over finding the proper word to describe the thing inside her "—my beast fought me. It...won."

A gleam of interest made his silver eyes glow. He moved closer. "You changed?"

"Yes." As shame flooded her, her entire body grew hot. "I did. But as soon as I could regain control, I changed back."

"You should have hunted with us." His tone, while fierce, also sounded gentle. "My brothers and I would have welcomed your company."

Horrified, she could only stare at him, wondering if he'd lost his mind. "I thought you understood." Her voice broke. "Whatever those people at Sanctuary did to me..."

Unable to finish, she turned away, unwilling to let him see that her eyes had filled with tears.

Grateful when he didn't comment, she used the time to pull herself together. Of course he didn't understand. He hadn't been there. He hadn't seen. He didn't realize the thing inside her was a danger to him and any male it came into contact with.

As he lifted her head, the words hovered on the tip of her tongue, but the look on his face stopped her. Pity.

Pity from the last person she wanted it from. Pity from the only one she'd thought she could trust.

Chapter 8

Watching as Lilly tried not to weep, Kane had to clench his fists to keep from going to her and taking her in his arms.

At last he finally understood. Like an anorexic who, when looking in the mirror, always saw a heavy body, Lilly truly believed her wolf was deformed, some kind of monster. Part of her healing process would be confronting her wolf self and discovering that she was a wolf, nothing more. Nothing worse.

Looking at him, she gasped. "Don't." She shook her head so rapidly her long hair whipped around her. She sounded broken.

Damn propriety. In three strides he reached her and hauled her up against him. With her head tucked under his chin, he inhaled the shampoo scent in her hair. "I'm sorry," he murmured, meaning it.

"Don't be." Holding herself stiffly, her low voice vibrated with pain. "I'll be fine."

When she pulled out of his arms, he had no choice but to let her go. And ache as he watched her, back to him, struggle mightily to keep all of her emotions buried inside her.

He wished she'd simply get angry, beat on him with her fists, something. Anything would be better than pretending she didn't feel anything.

Maybe some exercise would help her. "Go and put on some loose-fitting clothes."

Clearly shocked, she swung around to face him. "What?"

"We're going to my sister's house. She and her husband have a state-of-the-art workout studio out back. It's time you start learning a few self-defense moves."

"Okay," she said, surprising him, before disappearing into her bedroom, closing the door after her.

While she changed, he located a pair of gym shorts and put those on. As he was lacing up a pair of sneakers, she emerged. She'd tied her hair back in a ponytail and wore what looked like expensive yoga clothes. He tried not to notice the way the workout shorts clung to her shapely bottom, or the way her fitted yoga top highlighted her new lush curves.

Despite himself, his body stirred. He turned away, disgusted with himself. Of all the times for his libido to start acting up.

Since Kathy lived right around the corner, they were there in under a minute. Kane had an open invitation to use the gym so he didn't have to phone ahead. He retrieved the key from its hiding place inside a fake rock and unlocked the door.

Once he flicked on the light switch, he stepped aside so that Lilly could enter.

"Wow, this is really nice." She stood just inside the

doorway, surveying the large open space with one mirrored wall and all kinds of professional gym equipment. With the sunlight illuminating her dirty-blond hair, her aura had taken on a golden glow. It looked almost healthy.

"Kathy's husband must be serious about working out," she continued.

"He is. Tom used to be a professional bodybuilder," Kane told her.

Moving to the center of the room, he took out two mats and placed them on the floor.

Lilly followed, constantly turning to take in every aspect of the room. He didn't blame her. The entire family always joked that Tom could turn the place into a paying gym if he wanted to.

"So what now?" she asked.

"First, we warm up. Do what I do." Smiling at her, he began to move. "Do what I do." He ran through a serious of jumping jacks, push-ups, sit-ups, then stretching. Finally, he showed her a few basic kicks.

Her form looked good and she completed every exercise. By the time they'd finished the warm-up, a light sheen of perspiration covered her forehead, making her creamy skin appear to glow. This captivated him for a moment, before he shook it off. Still, he had to wonder what the hell was wrong with him. Focus. He needed to focus.

"What else?" Balancing on the balls of her feet, she appeared energized by the exercise. "I'm ready to learn how to fight."

He grinned. "Bloodthirsty, aren't we?"

Grinning right back, she gave an exaggerated shrug. "It feels good to be in control, even if it's only practice."

Again, he felt another flush of attraction, which he managed to ignore. "Good. Now remember an assailant isn't going to walk up to you and calmly ask you to go with him or her. Most likely, they'll be jumpy and jittery. You can turn that against them."

She nodded, appearing focused and comfortable.

"You look relaxed."

She flashed him a smile. "I am."

"Don't be. Adrenaline is important," he told her. "You can use it as a tool. We're going to run through some attack scenarios. Start by targeting your attacks to the body's most vulnerable points. The eyes, neck or throat, face, groin, ribs, knee, foot, fingers, etcetera. You hit them where they're most vulnerable. Your goal is to counterattack as quickly as possible."

"In other words, how to end it efficiently." Her tight lipped smile looked more like a grimace.

"Yes. In addition to that, you have to develop an awareness of your surroundings so you can escape if possible."

"I'm ready."

"Then let's go." First he walked her through a potential choking situation, showing her how to break the hold and also what not to do. He split each move into steps and they practiced one at a time. First a block, then a palm strike and ending with a quick knee to the groin.

Once it seemed she had all the moves down, the time had come to try it at full speed.

Surprisingly, she balked at this. "I don't want to hurt you."

He couldn't help himself; he laughed. After a startled second, she did, too. It felt good, releasing the lingering tightness in his chest.

"I'm sorry." Biting her lip, she peered up at him through her long lashes, looking not the least bit contrite. "But I sometimes don't even know my own strength."

"You need to learn."

She nodded. "All right. I'm ready."

The first time, he took care to be gentle, holding back a large portion of his might. She flipped him easily, partly because he anticipated it.

Frowning at him, she shook her head. "Don't hold back."

He gave her own words back to her. "I don't want to hurt you."

"It doesn't matter whether I'm hurt or not. I want to learn. If they come for me, the last thing they're going to care about is not hurting me."

Because she had a valid point, he pushed up from the floor and launched himself at her. At the instant before he connected, she twisted, ducked sideways, and took him down with a swift kick to the knee.

Stunned, he didn't have time to protect himself and fell, his right hip taking the full weight of his body.

"What the…"

She'd taken a step back, looking as shocked as he felt. In that second, he realized what the wrong response would do to her already fragile self-confidence.

"Excellent!" Steeling himself not to wince as pain stabbed through him, he pushed to his feet. "Again."

This time, he made his movements more deliberate. Still, she managed to elude him, shaking off his grip while at the same moment landing a powerful kick to his stomach.

Winded, he grinned at her while he tried to recapture his breath. "Good job."

Though she didn't appear entirely convinced, she flashed a quick smile and came closer, extending her hand. "Are you all right?"

"Fine," he huffed, even as he realized he wanted to

grab her fingers and pull her down beside him so he could kiss her. Just the thought was enough to catapult him to his feet.

Careful not to look at her in case she read his desire in his eyes, he crossed to the small refrigerator and pulled out a couple of bottles of water. "Want one?" he offered.

"Please." When she reached for it, their hands connected. A jolt of pure lust ran through him, fingertip to arm, straight to his groin. He covered this by opening his water and draining the bottle.

After a moment, she did the same, though she only drank half of hers. "Are we done?"

Was that his imagination, or had her voice gone husky? Quickly, he decided he was hearing things thanks to his overheated libido.

"Not yet." He managed a casual smile. "We're going to do more push-ups, but this time I want you to jump up into a palm strike. Kind of like a burpee with a punch. This will prepare you in case you ever get knocked to the ground and have to fight for your life."

She nodded. "Now?"

Though his hip still ached from his fall, and his abs still felt the impact of her blow, he nodded. "Now."

A few rounds of this and he called it. "I think we've done enough for one day."

Though she was barely breathing hard, she agreed. "I'd like to go back to the cabin and shower. Then I want to spend the rest of the afternoon relaxing."

About to take her arm, he thought better of it. "You've earned it."

"So have you." The warm gratitude in her smile matched the glow in her blue eyes.

Raw need had his blood heating. The surge of desire again angered him at its inappropriateness. He was her

Protector, not her seducer. Yet even that knowledge didn't stop him from desiring her.

"Let's go." Though he knew he sounded gruff, there was no help for that. He led the way out the door, stepping aside to allow her past, before locking up and replacing the key in its hiding place.

Lilly couldn't decide what she'd done. Kane had been the epitome of friendliness, grinning his devilish grin at her and helping her learn how to take an assailant down quickly.

But then, something had changed. Surely he wasn't angry that she'd knocked him to the floor? She'd only done what he'd taught her to do.

No, she believed she knew him well enough now to know that wasn't it. Then what?

Every time she thought about asking him, the words stuck in her throat. Truth be told, she wasn't entirely sure she wanted to know.

She wanted to kiss him. And maybe more. At fifteen, when she'd been imprisoned, she'd been a complete innocent. In the fifteen years since, that hadn't changed. Though she realized she might be the only thirty-year-old virgin around, she hadn't been free, or normal, long enough to change that. And she wasn't even certain she wanted to.

Until now. Kane made her want things she couldn't even articulate. She ached for his touch and dreamed about his kiss. This had to be a crush, much like the ones she'd had when she'd been fourteen, a kind of formless yearning. Kane would probably laugh if he knew.

They arrived back at the cabin only to find Kane's mother had left some sandwiches and chips on the table for them. They ate together, which felt both familiar and uncomfortable. Every time Kane's glance touched on her, Lilly burned.

When they'd finished, she murmured something about needing to rest, and promptly disappeared into her bedroom.

Instead, she showered again, as if by doing so she could wash off the strong pull of desire. Clean, she put on a pair of denim shorts and a T-shirt and blow-dried her hair.

As she debated checking out the latest fashion magazine Kathy or one of the others had left for her, Lilly heard the clear notes of Kane's guitar. Cocking her head, she stood still and listened, waiting for the music to quiet the ever-present struggle still roiling inside her.

Instead, he stopped playing. Disappointed, she opened her door, realizing he'd gone outside on the front porch. She stood still, waiting as she heard him pick out another note or two.

Again silence fell. Intrigued, she went outside.

He sat on the edge of the steps, with his guitar and a pad of paper.

"What are you doing?"

When he looked up, his mouth curved into an unconsciously seductive smile. "Trying to write a song. I used to do this for fun, but it's been too long." As if to demonstrate, he strummed a few more chords. "Listen to this." And he played the better part of a melody.

Something about it touched her deep inside. Though she wasn't vain enough to think he might have written it for her or about her, the melody felt personal.

He played it once more. "What do you think?"

"I like it." She smiled, tentative. "I actually feel as if I could be good at making up words to that particular tune."

"Do you?" He smiled back, encouraging. "Why don't you try then? Let me hear what you've got."

And he strummed the guitar and began to play once more.

Though she hadn't sung out loud since she'd been a child, Lilly couldn't help herself. She'd never had a reason to, not before. Music equaled contentment, happiness, joy and peace. And perhaps something more. All she knew, right now, was the time was right.

So she began singing, some of the words fragments that had been running through her head ever since she'd left Seattle. The others, she made up as she went along. She didn't know if she had a good voice or bad, she only knew with music, she felt free of her demons. The time had come to let her voice free.

And she sang.

After one, quick, startled look, Kane nodded and continued playing. As if they'd worked together before, he fell into the rhythm. Joining with her, as if they were inside each other's minds. Creating, making music.

Glorious.

She let her voice soar, abdicating rational thought or limitations, vaguely aware that this song connected the monster inside her with her true self, in ways that felt real and right. And maybe, not so evil after all.

Darkness swirled, lightening into something seductive, and she glanced at Kane. He watched her, expression savage, as though need and yearning and desire had transformed him into something else.

Something else… She didn't understand, but she realized it had something to do with her voice, with the song. Heart sinking, she understood the awful power she could wield over this man. Those damn experiments they'd done on her—she had no idea of all the changes those doctors at Sanctuary had made to her psyche. Had this been one of them?

Horrified, she closed her mouth, turning to run from him, not wanting to see what she'd done. Too late. He shoved aside his guitar, uncaring when the instrument hit the floor with a discordant clang. Even as she leaped forward, he was faster, and his fingers closed around her arm, the opposite of gentle.

Desire made his eyes molten silver. He yanked her toward him, letting her feel the strength of his arousal. She knew what he was about to do. Oh, she knew and some small part of her reveled in it. The power, the craving, the need, all tangled up together like some horrific spider's web, leaving nothing but chaos in its wake.

He slanted his mouth over hers, his lips hard and cruel and possessive. Not like him at all, she felt, then gave up any attempt to think. Heat flared, feeding her hunger. Angry, she wanted him to ravish her, even as she struggled to escape his hold.

Ecstasy flared, dark and bright and urgent, all at the same time.

This wasn't her, yet was. And Kane, he'd become a savage stranger, the blankness of his gaze telling her he knew not what he did.

She wanted him, but not like this. This wasn't real, wasn't about her at all. Something else, her siren's song, compelled him. It would be up to her to bring this to a crashing halt. If…she wanted to.

Her senses reeled, sending her equilibrium diving and crashing. Blood pounded through her body, searing her with a fire that craved only one release. Him. Buried deep inside her.

She gasped as his mouth seared a path down her throat. Her legs turned to putty, and she sagged against him, even as her hands moved of their own volition to the bulge in the front of his jeans.

No. What was she doing? From a distance, she heard herself protest, then heard herself scream. Somehow, she found the strength to push him away. Expression glazed with passion, he came at her again. He was strong, too strong for her to overcome, and she knew her only chance would be to try to reach inside to the man he truly was.

"Kane." Her voice, hesitant and frightened, didn't reach him. She tried again. "Kane. Stop. Right now."

Something flickered in the liquid silver of his gaze. Recognition? Sidestepping, she managed again to evade him, though every bone in her body ached to let him crush her against him once more.

"Kane." Louder. "You don't want to do this. Wake up. It's me, Lilly." Her voice rose. "Kane. You're supposed to be protecting me."

That reached him, she could tell. He froze, shook his head as forcefully as a wounded bear and growled. When he blinked, she saw him come back to himself. "Lilly?"

"It's okay," she soothed, aware of the bitter irony. "You're all right."

"What have I…" The instant his arousal registered, he flushed a dark red. "I don't understand. I…apologize." Turning away, he bowed his head. "You need to leave."

Though she didn't want to, she couldn't help but see the wisdom in that. Still, despite that, she stood her ground. "I need to explain."

"Not. Now." He ground the words out through what sounded like clenched teeth.

For the first time, she sensed that maybe his arousal hurt him. She who had zero experience with men or sex had no idea if that was possible or not. "Fine." Conceding, she spun around and headed into her bedroom. "Call me when you're ready to talk. I suspect I've got a lot of explaining to do."

Kane watched her go, his body throbbing. What the hell had just happened? He had no clear memory of it; the last thing he knew, he'd been strumming his guitar and then Lilly had come into the room and started singing. Even the memory of her seductive voice sent a thrum of desire through his blood.

Hell hounds. He'd played some chords, and she'd started to sing. They'd been writing music, he thought. What had happened after that, he couldn't remember.

Obviously, she knew what had happened and why. And as soon as he got his overheated body under control, he meant to get some answers. For now, he gulped in air, wondering why he had to struggle even to breathe.

As soon as he could walk normally again, he made it into the kitchen, popped open a beer, and drank half the can in a few swallows. He wiped his mouth with the back of his hand. Again, he pictured Lilly. Her mouth had appeared bruised and swollen, matching the tingling in his. Had they kissed? He knew damn well he'd definitely remember if they had. Instead, he drew a complete blank. How on earth could he have no memory of something so momentous?

Stepping outside, he breathed deeply, hoping the pine-scented air would help clear his head.

He glanced at the chair, his guitar next to it, decided no, and kept on going. He needed to go, he needed to run. Yet, he realized he couldn't outrun her. Hell, he couldn't leave her. He was her Protector.

But who the hell was going to protect him from himself?

He wanted her. Of course he did. He'd felt that click of connection the first time he'd seen her, when he'd been part of the team who'd rescued her from the basement underneath Sanctuary. Then, he'd thought it was because he'd become friends with her twin brother. But later, during one of his many visits to her while she'd been hospitalized, he'd come to understand it was more. Deeper. Deeper than it should be, perhaps. But he'd believed he could handle it, aware of the strength of the barriers he'd erected around his self-control. He had not the slightest doubt he could keep them intact, no matter the provocation.

And now this. How the hell he could black out while playing music and then come to, fully aroused, was beyond him. Especially since he knew if he ever got together with Lilly, he'd sure as heck remember.

As he moved off the front porch, his cell phone rang. Not his regular one, but the disposable phone he'd purchased to keep in touch with Lucas. Lucas had the exact same phone.

"What's up?" Kane asked.

"They burned my house," Lucas said, sounding furious. "Broke in while we were all out to dinner and torched the place."

Kane cursed. "No one was hurt?"

"That's the only good thing. The fire department came right away, but the place is a total loss."

"You're sure it was them?"

"Oh, yeah." Now the other man's voice rasped, positively savage. Previously, Kane had only heard his friend use that tone when planning the assault of Sanctuary to free Blythe and her daughter. "Even in my human form, I can smell the accelerant. Worse, the fire department's arson investigator wants me to come in for questioning. They think I set my own home on fire!"

"What are you going to do?"

"After I deal with the arson investigator and the police, who also want to talk to me, I'm taking Blythe and Hailey and disappearing for a while. We're heading to my cabin."

"Good idea." Kane had always envied Lucas his isolated retreat in the Colorado mountains. It would be the perfect place for him to shield his family from the madness engendered by the crazy followers of Jacob Gideon. "Even though their leader's in prison, they just don't give up, do they?"

"My guess is that whatever they did to my sister is extensive enough that they feel they've got to get her back. Has she told you any information about her time while in captivity?"

"Not yet." Even with her twin, Lilly had been extremely reluctant to share the horrors she'd endured.

"She alluded to experiments," Lucas continued. "But other than saying her inner wolf was no longer a wolf, she refused to elaborate. Which fits in with what they tried to do to Blythe while she was there. I imagine they perfected their methods on Lilly since they had fifteen years to implement them."

The anger that surged through Kane stunned him. He wanted to break something, punch someone, or rip something in half. "I need to change," he muttered.

Lucas's short bark of laughter told him the other man knew exactly what he meant. "I bet you do." His tone lowered, became serious. "Just be careful around Lilly. She freaked out the few times I mentioned it to her."

"Same here. But she's going to have to do it sometime," Kane mused. "Otherwise she's going to start having other problems."

"I think…" Lucas's hesitation completed his sentence. Kane knew Lucas thought that some of the problems experienced by shifters who went too long without changing had already manifested in his sister.

For all Kane knew, he might be right. "Do you know if such things are reversible?"

"That's a question for the Healer."

Kane agreed. "I've already started a list. I've been instructed to contact her, but not until I have a good handle on things."

"Keep me informed," Lucas said. "Listen, I'm going to go. I wanted to let you know where we're going to be. We've got to get out of Seattle before those idiots come back and decided to try for Blythe or Hailey."

"Make sure you're not followed."

"Of course. Talk to you later." Lucas ended the call.

"Who was that?"

Kane turned, finding Lilly eyeing him thoughtfully. He wondered how much of the conversation she'd heard, and then wondered why he hadn't heard her approach. At the very least, the sound of the dead leaves under her feet should have alerted him.

Quickly, he filled her in on what had happened to her brother.

"He loved that house," she said numbly. "He and Blythe were in the middle of renovating it. Why would someone do something like that?"

Though he hated to tell her, she needed to know the truth. "To get to you. They're trying to flush you out."

The stubborn tilt of her chin told him she wasn't buying it. "That makes no sense. I wasn't there. Lucas and his family weren't even there, thank goodness. It sounds like they're trying to prove a point."

Relieved, he nodded. "That's right. In a way, they are. They want to make sure we know they mean business."

"Even though their leader is in prison?" She frowned, her expression troubled. "Sanctuary has been disbanded. Their building is empty. What could they possibly hope to gain?"

"You."

Grim-faced, she nodded. "But why? What are they going to do once they have me?"

Though he didn't even like to consider the possibility, he managed to shrug. "Maybe since they apparently still regard Jacob Gideon as their prophet, they expect him to raise Sanctuary up from the ashes once he's freed."

"That's not going to be for a long time."

Unless he escaped. Briefly, Kane wondered if the Protectors had even considered this possibility. Of course they had. He decided not to mention it to Lilly.

"Who knows what whackos like that think? The important thing is that Lucas and his family are safe."

"True. Where are they going to go now that their home is gone?"

"He has another place, hidden away."

She nodded. "It's probably best that I don't know."

Another flash of misgiving. Was she aware of something that might happen, something he wasn't? He pushed away the supposition, well aware that in situations like this, he could only act on facts, not speculation.

"In case I'm captured," she elaborated, looking grim. "They're awfully good at torture, you know."

Then he understood. She could only face little pieces of her horrific past at a time.

His heart clenched. "Come on. We need to talk."

Looking down, she studied her hands. "I was afraid of that."

Chapter 9

Once they reached the cabin, Lilly hurried inside, heading straight for the kitchen. She looked up, flashing a sheepish smile. "I feel better if I can keep busy. I might as well get something started for dinner."

As she stood up on tiptoe to inspect the contents of the top shelf of the pantry, he couldn't help but admire her slender curves and the way her legs in her denim shorts seemed to go on forever. Instead of her earlier ponytail, she wore her hair lose, and the silky strands swirled around her shoulders. She moved like a dancer, completely unaware of either her beauty or her grace.

Kane swallowed hard, battling the urge to go to her and take her in his arms.

Instead, he crossed to the other side of the breakfast bar, keeping it between them, and climbed up on a stool.

"Do you want to tell me what happened earlier?"

She froze, turning slowly. "I don't know, exactly."

Lowering her lashes, she flicked an imaginary insect off her arm.

"Try."

"I started singing and you…had a strange reaction."

Though he knew she had no idea how sensual he found her voice, desire once again stabbed him.

"I can assure you," she muttered hastily. "I won't let that happen again."

"Let *what* happen again," he pressed, keeping his tone calm and patient.

Expression miserable, she dropped her chin. "I'm not sure, but I think it has something to do with all the experiments the doctors were doing on me at Sanctuary."

The words, hung there, almost sounding like deluded ramblings, except for one thing. Kane had been in the laboratory at Sanctuary; he'd seen. And he recognized the possible ring of truth in what she said.

A shudder of foreboding passed through him. The Pack Protectors would have to be notified as soon as he had the full story.

Lilly had already been through more than most. More than enough. If the three missing members of Sanctuary were to recapture her, he could only imagine what they'd try to do. Their experiments would be accelerated since they would be aware they could be captured at any moment.

Lilly would once again be nothing more than a lab rat.

The thought of this made his gut twist. He couldn't let anything like that happen to her. Not only would he have to protect her from the Sanctuary fanatics who were searching for her, but from her own, inner psyche. Damn.

"Sit." Releasing her, he indicated the rocking chair. He waited until she was seated before lowering his bulk into the one next to her. "How much did they tell you?"

"About what they were doing to me?" Her full lower lip trembled, giving him the urge to softly run his thumb over it. "They taunted me with it every day. But I don't have any idea what was truth and what was lies."

He saw agitation boiling up under her outward demeanor. While he desperately wanted to know, gut instinct told him that here, he needed to go slow.

"It's not your fault." Reaching over, he gave her shoulder an awkward pat, aware what he really wanted to do was pull her onto his lap and hold her. Kiss her. And more.

Dammit. He shut the thought down. "You can tell me more when you think you're up to it," he said, feeling the warmth of her grateful smile.

"There's not much more to tell. They barely spoke to me, except when they prayed for the demons to release their hold on my soul."

He shuddered. "You do know they are insane, right?"

As she stared at him, one corner of her mouth lifted in the beginning of a smile. "The longer I'm away from them, the more I've come to see this."

He refused to let himself smile back. Pushing up from the stool, he moved toward the bathroom. "Let me get cleaned up, and then I'll help you make something to eat."

Lilly refused to let Kane help with the cooking. She wanted to try out her extremely limited culinary skills. She made grilled cheese sandwiches and canned tomato soup for their dinner. Kane devoured his with as much pleasure as if she'd prepared a gourmet feast. She found herself watching him instead of eating, wishing she could take that much pleasure in something. She'd bet he dreamed in vivid color rather than the muted shades of gray that made up her own dreams.

"How about we pay a visit to my family?"

His voice, deliberately casual, startled her. She'd just carried the plates to the sink and started cleaning up the kitchen after their meal.

"Your family?" Stalling, she couldn't come out and tell him how much his boisterous kinfolk frightened her. Anyway, she guessed he already knew.

"We can't avoid them the entire time we're here," he pointed out, still sounding calm and reasonable. "If we try, they're just going to show up here at our cabin. I'd rather keep what privacy we have and meet them on their own turf."

Put that way, she understood. "I don't mean to be so…"

"It's okay." He squeezed her shoulder, a friendly touch which reassured her. "I promise they don't bite."

Again, the image of a wolf, jaws open, sharp teeth gleaming, flashed into her mind. She couldn't help but shudder, wondering how they dealt with such a vicious animal inside them. She'd tried to talk to her brother about that, but Lucas hadn't understood and she'd given up. Since then, she'd known better than to try to explain her feelings to anyone, including the therapist she'd seen in Seattle several times.

She sure as heck wasn't mentioning it to Kane.

"All right," she finally said. "Let's go."

At least this time, they were headed up to the main house after the rest of the family was sure to have finished eating.

She liked that he also knew when to be quiet. They set out side-by-side from their cabin, each lost in their own thoughts. She could tell he also enjoyed the myriad of sounds that meant the wood creatures were awakening and felt no need to warn the animals of their presence with needless chatter.

The feeling of companionship, of kinship with this tall, muscular man—though it puzzled her if she thought too hard about it—was something to be savored and appreciated.

As they rounded the corner in the path, side-by-side, the front door opened and several of the older children spilled out. Laughing and jumping and wrestling, they chased each other on the small patch of lawn, weaving in and out of the trees.

The adults followed, moving more slowly, but talking and gesturing with as much animation. Kane's family lived with vibrancy and a love of life they were willing to share with anyone lucky enough to pass into their orbit. They'd certainly reached out and welcomed her time and time again, undeterred by her repeated efforts to distance herself. Sometimes she thought they somehow knew how badly she wanted to share in their world and how badly her fear held her back.

No one had noticed Kane and Lilly yet. They were moving toward a footpath that led through the trees up a hill to the east of the main house, talking and joking. The scent of pipe tobacco drifted back from Kane's father's pipe.

Kane watched his family with a sort of bemused envy. She guessed he badly wanted to go with them, whereever they were headed.

"What's going on?" Lilly asked, frowning. "It'll be twilight soon."

He glanced at her, the light in his eyes fading. "They're heading up to a part of the woods that adjoins the Catskill Forest Preserve. It's really isolated and not accessible by vehicle."

"Why? To hike? Do you want to join them?"

Slowly he shook his head, never taking his gaze off

her. "No. I completely forgot that they told me they're going into the forest to change tonight. You know, shape-shift into wolves. They invited us to join them, but after your reaction last time, I said no."

She stared, ignoring the tiny flutter of panic. "I can't…" she said, expecting him to try to change her mind.

Instead, he nodded. "I know. It's okay. Everything will come with time."

Not this, she vowed silently. He and his family had no idea what kind of thing lived inside of her. Nor would they ever find out, at least as long as she drew breath.

Together they watched silently as his family trouped up the hill and vanished from sight. Lilly found herself wishing she had enough nerve to take his hand.

"Come on," he said, as the last person disappeared over the hill. "How about you and I do a bit of exploring on our own?"

Another frisson of fear. "Won't we get in their way? I'd hate to run into them."

A shadow crossed his face. Regret? She wasn't sure.

"We won't. They'll be far enough that we shouldn't, but just to make certain, we'll go the opposite direction. Don't worry, I'm familiar enough with these woods that we won't have a problem."

Aware he was making sacrifices for her, she shook her head. "Why don't you go and join them. I promise I'll go back to our cabin and wait for you."

"Absolutely not." He didn't even hesitate. "I'm not leaving you here alone." Glancing at the house, he flashed a smile. "I have an idea. We'll grab a few things from the house—I know my mother baked lots of treats—and we'll have a hike and a dessert picnic. Desserts and champagne. Would you like that?"

Her heart melted at his almost boyish eagerness. Still, she hesitated. "It's going to be dark soon."

"So? We've got flashlights and lanterns. Plus the moon's still close to full. It'll provide a lot of light."

Though she had her misgivings, she had to admit it sounded like fun. Or at least better than another night alone with him in the cabin, each of them trying too hard to be like friends. "Okay."

"Great!" Grabbing her hand, he tugged her toward the main house. "This is going to be awesome."

His enthusiasm appeared to be contagious. Heart skipping, she let him pull her. They hurried along, through the front door, toward the kitchen. Passing the main refrigerator, he headed toward the laundry room. "She keeps a second one in here," he said. Sure enough, there was another one nearly as big as the first.

He let go of her hand to open the stainless-steel door. "Jackpot!"

Inside were cakes, pies and assorted other sweets. She counted at least four kinds of cookies, chocolate-covered strawberries, which made her mouth water, and what looked like custards and puddings or flan.

"My goodness. There's enough here to feed a small army."

His grin widened. "Exactly."

"Are you sure she won't mind?"

"Are you kidding me?" He shook his head, continuing before she could even answer. "This is what my mom lives for. She loves to cook and bake, and feeding people is her vocation. So look around and pick out whatever you'd like."

While she deliberated, he grabbed a basket from a stack on a shelf. "She keeps these here in case any of her kids or grandkids want to take food home or have a picnic."

Inside, she saw a red-checked cloth, plastic cutlery, paper plates and napkins. "Ready-made picnic?"

"Yep."

She picked out a few things that looked appetizing, including the chocolate-covered strawberries, then backed away and let him choose the rest. He grabbed a bottle of champagne from the door of the fridge, two plastic glasses and a corkscrew, and closed the basket.

"All ready." He sounded so happy, she couldn't help but smile.

"I wouldn't peg you for someone with a sweet tooth," she commented.

His only response was a conspiratorial grin.

Once outside again, he led her in the opposite direction from that his family had gone in. This helped quell some of her nervousness. "How much land does your family own?"

"Forty acres. And beyond that is the Catskill Forest Preserve. So we're pretty isolated out here."

Which she supposed was good if one was a Shapeshifter.

"What about the people who live in town? Where do they go when they want to change into wolves?"

"The preserve, mostly. No one would trespass on our land without being invited."

Though she knew he'd added the last to reassure her, she couldn't help but glance out into the thick forest. They reached a clearing, a small glade really, with a couple of large boulders stacked on top of each other.

"Here we are." He set down the basket. "When I was a kid, I loved to use this rock as my own personal fort."

Helping her up, she marveled at the way her skin

seemed to tingle where his hands touched. He passed her the basket, which was surprisingly heavy, before climbing up and joining her.

Once he'd gotten settled, he spread the checkered cloth on the flat part of the rock, placed a few paper plates, and then removed all the delicacies he'd packed in the basket. Once they were all on display, in their delectable, tempting beauty, he popped the cork on the champagne.

"Only a small glass for me," she cautioned, as she popped a chocolate-covered strawberry into her mouth.

Ignoring her, he filled the plastic glass before handing it to her. "Here you go."

She watched as he sampled one of everything, finally settling on a large slice of cheesecake. He ate with relish, the way he did everything, and she enjoyed watching him.

After eating a couple more strawberries and taking a few more sips of champagne, she settled with her back against the large boulder, and looked around at the wilderness. "Will you be able to find our way back once it gets dark?"

For an answer, he reached inside the basket and brought out a flashlight. "Yep, with this to help us."

Before she could respond, a howl drifted on the breeze, otherworldly and eerie. The sound sent a shiver up her spine.

Kane noticed. "No worries. They're a good distance away."

Glancing at him, she nodded. Then she took a second look. His aura...for a moment the vague glow had coalesced, resembling one of the wolves that haunted her dreams.

"Are you..." Hesitant, she asked, "Are you okay?"

One dark brow rose. "Sure. Are you?"

His profile seemed to waver, flashing from human

to wolf and back again. Suddenly nervous again, she couldn't help but wonder if he was about to change shape. She didn't know how she'd react to this, and she really didn't want to find out.

More howls, several together, the sound rising and falling and drifting into the air.

The monster inside her woke, stretching, reaching out with razor-sharp claws. Reacting.

She swallowed hard and slammed down her mental prison. "What's going on?" she asked, unable to keep the rising panic out of her voice. "Are you about to shift into a wolf? Is the sound of your family as wolves affecting you?"

"Maybe a little," he admitted. "But it's all right. I'll change later, after you go to sleep. Don't worry, I'm not going to go all lupine on you."

"Lupine?" And then she knew. The word meant *wolf.*

A veritable chorus of howls made talking difficult. "I don't know about you," she said, her breath catching. "But I think they're getting closer."

He cocked his head, listening. "Maybe you're right. Though that doesn't make sense. We never venture over this way unless…"

Twisting her hands in her lap, she waited for him to finish. When he didn't, she prodded him. "Unless what?"

Unfolding his long legs, he pushed up from the ground, holding out his hand and pulling her to her feet. "Unless they're following prey. They're hunting after all. Come on, I'd better get you back to the cabin."

Blind terror made it difficult to see. She hated this about herself. Despised the unreasonable panic, the character flaw that had taken away any backbone she might have once had. Intellectually, she knew this was due to years of conditioning and suffering as Jacob Gideon's captive, but emotionally the frustration could be overwhelming.

Worse, the instant she let down her guard, the thing inside her tried to fight its way free.

"No." Gripping Kane's hand, she leaned into him, taking strength from the warmth of his body.

"You don't want to go?" Sounding surprised, he squinted at her. "I mean, I know they wouldn't hurt you, but I thought you…"

His words barely registered as she struggled internally. Heaven help them all if her monster managed to break free around anyone else. It had happened once, in the lab. Before they'd shot the tranquilizer dart into her, she'd killed two lab technicians and a doctor. Worse, she had absolutely no memory of doing it.

The numerous tortures that followed had ensured she'd been well and painfully punished for that.

She wouldn't change, couldn't allow the beast inside her to win. Not now, not ever. But was she strong enough to hold it back when it had become this determined?

"Help. Me." She pushed the words from her, reaching out blindly, hoping and praying she could somehow add his strength to her own.

More howls. The sound excited her beast, energizing it and encouraging it to double the attempt to force her to change.

She felt her bones begin to lengthen. "No," she cried, writhing in pain. "I can't let this happen."

At that, he pulled her close, wrapping his strong arms around her. Her inner animal didn't know how to react to this, and Lilly seized this advantage to force it back inside its mental cage.

As she struggled, Kane continued to hold her. Gradually, she became aware of the sound of his heartbeat under her ear.

"Shh." His large hand swept over her hair. "It's all right. I won't let anything happen to you, I swear."

Did he still think his family's wolf howls frightened her? The next second, she had her answer.

"Lilly, if you want to change, I'll help you. I can stay human if you'd like, or change right along with you."

Horrified, she pushed him away. "You have no idea what you're saying."

"I think I do. Your inner wolf responded to the sound of the howls. That's all right—mine did, too. I know it's been a while for you and Lucas also told me how those idiots at Sanctuary conditioned you to think shape-shifting was evil. I promise you, once you let yourself go, release your wolf, you'll feel better. You'll see. You'll feel like a different person."

"There is no wolf," she told him, her voice flat. "That's what you and my brother don't understand. The people of Sanctuary killed it. They destroyed my wolf and left something twisted and misshapen in its place. I've seen it and I promise you, it's truly hideous."

He stared at her. Was that *pity* she saw in his handsome face? She knew he thought she was crazy. She'd seen the exact same expression in her brother's eyes when she'd attempted to explain it to him.

Turning away, she shook her head, swiping at the lone tear that escaped from her eye. He didn't understand. How could he? He hadn't been there to see. All those that had been were now dead or in prison.

Except for the three that hunted her still.

A shudder wracked her. Once more, her monster snarled and tested the edge of its cage, which thankfully held. "I'd like to go back now," she said, ice in her voice and her spine. "If you want to stay out here and try to find your family, I'm sure I can make my way back alone."

"I'll go with you."

She glanced at him, and a growl split the air in the underbrush nearby them. Instinctively, they both turned.

Something—a black blur—launched itself out of the bushes at them.

Kane snarled as his human form wavered. Hands up, he caught the thing, holding it away from him as it made rumble sounds and bared its tiny, sharp, white teeth.

"A wolf pup," he said, sounding relieved. "One of the youngsters must have wandered away from the pack."

He held the squirming creature up, revealing a small, furry thing whose fierce show of bravado changed to wiggling, tail wagging, submissive friendliness.

"My nephew Reggie." Shaking his head, he set the puppy on the ground. It sat, panting, tongue lolling.

"Your mother is going to be very upset with you," Kane admonished. "You may as well change back to a boy."

Head down, the pup slunk back into the bushes, apparently to do exactly that.

"I thought young children weren't able to shape-shift yet," Lilly said.

"That's right, they can't." Kane nodded. "But he's not that young. I don't know if you noticed, but the smaller kids didn't accompany everyone into the forest. One of the parents stayed back to watch them. Usually in order to change, one has to be at least a preteen. Reggie's twelve."

As she and Lucas had been the first time. Lilly had never forgotten the first time she'd changed. She and her twin brother had been amazed and excited. They'd spent the first few years learning what their wolf selves could do. Thinking back, she was surprised they'd been able to keep it secret for as long as they had. Especially given the depth of Jacob Gideon's hatred for what he called demons.

A fierce longing seized her. How she wished she could simply step away, shed her clothing, drop to the ground and change into a wolf. Like she and Lucas used to do when they were teenagers. Back then, she'd found joy in the other part of her.

No so much now. Because her wolf had been distorted, ruined, until the beast had become a monster of death and ugliness. Changing no longer brought happiness, just agony and rage.

The thing inside her snarled, feeling her hatred. She snarled right back. She wanted it gone and her wolf returned. Now. Being among Kane's family, this town, a group of other people who were like her, who *celebrated* what they were, made her long to be able to share in their joy.

Fists curled so tightly her fingernails dug into her palms, she tried to move, to break away from Kane so she could make a run for the cabin.

Instead, Kane grabbed her arm. Startled, she rounded on him, letting down her inner guard for just a fraction of a second. A crack but enough for her monster to try to slip through.

Again her bones began to lengthen and shift painfully. She screamed, a shrill cry of pain.

"Lilly." Hauling her against him, he put his face so close to hers that his breath tickled her cheek. "Sweetheart, it's all right. I won't let anything happen to you."

Barely conscious, she moaned. She couldn't let her beast hurt him. She wouldn't. With everything that she was, she hung on to this thought, clinging to him.

"Get me inside," she managed to croak.

Just like that, he scooped her up in his arms and, leaving the picnic basket behind, headed back the way they'd originally come.

Chapter 10

Once he reached the cabin, he stopped, breathing hard. Lilly had gone so still in his arms, he feared she'd lost consciousness.

Carefully, he set her down in the porch chair. Though she slumped a little to the side, her amazing blue eyes were open, though fixed on nothing.

"Lilly?" Keeping his movements slow and gentle, he stroked her cheek. "Are you okay?"

She blinked, stirring as though awakening after a deep sleep. "Hey, Kane." A tiny frown creased her brow. She gasped and sat up, remembering. "Did I…"

"No. You did not."

Heaving a sigh of relief, she stood, appearing shaky. "I'm sorry I ruined your picnic."

"You didn't." He managed a smile, aware he couldn't reveal how badly she'd worried him. "We got to eat, that's the important part."

"What about the champagne? And the basket?"

He shrugged. "I left it in the woods. I'll go back and get it later."

"Maybe you'd better get it now. You don't want a bunch of drunken wild animals roaming your land." Her tentative smile made him realize she was trying to joke with him.

"It's almost dark," he told her. "Why don't we get you inside."

"And then you'll go retrieve it?"

Holding the door open, he stood aside to let her pass. "I don't know if I should leave you here by yourself."

She waved away his concern. "The danger has passed. I'll be fine. In fact, if you want to join your family on their hunt, go ahead. I'm just going to clean up and read some before I go to bed."

"No," he said, more to dispel the instant flash of carnal images at the thought of her going to bed. "I'll run out and get the basket and the bottle and be right back. Shouldn't take me more than a couple of minutes."

One elegant shoulder lifted in a shrug. Even this, he found sensual.

"Suit yourself," she said, barely hiding a yawn. "I'm going to go change into something more comfortable."

The old, tired line took on new meaning when she said it in that silky, sensual voice of hers. For a second he forgot what he was about to do and simply stood, staring at her.

She took a step back, making him realize the raw desire had most likely shown in his face.

"I'll be right back," he said brusquely, and then turned and headed right back out the door before he did something he was going to regret.

He could only hope like hell he had himself under control by the time he got back. He'd pocketed the flashlight, so he used that to retrace their earlier steps.

Once he'd gone deeper into the woods, the tell-tale signs of his family's hunt revealed exactly how close they'd come to him and Lilly. They'd killed something large, a deer from the looks of it, and dragged the carcass away. The bloodstains and bits of bone testified to the fact that they'd already begun to feed.

He had no idea where they were now, but he couldn't smell or hear them. Oh, he could follow the scent of the deer, but right now he just wanted to get the damn basket and champagne and get back to Lilly.

He found everything where he'd dropped it, though the champagne had run out of the bottle into the ground. Gathering it all together, he hurried back to the cabin.

As he approached, the yellow light beaming from the windows appeared welcoming. His heart—*dammit*— started to pound as he pictured Lilly in whatever "get into something comfortable" meant to her. Though she'd probably been talking about a T-shirt and jeans, his imagination took him to some other interesting outfits.

More proof that he was acting like a fool.

Opening the front door, he stopped just inside. Curled up on the couch, Lilly appeared engrossed in one of the books on Shifter history he'd given her.

She looked up, her slow smile taking his breath away. "This is good stuff," she said, brandishing the book. "I had no idea. I wish I could share this with Lucas."

"I'm sure your brother has learned a little about his heritage," he said, smiling back. "But in case he hasn't, we can always let him borrow it."

This seemed to reassure her. "Thanks."

"Are you ready to call it a night and try and get some sleep?"

She stood, absently running her fingers thought her long, luxurious wealth of hair. Remaining motionless for a moment, she seemed to struggle with her own emotions. "I don't know what happened out there," she began.

"No worries," he reassured her, aware he had his own struggles to face. "And no pressure, either."

Finally, she nodded and looked up, a grateful smile curving lips that begged for his kiss. Again, he had to shut his thoughts down. He had to figure out how to stop wanting her, but that was his problem, not hers.

"There's more I want to teach you," he continued. "In addition to the basic self-defense moves we've practiced, I want to teach you how to feel comfortable with a gun."

She eyed him, not protesting, despite her uncertain expression. "I'm not sure I can—"

"You'll do fine," he assured her.

Still she seemed doubtful. "How do you know these things? I mean, you said you were a veterinarian by trade."

"And a Pack Protector. I'm in the reserves. Just like the U.S. military. And I received extensive training." He smiled. "Plus I occasionally teach a woman's self-defense course in Fort Worth."

Nodding, she appeared impressed, though he found her poker-faced expression difficult to read.

"Where do you go to shoot a gun? Are we driving to a shooting range or something?"

"Nope. The nearest shooting range is fifty miles away," he told her. "There's a meadow where I used to go at sunrise to do my tai chi. It's big and flat. We'll set up some targets and shoot there."

A worried frown creased her brow. "When?" she asked.

"We'll play it by ear. Maybe tomorrow morning. Pretty early, before the heat of the day sets in."

Lilly lay awake in her bed long after she'd turned out the light. An entire new world had opened up for her since Kane had taken her away from Seattle. Remembering her performance in the self-defense training, she felt a flush of pride.

A gun was a different matter. She wasn't sure how she felt about Kane's desire that she learn to handle one. She decided to simply, as Kane had put it, play it by ear.

And thinking of Kane, with his large, capable hands on her body, she became aware of a low thrum of desire. She finally fell asleep aching with need.

That night, instead of pleasant dreams, the old nightmares returned. She found herself back in Sanctuary, strapped to the metal laboratory table as the doctors came at her with needles and knives.

Somewhere in the dark of the night she awoke gasping, drenched in perspiration. She knew they'd come for her in darkness. Lying in her bed, alone and aching for Kane, she felt a frisson of fear. Who knew how these acolytes of the church of Sanctuary would manage to find her and worse, what they wanted to do to her. Had she been slated for death, a decree given by the man who'd claimed to be her father, while he served time in prison?

He'd certainly been furious enough for that.

Grabbing her small flashlight, she got out of the bed and opened her door, taking care to move quietly so she wouldn't disturb Kane.

Straight through the living room she went, unlocking the front door and stepping outside on to the front porch. She dropped into the chair, breathing deeply of the fresh night air. The waning moon provided enough light that she was able to turn off her flashlight.

At first, the crickets had gone silent when she emerged. They started up again in full force, which made her smile. She felt the tension leach out of her, enjoying the energy of nature. For the first time since she'd arrived in Leaning Tree, she didn't allow the monster inside her to ruin the moment. She'd suffered enough in the past and now, thanks to Kane, she'd begun to step outside of her shell. She liked the flush of confidence learning self-defense had given, liked even more the heady sensuality she experienced when she was around Kane.

As if thinking about him had summoned him, the front door creaked open and Kane emerged. He had a serious case of bed head, which somehow made him look edgy and even more sexy.

"Hey," he greeted her, taking the chair next to hers. "You couldn't sleep, either?"

She gave him a rueful smile. "Oh, I could sleep. It was the nightmares that got me up."

When he nodded rather than pressing her for details, she silently thanked him. Reliving the terrors of those dreams wasn't pleasant, whether awake or asleep.

"We need to talk," he said, his deep voice serious. "I'm coming to understand that there's a lot more to you than I, or anyone else, realizes."

"I warned you I was messed up." She tried to keep it light, and failed miserably. "Fifteen years of captivity will do that to a person."

He took her hand, stunning her into temporary silence. "It was more than just captivity, I know. You mentioned they experimented on you."

Her nod was the only answer she could manage.

"Do you know if they were…successful with any of the experiments?"

"Successful?" The concept was so foreign to her, the word might almost have been in another language. "I know what they wanted to do with me." And what they'd tried to turn her into. She thought of what the doctors had called the Siren, and realized, yes, they'd succeeded. At least in that.

As if she'd spoken out loud, he leaned closer. "Lilly, I need you to tell me what happened to me when you sang."

Once, she would have hung her head. In fact, the person she used to be would have stammered out an apology. But this was not her fault. None of it was. So she lifted her chin and looked Kane directly in the eyes.

"I don't know." She shrugged, refusing to allow herself to feel dejected. "It had to be because of what they did to me at Sanctuary. I don't understand all the technical aspects. I just know they tried to make modification after modification to me. To my DNA, my body, my spirit and my beast. If they could have figured out a way to get to my soul, I have no doubt they would have."

Still holding her hand, he nodded, waiting for her to continue.

She shrugged, refusing to give in to her embarrassment. "I don't know how or why, but apparently when I sing, my voice is like the mythical sirens', compelling men. As it did you."

Narrow-eyed, he stared. "Then why can't I remember? Even if you could make me do something, you shouldn't be able to make me forget."

Now she did look down, knowing how much this proud, strong man would hate what he'd momentarily become under her spell. "I don't know. But you kissed me." Her face heated, which meant she was most likely a fiery red. "And you wanted to do more, but I was able to stop you."

"Stop me? You say that like I tried to force myself on you or something."

She let her silence be her answer.

His lowered brows told her what he thought of that.

Watching him as he wrestled with this knowledge actually brought her physical pain, low under her breastbone.

Because that sensation felt unbearably uncomfortable, she yanked her hand free, pushed herself up out of the chair and went back inside the cabin, leaving him alone on the porch.

Still trying to make sense of her words, Kane didn't react. He was too busy trying to figure out what the hell had happened when she sang. Nothing she'd said made any sense. Even if her singing could somehow intensify the desire that already simmered constantly in his veins, how could her voice make him lose all memory of what he'd done?

She'd hinted that he'd tried to force himself on her.

No, no way. He wasn't that kind of man. He didn't force women to do anything, not ever.

Too restless for sleep, he got up and followed her back into the cabin.

She stood in the kitchen, her back to him, the lights still off.

"You know, you're eventually going to have to change." As he spoke, he flicked on the light switch.

She spun around to face him. He didn't miss the spark of panic that flashed into her eyes.

"Why?" Crossing her arms, she lifted her chin. "Are you punishing me now for what happened when I sang?"

Shocked, he recoiled. "Of course not."

"Then why? I don't see the need."

"Lilly." He softened his voice, aware that what he had to say next might be news to her. "Every Shifter has to change periodically. If they don't, they'll go insane."

To his surprise, she greeted this statement with a short bark of humorless laughter. "Insane? I think that ship already sailed. It's too late for me, Kane."

"Don't say that." He couldn't help himself; even though she wasn't looking for sympathy, he pulled her into his arms. Once he had her, inhaling the sweet scent of her freshly shampooed hair, he wondered how he'd ever let her go.

Lilly decided that for him. Pushing him away, she fixed him with a glare. "I'm not joking."

"I didn't think you were. But still, you're a long way from the kind of insanity I'm talking about."

From the way she cocked her head, he could tell she didn't believe him.

"I've seen it," he continued quietly, aching now that he no longer had her in his arms. "People driven so mad they were reduced to rabid beasts, foaming at the mouth and tearing at their own skin with their fingernails. And not only were they a danger to themselves, but to others."

Something in his voice must have gotten through to her. Sorrow softened her expression as she relaxed her stance. "How is it possible that you've seen such things?"

"The Protectors," he told her, remembered horrors still clutching him. "Once, not too long ago, these Shifters were called Ferals. Those that lived outside society for whatever reason. Our task was to hunt them and bring them in."

"For what?" Now she watched him as though she expected another monster to emerge. "Please tell me you didn't experiment and torture them like the people of Sanctuary did."

"Of course not." He sighed. "This was a dark period in our organization's history. Corrupt and evil men had gained power, and they overstepped the bounds of decency. But Protectors revolted against them, because by our very name we knew we'd been charged with Protecting our own kind, nothing more, nothing less."

She still hadn't moved. "What did you do to them, these Ferals?"

"They were offered a chance to be rehabilitated." This said, he prayed she didn't ask about the others, who refused this offer.

"Define rehabilitated."

"They were given medical and mental-health care and once healed, were trained to reassimilate themselves back into society."

Staring past her, he remembered the chaos, the unnecessary bloodshed, and the brave revolt. "Now our organization has been cleaned up. The corrupt officials were arrested and stood trial."

Though she nodded, her gaze still appeared troubled. "What about the ones that refused?"

Crap.

"Refused?" he asked carefully. "That was an extremely rare occurrence."

"Still, it happened, right?"

Reluctant, he nodded.

"So what did you do to them?"

He wanted to balk, wished he could lie. But the one thing above all others that Lilly deserved was honesty, whether she liked the answer or not.

"The directive given at the time was extermination."

"What?" Clearly shocked, she recoiled. "You...you killed them?"

"I didn't, not personally. I was one of the ones who refused. I was put on furlough while they considered whether or not to put me up for court-marshal."

To his disbelief, she came close and put her small hand on his arm. "Thank you," she said, confusing him.

"For what? I wrestled with my conscience back then. I respect the Society of Pack Protectors. I believe in them, always have, even then. You don't know how closely I came to blindly following orders."

"But you didn't." Her dulcet voice hummed with pleasure. "Because you're not that kind of man."

In the end, he hadn't been. He and many others had refused to brutally slaughter the Ferals. Some had been mentally ill and were able to get help. Others...they'd preferred to live in the wild, outside the radar. As long as they weren't a danger to others, the new directive had been to let them be.

"Thank you," she said, pressing a soft kiss against his throat.

At the gesture, desire flared, thickening his blood and his body. He half turned, aching to capture her mouth with his. But when he saw the tears trembling on the edge of her eyelashes, he managed to rein himself in.

"What's wrong?" Gruff voiced, he pulled her in for a platonic hug, angling his body so she wouldn't feel the strength of his need for her.

"I can't stop thinking of all the ones who lost their lives." Her voice caught. "I wonder if they suffered, the way we suffered at Sanctuary."

"We?" He watched her closely. One of the things he and her brother, Lucas, had wondered had been how much Lilly had known about the others. She hadn't been the only Shifter Jacob Gideon had captured for his barbaric practices. He'd been taking children, apparently believing their young spirits would be easy to bend to his will.

But she shook her head and wiped at her eyes with the back of her hand. "Enough of this talk," she declared.

"Agreed. We circled around what I originally wanted to talk to you about."

Her quick nod told him she was completely aware of that.

"You need to change."

She sighed. "You never give up, do you?"

"Not when it comes to keeping you safe and healthy."

Head down, she didn't immediately reply. When she lifted her head, the stark agony in her face made his breath catch in his throat.

"I'm a monster."

Once again he pulled her close, smoothing her hair and wishing he knew the best way to reassure her. "You're not. That's Jacob Gideon's brainwashing speaking. We're Shape-shifters. Humans and wolves. Not monsters."

"Maybe you are." Leaning back, she looked up into his eyes and shook her head. "But not me. I'm not normal."

He knew he had to try a different tack. "How do you know? Have you actually seen yourself, like in a mirror?"

"No." Briefly, she closed her eyes. "You don't understand, Kane. They had me change once, there in the lab. I must have blacked out because I don't remember anything about what happened. But when I changed into a human again, one of their doctors and two lab technicians were dead. The carnage was unbelievable."

"How do you know it was you who killed them?"

Mouth twisting, she waved his question away. "Who else? Those that survived, they saw. Somehow, they'd managed to get me chained up."

"So you took their word for it? How do you know they didn't stage this, to make you think it was you?"

An utterly flat and lifeless look came into her eyes. "Because, Kane. Because when I came to, chained and shackled to that damn laboratory table, I was covered in blood."

He didn't know what to say. He supposed, given time, he could come up with dozens of reasonable explanations, other arguments, but not now, not at this instant. Instead, he held her, aching and wishing he could discover a way to help her find herself.

Only then, could the healing begin.

"How about this?" He kept his voice level, as if what he was about to ask was perfectly logical and reasonable. "How about I help you change?"

"Are you crazy?" Chest heaving, she shook her head. "There's no way. I couldn't risk it. What if I hurt you?"

"You won't. Your beast is fighting you. I've seen it several times. Wouldn't it be much better—and safer—to manage the time and place of the change, rather than simply let your wolf self wrest control?"

While she appeared unconvinced, at least she still listened.

"Plus, once you let your wolf out, allow him to hunt and run and just be, he'll be sated and quiet. You'll get a much needed rest from constantly battling him."

This appealed to her, he could tell. She swallowed, quietly considering. "Maybe," she finally conceded, making him feel as if he'd won a huge victory. "If there were safeguards in place to ensure no harm would come to others."

"When?" Now that she'd agreed, he knew he had to keep pushing, or she'd overthink things and refuse.

"I don't know." She shot him a cross look. "Not right now."

"Why not?" he persisted. "The timing couldn't be any more perfect. It's the middle of the night, no one else is around, and the weather is comfortable."

Her eyes widened. "Are you serious?"

"Yes. In fact, there are a couple of caves up on some cliffs about a half mile away. We can go there."

Biting her lip, she swallowed. "Do you have chains or rope?"

"What for?"

"Restraints." Her chin came up. "You've got to make sure I'm restrained, tied up. Otherwise, once I give that monster full rein, he could go after you or your family."

Though he felt 99 percent convinced that the monster part was a product of the intensive conditioning she'd received and thus, all in her mind, he nodded. "I have rope. Though I'm not sure I like the idea of tying you up."

Her chin came up. "That's the only way I'll agree to this."

"Then rope it is. I have some in the trunk of my Vette." He took her arm. "You can come with me and get it."

Despite his gentle prodding, she still didn't move. When she looked up and met his gaze, the stark terror in her eyes made his heart ache. "It's going to be all right," he said. "I promise."

"I'm not sure I can do this." But this time, when he took a step toward the door, she moved with him.

Outside, he kept her close while he retrieved the rope from his trunk. Doing this made him feel vaguely criminal, and also vaguely kinky, like they were going into the woods for a bit of S and M.

Pushing away these thoughts, along with his own misgivings, he took her hand firmly in his and, using a small flashlight, led her unerringly along a path, past the small grove where he and his brothers often went to change, and up a rocky hill.

"Here we are," he said, trying to sound as normal as possible. "Check out these caves. Bats live there during the day, but they're out hunting right now."

She tugged her hand free. "Let me borrow your flashlight." Once he handed it to her, she turned a slow circle, shining the light into the mouth of the nearest cave. Next, she began walking, appearing to study the surrounding trees. "This one," she finally said, indicating a sturdy oak.

At first he wasn't sure what she meant. Then, glancing down at the rope in his hands, he understood. She wanted him to tie her to that tree.

Though he'd sort of promised, he still had to try to dissuade her. "Lilly, I really think—"

"No." Voice sharp, she cut him off. "That's a dealbreaker. Either I'm tied up, or I don't change."

Again he looked down at the rope. "But how? If I tie you up when you're human, when you're body becomes a wolf, the ropes will simply fall off."

"Not if you tied it around my neck."

Horrified, he started to protest. This time, she held up her hand to stop him, as if she already knew what he would say.

"It's no worse than a dog on a leash." Though she tried to sound nonchalant, the waver in her voice let him know how she really felt. Still absolutely terrified.

He wanted to reassure her, but knew there were no words capable of doing that, so he kept his silence.

"Give me that." Taking the rope out of his hands, she looped it around her neck. He was relieved to see she didn't make the type of collar that would choke her. Instead, she tied off a circle, just loose enough to accommodate the neck of a wolf, knotting it securely before handing the rope back to him.

"Tie it to that tree, please," she said. "And make sure you get a couple of good knots."

For some reason, seeing that rough rope around the creamy skin of her delicate neck, he couldn't make his feet move.

Then she tugged on the rope. "Kane? If you want to do this, please get that rope tied up before I completely lose my nerve. I think I'm pretty strong once I become—" she swallowed hard "—the other thing."

This galvanized him into action. "It's called a wolf, Lilly," he chided her with a teasing smile in the hopes of reassuring her.

Taking the rope, he wrapped it around the tree and made sure to leave her enough room to move around before tying a secure knot. He hated the idea of confining her wolf but knew this was necessary this first time, until she could see there was nothing to be afraid of.

It did cross his mind to wonder, briefly, what would happen if she was right and the horrible experiments and torture she'd endured had somehow harmed her wolf self.

He'd deal with that if it happened. He'd consult the Pack Healer, Samantha. For right now, he didn't need any negative thoughts. He had to believe this would work. He didn't know what he'd do if it didn't.

After she'd inspected the rope and was satisfied, she wiped her hands on the front of her jean shorts and faced him. "What now?"

"With my family, we strip, drop to the ground and shape-shift."

"Strip?" Her question came out a nervous squeak. "I don't know if I can do that."

"If you don't, you'll rip your clothes." He tried to move

past the searing image of her naked. "Would you rather I changed first? That way I'll be wolf before you have to undress."

Exhaling loudly, she nodded. "Yes, thank you. You change to wolf, and then...I will, too."

Though he could scarcely see her in the shadowed forest, he could hear the sincerity in her shaky voice.

"I won't let anything happen to you, Lilly," he promised. "Trust me on that."

Chapter 11

Though terror had Lilly shaking so hard she could hardly keep her teeth from chattering, she was still curious to see Kane shape-shift into a wolf.

She held her breath, trying not to stare as he removed first his T-shirt, then his khaki shorts. He showed no embarrassment as he stood before her clad in nothing but boxer shorts, but then why should he? The man had the kind of broad-shouldered, narrow-waisted body seen only in athletes and movie stars. His muscles rippled in the partial moonlight as he moved with a nonchalant grace a few feet away.

Slowly, as she watched, he stripped off his last scrap of clothing, making her mouth go dry. Then, while she unabashedly stared, he dropped to the ground on all four legs and began the change.

She held her breath. Not since she and her brother had shape-shifted as teens had she witnessed another person change into a wolf. Fascinated, she grimaced as his bones began to lengthen. A myriad of bright floating sparkles appeared around him, bathing him in a flickering glow.

She moved a tiny bit closer. Though the flickering lights were beautiful, she needed to see past them to Kane. But the swirl of colors was so thick, it was impossible to see. Still, she tried. As if her thoughts had become movement, the sparkles vanished. Lilly gasped out loud. A huge wolf stood where Kane had been.

The majestic black-coated beast padded toward her. Instinctively, she moved back. When she did, the wolf paused, lifting one large paw and cocking his head inquisitively.

Kane. This was Kane. She made herself move closer, her heart trip-hammering in her chest. Kane. Just Kane.

Finally, just a foot away, she stopped, reaching out with a tentative movement and tangling her fingers in the luxurious black fur. He allowed this, holding himself with a regal bearing that so much reminded her of the human Kane, she nearly laughed out loud.

Wolf Kane made a sound, a cross between a bark and a growl. Somehow she understood. He was merely reminding her that her turn had come to shape-shift.

Panic rose like bile in her throat, choking her so badly she almost clawed at the rope around her neck, wanting it off. No, that wasn't really her, it had to be the monster inside her, trying to trick her into doing something foolish and setting it loose.

At the thought, the knowledge of what she was about to attempt, her beast broke free. This time, the change easily overpowered her human will, though maybe this was because she had already anticipated this and permitted it to happen.

Battling to slow the change down for a few seconds,

she ripped off her clothes and, imitating Kane, dropped to the ground. Just in time, for the instant she dug her nails into the damp forest dirt, the change initiated in earnest.

Ahh! It hurt. Was it supposed to hurt so much?

As her bones lengthened, she tried to look for the same sparkling light show as Kane's, but the pain became too intense for her to do anything but try to keep it from overwhelming her.

Gradually, the agony subsided and she rose up, wondering what kind of thing she'd become. Sniffing her furred leg, she smelled her own scent, which her brain told her was wolf, like Kane.

Even better, she felt like herself, in full possession of her facilities. Not crazy. Not full of a murderous rage. With pleasure, she sniffed the dead leaves and earth underneath her, amazed at the myriad of smells. Her lupine nose had her human one beat.

She sat. Glancing down at her belly, she believed she had become a wolf. Not distorted or twisted, but a true wolf, similar to Kane, though much less massive. Her soft gray fur glowed in the shadowy light. Pleased, she thought it kind of pretty.

Kane made a chuffing sound, drawing her attention. Full of joy, she looked up, caught sight of him, and then tried to rush toward him.

When she reached the end of her rope, the resulting tug jerked her off her feet. A yelp escaped her. Stunned, she staggered back to her feet, neck burning.

Kane shook his massive head and lay down. Again the firefly lights arrived, and then human Kane had returned. He padded over to her, his fingers working at the knots. A few minutes later, he'd managed to untie her.

As soon as he had, he went back to his spot, got down

again on all fours and shape-shifted back into a wolf while she waited.

Barely able to contain her excitement, the instant he had regained his wolf shape, she rushed him, bowing playfully before nipping him on the hindquarters and running off.

They chased each other, rolling and play biting. He tore off through the woods and she followed.

When he slid to an abrupt stop, she plowed into him. Shaking her off, he nudged her, making her turn. The sliver of moon shone in a small pond, the still water peaceful.

He nudged her again, as though trying to make her understand. As she edged forward, she realized the pond made a pretty darn good mirror. Standing at the edge, if she leaned her neck out, she could see herself pretty clearly.

A wolf. Stunned, she looked again. She couldn't believe it. When she looked in the water, a pretty silver wolf looked back at her. She'd become a wolf. Exactly like she was supposed to. Nothing more, nothing less. No monster. No rage-filled killing machine. Which meant they'd either lied to her, or injected her with something to bring on hallucinations and madness.

Though either scenario was possible, she'd put money on the second.

But what about the deaths? She'd seen the blood and the bodies with her own two eyes. Had it all been staged? Or had someone else done the killing and made it appear as though it had been her?

Kane nudged her, his plumed tail high over his back. Then he took off running, appearing as if he was laughing over his shoulder at her.

For one frozen second, she stood, uncertain. Finally, her heart light, she took off after him, giving chase.

They ran and ran and then, tongues lolling, they rested. Finally, stealing into the nighttime forest, they hunted.

By the time they returned to the clearing, the sky had begun to lighten, signaling dawn would soon arrive. Sated and more relaxed than she'd felt…well, since she'd been fifteen, Lilly lay belly down on the damp forest floor. Next to her, the beautiful black wolf that was Kane watched her through golden wolf eyes.

This time, though she longed to remain a wolf a little longer, she initiated the change first. To her surprise, her wolf acquiesced readily. This time, the shift back to human wasn't painful. Instead, her body welcomed it.

Once she could see normally again, she blinked, automatically looking for Kane. While she was becoming human, he'd changed, too. Naked, he lay propped on one elbow and watched her.

"Welcome back." The sound of his husky voice sent a shudder of heat straight to her center. "Did you enjoy yourself?"

Mouth dry, she could only nod. Her entire body ached for his touch and she had to fight not to crawl over and climb on top of him.

"I…um." Licking her lips, she closed her eyes, hoping to blot out the temptation of his gorgeously naked body.

To her shock, he laughed. The masculine sound only served to make her want him more. Desire was foreign to her, something she'd never thought she'd feel since while at Sanctuary she'd not only been tortured and experimented on, but raped, as well.

This…feeling seemed about as far from that as her wolf did from the monster she'd pictured.

"I forgot to warn you," he said, as she kept her eyes

screwed shut. "Most Shifters are used to it, but for whatever reason, changing back to human form makes us horny."

Horny? Great.

"This…didn't happen to me when I changed before."

"You were only fifteen. The desire part doesn't happen until you're fully grown."

Desire part. To her fogged and overheated brain, all she could think about was what part of him she wanted inside of her. She'd been brave enough to try what had been her greatest fear. Surely she could be bold enough to claim her reward.

Slowly, she opened her eyes, looking into his gaze. "I want you."

He swallowed, his gray eyes going dark. "I want you, too, but that's just the effects of changing. No worries. I'm used to it. I can control it."

Inhaling, she stood, letting him get a good look at her naked body, erect nipples and all. She crossed the distance between them, standing over him and speaking clearly and distinctly. "I don't want you to control it. I'm on fire, Kane. I need you."

His sharp inhalation of breath was the only sound he made as he stared up at her. With his gaze at first riveted on her face, he let it slowly roam over her, soft as a caress. The tingling in her nether regions made her melt inside.

He stood, his look a smoldering flame, and turned. He kept his back to her and slowly moved a few steps away, breaking her heart.

"You don't want me?" To her horror, she realized she was on the verge of tears. Even worse, his apparent rejection of her did nothing to lessen her craving for him.

"Lilly, I want you so badly I can hardly walk."

Though she wanted to, she didn't believe him. Her disbelief must have shown in her face. He shook his head.

"Look," he said simply, turning so she could see him, all of him, but most especially his massive erection.

She tried to throttle the explosive desire that consumed her, but her knees had gone weak. She could scarcely breathe, but somehow she took a step or two toward him, making a cry of desire low in her throat.

Pulse pounding, heart jolting, body aching and melting, she threw herself at him, trusting him to catch her, thrilling to the feel of the long, hard length of him pressing into her belly.

A ripple of excitement made her shiver as she felt him give what had to be an involuntary push against her.

"Lilly," he rasped. "Please stop."

Heady with power, buzzing with desire, she ignored him. Using her womanly instincts, she rubbed up against him, like a cat hungry for cream.

His reaction was swift, and violent. Grabbing her by both upper arms, he tried to hold her still. "Seriously. Stop."

"I don't want to," she purred, raw wanting making her dizzy. She inhaled sharply as he pulled her roughly against him.

"Don't start something you can't finish," he grated.

She had a second of misgiving as he let her feel the full weight of his arousal. Trembling, she clung to him as he moved against her. He no longer used his hands merely to hold her in place, but to caress her. Her skin tingled everywhere he touched her.

When he cupped her breast, her heart lurched. Body already throbbing, she gasped in delight, welcoming the strength and heat of his flesh as he surged against her.

A moan escaped her, the heat building inside of her rushed to every spot his hands caressed.

Belatedly, she began to hesitantly mimic the way he touched her, thrilling the muscles rippling under his firm flesh. He groaned as she slid her hand down his pecs, about to dare to go lower when his hand captured her, stopping her.

"Lilly, I—"

Raising on tiptoe, she pressed her mouth against his. When he responded to her as though starving, sending spirals of ecstasy through her, she knew they both were lost.

She curled into his body, went with him as he lowered her to the ground. As he kissed her, their tongues mated, and she writhed against him, wanting more.

Savage, intense, his eyes glittered with heat as his body imprisoned her in a pulse of growing arousal. "Are you very, very sure?" he asked, as he kissed the hollow at the base of her throat, making her shiver.

She wasn't sure of anything, other than the fact that she wanted this man more than she'd ever wanted anything in her entire life. Caressing the tendons in his muscular shoulders, she let her body answer for her.

He entered her with one swift movement, the sheer size of him filling her completely, making her cry out. His hard body fit with hers, as if they'd been made for each other.

And when he moved…the heavens and the earth moved with him.

Tangled together, bodies slick with passion, he moved, and she moved with him, taking the full length of him, her body clenching with each powerful thrust.

Drowning, soaring, all at once. They danced, mated. Her blood pounded with passion, nearly shattering her.

All at once, at the same time, she was on fire, she was on ice, as he made love to her.

And then…and then…gasping in sweet, perfect agony, she felt a shower of sparks explode as her body shuddered around him, tightening as if she wanted to wring every last ounce of passion out of him.

He cried out, a sound of triumph, of pleasure and of pain.

She held him while he emptied his essence into her, held him while their heartbeats slowed and their breathing quieted.

Savoring the scent of their lovemaking, she wanted to capture this instant forever, to take out and look at in those dark, lonely times that were sure to come.

"This has been the absolutely, most perfect day," she told him, meaning it.

He groaned, though he didn't push her away. "I'm already having regrets."

"Regrets?" She refused to let his words hurt. "Don't you dare. You've given me the gift of my wolf self, and then this. We're both adults. There's nothing wrong with what we did and if you say there is, I just might have to smack you."

"You were vulnerable," he protested. "I shouldn't have taken advantage of you."

"Advantage?" Slowly she shook her head. "You've healed me. In more ways than you could ever imagine."

The bleak look in his eyes told her he refused to believe her. She knew that this time, she'd have to be strong, to keep him from beating himself up with guilt.

Gently, she slid out from under him and, brushing herself off, got to her feet. After a second, he did the same. Naked, they stood looking at each other. She drank in his male perfection with her gaze before taking a deep breath.

"Kane, all my body has known before today was abuse and pain. I've never…" She blushed as words momentarily failed her. Lifting her chin, she continued. "You showed me that two people can come together with pleasure and joy. Please don't try and take that away from me."

He made a strangled sound as he reached for her. This time, she evaded his grasp, wanting anything from him but his pity. "Come on." Turning her back to him, she snatched her clothes up from the ground. "Let's get dressed and go back to the cabin. If we're lucky, we might be able to get in a few hours of sleep."

Struck speechless, Kane wasn't sure what to make of this calmly assertive, and sexy, Lilly. He'd always known she'd eventually find an inner strength, but this sensual, confident aspect of her wasn't something he'd anticipated so soon.

Though she'd assured him otherwise, he couldn't help but feel as though he'd taken advantage of her in a weakened state. He was supposed to be her Protector. He knew how the change back to human form made Shifters horny. Not only that, but he'd made love to her without protection. There could be a consequence. He stifled a groan. He should've taken precautions. Lilly had enough to deal with right now without having to handle an unexpected pregnancy.

Despite this possibility, she'd still claimed he'd given her a gift, when in fact it had been the other way around. He'd known lots of women in his lifetime and the sex had ranged from mediocre to fantastic. But this, this had been different. Not once with any of the others had he been even remotely tempted to call it *making love*.

Damn. Maybe he was the one in trouble, rather than Lilly.

Again he remembered her horrible imprisonment at Sanctuary. When he'd first seen her huddled in a metal bunk in a cold and damp basement, emaciated and filthy, he'd wanted to find the people who'd done this to her and make them pay. Only the fact that he was there as a professional law enforcement officer had kept him rational.

And now this. While he'd guessed she'd probably been raped while a prisoner at Sanctuary, hearing her confirm it in the same breath as she discussed the physical act they'd just shared, had been disconcerting, to say the least.

When they reached the cabin, she disappeared inside without a backward glance. He followed more slowly, wishing he could find the right words to straighten this mess out.

To his surprise, when he went in, Lilly waited for him in the kitchen.

"We need to talk," she said, getting two glasses of tap water and placing them on the countertop.

Instead of trepidation, he felt relief. "Yes, we do."

"I'm a wolf," she said. "An honest-to-heavens wolf. Not some sort of monster."

He nodded. "Yes, you are. And now you can shape-shift whenever you want."

"And I don't have to worry about anyone else getting hurt. What I don't understand is how the crazies at Sanctuary had me convinced I was some sort of monster."

Some of the tension eased from him. Taking a long swallow of water, he sighed. "I'm still not sure what they were trying to do. What could they hope to accomplish by making you think you'd change into some sort of fire-breathing dragon type thing?"

She bit her lip, looking surprisingly vulnerable. "Yeah, but apparently they succeeded with the singing thing."

"I'm going to have you do that again, but only when someone else, preferably female, is here to help you. I want it videotaped."

"Why female?"

"So they won't be susceptible." He smiled at her, trying for gentle, but knowing he probably looked grim. Just the thought of some other man being compelled by her song and putting his hands on her…made Kane feel violent.

She yawned, making him feel contrite. Glancing at the clock on the wall, he saw it was after 5:00 a.m. "I didn't realize it was so late—or early. We stayed out a long time. Maybe you should just go ahead and try and get some rest."

Her gaze, so intensely blue, seemed bemused. "Oddly enough, I'm not tired. I'm more energized than anything else. What about you?"

"I'm going to make a pot of coffee," he told her, grinning. "You're welcome to join me."

"Sure." She grinned right back. He was pleased at the absence of the shadows that usually haunted her. While he wasn't foolish enough to think they'd all been vanquished, the events of that night had evidently gone a long way toward healing her.

As he made the coffee, she sat silently and watched him. He liked that she didn't feel the need to fill the silence with chatter. Once the coffee had started brewing, he turned and let his gaze drink her in. Despite just having made love to her, he felt the same tug of attraction. Pushing that away, he took a deep breath, telling himself to focus.

"Uh, Kane? There's one more thing we need to discuss."

The tiny tremble in her voice alerted him. "What?"

"I need to make sure you understand…" Hesitating, she swallowed, and then raised her chin and met his gaze. "Despite the sex, there can never be anything between us."

He wasn't prepared for the emotions that slammed into him. Shock and surprise, of course, but more than anything he wanted to deny the truth of her words, and prove to her that she was wrong. Completely wrong.

Instead, he tried rationality. "If you think it's because you've got too many issues, I want you to know—"

"No." Her blue eyes had gone cold. "I know you're willing to work with me on those, and I thank you for that. It's not you at all, it's me."

The clichéd break up line seemed totally out of place coming from her, especially since they'd never been a couple. Had they?

"I've spent half my life in captivity," she continued. "I've never learned how to be strong enough to live on my own. You've shown me that it's possible, and I owe you for that."

She *owed him*?

"But I can't start any kind of relationship." Her earnest voice seemed at odds with her frozen expression. He had the sense she might be retreating again, hiding behind an inner wall for her own protection. To keep herself from being hurt.

Or that might have been just wishful thinking on his part.

"That's fine," he heard himself say, managing to sound

relatively normal. "I wasn't looking for a relationship anyways."

Though he'd begun believing he spoke only the truth, the instant he'd said it he realized it was the first time he'd ever lied to her.

"Thank goodness," she said, sounding relieved. She cleared her throat, keeping her gaze averted. "So what's on the agenda for us today?"

Normalcy. Good. Better to get back on track and minimize the danger of saying something he didn't mean to say.

"I'd planned for us to practice shooting today, but I think we'll do that another day." He cleared his throat. "I want us both to be well-rested and sharp."

She nodded, still appearing skittish, which irritated him more than it should have. "We can always take a nap."

Again, the images that flashed into his mind made him lose the capacity for speech. Though he knew she'd meant actually resting, all he could picture was the two of them, curled into each other on the bed. There were a lot of things he'd like to do with her, and sleeping was the least of them.

He swallowed hard, reached into the cupboard and pulled out a couple of mugs. Keeping himself occupied would help him get his libido settled down. He didn't know what it was about her, but Lilly affected him, arousing him with a single look of her long-lashed baby blues.

She accepted her coffee with a lopsided smile, making him see he'd added powdered creamer and one sugar without even asking.

"Just the way I like it," she said, taking a small sip.

Together they watched as the sky outside the kitchen window began to lighten. He felt a sense of peace, something he usually only felt occasionally, and then only when he was around his family.

"Thank you." Her silken-voice yanked him out of his introspection.

Finishing his first cup, he grabbed her nearly empty one and made them each a second. He knew he was enjoying this more than he should have, but he decided to just go with it.

"It's hard to believe you grew up here," she said. "What was it like?"

"Not much different than it is now." He chuckled. "My two brothers and I ganged up on my sister. We had the entire woods as a playground. We had tree forts and spent most of the summer days outside. It was a great place to grow up. What about you?"

The instant the question left his mouth, he wanted to call it back. "Sorry. I'm guessing you grew up at Sanctuary."

She nodded. "For as long as I can remember. Still, Lucas and I did the best we could to have some sort of normal life."

"Did you go to public school?"

A shadow crossed her face. "Yes, at least until eighth grade. We were outcasts at school anyway, and then Jacob decided to homeschool us, which essentially cut off all of our contact with the outside world. At least I had my brother."

The sharp rap on the front door startled them both. Glancing at her, he tried to hide the way he automatically tensed. Especially since dawn had barely broken.

"Wait here," Kane told her. Since there was no peephole, he tried looking out the front window, but couldn't get a good view of the front porch. Deciding he was being too paranoid, he cracked open the front door.

"Morning." His brother Kyle looked as if he hadn't slept much either.

"Barely," Kane responded. "It's 6:00 a.m. What's going on? Are Mom and Pop okay?"

"Yeah, everyone's fine. I came because Muriel Redstone just called. I don't know if you remember her, but she works the front desk at the Value Five Motel. Wanted to know if we had room for a party of three."

"Okay." Opening the door wider to allow Kyle entrance, Kane led the way into the kitchen. "Coffee?"

"That would be wonderful." Accepting the steaming mug gratefully, Kyle drank with appreciation.

Kane and Lilly exchanged looks. Finally, Kane shrugged.

"So you came over to tell me Muriel referred a party of three? Isn't that pretty standard since we are the only other lodging in town?"

Setting his mug down on the counter, Kyle's expression turned intense. "Three people—think about it." When Kane didn't respond, Kyle rolled his eyes. "They're asking about a woman from Texas. Even showed Muriel a photo. From what she described, they're looking for Lilly."

Chapter 12

Kyle barely finished speaking when Kane exploded into action. Locating his cell phone, he dialed the emergency number for the Protectors and punched in the prearranged code. The instant that was done, he started to call Lilly's brother, then remembered it would only be 4:00 a.m. in Colorado.

When he looked up, both Kyle and Lilly were looking at him as if he'd lost his mind.

"Are you okay?" Kyle asked.

"Never been better." He flashed them both a savage grin. Adrenaline felt a thousand times superior to simply waiting for something to happen, as they'd been doing. Now that it had, he could deal with it and eliminate the threat. Exactly as he'd been trained.

"What did you just do?" Lilly asked, the tiny wrinkle between her eyes attesting to her worry.

Though he wanted to go to her, wrap her tightly in

his arms and assure her she'd be safe, he knew if he did, his brother would read too much into the reassuring gesture. He settled for what he hoped was a reassuring look.

"I activated the Protectors. I dialed a number and punched in a code. They'll send a team, incognito." Kane inclined his head at his brother. "There should be six and they'll be here before sunset. Can we make room for them?"

"I've got one cabin available." Looking bemused, Kyle scratched his chin. "Though I told Muriel we had no vacancies. I knew there was no way we wanted those three on our premises."

"So we don't know where they'll be staying?"

Kyle shrugged. "Who knows? Maybe, since there's no room at the inn, they'll just move on and leave us alone."

"I wouldn't count on that." Truth be told, Kane hoped they wouldn't. Once his colleagues swept in, they'd take care of everything, removing the threat that had hung over Lilly's pretty head ever since she'd been freed.

"Kane's right." Standing, Lilly walked to the front window and peeked through the blinds as if she expected to see them strolling up the path at any moment. "Not these people," she said, her tone flat and emotionless. "They don't give up so easily."

From her tone, he could tell she was remembering the unspeakable horrors the followers of Sanctuary had already visited up her.

His brother's opinion be damned. Kane crossed the room, went up behind her and wrapped her in his arms, holding her close. "Don't worry, I won't let them get anywhere near you."

"I'm not worried," she said, her stiff posture contradicting her words. Her heart beat a frantic tattoo under his palm.

Behind them, Kyle made a sound, low in his throat. Kane turned to find his brother eyeing him, a concerned expression on his face.

"What?" Kane asked, even though he knew.

Kyle shook his head. "Never mind." Picking up his coffee, he drained the mug and set it back on the counter. "Thanks for the java. I'm heading back to the main house to enlist help getting that last cabin ready for our guests."

"Thanks, man." Though he didn't want to let Lilly go, Kane released her, taking a step back. She didn't turn from the window so, after a moment, Kane crossed to his brother, and walked with him out the door and onto the porch.

"I really appreciate this," Kane began.

"Yeah. You got a minute?" Kyle asked, his tone still pitched low. Serious. "There's something else I need to talk to you about."

Kane looked up, and the worried expression in his brother's gray eyes caused his gut to clench. "There's more, isn't there?"

"Not about the three strangers. I told you everything I know about them. This has nothing to do with them."

"Then what's wrong? Kathy's all right, isn't she?" Their sister and her husband had tried for a baby for a very long time. If something happened to mess this up, Kane wasn't sure how Kathy would take it.

"Kathy's fine, as far as I know." Kyle waved his concern away. "Calm down. Let's go for a walk."

Glancing back at the cabin, Kane shook his head. "Not right now. I really don't want to go too far from Lilly. She's freaking out."

"I understand." Kyle glanced at the still closed door and grimaced. "But I don't think you want her to hear what I have to say. How about we go to the edge of the yard?"

"Okay." Perplexed, Kane fell into step beside his brother. "Are you sure this couldn't wait? We've got enough going on right now as it is."

With a shrug, Kyle conceded the point. "It probably could. But I can't think of a better time for us to discuss it."

Kane nodded. "Fine. Though I can't imagine what it could be, I'm game. Go ahead."

"Just a minute." When they reached the spot where the circular drive went into the main path, Kyle stopped. "I wanted to talk to you about Lilly," he said, his expression tight. He held up his hand before Kane could speak. "Now you might tell me to go to hell, or that it's none of my business, but I feel I have to speak my piece."

Though Kane nodded, he had no idea what his brother could possibly have to say about Lilly. "Go ahead."

"From what you told me, you promised Lilly's brother you'd be her bodyguard, right? That you'd protect her from whatever people are searching for her?"

"True." As they continued walking, taking the trail up to the high ridge where as boys they'd often played, Kane thought he knew where Kyle was going. "Look, until now no one has surfaced looking for her, but believe me, if these three who just showed up are who I think they are, they're extremely dangerous. The Protectors have been actively searching for them. We need to bring those nut jobs from Sanctuary in—dead or alive. But I promise you, Lilly will never be in any danger."

"I don't doubt that." Kyle shot a sideways glance toward him, his gray eyes troubled. "This isn't about you keeping Lilly safe from them."

"Okay." More puzzled than ever, Kane eyed his brother. "Then what?"

"This is about keeping her safe from you."

"From me?" Stunned, Kane stared. "I'm not sure what you mean." But he knew. Deep down inside, the sinking in his gut added weight to the possibility Kyle was right. He'd already taken advantage once. Still, he felt he had to protest. Kyle didn't know about that. He couldn't. "You're not making sense."

"Bear with me and let me finish. You also told me you wanted to train her how to be self-sufficient, how to take care of herself once she is on her own."

Again stumped, Kane nodded. "And I am. She's had a self-defense lesson, and I'm planning to teach her how to feel comfortable with a pistol. We've only just gotten started, but by the time she leaves here, I'm confident Lilly will be able to handle herself in any situation."

"Will she?" Kyle stopped, lightly squeezing Kane's shoulder. "I have eyes, Kane. I see how you are together. Don't you think she's becoming a little too dependent on you?"

Dependent on him? How could his brother not see it was the other way around?

Kane couldn't help it—he laughed out loud. "Come on, Kyle." He shook his head. "Enough playing around. What did you really want to talk to me about?"

A muscle worked in his brother's jaw. "Dude, I'm serious. I know you're trying to help Lilly, but she relies on you for everything. I think once you bow out of her life, she'll be lost."

About to argue, Kane swallowed back the words. Kyle's particular phrasing had given him pause. Once he *bowed out* of Lilly's life. As he'd always planned to, as he'd known he'd have to eventually.

Then why did the thought make him feel so hollow and empty?

His churning emotions must have shown on his face.

"Hellhounds," his brother said, incredulous. "You're in love with her."

"No." Kane denied it without hesitation. "I care about her, but…"

"You should have seen your expression," Kyle persisted. "You love her. I recognize love when I see it. I've been there, brother. You can't stomach the idea of life without her."

Kane opened his mouth, and then closed it. "I…"

"Damn." Kyle clapped him on the back, suddenly gleeful. "Forget I said anything. Turns out I was worried for nothing. If you're not going to bail on the girl, then it's all good."

"What do you mean?" Kane narrowed his eyes. "Of course I'm not going to bail on her. I'm simply going to return her to her family once the danger is eliminated."

"Sure you are." Grinning from ear to ear, Kyle rolled his shoulder, shaking himself out as if he was in wolf form rather than human. As he moved away, he lifted his hand in a wave. "My work is done here. I'm heading back now." He quickened his steps, glancing back over his shoulder, still grinning. "I can't wait to tell Kris."

"Wait a minute." Kane hurried to catch up. "Tell him what? The way you're talking is crazy."

Increasing his speed, Kyle kept going. "Is it? I'm married, remember? I recognize the symptoms."

When his brother sprinted away, Kane let him go. Though he'd been away awhile, he should be used to his brother's teasing. Yet something about this cut too close to home.

Was Kyle right?

No. Not just no, but hell no. Kane had never been in love, nor did he intend to start now. What he felt for Lilly was protective, wasn't it?

An image flashed into his mind of her naked, writhing beneath him. Maybe more. Maybe just a little bit more.

He cursed. He didn't need this muddling up his thought processes right now. He had other, more important things to worry about.

Lilly wished she'd been able to catch some shut-eye, because with the tension so high, taking a nap would be damn near impossible. She drank a third cup of coffee and then regretted it. She really didn't need the caffeine. Her nerves were thrumming, and the constant adrenaline made her constantly battle the instinct to run away. She wanted to put as much distance between the sadistic doctors from Sanctuary and herself as possible. Even the possibility of seeing them again terrified her, making her want to retreat back inside her shell. A long time ago, she'd learned how to hide without going anywhere. She might not have been able to entirely keep her body safe, but at least she could throw up some kind of protection for her mind.

Now, even though Kane had done his best to show her how to be self-sufficient, and she'd made some real progress, she felt as if she'd lost significant ground.

Pretty much in combat mode, Kane ignored her, making her feel even more lost. He spent a lot of time on his phone, talking to his agency. When he finally called her brother, waking Lucas and Blythe despite his attempt to wait until a decent hour, he didn't even offer to let Lilly talk to her family.

Which was okay, she supposed. She wasn't exactly sure what she would have said anyway. She certainly didn't want her brother to decide she needed to leave here. Despite the threat, she trusted Kane implicitly to protect her.

Finally, he put his phone down. When he raised his head to find her watching him, the fierceness blazing from his eyes made her want to go over to him and let him wrap her in his arms and kiss her fears away. She longed to hang on to him, grab him by the shirt, and demand he promise her that she'd be safe.

With difficulty, she stifled the notion. She didn't want him to know how quickly her newfound self-assurance had disappeared. "Are you okay?" she asked instead, hating that her voice came out quavering.

He blinked. "Shouldn't I be asking you that?"

"How was my brother?" she asked instead of answering.

"Alarmed." Standing, he held out his hand. "I didn't let you talk to him because I didn't want him to get you all worried, even worse than you probably are."

"I'm not." Blurting out the false words, she slipped her fingers through his, wondering if he'd notice how badly she trembled. To distract him, she gave in to temptation and placed her lips in a soft kiss on his neck, inhaling the masculine scent of him. "I trust you to take care of me."

He shuddered, every muscle going tight, making her pull back in surprise. When she looked at him, he smiled at her, a tight smile that did nothing to soften the flat expression in his eyes. Gently, he unwound her arms from around him, taking a stiff step back.

"Me and six others," he said, the harshness of his voice at odds with his pleasant yet remote, expression. "Remember, the Protectors are coming in. They'll round up those three Sanctuary crazies. I won't have very much to do with it."

"And then I'll be safe?" Wrapping her arms around herself as if by doing so, she could find comfort, she leaned her head back. She held his gaze, feeling almost belligerent. She didn't understand exactly why it felt as if he withdrew more with every second that passed.

"Yes. Then you'll be safe."

She wanted to ask what would happen after that, but didn't. She wasn't sure she wanted to know. Ideally, he'd keep her around until he'd finished her training, but she had a feeling that once the threat had been eliminated, he'd return her to the care of her brother and disappear forever out of her life.

Why this made her feel like her heart were hollow, she didn't even want to know.

"Let's go get some breakfast," he said, abruptly breaking into her thoughts.

She nodded. "Okay. Where?"

Again he flashed that generic smile. "The main house. Where else?"

This time, they drove instead of walking. Judging by the number of vehicles parked out front, everyone else had had the same idea.

Though nerves had her stomach churning, Lilly squared her shoulders and lifted her chin. She walked in to the crowded room trying to make herself feel as if she belonged.

The entire family had gathered around a restaurant-quality buffet. Chatter briefly ceased when she and Kane walked in, but picked up almost immediately. Lilly was glad to see there were no outsiders there. Evidently any guests had already been fed.

"What's the plan, son?" the senior McGraw asked eagerly, smoothing a lined hand over his shiny bald head.

He wore his customary button-down short-sleeve shirt and jeans.

"No plan, Dad." Kane smiled, a cold tight smile that told Lilly he was back in what she thought of as his Protector mode. "The rest of the Protectors will be here soon. They'll take care of this."

"We want to help," Kyle said firmly. Kris and his father echoed the sentiment.

"I appreciate that, but…" Though Kane smiled, his silver gaze had turned to steel. "They're a team, specially trained to handle this kind of thing. The rest of you will need to stay out of their way."

His father and brothers looked as if they wanted to argue, but after Kane eyed them one at a time, his stare unflinching, no one else commented. Even the Senior McGraw finally grimaced and continued munching on his bacon.

After the brief moment of tension dissipated, everyone went back to piling food on their plates and eating. As Kane moved away, Lilly stared at the buffet, not only amazed at the sheer amount of food, but the variety. There were scrambled eggs, pancakes, French toast, hash browns, sausage, bacon and ham, as well as two kinds of toast—white and wheat. On a table near the food, she spied a coffee urn, and pitchers of what appeared to be orange juice and tomato juice.

Glancing at Kane's mother, Lilly wondered if the poor woman had cooked all this herself, or if she'd had help.

Kathy came up beside Lilly, touching her arm and making her jump. "Hey, you. Are you all right?"

Heart in her throat, Lilly nodded. She couldn't help but wonder what Kane's sister would do if she told her the truth: no, she wasn't all right. She was scared and lost and on the verge of becoming a total mess. "I'm fine," she said, choosing to continue to lie. "But I'm so glad to have all of you around me. It helps, a lot more than you know."

Apparently, she'd said the right thing. Kathy beamed. "Go ahead and get something to eat." She pointed at the buffet. "You've got to keep your strength up."

Despite the beautiful array of beautifully cooked choices, the idea of food, any food, made Lilly's stomach roil. "I will," she lied again. "I just need to wake up first." This despite all the coffee she'd already consumed.

As Kathy moved away, Lilly watched as Kane strode over to the buffet and loaded up his plate with scrambled eggs, pancakes, sausage, bacon and hash browns. When he turned, he met her gaze and came over, holding out the plate. "Here."

She made no move to take it. "What's this?"

"Breakfast. For you," he said. "You haven't had anything to eat since we hunted last night."

"I couldn't—"

"Please. At least try." Now, he seemed relatively normal, as if the old Kane had returned. He leaned in close, nuzzling her ear, making her shiver and sigh. "Unless you want me to tell everyone how you shape-shifted last night," he murmured. "And what we did after."

The contradiction of the delicious delight brought on by his closeness and his actual words had her briefly speechless. "You're blackmailing me?" she asked, uncertain whether he was serious or not.

She glanced up. His teasing smile still seemed at odds with his flinty eyes, which had not yet begun to thaw.

"Yep." He nodded. "For your own good."

She gave in and accepted the plate, which felt surprisingly heavy. "Thanks," she said.

"Thank you," he replied. "Why don't you take a seat and let me get my own and we'll eat together."

Though the scent of the food wafting up to her made her think she might be sick, she only nodded.

There were two empty chairs next to each other at the end of the long table. The instant Lilly took one, Kris's wife Debi dropped into the empty seat next to her. Today she'd wrestled her wild dark hair into a ponytail, though curly strands had escaped to frame her olive-skinned face.

"Hello there."

"Hi." Lilly gave her a weak smile, unable to keep from looking to see what was keeping Kane.

"No worries," Debi said, her brightly painted lips still curving in a smile. "I just need a second. I wanted to apologize to you for what happened when we had girls' night."

Lilly had just opened her mouth to try a forkful of scrambled egg. She nearly choked. Chewing, she managed to swallow. "You didn't do anything wrong," she protested, as soon as she could speak. "I drank too much and wanted to walk home."

"Sharon and I shouldn't have let you."

The small bite of eggs sat like a rock in her stomach. "Let me?" Lilly asked, mildly. "Last time I checked, I was an adult. Neither of you is responsible for me."

Her firm declaration apparently startled the other woman. Debi started to speak, and then winced as Kane came up next to her. "I think I'm in your seat," she said, jumping to her feet.

She wouldn't meet Lilly's eyes as she hurried off.

"What was that all about?" Kane picked up a piece of crispy bacon and began eating it with obvious relish.

Lilly told him, trying another forkful of eggs when she'd finished. This time, she managed to swallow without gagging. Progress.

"Did you accept her apology?" Kane asked, his own fork poised over his towering stack of pancakes.

"I told her she had nothing to apologize for." Lilly shook her head. "You'd better eat up, or your food might get cold."

As delaying tactics went, that worked. Kane flashed a grin and then turned his attention to his meal. He dug in. After a moment, she tried to do the same. She managed to get down most of her eggs, one piece of toast, and the bacon. Eating the rest of the still-heaping plate was beyond her capabilities.

When all the women started clearing the dishes and breaking down the buffet, Lilly jumped up to help them. Staying busy would keep her from worrying.

After the meal, everyone drifted into the living room, where some sort of sports game played on the big-screen TV. The volume had been turned low, but all the men had their attention riveted on the game.

"Preseason football," Debi said, shaking her head and sending her long earrings flying. "Come on, we're starting a card game in the kitchen."

Lilly followed Debi and saw Sharon and Kane's mother were already seated at the dinette table.

"Do you know how to play gin rummy?" Sharon asked, her smile friendly. She, too, had put up her wavy red hair, though she'd made hers into a sock bun on top of her head.

"No." Lilly didn't know how to play any card games. "Maybe I'd better just watch."

"It's easy." Sharon patted the chair next to her. "Sit. We'll teach you."

Lilly won the first round. "Beginner's luck," Debi told her. "But we go to 500 points, so we've got plenty of time to catch up."

They played hand after hand. When the score finally topped 500, Kane's mother won by a landside. Lilly glanced at the clock, surprised to learn several hours had passed.

The football game was still on, but the men appeared to have lost interest. Kyle was glued to his phone, either checking email or playing a game. Kris and Kane were engaged in some sort of discussion, while their father alternated between watching the game and wearing a path from the couch to the front window. His wife watched him with an indulgent expression. "We get so little excitement around here," she told Lilly. "He's beside himself."

"I'd rather have the boring peace and quiet," Lilly confided.

"Me, too." Kane's mom slipped a friendly arm around Lilly's shoulders and gave her a quick hug.

Surprised, Lilly smiled her thanks, enjoying the glow of warmth the friendly gesture brought.

The Protectors arrived exactly as Kane had said they would. Lilly and he were still at the main house. Kane's father, who was at the front window, notified everyone of their arrival.

The quiet hum of conversation ceased as everyone went still.

"Wait inside," Kane told everyone. "At least until I make sure this is them."

Just then, his phone chimed, signaling a text message. "'We're here,'" he read out loud. "It's them."

Everyone started talking at once.

Lilly crossed the room to stand in front of Kane.

"So they're finally here."

He nodded.

"I want to go with you to meet them."

He studied her, and then nodded. "Only you," he said,

raising his voice for the benefit of the others. "The rest of you, please wait inside."

The grumble of protest which followed seemed mainly masculine. Ignoring this, Kane headed to the front door.

As Lilly followed Kane out, she studied the nondescript black SUV that had pulled up and parked. As she did, six men emerged from the vehicle. The first thing Lilly noticed was they looked like ordinary men, except for the fact that they were all dressed in black from head to toe. She did a double take. Scratch that. One of them was a woman.

They greeted Kane with the ease of long familiarity. Lilly noticed how everyone, including the lone female, treated Kane with respect.

"Let me show you where you'll be staying," Kane told them. "Once you're settled in, we can go over strategy."

"Strategy?" A large man with a bulbous nose laughed. "As far as I'm concerned, it's simple. We find these sons of bitches, arrest them and haul their asses off to jail."

The rest of his companions laughed.

"If only it's that easy, Sly," Kane said, clapping him on the back. "Grab your gear and follow me."

The cabin that had been allotted to the Protectors was the next one down from Kane and Lilly's. Though the building itself couldn't be seen from their front porch, a quick jog down the road and around a turn would put them there.

Lilly wished this knowledge made her feel safe. Instead, her gut instinct screamed at her to flee. Only the knowledge that she could now change into her wolf self and outrun any human was able to comfort her.

"We're just around the bend," Kane told the crew, pointing.

"Do you need a few minutes to decompress?"

This time the woman glared at him. "What do you think we are, trainees? What we need is to plot a quick strategy, change into civilian clothes, and head into town to do some recon work."

Kane smiled his approval. "Good deal. First check with Muriel, she's the front desk clerk at the Value Five Motel. It's an old place, back in the pines along Main Street."

"Got it." The large man with a silver flattop haircut tapped his phone. "All the info has already been relayed to us."

"Well, then. I'll leave you to it."

This clearly surprised them. They all glanced at each other in obvious confusion. "You're not coming with us?"

"Nope." Kane put a friendly arm around Lilly's stiff shoulders. "I have to stay here and protect the asset."

The Asset?

Though they all nodded and then went on about their business, Lilly kept herself absolutely still, seething. The asset? As if she was no longer a person, but an item. Worse, Kane had been the one to use it.

She eased out from under his arm, jaw tight, chest aching.

"What are you two going to do?" This from the female agent, standing a few feet away, the sympathy in her clear green eyes letting Lilly know she'd not only noticed, but understood.

"I'm thinking we might practice shooting after all," Kane answered, even though the other woman had been looking at Lilly when she spoke. Then, when Lilly made a soft sound that might have been a protest, he faced her.

His granite expression softened. "I want to make sure you can defend yourself if something happens to me."

Her anger evaporated. "Happens to you? What do you mean?"

"Yeah." The female Protector crossed her arms, her expression mocking. "Since you're staying here, what could possibly happen to you?"

Before he could answer, the rest of her team joined her.

"Yeah, McGraw," one of them said. "Is there something you know that you're not telling us?"

Once again Kane's expression turned to stone. "Nope. Just taking precautions for any possibility. You know that. It's part of our basic training."

Just like that, they all got busy doing something. Except Lilly. She wasn't part of any team, including the one she'd believed she and Kane had begun to form. For the first time since she'd been rescued from Sanctuary, she felt utterly and completely alone.

Chapter 13

"Come on." This time, when Kane reached for her, Lilly neatly evaded him. She marched to the door herself and stepped outside, not bothering to see if he followed her.

"Anger is good," he said, from right behind her. "You can use it to your advantage and channel that fierceness when working with the firearm. You'll be much more accurate."

She stared in disbelief. How was it possible for him to be that clueless? She climbed into his car without responding. She'd been ambivalent about the entire teach-Lilly-to-shoot thing before. Now she was pretty damn sure she didn't want to do it.

They drove the short distance down the road and stopped at their cabin. Kane asked Lilly to wait in the car while he went inside to retrieve a spare pistol and some ammunition. He didn't seem to notice her black mood or if he did, apparently assumed it had nothing to do with him.

When he returned to the car a few moments later, the happy tune he was whistling set her teeth on edge.

"All is apparently right with your world." She couldn't keep the furious hurt from her voice.

Clearly surprised, he cocked his head and looked at her, one hand on the ignition button he'd been about to press. "If everything goes as planned, everything will be perfect for you, too. Now that the Protectors are here, it won't be long until you're safe. Once those three nut jobs from Sanctuary are securely in custody, you won't need to worry anymore."

"True."

He made no move to start the car. "Yet you don't sound happy."

"Oh, this *asset* is perfectly fine." Though she fairly spat the words, the instant they were said she wished she could call them back. She knew learning to express her feelings had to be a good thing, but she wasn't sure she actually enjoyed doing so.

"That's what this is about? You're upset because I—"

"Referred to me as an object?" Crossing her arms, she glared at him.

"No, Lilly." Expression bemused, he dragged his left hand across his chin. "That's just Protector talk. The asset refers to whatever we must protect above all else. And that would be you."

His explanation didn't make her feel any better. "You're telling me you dehumanize people? That makes no sense."

"It's perfectly logical." Voice now fierce, his silver eyes flashed as he faced her. "In order to act efficiently as Protectors, we absolutely cannot allow emotion to get in the way. I won't risk you for anything, do you understand?"

Slowly, she nodded, even though she wasn't entirely clear on whether or not he'd managed to insult her again or given her the highest compliment.

When she didn't say anything else, he started the car and put it in gear. They drove out onto the main road, and then hung a quick right. "Are we going to your brother's place?" she asked.

"Nope. A little beyond there."

They pulled off the gravel and dirt road and he killed the engine. "Come on," he said.

Her head began to ache as she followed him. When they reached a large, grassy meadow, sheltered on all sides by dense underbrush and trees, her stomach had started hurting, too. Though part of her wanted to go along with his plan since he clearly only wanted to help her, even the idea of handling a firearm made her want to retch.

"Here you go."

She recoiled when he tried to hand her a shiny silver pistol. Instead of taking it, she stared, wondering what he'd say if she told him it reminded her of a poisonous snake. Dangerous and deadly. "What's this?"

"My favorite revolver. It shoots .38, which won't have too much recoil for you to handle."

Gathering up her courage, she made no move to take it. "I actually don't like guns."

He gave her a reassuring smile. "As long as they're handled properly, there's no need to be afraid of them. Respect them, always, but I want to get you armed so you can defend yourself if need be."

He wanted. Though she knew he was right, the aversion she felt to handling the pistol ran deep, unshakable.

In the time she'd spent with Kane, she'd grown strong and more confident. She realized if she didn't take a stand on this, she would be taking a giant leap backward.

"No," she told him, meeting his gaze without flinching. "I know you mean well, and your wanting me to know how to handle a weapon makes sense."

Watching her, he waited. "But?"

"But I don't want to." She took a deep breath, gathering her resolve. "Honestly, I couldn't do it. Even if I knew how to shoot a gun, at that moment when I found myself pointing it at another human being, I'd freeze. I wouldn't be able to shoot."

His mouth twisted. "Even if you knew you'd die if you didn't?"

"Even then."

Despite her words, he continued to hold the pistol as if he thought she'd change her mind. "You're telling me you'd rather be recaptured by those religious fanatics, held prisoner and tortured than defend yourself."

"No." Glaring at him, she shook her head. "Put the gun away. Please."

Finally he did, making her exhale with relief.

Still, the black look he gave her told of his unhappiness. "I need to know, Lilly. What would you do if you found yourself alone and surrounded, with the Sanctuary doctors about to take you prisoner?"

She opened her mouth to speak, but he forestalled her. "And don't say you'll have me to defend you, because I might not always be there."

Though the thought stung, his assumption also angered her. "I wasn't going to say that. You've made it quite clear that I need to learn to rely on myself."

"Good." But his harsh tone conveyed a different message. "Then tell me what you'd do in that situation."

"I'd change into a wolf and attack them," she answered. "Or run. Something. But I wouldn't shoot them. I couldn't."

"I'm only trying to keep you safe." Though he still looked fierce, the tight line of his mouth had softened somewhat. "And in all actuality, I'd prefer to see them all dead."

She couldn't resist. "Can't let them near *the asset,* now can you?"

He laughed and finally reholstered the gun. "You win. I'm not happy about it, but you've made your feelings quite clear."

Something about the way he acquiesced, the way he gave what she wanted precedence over his own wants and needs, touched her deeply. "Thank you."

His gaze felt like a caress. "I'm proud of you, you know."

The smoldering flame in his eyes lit a bonfire deep inside her. She took a step toward him, her heart pounding an erratic beat. A bolt of raw wanting ran through her.

He met her halfway, slanting his mouth over hers as if the touch of her lips was necessary for his survival.

Her entire body throbbed and she gave herself up to his kiss.

Then, as if someone had just dumped a bucket of ice water on him, he moved away, head and shoulders bent as though in some kind of pain.

"We shouldn't do this," he said, his rusty voice harsh. The obvious sign of his arousal gave lie to his words.

Aching, yet aware he was probably right, Lilly nodded.

"Come on, let's get you back to the cabin." Kane moved off without waiting to see if she followed. "We've got a lot more preparations to do if we want to keep you safe."

Though the hot ache inside her spread to her eyes, making her blink back unexpected tears, she nodded. Following his lead, she climbed into his car, buckled in and stared out the window as he drove them back to the cabin.

Kane had never been one for self-delusion. Calling Lilly the asset had been his last desperate attempt to return to the perfectly trained operative he'd always been.

Not only had it pissed her off, but it clearly hadn't worked.

And then she'd refused to learn how to handle a firearm. Not only had he not seen that coming, but he'd been ashamed at the relief that had flooded through him. He'd known that attempting to teach her to shoot would have become another exercise in torture. After all, he would have had to put his hands on her, to help show her the proper stance and way to hold the pistol and aim.

Even standing a few feet away from her, the scent of her made him dizzy as hell. Once he'd touched her, all bets would have been off.

The kiss had come out of nowhere, sending him dangerously close to losing all control. Though he'd fought it, he'd become so aroused he'd had to step back and clear his head or he'd have taken her right there in the meadow.

When they arrived back at the cabin, a shadow detached itself from the wall and moved to greet his car. Bronwyn, the female part of this particular Protector team.

"Wait here," he told Lilly, killing the ignition and reaching for the door handle.

"Like hell," she muttered, making him grin as she did the same.

"Where have the two of you been?" Bronwyn sounded

pleasant enough, but the tightness in her expression belied her attempt to appear casual.

"Why?" Crossing his arms, Kane gave Bronwyn a look that he hoped would communicate that he wanted her to cut to the chase.

Though the tiny jerk of her chin told him she got the message, the way she cut her eyes toward Lilly let him know she wasn't comfortable speaking in front of the asset.

Even thinking of Lilly that way felt wrong. He completely understood why she'd gotten so upset.

"It's okay, Bronwyn." He clapped his hand on her shoulder. "Lilly can hear whatever you have to say."

Her shrug effectively removed his hand. "It's your funeral. Anyway, we've been all over this town. No one has seen or heard from those three. The only person who has seen them is the woman who works in the motel."

"Muriel."

"Yes." Bronwyn glanced again at Lilly. "How reliable is she?"

"I've known her since I was a little kid. She'd never make something like that up. And furthermore, we've been pretty quiet about how many from Sanctuary are still running loose. She has no way of knowing there are three."

"True, but we can't figure out why the perps would arrive and ask exactly one single person about their quarry, and then disappear."

"Perps?" Lilly asked.

Kane smiled at her. "Short for perpetrator." He glanced at Bronwyn, who watched him with an odd expression on her face.

"That's right," she said. "And they're not acting like they should, especially if they think you're here."

"Which doesn't make sense," Kane put in. "Why else would they travel to Leaning Tree? We're a small town in the Catskills, not even a major tourist destination like Woodstock."

Lilly cleared her throat, drawing both of their attention. "They won't do things the way normal people would. My guess is they know more than you realize. They've found someplace where they can hole up and watch and wait."

"How would you know?" Bronwyn didn't bother to disguise her dismissal, as if she was delivering an unspoken message that Lilly should leave things to the professionals.

As Kane watched, his little Lilly lifted her chin. "How would I know?" she asked, her voice silk and steel. "I think I'd know better than anyone else what kind of crazy those people are. Especially since I was their prisoner for fifteen freaking years."

To Kane's amusement, Bronwyn's stiff, military demeanor vanished. She inclined her head, conceding the point to Lilly. "I apologize," she said quietly.

"Apology accepted." And Lilly smiled, making her appear radiantly beautiful. Again Kane had to battle with the urge to pull her against him and publically claim her as his. Which of course she wasn't. And could never be.

To his horror, Bronwyn appeared to pick up on this. She studied him intently. "Are you two...mates?"

Mates. The word he'd managed to avoid even thinking.

"No," he answered quietly, the ache in his chest making him feel like a liar. "We're not."

Bronwyn and Lilly exchanged a glance, the kind two women do when they're having a private conversation. Except this one didn't even have any words.

"What else?" he barked. "Surely you have more to tell

me than the sad fact that six trained Protectors can't locate three crazy cultists?"

His sharp tone didn't appear to faze her. Slowly, she
shook her head. "Nope."

"What's the plan?"

"We're going to stay awhile. I need you to clear this
with your parents. A few of us are going to try and get
jobs in town, and see if we can blend in. We're betting
the perps will surface eventually."

Behind him, Lilly made a sound low in her throat.
"This is going to take a while, then?"

Both Kane and Bronwyn turned to look at her.

"It would appear so," Bronwyn said, her sharp gaze
missing nothing. "I know you're probably ready to get
out of the boonies, aren't you?"

"Yes," Lilly answered, way too fast. The pink flush on
her cheeks told Kane she was lying, though he couldn't
understand why.

"Hey, you're not insulting me," he told her softly. "I
get stir-crazy if I spend too much time here. I don't blame
you for wanting to get out."

Bronwyn cleared her throat, making him realize he
and Lilly had locked gazes.

"I've filled you in, so I'll be going." Bronwyn's
amused smile told him she'd noticed. With a casual flip
of her hand, she took off.

As they watched her go, Lilly's pensive expression
made him wonder.

"Sorry." He went past and held the cabin door open
for her. "There's nothing I can do about your being stuck
here with me, at least not until all of this is over with."

Pushing on past him, she didn't respond. Once inside, she headed directly to the kitchen, where she began
rummaging in the cabinets as though looking for some-

thing to cook. The small frown line between her perfectly arched brows told him she still wasn't happy.

"Lighten up," he told her, fed up and surprisingly hurt, too. "For all you know, it might only be a couple more days."

Her head snapped up. "Do you think?"

"No." Passing deliberately close to her, he retrieved a soft drink from the fridge and popped the top. He took a long drink, set the can down on the counter and looked at her. "What's wrong, Lilly?"

"Nothing." But she wouldn't meet his gaze.

"It's only natural to be afraid."

"I'm not." Defiance blazed from her eyes. "I'm angry. I don't understand why they won't leave me alone. Why me? Haven't I suffered enough? Why can't they just go away and let me live my life?"

"I don't know." Though he wanted to gather her close, he resisted, sensing she wouldn't welcome his embrace, at least not right now. "But you're getting stronger, every single day. I think it's been good for you, being here."

Briefly, she lowered her lashes. "It has. I'm just feeling restless, that's all."

He thought he understood. "Ever since you learned the three Sanctuary doctors were in the area."

"I guess. I can't help thinking it's safer to go on the run."

"And then what?" Taking another drink of his cola, he sighed. "You can't spend the rest of your life fleeing."

Though she nodded, he could tell she wasn't entirely convinced.

Kane's cell rang. Caller ID showed his brother Kris's number. "What's up?" he asked.

Kris's voice rang with amusement. "You'd better come up to the main house. There's someone here to see you."

Kane sighed. "I don't have time for games."

"Games?" Kris sounded indignant. "This isn't a game, I promise. You really do have a visitor. Someone you haven't seen in a long time."

"Just spit it out. Who is it?"

"Anabel Lee."

"What?" Kane groaned, remembering Shawn Ferguson's claim that Anabel was on the prowl for him. He glanced at Lilly, also remembering that Shawn had said Kane would have to publicly claim her.

"Yeah," Kris continued. "She's in the kitchen, chatting it up with Mom. She acts exactly the way she did back in high school, when she used to come over and wait for you to get home from football practice."

"Just send her away." Kane didn't bother to keep the annoyance from his voice. "I don't have time for this."

"I'll try." Still chuckling, Kris ended the call.

"What's wrong?" Lilly asked softly.

"My old high school girlfriend is here." He sighed. "I have no desire to reconnect with her."

Her blue gaze roamed over his features. "Why not? Are you still in love with her?"

He couldn't help laughing at that. "Not hardly. But she's what they call a drama queen. I can only imagine she's here to make trouble."

"If you say so." She didn't appear convinced. "How long has it been since you've seen her?"

Trying to remember, he shrugged. "I don't know exactly, but it's been years."

"Listen." A shrill, feminine squeal came from outside. Kane grimaced. "Hellhounds. I know that sound."

He went to the window and cursed. "I was afraid of that," he said, as Lilly joined him. "Somehow, she talked Mom into telling her where I was staying."

Anabel wore a long black dress and a huge purple hat, the brim completely shadowing her face. She'd always favored an eclectic style of dress, but from what Kane could tell, she looked downright…old-fashioned and frumpy.

"But why is she circling your car?" Lilly asked. "And making sounds like that?"

"Apparently she likes red corvettes. As to the pig-squealing sound, she's always done that. It used to drive me insane."

Lilly grimaced. "Is she a witch? I don't mean the Wiccan kind, but the other, dark type. Assuming there are such things."

"Hey, there are vampires, werewolves and fairies," he said. "So I'm pretty sure there are a few of our kind who practice the darker arts."

"Scary." She shuddered. He couldn't tell if she was joking. "Though I don't think they have anything on the torture artists at Sanctuary."

Again he wanted to hold her. And once more, he understood he could not. "What the hell am I going to do? I want to send her away, but we need to be careful not to make any enemies in Leaning Tree."

She shot him a rueful look. "I guess you've got no choice but to go out and greet her."

He muttered a curse word. "Only if you come with me."

Smile broadening into an all-out grin, Lilly shook her head. "I will. That's what best friends do."

Best friends? Though Lilly claimed she couldn't handle a relationship, he wasn't sure he liked the idea of her thinking of him as a friend, best or not. Yet one more thing he'd have to get over.

"Come on then," he growled, holding out his arm before he changed his mind.

Taking it, she laughed again, apparently amused at his gruff expression. "Do you want me to pretend to be your girlfriend?"

Though her tone suggested she was kidding, he decided to take her seriously. "Yes. More than that, actually." Hesitating, he bit the bullet. "I need you to pretend to be my mate. Shawn tried to warn me that night we ate at his place. She's pushy, but even a woman like Anabel Lee won't try to come between mates."

Though Lilly had readily agreed, hearing Kane use the word *mate* did strange things to her equilibrium. The term seemed fraught with meaning, more intense than a mere *fiancée, wife* or *spouse,* suggesting a lifelong commitment that had been predetermined at birth.

Worse, hearing it applied to her and Kane…the word *mate* fit somehow. Which was not only a foolish thought, but a dangerous one, as well. A man like Kane could never be saddled with a woman like her. He'd pity her if he knew how badly she wanted him.

As Kane yanked the front door open and pulled her outside, she had to admit she was curious about what kind of woman Kane had dated in the past.

Her first up-close glimpse of Anabel Lee made her think someone had taken being named after a character in an Edgar Allen Poe story a bit too seriously. Her raven colored hair was long, almost to her waist, and straight. Anabel also wore a floppy purple hat and flowing black dress that might have been patterned after one from an earlier era.

She turned with a flounce as Kane and Lilly approached, removing her hat and flipping her hair back over her shoulder in a gesture as antiquated as her appearance. Her heavily mascara'd brown-eyed gaze devoured Kane. She ignored Lilly completely.

"Kane!" She uttered a shrill squeal before throwing herself into Kane's arms.

Luckily for her, he managed to catch her. Holding her at arm's length, he shot Lilly a look so pleading she almost laughed.

Instead, she sidled up to the two of them and cocked her head. "Hello," she said, looking Anabel up and down and hoping her expression appeared friendly enough. What Kane had said made sense. They didn't want to risk alienating anyone who might come into contact with the Protectors or the doctors from Sanctuary.

Anabel straightened her spine and collected herself as Kane released her. Dusting off her arms where he'd held her, she gave Lilly a narrow-eyed, appraising look. "Who are you?" she demanded.

"I'm Lilly Gid— Er, Green," Lilly said, relieved she hadn't inadvertently blurted out her real name. She considered holding out her hand and then thought better of it, inclining her chin instead. "And you must be Anabel Lee."

"I am." Anabel glared at her. "What are you doing here?"

"Lilly's my fiancée," Kane put in, ever helpful, though Lilly couldn't help but notice how he kept his distance from both of them.

"Fiancée?" Anabel went completely still. The way she'd outlined both her eyes in heavy black eyeliner gave her a racoonish appearance. Kane's words appeared to stun her. Pain flashed across her face. She looked from Kane to Lilly. "That's not possible. Kane, you can't marry her. You're my mate. You belong with me."

For one stunned moment, her words seemed to hang

there, bald and unbelievable. Anabel winced, apparently aware that now she'd just exposed her inner emotions without warning, she'd also set herself up for the possibility of being hurt.

Lilly felt a stab of sympathy for her.

"Anabel." Kane lowered his voice, sounding oddly gentle. "I haven't seen you since high school. We only dated casually in our senior year. You know we aren't mates. We never were."

"Liar." Anabel's eyes filled with tears, smudging her mascara and eyeliner. "I've waited for you all these years. Ask anyone." Her voice rose. "I gave Kathy letters once a week to send to you."

"Letters?" Now Kane blinked with bafflement.

Anabel narrowed her gaze. "Don't tell me your sister didn't give them to you."

"Of course she did," Kane responded quickly. Since even Lilly could tell he wasn't telling the truth, she had no doubt Anabel could, as well.

"Why didn't you ever write back?" The plaintive note in her voice was both disturbing and, for whatever reason, tugged at Lilly's heart.

Kane shook his head. "Enough, Anabel. I really think it's time for you to go."

"I just got here," Anabel screeched. "I wait years for you to return to me and you finally come home, but you bring this…" Swallowing back a sob, she gestured at Lilly, her hurt and angry expression letting them know whatever term she eventually chose, it wouldn't be pretty.

Yet despite all this, the raw wretchedness in her face made Lilly want to comfort her. Crazy? Maybe. Or just confused. Whatever she might be, her raw sense of loss appeared palpable, as if she honestly believed every word she'd said.

As Lilly stared at her, at a complete loss for words, Anabel's wolf became visible, like a projector image superimposed over her face. It snarled and lunged at her. Lilly took a step back, right into Kane's arms.

She would have moved away, but he held her in place with a steel grip, shielding her in case the other woman did something crazy.

Meanwhile, Anabel covered her face with trembling hands and sobbed, giving voice to her sense of loss. "First my David goes and leaves me, and now you."

"Anabel, I'm sorry for your loss. But I really think you need to leave."

At Kane's sharp tone, Anabel appeared to physically pull herself together. She wiped at her tears, swallowing back a sob. As she stared at Kane, a mocking smile hovered over her hot-pink painted lips. "I know what you're doing here," she said, her cool tone containing a subtle threat. "And while I don't understand how you can break my heart just to protect her, I want you to know that I'll continue waiting. For as long as it takes."

After delivering that pronouncement, Anabel spun around and marched away.

Lilly watched her go in stunned silence. "What was that?" she asked, finally having the presence of mind to move out of Kane's arms.

"I don't know." His grim tone contained a note of worry. "Shawn told me she lost her husband six months ago in Afghanistan. Evidently the grief got to her and she's gone slightly nuts."

"I feel bad for her."

"I'm more concerned with the way she claims to know who you are."

"She didn't say that. She said she knew what I was doing here."

"Same difference." He dragged his hand through his hair. "I need to fill the team in. Just in case Anabel turns out to be a threat."

"Don't you think she's too obvious?" Lilly sighed. "I saw genuine hurt in her eyes. If it weren't for that, I would have thought the entire performance was an act."

"Hurt?" He shook his head. "She has no reason to feel hurt. None at all. She has to have some ulterior motive behind acting that way."

"She's grieving. Sorrow can do awful things to some people."

"Maybe. But I still need to talk to the team. I also need to get with my brothers and some of my old friends in town. Maybe they can shed some light on to what's going on with her."

"What about the letters she says she sent?"

"Kathy will know if that part's true or not."

Lilly cleared her throat. "From what I understand, if Anabel truly believes you're her mate, there's a very real possibility that you might be."

"No." He didn't even hesitate. "Anabel is most definitely *not* my mate."

Though the idea of him with anyone else made her entire body hurt, more than anything Lilly wanted Kane to find happiness. If Anabel might be his future, she had to give him a chance to find out. "I think you should go talk to her, just the two of you."

His eyes darkened dangerously. "Have you lost your mind? Why would I do that?"

Since she needed a good reason, she said the first thing that came to mind. "Because Anabel might just be the one person the 'perps,' as you call them, need to get to me. I think it's better if you don't make any enemies."

He cursed under his breath, but she could tell from his expression he knew she was right.

"I'll think about it," he finally told her.

"When?" she pushed. Then, because she couldn't help herself, she took a deep breath. "I'd hate to be keeping you from your destiny."

At her words, he went absolutely still. "I don't believe in destiny," he snarled, then strode into the bathroom and closed the door.

A moment later she heard the shower start up.

Staring after him, Lilly knew he had to give Anabel a chance. Even if in the end, he wasn't the man for her, the poor woman didn't deserve to live with such sorrow and regret. During her time in captivity, Lilly had become intimately familiar with grief and an overwhelming sense of loss. She'd spent fifteen years mourning the loss of her brother, only to learn Lucas not only lived, but had believed her dead also. They'd found each other and in the process, Lucas had found Blythe, his mate. Lilly had been delighted at the happiness radiating from them. This sort of joy was exactly what Kane needed.

And if Anabel might be able to give it to him, so much the better. If not, Lilly wanted to find a way to help the other woman move on, because there had to be something else over the next horizon.

Now she sounded maudlin. Kane would order her to take off her rose-colored glasses and face reality. Lilly had spent most of her life staring a mean and painful reality in the eye. She was ready for a little happily-ever-after.

Fine, Lilly decided. If Kane didn't want to befriend Anabel, then she'd have to do it.

Chapter 14

That night, the raw sorrow Lilly had seen in Anabel's brown eyes kept haunting her. Though she knew she shouldn't take it personally, she couldn't help but identify with the other woman. Maybe it was the simple fact that she, having suffered so much at the hands of others, simply could relate to pain.

While she wanted Anabel on their side, she wanted to help her even more. And if by doing so, she could help Kane, then all the better.

Yet, the gamut of emotions that flooded her at the thought of Kane with Anabel tore Lilly up inside. Wanting him made her selfish, especially since she knew he deserved so much more than someone like her, broken inside. Maybe if she found him true happiness, leaving him wouldn't be so damn difficult.

Lilly tried to come up with a plan, but couldn't. Since Kane insisted on staying near her 24/7, meeting up with

Anabel by herself would be difficult. She'd need help. Though she liked Kane's brothers' wives well enough, neither Debi nor Sharon seemed like the type to keep a secret. That left Kane's sister, Kathy. Who apparently had remained in touch with Anabel, at least accepting the letters for Kane. Lilly had to wonder why she hadn't forwarded them on.

"I haven't seen Kathy around lately," Lilly mentioned casually the next morning. She'd just poured them each a fragrant cup of coffee and Kane had promised to make them scrambled eggs. She loved the way he looked first thing in the morning, with his short dark hair all spiky and his silver eyes still molten liquid from sleep.

"That's because we haven't been up to the house around dinnertime," he said. "But I do need to talk to her. I want to ask her about those letters Anabel supposedly gave to her."

Opening the egg carton, he swore. "We only have two eggs."

Which gave her the perfect opening. Maybe, just maybe, if they had breakfast at the main house, Kathy would be there and Lilly could have a word with her separately from Kane.

"How about we have breakfast with your folks?" she said, acting as if she didn't care one way or another. "Maybe Kathy will be there and you can talk to her." She felt a flash of guilt as pleasure replaced the surprise in Kane's expression.

"I'd love that," he said quietly. "Let's go."

Outside, the breeze felt chilly despite the sun. They drove the short distance instead of walking, as Kane said he was too hungry to wait too long. When they entered the house through the back door which led directly into the kitchen, Lilly was disappointed to see no sign of Kathy.

Kane's mother beamed. "Welcome, you two. You're just in time for my famous cinnamon French toast. Kathy and Tom are on the way, too."

"Great." After kissing his mother's cheek, Kane squeezed his father's shoulder and then pulled out a chair for Lilly. Once she'd taken her seat, he dropped down next to her. "Where are Kris and Kane and the bunch?"

"They went into town to help with the planning committee for this year's Labor Day Parade. Preparations have been in full swing for a couple of weeks. They're already building the floats."

Kane shook his head. "It's hard to believe summer is almost over."

"Labor Day is tomorrow." Mr. McGraw smiled at Lilly. "They need all the hands they can get. Maybe the two of you should volunteer to help. I think Lilly would enjoy it."

Lilly couldn't resist glancing at Kane. He knew her well enough to know how much she'd hate something like that. One corner of his mouth twitched in the beginning of a smile. "We'll keep that in mind, Dad."

Kathy and Tom blew in. Kathy's glorious mass of wavy hair had been pulled back into an untidy ponytail and she appeared radiant with happiness. "Look!" With a dramatic flourish, she pointed to her stomach. "I finally have a baby bump!"

Mama McGraw rushed over and enveloped her daughter in a hug. "I hope you're hungry. Sit, and let me get started cooking. You need to eat lots—remember, you're eating for two!"

Grinning at his wife, Tom pulled out a chair next to Lilly, fussing over Kathy as she settled herself in her seat.

"Good morning, Lilly," Kathy fairly sang the words. "Do you want to feel my belly?"

Taken aback, Lilly wasn't sure how to react. Finally, she held her breath and placed her hand on Kathy's newly rounded abdomen. "Will I feel it kick?" she asked.

Kathy smiled. "Not yet. I can't wait for that. If you're still here, I promise to let you feel once the baby does."

If you're still here. Funny, how the casual words wounded her. Lilly managed to smile and nod, gently moving her hand away.

Luckily, Kane's mother returned with a huge platter of French toast. "Here you go," she said, setting it down. "I've warmed maple syrup. I just need to fetch it from the kitchen. There's butter in the bowl in the center of the table."

Mrs. McGraw returned with the syrup as everyone helped themselves. Silence fell, while they dug in.

Lilly nearly moaned out loud as the first bite melted in her mouth. "This is wonderful," she said, meaning it. Around her, everyone smiled and nodded and just kept right on eating.

When the platter had been emptied, Mrs. McGraw stood and began gathering the plates.

"Let me help you, Mom," Kathy said, pushing to her feet and reaching for the silverware.

Lilly saw her perfect opportunity. "I'll help, too."

"Let me assist you lovely ladies," Kane put in.

"Sit," Lilly ordered, before she had time to think. "I need a break from you." Everyone stared at her, looking amused. She thought about trying to explain, and then decided against it.

Surprisingly, Kane looked stung. But he remained where he was and Lilly continued to help clear the table.

Once everything had been gathered up, she followed Kathy and her mother into the kitchen.

"Dishwasher's broken, ladies," Mrs. McGraw told them. "We'll have to wash this batch by hand."

"Mama, go relax." Placing her plates on the counter near the sink, Kathy shooed her back towards the dining room. "You've done enough, cooking all this. Lilly and I can take care of the dishes."

Laughing, the older woman wasted no time returning to the rest of her family.

"I'll wash and you dry." Kathy handed her a towel. "Is that all right with you?"

Lilly nodded. "I've helped my brother's wife, Blythe, do this a lot back home."

After rinsing off the dishes and filling the sink with soapy water, Kathy began scrubbing. "Where's home to you?"

For some reason Lilly thought of Kane. Which confused the heck out of her. "I grew up in Texas," she managed to say without wincing. "And before here, I lived with my brother and his wife in Seattle."

"I love that city." Kathy handed her the first plate. Lilly carefully dried it before placing it in the dish rack on the counter.

They chatted a bit, working through the dishes, while Lilly tried to figure out how to ask her question. Finally, she simply inhaled and plunged into a gap in the conversation.

"Kane and I had a strange visitor yesterday," she said. "A woman named Anabel."

Though Kathy continued working on cleaning the silverware, Lilly noticed a kind of watchful stillness in the other woman.

"Really?" Kathy's brows rose. "I'm surprised I haven't heard about that yet. How'd it go?"

"She claimed Kane is her mate. And she also said she's been giving you letters to give to Kane."

"Letters?" Now Kathy turned to face Lilly, frowning. "That doesn't make sense. She has his email. Everyone does. His veterinary practice has a website." She paused, then reached for another handful of silverware. "I wonder if she's confusing him with her husband, David. She used to send him care packages along with handwritten letters. I know because I helped her box them up a couple of times."

Lilly pondered this. "Is she mentally ill?"

"Probably." Kathy didn't hesitate. "She stopped going to grief counseling after she fell apart in one of the sessions. I feel bad for her, but she won't let anyone help her. She's become a recluse these past few months. Rarely leaves her home and when she does, she dresses in an outfit that looks like a Halloween witch costume."

It was a pretty accurate description.

"And now she's fixated on Kane."

Kathy made a sound. "Poor him. How'd he deal with that?"

"He was kind," Lilly said, feeling compelled to defend him. "And firm. He told her they were never mates and asked her to leave."

"He's right about that. They aren't mates." Tone firm and no-nonsense, Kathy just looked at Lilly. "You do realize that, don't you?"

Lilly shrugged. "I don't know how to tell."

The strangled sound coming from Kathy might have been laughter, or something else entirely. "You honestly don't know?"

Slowly, Lilly shook her head.

"Kane and Anabel aren't mates, because you and he are. Anyone with eyes in their head can see that." Handing Lilly the last of the silverware, Kathy pulled the drain plug and began draining the sink.

Meanwhile, Lilly stood frozen, clutching a bunch of wet forks and knives before belatedly placing them on her dish towel. "No," she said faintly. "He and I aren't mates. We can't be."

"Why's that, hon?" Grabbing the dish towel from her, Kathy gently removed the pieces from Lilly's hands and dried them. "Why can't you and my brother be together?"

"We just can't." Oddly enough, Lilly felt like she might be about to weep. "Please, just leave it at that."

Kathy stared at her for a moment in silence, and finally nodded. "Have it your way," she said. "Come on, let's go rejoin the others."

"Wait." Lilly grabbed her arm. "I need your help." She glanced at the still-closed door. "I want to talk to Anabel without Kane."

Kathy studied her through narrowed eyes. Just now, the dove-gray color appeared more silver, like Kane's. "Why?"

"I think I can help her."

"You'd better talk to Kane about that." Kathy sighed. "I can't help you do anything that might not be safe. And with Anabel's fragile state of mind…"

"Please." Lilly continued to hold Kathy's arm. "It can be in a public place, and you can be there, too. I just need a few minutes with her. That's all."

Kathy's hand crept up to rest on her slightly rounded belly. "I still don't understand what exactly you're trying to do."

"Just talk. Nothing more."

"We need to run it by Kane." The firm set of Kathy's jaw told Lilly she wasn't budging on this.

Which meant Lilly wouldn't be meeting with Anabel. "How about giving me her phone number?" Lilly tried to keep her voice casual. "That'd be nearly as good. I can speak to her on the phone instead."

"I don't know…" Kathy glanced at Kane before looking back at Lilly. "All right," she finally said. "I can give you her number. I can't guarantee that she'll even talk to you, and I want your word you won't try to sneak off and meet with her."

"You have it." Lilly smiled as Kathy scribbled the number on a paper napkin. Pocketing it, she thanked her.

"What I don't understand is why you want to get involved in this," Kathy mused. "You have enough crazy stuff to deal with as it is. Why add more?"

"Because I truly believe I can help her. Since I was rescued, I've done nothing but accept assistance from others. It's time I give back."

Kathy smiled. "That's really nice. Good luck with it." They went back in the room and sat. For a while, everyone sipped coffee, sated and relaxed.

After they'd socialized for another half hour, Kane got up. "Come on, Lilly. We need to stop at the cabin before our drive."

Drive? Lilly knew better than to ask in front of Kane's family. Pushing to her feet, Lilly thanked Kane's mother for a wonderful meal. The older woman beamed at the praise.

Outside, the morning air still carried a bit of a chill, hinting that fall was just around the corner.

Once they were in the Corvette, Kane started the engine.

"I understand you want to talk to Anabel," he said, the instant they pulled away from the main house.

Her stomach clenched. "Kathy told you."

"Of course she did. I'm trying to keep you safe. I can't do that if you go around contacting people like Anabel. You don't even know her. Why would you want to do that anyway?"

She swallowed. "Because she's hurting and I know how that is. I identify with her. And I think she's just fixated on you as a way to cope with the loss of her husband." She lowered her voice. "I want to try and help her. Because if there'd just been one person during all my years as a prisoner, a simple kindness like a conversation would have meant the world to me."

His expression changed. "Just don't be hurt if she rebuffs you."

"I won't." She gave him a smile. "And don't be surprised if she doesn't."

One hand on the steering wheel, he handed her a cell phone. "Here. You can keep this. It's a spare prepaid one I bought before we came out here. Have at it."

Despite her brave assurances, Lilly's heart was in her throat as she dialed the number Kathy had written.

It went straight to voice mail. Lilly sighed, debated hanging up, and left a message instead. "This is Lilly Green. I met you yesterday, out at Wolf Hollow. I was hoping to talk to you. We have quite a bit in common. Please call me back at this number."

After disconnecting the call, she sighed. "Now I just need to wait and see what happens."

Kane shook his head as they pulled up to their cabin. "I doubt she'll call you back."

"Well, until she does, since you mentioned we were going for a drive, I'd like to go into town. I need to buy a few things."

"You can't," he said, grimacing. "Too risky until we

find out where the cultists are. If you'll give me a list, I'll have Kathy or Debi or Sharon pick up whatever you need."

Her cheeks warmed. "How about we go to the next town over? It's been ages since I went shopping. Shopping is one of the things I really enjoy."

"What woman doesn't?" He chuckled. "All right. We'll stop in Kingston while we're over that way."

"Where are we going?" Fairly bouncing in the seat, she couldn't hide her anticipation.

"I thought I'd take you over to Woodstock. It's a touristy sort of place and at this time of the year it should be crawling with people. I figure it'll be safer that way."

"Safer." Though she nodded, a sudden realization struck her. "You know, since coming here, I've been almost as much of a prisoner as I was before."

His smile disappeared. "Ouch. I'm sorry you feel like that. Everything we do is only to protect you."

"I know that." Without thinking, she lightly touched his arm. He tensed under her fingers. "It's just that I've been feeling a bit like a butterfly, emerging from a cocoon. No." She waved away any potential comments. "Let me rephrase that. Like a bear waking up after hibernating all winter." She laughed, amused at her admittedly rough analogy. "I'm eager to discover and learn and fierce to protect my right to explore."

After a startled second, he laughed with her. He took a deep breath. "You've been doing so well with your self-confidence. I've seen a side of you I didn't expect to see, at least not so soon."

She smiled at the compliment.

They parked in front of the cabin. "You can wait here if you want. I just need to grab my backpack."

"I need to freshen up." She got out, closing her door

quietly and hurrying in ahead of him. She felt like a kid, getting a day off from school to do something fun. Just because she was getting to do an ordinary thing, something other people didn't even think about before doing.

The instant Lilly disappeared into the bathroom, Kane sent a text to Sly, the leader of the Protector team on-site. He requested backup, needing someone to shadow them while they took in the sights. The most important aspect was that Lilly not notice. Her newfound independence might be fragile. He didn't want to upset it.

After receiving the text response assuring him that Sly would have the situation handled, Kane relaxed. He grabbed his backpack, checking to make sure his camera battery was fully charged, and sat down on the couch to wait for Lilly.

When she emerged, his heart turned over. She'd put on a brightly patterned sundress, which showcased her long, creamy legs. Her soft, ivory shoulders and slender body made her look dainty and graceful. The low-cut bodice highlighted her shapely figure. She was a pleasing contrast of wholesome yet seductive.

Just like that, he burned for her.

Stunned speechless, he tried to find the right words to compliment her without betraying the way she affected him.

He knew he was staring, but he couldn't help it. Slowly, he rose to his feet, holding his backpack in front of him like a shield. "You look great," he rasped. He kept his gaze riveted on her face, but then, unable to help himself, let it travel over her once again slowly. As if he were photographing her with his eyes.

"Thanks." Her porcelain complexion turned pink. "Are you ready to go?"

Inside, his wolf roared. Looking at her, he swore he could see the faint suggestion of hers, doing the same.

Shaking it off, he turned and held the door for her. The light, floral scent she wore drifted to him as she passed, making him ache.

"It's a bit of a drive," he told Lilly. "But scenic. So relax and enjoy. On the way home, there's a great fruit-and-vegetable stand I want to stop at. Mom always likes for me to pick up stuff for her there."

She smiled back. "Sounds lovely."

The winding road meandered through the occasional older neighborhoods, large two-story houses set way back off the road. Traveling to the highway was easier if he drove directly through town, but he wanted to keep Lilly away from Leaning Tree, so he took the long way. This involved making a circle around town, cutting around the reservoir, and finally reaching the main road.

"I love this." Cheeks still flushed, eyes bright with excitement, Lilly seemed enthralled with their surroundings. "I bet it's really beautiful once the leaves start turning."

"It is."

As he hit the interstate, his cell phone rang. His brother Kris.

"Hey, Kane." Kris's voice sounded strange, completely unlike his usual jubilant self. "I'm just leaving town, but Mom called. She says there's a guy up at the main house with some sort of law enforcement credentials. He's asking a lot of questions about a missing woman who he claims has been abducted."

Kane swore. "Why didn't she call me?"

"She says I'm closer. She knew you were taking Lilly over to Woodstock today."

"Do you know if he has a picture of the woman he's looking for?"

"She said if he does, he hasn't gotten around to showing her yet." Kris sounded agitated. "I'm driving as fast as I can, but we're still a few minutes out. I have a bad feeling about this."

"I do, too. Why'd Mom let him in?"

"No idea. You know how she is. Too damn trusting. Why don't you call your Protectors and see if there's one still on the premises. If so, have them get over to her."

"Will do. And I'm on my way also."

"Kane," Kris cut in swiftly. "Absolutely not. Think, man. You need to take Lilly and disappear into the woods. Change if you need to, but get her the hell away from here."

He was right. But also wrong. "I'm not leaving Mom and Dad unprotected."

"I doubt it will come to that." But Kris didn't sound certain. "They're not here for her or us."

"Let me notify them. I'll call you right back." Kane ended the call and immediately dialed Sly's number. He passed on what his brother had told him.

"Hellhounds." Sly sounded furious. "No one's there. I'm the closest. I can be there in under ten minutes."

"Good. Get there as quickly as you can." Kane pressed End and called Kris back. "Sly is on his way. Who's all at the house with Mom?" Kane prayed Kathy and her husband had gone home.

"Just Mom. I think Dad went into town."

"Good." Kane took a deep breath. "Is Kyle heading back with you?"

"Yes. He's right here. We had Debi take Sharon and the kiddos home."

"Excellent. Do you and Kyle have access to weapons?"

"Weapons?" Kris sounded grim. "Of course we do, but do you really think—"

"The fact that you called me tells me you do, too. In situations like this, go with your gut. Do not let any harm come to Mom. Swear to me you'll do your best to protect her."

"Of course I will. But Kane—"

"Just go. Don't call me back until you know she's safe."

He savagely punched off, then tossed his phone onto the console. Damn. Kane glanced at Lilly. Blue eyes wide, she stared.

"What's going on?" she asked, fear vibrating in her voice.

"No time to explain." Pulling over to the side of the road, he grabbed her hand. "Lilly, I want you to listen to me and do exactly as I tell you. Do you understand?"

Terror darkening her gaze, she nodded.

"Good. You're going to run into the woods and change. I want you to put as much distance between yourself and here as possible."

"What about you? Aren't you going with me?"

"I can't leave my family undefended. You'll be fine, as long as you follow instructions. Remember those caves, I showed you?"

When she nodded again, he exhaled. "Go there as a wolf, and hide. I'll come for you when it's safe."

"Why as a wolf?"

"Because all your senses are sharper. You'll be able to hear them coming from much farther away. And you can use your snout, too." Getting out, he yanked open the door and grabbed her. "Take off. Now."

Again she hesitated. Chest tight, he gave her a small tug. "Hurry, Lilly. Go."

Finally, she went, crashing into the woods and head-

ing away from Wolf Hollow. He watched until he could
no longer see her, feeling as if he was sending away his
heart. Then he stiffened his spine, grabbed both his pis-
tols and, after checking to make sure they were loaded,
stuffed them into his hidden holsters. Jumping back into
his car, he turned around and stomped on the accelera-
tor, headed back home.

Heart pounding, Lilly took off running, exactly as
Kane had ordered. She made it to the first clearing,
stripped off her clothing, carefully folding her new dress,
and initiated the change to wolf. Even in her animal form,
she couldn't stop thinking about Kane's parents and the
fact that they were in danger. Because of her.

And she was about to run and hide in a cave like a
coward. She might have been able to do such a thing
once, but not now. She was no longer the terrified victim she'd been.

As a wolf, she circled around, heading back to the
main house, keeping her ears open for any out-of-the-
ordinary sounds.

While she ran, she periodically scented the air, just
in case. She didn't expect them, if in fact, this stranger
was part of Sanctuary, to be out beating the brush for
her. Not yet.

But she owed it to Kane and his family to make sure
no one got hurt. They wanted her, not them. Well, she'd
damn sure make certain they got exactly what they
wanted.

Chapter 15

Though journeying on foot, even as a wolf, would be much slower than Kane traveling by car, Lilly kept moving. As a human, she had absolutely no sense of direction. As a wolf, she knew exactly which way to go.

She paced herself, keeping to a lope rather than a run, aware she had quite a few miles to go. When she reached the first road, one of the winding ones she and Kane had taken to reach the interstate, she looked both ways and waited until there were no cars in sight before crossing.

Since she had no watch, she wasn't sure how much time passed. Judging from the position of the sun, it took her close to an hour before she reached the boundaries of Wolf Hollow's land. She only hoped she wasn't too late.

Keeping to the ridge above, she remained in the shadows of the giant oaks when she finally reached the main house. Below, the place appeared quiet, like an ordinary morning at Wolf Hollow Motor Court. Kane's Corvette was parked in front, as was Kris's minivan and the elder McGraws' sedan. There were no other vehicles, nothing to indicate the stranger might still be there.

A slight rustle of sound caught her attention. She spotted two of the Protectors, weapons drawn, creeping up on the house from the back. They passed directly below her, not seeing her.

She watched as they reached the back door and tried the handle. Apparently they found it unlocked. Glancing at each other, guns still drawn, they opened it and slipped inside. All was quiet once more.

Now what? She wanted to do something, anything, to help, but didn't want to be in the way. If she was too late and the intruder had gone, at least she'd tried. If not, she'd be waiting while he made his escape.

Creeping closer, Lilly waited for several minutes. Holding herself absolutely still, she listened for any sounds of a scuffle or, heaven forbid, a gunshot. She heard nothing but the ordinary sounds of the forest. Birdsong and small creatures rummaging through the underbrush. The sounds of peace.

Should she try to enter the house? Remain wolf, or change back into a human? Since she had no clothing, she elected to stay wolf.

She cocked her head, listening. She heard the low thrum of voices, but detected no alarm or tension. Still, she knew she needed to be careful.

Cautiously, she circled around, heading toward the east side where the sliding glass door should provide a decent view of the inside. She kept low to the ground as she moved closer, every sense on full alert.

Reaching a decision, she rushed the same back door the two Protectors had just entered. Gripping the knob with her teeth, she managed to turn it enough so she could push the door open with her body. Moving silently, in full-out hunting mode, she entered the house.

It took a few minutes for Kane's heart to stop pounding. Adrenaline still flowed as he faced his parents, who were flanked by his two brothers. Sly and one of his team stood on the other side of the room, as though they'd formed sides and faced off. Everyone had turned and stared at him when he rushed into the room, weapon drawn.

"Put the gun away," Kris said. "He's gone."

Slowly, Kane thumbed the safety back on and holstered his pistol. Too late. Still, a quick survey of the room told him no one had been harmed.

His mother stood, head up, arms crossed, unharmed and unshaken. His father stood next to her, glowering at Sly as if the next move the Protector made would be his last.

"Mom." Kane moved forward, cutting off Sly and enveloping his mother in a hug. "Are you all right?"

"Of course I am," she said, her voice as unflappable as always. "I've already told your father and both your brothers, and now this man—" she glared at Sly "—has made me repeat it yet again. I don't know what the big deal is. The man who was here asking questions is gone. And I didn't give anything away."

"Of course you didn't," Kane soothed, shooting Sly a look that plainly told him to back off. "What did the stranger want?"

"He was on a fishing expedition," she continued, lifting her chin, pale blue eyes glinting. "Plain and simple. He was here trying to find out if Lilly is staying with us."

"What did you tell him?"

Her frustrated sigh reminded him of when he'd been a

child and she'd caught him and his brothers doing something they weren't supposed to. "Absolutely nothing that could harm anyone. Sure, he asked about Lilly. I told him I hadn't seen her. But Kane, he seemed way more interested in you."

Kane exchanged a look with Sly. Without exchanging a word, they both knew what this meant. Somehow, the cultists knew Lilly was with Kane. They'd come here because they'd learned this was where his family lived. In other words, he'd led them right to her.

"Are you even sure this man was the one you're looking for?" his mother continued. "He might have just been an old friend of yours or maybe someone from college, trying to track you down. I swear he looked perfectly normal to me."

"Normal?" Kane gestured at Sly. One of the team members handed over a computer tablet. "Tell me mom, was it one of these men?"

He pulled up the file and opened it. When he passed it over to his mother, pictures of the two remaining male Sanctuary members showed.

Her eyebrows rose. "Well, I'll be darned. Yes, it was this man right here." She stabbed her index finger at the one on the left, who had an afro and large aviator glasses. "He sure doesn't look like a member of a religious cult. Where's the third? I thought you said there were three?"

"There are." Sly answered for him. "The third one is a female."

A sound from the kitchen made everyone freeze. Kane and the Protectors all withdrew their weapons, motioning at everyone else to move away and take cover.

As soon as everyone was safely around the wall and in the hallway, Kane opened his mouth to ask who was there. Before he could, a beautiful gray wolf padded into the room.

"Lilly?"

At her name, the wolf turned toward him, staring at him with Lilly's stunning blue eyes.

"Stand down," Kane ordered, even though Sly should have been the one to give the command. "It's only Lilly." He put away his gun.

Instantly, the other men did the same.

"Lilly?" Kane's mother breathed. Kane hadn't even heard her reenter the room. "Oh, you're so beautiful, sweetheart."

Then, with everyone looking on in amazement, the older woman dropped to her knees and held out her arms. "Come here, Lilly, and let me have a look at you."

Casting Kane one more swift look, wolf Lilly did as his mother asked. The two women—one wolf, one human—touched noses, a sign of respect. Lilly allowed the older woman to coo over her, stroke her fur, and she even lifted her paw in a gesture of friendship.

When his mother had finished admiring Lilly, Kane showed her the way to the spare bedroom, borrowed a T-shirt and shorts from his mother, and left her alone to change back to her human form. Though the clothes would hang loosely on her, they'd have to do until he could take her back to the caves and retrieve her own clothing. Briefly he remembered her brightly colored sundress and wondered if it had been ruined.

Most of all, he couldn't believe Lilly had put herself at risk and come back to Wolf Hollow.

Anger had replaced the adrenaline now. When Lilly emerged, looking like a street person from the alleys of New York City, he grabbed her arm and led her outside.

"What are you doing here?" he demanded. "You promised me you'd stay safe at the caves."

"I did no such thing." When she lifted her face to his, her enlarged pupils took his breath away. Since she'd just changed back into human form, he knew she was fighting her own arousal.

The thought, and the sight of her swaying before him, was enough to set his body on fire. Using every ounce of willpower he possessed, he fought his own sharp stab of desire. He even jammed his hands into his pockets to make sure he didn't reach for her.

"At first, I did as you wanted," she told him softly, the sensual thrum in her voice tantalizing his already overheated body. "And while I was running, I realized I could no longer cower in the shadows, hiding from danger."

The cost of this bravery, the amount of courage it had to have taken for Lilly to decide to face her demons head on, wasn't lost in him. Wasn't this what he'd been trying to teach her all along?

Then why the fury? While he wanted her to have more confidence, there was a difference between being self-assured and acting foolishly. He just couldn't get past the idea that she'd willingly placed herself in danger for no good reason. Imagining what could have happened to her made him break out in a cold sweat. Yet since she'd come so far, he knew he had to choose his words carefully.

"Lilly, it's fantastic that you want to stand up to a threat." Unable to help himself, he leaned forward and placed a chaste kiss on her forward. As he did, she moved closer to him, apparently aware he was already rock hard.

In desperation, he took a step back, forgetting what he'd been about to say.

"Thank you," she said, her husky voice nearly a purr.

"I can honestly say my progress in that area is entirely due to you."

Her voice caressed his nerve endings. He swallowed, realizing he was perilously close to losing all control. "I know you just changed back."

Purposely making his tone as harsh and cold as he could, he turned his back to her, breathing rapidly and fighting for self-control. "We need to go find that pretty little dress you were wearing earlier. After that, I need to meet with Sly and his crew. We'll need to develop a plan of action now that they've made their presence known."

"Okay." Her voice was right behind him. Close. Too close.

He wondered if she knew how he had to struggle to keep from taking her in his arms. Hell, taking her period, right there on the front lawn of his parents' house. As if he had no self-control left. Like the night she'd sung to him and he'd blacked out. Yet one more aspect of Lilly he needed to investigate.

She was dangerous to him. Even without her singing. He'd always been known for his unshakable self-control. And now part of him ached to forget his training, the situation, and reach for her, so he could luxuriate in the pleasure they gave each other.

This would be wrong, in more ways than one.

Luckily, the other part of him, the rational side, still had the upper hand. As of right this moment, at least.

Clearing his throat, he tried to find words. Any words, as long as they weren't *come to me*.

"So, do you want to go get my dress now?" Even with his back turned, he could hear the sensual smile in her voice. No doubt she had visions of the two of them, alone in the woods, desire pulsing like a living thing between them.

Dangerous. And he couldn't allow himself to be distracted, especially not now, when things might be coming to a head.

Without turning, he nodded. "I'm going to send you up there with Kris or Kyle. I've got to get with Sly right away."

She protested, as he'd thought she would. "I want to be in on the meeting with Sly and the team."

"Why?" He didn't want to hurt her, but every aching moment he spent near her only increased his arousal.

"I want an update."

"I'll make sure that you get one, as soon as I can."

"But—"

"Lilly." He cut her off. "We don't have time for this right now. Wait here, I'll send my brother out, and he'll go with you to retrieve your dress."

Unbelievably, she still argued. "I know the way. I can go myself."

Though he realized it was out of proportion, infuriated, he turned. First mistake. He saw her expression the instant she caught sight of the bulge in the front of his jeans. Desire, raw and primitive, blazed from her amazing blue eyes.

"Oh, Kane…" She took a step toward him.

He took a step back. "Yes, I want you. No, we can't. Not right now." He spoke through clenched teeth. "Now please. Go inside the house and get one of my brothers. Kyle or Kris, I don't care. Tell him what I need him to do."

Finally, she lowered her head, giving in. "Fine. Where are you going?"

Feeling savage, he had to bite back a snarl. "I'm taking a quick walk. Alone. Once I have myself under control, I need to go talk to Sly and his crew."

"We can walk up to the caves together," she offered.

"Lilly." His tone carried a wealth of warning.

Without another word, she turned and went back inside, her back ramrod straight.

Despite it all, he couldn't help but grin. Any other time, in any other situation, he would have loved to explore her emerging feistiness.

He took off in the opposite direction from the caves. He hadn't gone far when he heard the sound of his brother's minivan starting. Good. Walking calmed his overheated body. Lilly's absence helped even more. By the time he reached the cabin where the Protectors were staying, he had himself back under control.

Sly and Bronwyn were waiting on the front porch. "I've already sent two teams of two out to try to sniff out that guy," Sly said by way of greeting.

"Good." Kane sighed. "I'm trying to decide if I should just take Lilly and get the hell out of here."

Both Sly and Bronwyn protested. "You can't. Not when we're so close. They took a huge risk today, sending one of their people out here. Sounds to me like they're getting desperate."

"Desperate?" Kane's short bark of laughter contained not one iota of humor. "You've been here a while. What's the status? Have any of your team even been able to locate where they're staying?"

Sly shook his head. "No. I'm not sure what's going on, but no one has seen those three since the desk clerk told them she had no room at her motel. They haven't shown up in town at all."

"Except today."

"Yeah." Grimacing, Sly and Bronwyn exchanged a glance. "If they hadn't made that move today, we were about to believe they might have moved on."

"Moved on?" This time, Kane didn't bother to hide

his disdain. "Not likely. I don't think they'd give up so easily."

"I agree." Bronwyn cast a sidelong look at Sly. "We're thinking since they sent that one to question your mother, they know she's with you."

Crossing his arms, he waited her out.

After a second or two, she continued. "We're hoping they'll eventually start canvassing the town. They've got to. They're here for a reason. For them to just go underground like this makes no sense."

"Unless they know you're on to them." Kane kicked at a rock with the toe of his boot. "We need to find out what brought them to Leaning Tree in the first place. They have no reason to suspect Lilly would be here. Lucas and Blythe, her brother and his wife, have no ties to this place. I'm thinking someone must have tipped them off."

This time Sly responded. "Maybe. It's possible. But who?"

Jamming his hands in his pockets, Kane paced. "I don't know. My family are the only ones who know Lilly's true identity, and they wouldn't betray my trust. As far as the missing Sanctuary people know, she could be anywhere in the U.S. So why have they come here? What brought them to our small town here in the Catskills?"

Again Sly and Bronwyn exchanged a look.

"What?" Kane stopped, glancing from one to the other. "What are you not telling me?"

Sly stepped forward. "I'm going to venture a guess, even though I know you're not going to like it."

"Go ahead."

Sly nodded. "I figure you've probably already thought this through, so it won't come as a total surprise. We're thinking they tracked you."

Kane blinked. "Dammit."

"We're checking in to that now."

"It's possible since I worked undercover at Sanctuary," Kane said.

"And were instrumental at bringing down Jacob Gideon," Sly reminded him. "It could be you're high on their list of targets."

"If they even have one, which I doubt." Staring off into the distance, Kane tried to think. "I swear, if I find out that I'm responsible for leading them to her..." He didn't finish the sentence. He didn't have to. Sly and Bronwyn completely understood.

"Look." Sly clapped him on the shoulder. "They aren't professionals. They've got to make a mistake. When they do, we'll be there to grab them."

Lilly went silent as Kyle drove her to the same general area where Kane had let her out of the car earlier. He was talkative, full of questions, but after receiving several monosyllabic responses, he stopped asking.

"You can walk to the caves from here." He pointed. "I'll wait. It should only take you a minute."

Though she knew Kane would have wanted Kyle to stay with her for safety reasons, glad of the chance for solitude, she simply nodded and got out of the car.

She couldn't remember how far she'd gone before she'd disrobed and changed. Either way, tromping through the woods would help her mood. She needed to purge her body of this insane desire for a man who clearly didn't want her.

Kane. She didn't want to need him, especially since she'd decided she had to be strong and learn how to make it on her own. When this was over, she had no plans to go back to live with her brother and his wife. She wanted to find a job, doing what, she didn't know exactly, and she wanted to experience the joys and the terrors of a self-sufficient life.

She thought. She wasn't sure she had it entirely right, assuming it would be a weakness to need or rely on anyone else.

Either way, she owed Kane an apology. She might not have much experience at life, but even she knew it was wrong to use someone physically.

The sad thing was, if Kane would let it, she knew their relationship had the potential of being so much more.

But she didn't want his pity. Not that, never that. She wished she could have met him as his equal, someone to be admired rather than one who evoked sympathy.

Sighing, she spotted the bright patterned material of her dress and hurried toward it. Once she had it in hand, she hurried back to where Kyle waited and climbed in his car.

"Good job," he said, smiling at her. He was handsome, too, she noted dispassionately, but without the touch of rugged masculinity that made Kane so attractive.

"Thanks." She smiled back. "I'm glad nothing happened to this dress. Today was the first time I've worn it."

He nodded. "Where to?"

The question surprised her. "I guess I'll go back to the cabin. I need to talk to Kane when he returns."

Again the nod. Shifting into Drive, he turned them around and they headed back to Wolf Hollow.

When they reached the cabin, Kyle parked. This time, he got out of the car.

"No need," she said, waving him back.

"I want to make sure Kane's here before I go. He'd have a fit if I left you here unattended."

She began to wish she'd taken a bit longer in the

woods. Solitude had become a rare commodity in her life these days.

As they stepped on to the porch, the front door opened and Kane came out. Her stomach did its usual dip and swoop at the sight of him.

"You found it?" he asked, his shuttered gaze going to the dress. When Lilly nodded, he strode to his brother and gripped his shoulder in a man hug. "I appreciate it," he said.

"No problem." Dipping his head in a nod, Kyle took off.

Lilly stood outside until the sight and sound of his vehicle had completely disappeared. Finally, aware she could put it off no longer, she squared her shoulders and faced Kane.

"I'm sorry," she began.

"Don't worry," he said at the same time. One corner of his mouth quirked in a smile. "Go ahead."

"You first." Moving past him into the house, she took a seat on the couch.

"I met with Sly and Bronwyn," he told her. "Four men are out looking for the guy who was here today."

"Do you really think they'll find him?" She didn't mean to sound skeptical.

"I hope so. Especially since it's Sly's opinion that I'm the way they tracked here."

"Because you helped take down Sanctuary."

"Yes. And because your brother and I became good friends."

She made a sound of dismay.

"It's okay. We're prepared," he reassured her. "The Protectors are going to be staying here awhile. At least until they've caught those three."

Awhile. She tried not to show her dismay. More time

while she felt increasingly like a lightning bug, trapped inside a jar. "And then what?"

"And then you can go on with your life."

She winced, then immediately tried to hide it. She didn't want him to realize how his words brought her pain. While she pretended to consider, she attempted to keep from staring at the way his muscles rippled when he moved his arm.

When his gaze met hers again, the intensity blazing from his made her inhale sharply. "That is what you want, isn't it?"

With him near, she no longer knew what she wanted. With one exception. Him. She wanted him.

All the logic she'd worked out while in the woods disappeared. She'd planned to apologize, to make promises she couldn't keep. In the end, she'd let him choose. She craved him, the same way she craved air to breathe. She'd let him know and allow him to make the choice. When... *if* she found enough courage to do so.

"Lilly?" His tone sounded savage. "Are you going to answer me?"

Pushing to her feet, she crossed to him and wrapped her arms around his neck, curling her body into his. Her mouth found his and this one touch was all it took.

Passion instantly blazed between them. Familiar and exhilarating. And welcome. When they were together, she didn't have to think about anything other than how good he felt.

Another way of running from reality? Maybe. But she truly didn't care.

Suddenly, the words Kane had said once came back to haunt her. She lifted her mouth from his, breathing hard. "I don't want to spend the rest of my life running from them."

"You won't," he hastened to reassure her. "We'll apprehend them soon."

"Will you?" Restless again, she twisted out of his arms. "What if you don't?"

"We'll deal with that if it happens." He reached for her. She sidestepped, biting back her frustration, pushing away her desire.

"No." The fierceness in her voice finally reached him. Crossing his arms, he waited.

"I want to go after them," she said. "I've put a lot of thought into it, and that's the only way we can catch them."

"What do you mean, exactly?" He spoke carefully, making her aware he already knew what she was going to say.

"They want me. We want them. It's pointless for those Protectors to hang around waiting for them to put in an appearance and you know it."

He took a deep breath, bringing his breathing down to match hers. "True, but we have no other options."

She smiled sadly. "But we do. We can make it look as if they're going to get me. I've got you and six well-trained Protectors to keep me safe. Put me out there for them to try and grab. Instead, we'll set a trap."

"Bait." A warning settled over his rugged face. He reached out to her, gripping her upper arms. "You want me to allow you to be used as bait."

Allow?

"Yes." Gently, she pried his fingers loose, so he could see the faint red marks on her pale skin. "It's the only way. I want this over with."

She thought he'd refuse, expected the next words out of his mouth to be "absolutely not." Instead, he cocked his head, staring off into the distance, as though giving her suggestion careful consideration. Meanwhile, the scent and power of their mutual desire lingered, swirling around them like a potent smoke.

Her body wanted him. Only her body. This wasn't what mattered right now, she told herself fiercely. He had to see the logic in her words.

"You know, you might be on to something," Kane finally said, studying her with a critical, narrow gaze. "As long as the proper safeguards are in place so you're not at risk. I'll take it up with the others."

"When?" she pressed. "I'll go with you." She wasn't going to give him a chance to stall. "Let's talk to them now."

Again he surprised her. "Okay. But let me lay the ground rules."

He held out his hand and she took it, without hesitation. Each day she grew stronger and more self-confident. Rather than holding her back, Kane appeared to have stepped back, giving her the necessary room to spread her newfound wings. A firefly, about to escape from the jar.

She almost grinned at the corny analogy.

Chapter 16

Watching Lilly, so full of newfound bravado, Kane felt a flush of pride combined with a grim sort of panic. It took every instinct he had not to sit her down and caution her about the reality of life. Though she'd emerged alive from fifteen years in hell, she hadn't been unscathed. Damned if he'd stand by and let her take a chance of getting hurt again.

Yet as she stared at him with that self-assured smile, her blue eyes bright with confidence, he hadn't the heart.

"Well?" She all but tapped her foot. "Let's put this thing in motion."

"Someone's been watching too many TV movies." Somehow he managed to tease her. He'd wanted to swear when she came up with her plan, wanted to grab her and hold her close and tell her absolutely not, no way in hell.

"Nope. I've been reading a lot of thrillers and romantic suspense books," she said. "Come on, tell me. What do you think?"

"Give me a minute." He looked down, holding his tongue while he pretended to consider her idea, which he hated. There was no real choice and she probably knew it. He'd realized she was right. They had to use her as bait. It was the only way. Simple and exactly the opposite of what the cultists would expect them to do. After all, they were Protectors. Their job was to protect, to keep Lilly safe.

Not to put her up for target practice.

If he believed they wanted her dead, he never would have agreed to her plan. But since they both knew the remaining doctors from Sanctuary wanted to capture her alive, so they could continue their horrible experiments, that was one risk they didn't have to worry about.

"We can try it," he said, keeping his tone cautious.

She met his gaze and dipped her chin. "Thank you."

They decided to walk over to the Protectors' cabin. Sly, Bronwyn and two other members of his team were gathered around the kitchen table having a quick meal.

"Come on in." Sly stepped aside, motioning them past. "I reheated some barbecued beef we picked up in town and we're having sandwiches. You're welcome to eat with us."

Though the aroma wafting from the table made Kane's stomach rumble, he shook his head. "No, thank you. I wanted to run something by you. Lilly's come up with a plan and, as much as I hate it, I think it might work."

Briefly, he outlined Lilly's suggestion that they use her as a lure to trap the cultists.

After a moment of silence, Bronwyn jumped to her feet. "I like it," she said. "And I really think it has a viable chance."

Sly and the others seconded her comment.

"Great." Lilly greeted their acceptance with a shy smile. "Now all we need to do is work out the details."

"We will." Sly gave her a high five.

The way the Protectors greeted the idea disturbed the hell out of Kane. He'd expected some reservations at the very least, not this outright enthusiastic response.

He glanced at Sly, trying to catch the other man's eye, but the team leader was busy giving Lilly a quick bear hug. "Quite the little she-wolf you've turned out to be."

Kane barely suppressed an instinctive growl. While Lilly had no way of knowing this was the highest compliment a male Shifter could give a female, Kane did. As his wolf self tried to protest, he realized he also didn't appreciate the way the other man was eyeing Lilly. Every instinct within Kane had him wanting to grab Sly and inform him in no uncertain terms that Lilly was his. *His.*

Except she wasn't. Never would be. And Protectors never lied to their teams.

"We've got to plan this carefully," Sly said, indicating Kane and Lilly should both take a seat. "I'm expecting the two remaining team members any minute, so we'll wait for them before we get started. Several of us have started working in town, so we're making contacts there. Still no sign of the cultists, though."

"That's what Kane was telling me," Lilly murmured, dropping into an empty seat next to Bronwyn.

As Sly made his way back to his chair at the head of the table, Kane remained standing. Seeing this, Sly stood also.

A sound outside had Kane's hand going instinctively to his weapon. Sly strode over to the window and peered out. "Stand down, man. It's just Drake and Stu."

He'd barely finished his statement when the last two

Protectors stomped inside. "I can smell that barbeque outside," one of them said. "We're starving."

Sly jerked his thumb toward Kane. "We've got company."

"They can eat," Kane put in. "Hell, everyone go ahead and have your sandwiches. Everyone thinks better on a full stomach anyway."

No one needed a second urging. Even Sly resumed his interrupted meal. "You might as well grab a bite," Sly told him.

About to shake his head, Kane's stomach chose that moment to protest. Loudly. Grimacing, he snagged a seat on Lilly's other side and loaded up one of the paper plates.

Silence fell while they all ate. Lilly made quick work of polishing off her single sandwich and then she watched quietly while the rest of them had seconds and even thirds.

Once everyone had pushed their paper plate away, Sly leaned forward. "Here's what I'm thinking. We've got to orchestrate this carefully. We'll figure out a way to put the word out that you're going to be in town. First up, we need to create a 'leak' as to who you actually are."

Kane glanced at Lilly. From her weak nod and queasy expression, he could tell she didn't like this, even though it had been her idea. Neither did he, but they'd both already committed.

"You can always change your mind and back out," Kane murmured.

"But you won't, because it's necessary," Sly said, apparently also correctly interpreting her expression.

Glancing from Kane to Sly and then back again, Lilly slowly nodded. "I won't back out. Your plan makes sense."

"How will we keep them from coming to Wolf Hollow to try and get her?" Kane asked, his tone a bit more savage than he'd intended. "I do not want to put my family at risk in any way, shape or form."

"Timing, my man." Clearly unfazed by Kane's tone, Sly continued. "We leak the info in the morning, and then have Lilly go into town in the afternoon. I'm going to arrange to make this a big deal. I have contacts at the local news station from Albany. I'll arrange for a live interview. We'll get newspaper coverage, and put the word out on social media."

Lilly blinked. "But why? Why would any of that even happen?"

Sly grinned. "Your book deal."

"My what?"

Kane understood immediately. He had to admit it was a damn good plan. "He's going to put the word out that you've signed a major book deal to tell your story. This will infuriate the Sanctuary people and might make them act less rationally."

"As if they were ever rational." Lilly lifted her chin, her blue eyes blazing. "I like it. When do you want to do this?"

"How about now?" Sly asked.

"No. Tomorrow is the big Labor Day celebration and parade," Kane put in. "There'll be too many people in town, which will not only make it difficult to keep on top of things, but will put too many civilians in danger of getting hurt."

Though he looked as if he wanted to argue, eventually, Sly capitulated. "Two days after the parade," Sly said.

Kane agreed. The remainder of the team watched the debate in silence, apparently willing to go along with whatever Kane and Sly decided.

"What do I do until then?" Lilly asked.

"For one thing, we're going to continue your self-defense classes," Kane told her, hating how she looked like a wild animal caught in a trap. "And I really wish you'd reconsider learning to handle a firearm."

"No." Lilly had begun shaking her head before Kane even finished. "No guns. I can fight with my hands or change into a wolf and fight with teeth and claws."

Looking from her to Kane and back again, Sly frowned. "But what if they have guns?" he pointed out. "You'd stand a much better chance if you were armed."

"That's what I have you for." Lilly's icy tone made the other man cock his head. "I want you and your team to make sure it doesn't come to that."

The hell with it. Kane pushed back his chair. Crouching in front of her, he placed his hands on her shoulders and looked her right in the eye. "You have my word, Lilly. There's no way I'm letting those nuts get their hands on you ever again."

Gaze locked on his, slowly she nodded.

Sly's eyes gleamed as he looked from one to the other. "In the meantime, we'll continue to work the town. Since this parade is such a big deal, we'll fan out and keep searching the crowd. Maybe we'll get lucky and grab those cult members before we have to resort to our other plan."

The morning of the parade dawned with an overcast sky, the dark gray clouds threatening rain. Despite that, Kane seemed cheerful.

"It won't dare rain," he promised. "As far as I know, our Labor Day parade has never been rained out."

Though Lilly was skeptical, she decided to go with the flow. "I've never been to a parade before."

From the shocked expression on Kane's handsome

face, she might as well have confessed to never having eaten ice cream, or something equally unbelievable.

"I thought you and Lucas were allowed to occasionally go into town. Surely even small Texas towns have the occasional parade."

She shrugged. "I imagine they do, but we were never there when they had one. I remember watching the big Macy's one at Thanksgiving, but I've never seen one in real life."

"That's a crime," he said, his silver eyes going briefly gray. "Well, that's about to change today."

Since attending the parade would mean going into town, Lilly's heart fluttered. "Did you change your mind then? Is today when we're going to implement our plan to use me as bait?"

"No." He shook his head. "Sly kept pressing for that, even after our meeting, but I overruled them. The town is too crowded. There'll be hundreds of civilians there. Kids and elderly people. Families. I don't want to take a chance on someone getting hurt."

Relieved, she nodded. "Then how are you going to disguise me so I can watch the parade? If I go into town, even with a ball cap and dark glasses, people will know who I am."

Now he grinned, a wicked, wolfish light coming into his eyes. "Kathy helped me put together a costume." He brandished a shopping bag. "Once we get you decked out in this, there's no way anyone is going to recognize you."

Wary and also resigned, she looked at the bag. "Hand it over. I might as well see what you two have in store for me."

Amusement still shone in his face as he passed her the bag. "You might need some help with part of that. If you do, just yell."

"I will." More curious than anything else, she carried the bag into the bathroom. When she pulled out the getup Kane and his sister had assembled, she couldn't help but laugh. A curly red wig, maternity dress and sensible shoes were the first things she saw. Lastly, there was some sort of stuffed pillow with straps. As she puzzled over that, she realized it was a pretend baby bump.

Kane was right. No one would recognize her, not even his family.

She got dressed with mirth bubbling up inside of her. She'd always heard pregnant women glowed. Maybe, just maybe, she could actually pull this disguise off. It would be absolutely heavenly to go out in public and not have to worry about some crazy from Sanctuary snatching her.

The maternity dress Kathy had chosen for her was a matronly navy color, with an empire waist. The sensible flats were also dark blue and they made up in comfort for their ugliness.

After putting on the red frizzy wig, Lilly almost took it right back off. But after she adjusted it, picking at the curls, she realized she looked like an adult—and pregnant—version of Little Orphan Annie.

When she emerged, waddling slightly, Kane took one look at her and cracked up. She loved the way he laughed, all husky and rich and, oh, so masculine. The sound made her want to hug him…and she might have if her enormous belly hadn't been in the way.

"So now that I'm a pregnant lady, who are you going to be?" she asked, fluttering her long eyelashes.

His smile faded as he gave her a long, serious look. "I'm escorting you and Kathy, since Tom is working the parade. You're Kathy's pregnant girlfriend from the city."

"Perfect!" She clapped. "I'm ready, let's go."

All the way into town, Kane kept shooting sideways

glances at her. At first, she thought he was still marveling over the costume. Then she wondered if her wig had slipped, or she'd misapplied her makeup. Finally, she couldn't take it anymore.

"What?" she asked. "Why do you keep looking at me?"

"I'm wondering if that disguise will even fool anyone. Especially if the cultists are watching me."

She gave him her most gentle smile. "If it doesn't, then we'll have to implement our plan early. You're still going to have me surrounded, just in case, right?"

"Yes." He still sounded glum. "The entire team is in plain clothes and in place. No one will be able to get within a few feet of you."

"Perfect. Then if someone makes an attempt…"

"We'll grab them. The only problem is there's three of them. I don't want to take a chance on any of them getting away."

"We'll be fine." She wished she could lend him some of her newfound confidence. For whatever reason, the fear and trepidation that had dogged her most of her life had disappeared. "I want those creeps caught."

"I do, too." His fervent reply made her smile.

"And if they are going to make some sort of move today, then I really, really hope they wait until after I've seen the parade."

Though the town had already begun to fill up and parking was at a premium, Kane's brother had saved him a spot in the grassy field behind the high school. He'd actually removed a lawn chair from his van and parked himself in the spot, so no one else could park there.

"Here we are," Kane said, grinning at his brother.

Lilly couldn't help but laugh. "That's nice of him."

Kris laughed when he caught sight of Lilly in her disguise. "Nice," he said. "You and Kathy look like two of a kind."

"We ought to," Lilly replied. "This is her dress, after all."

Once Kane had parked his Corvette and Kris had stowed his chair back in his van, the three of them headed toward Main Street. In the distance, they could hear the sound of the high school band playing. And the closer they got, the stronger the scent of burgers and hot dogs cooking became.

"This is the biggest crowd yet," Kris said, glancing to his left.

Kane nodded, though he didn't respond. Lilly eyed them. He and Kris were busy casting furtive glances around them, clearly trying not to be noticeable. The way they were acting made her wonder if they expected someone to jump out from behind every parked car.

Once they crossed from the alley onto Main Street, the crowded sidewalk made walking slow. They moved through throngs of people, sidestepping babies in strollers and the occasional dog on a leash. Her fake baby bump made walking a bit difficult, and she soon found herself out of breath.

"Will you two please wait up?" she chided. "Being pregnant forces me to move much more slowly."

The two men slowed their steps for her. Lilly found herself wondering what it was like to really be pregnant. She couldn't imagine how it must feel to know a little life was growing inside you. For the first time, she wondered if she'd ever experience such a miracle.

All along the sidewalk, vendors had set up little booths with brightly colored awnings. All kinds of goods were for sale, from homemade jewelry and baked goods to artwork made by local artists. In between these were booths selling freshly made burgers or hot dogs, turkey legs and funnel cake.

People were everywhere, dressed in shorts and T-shirts. There were strollers and toddlers and children running and playing, laughing as they dodged in and out of the crowd. The noise and the scent were overwhelming. But delicious, too. Lilly wanted to stop and take it all in.

But Kane and Kyle continued to plow determinedly through the throngs of people. Lilly finally had to take hold of Kane's back belt loop to keep from being left behind. He turned and smiled at her, the brightness of that smile nearly making her lean in for a quick, unthinking kiss. Luckily, she caught herself in time.

"Where are we going?" she finally asked, huffing a little.

"Where the family is waiting for us," Kane answered.

"Everyone's staked out our usual spot in front of the shoe store," Kris elaborated. He glanced at Lilly, his gray eyes a paler imitation of Kane's, and then winked. "Kathy wants you right next to her."

The festive air and the happy vibes everyone gave off made her want to laugh. Still feeling giddy despite her breathlessness, she nodded. "Where else would I be? We pregnant women have to stick together."

"There they are." Kris waved. "They haven't seen us yet."

Though Lilly squinted, she couldn't make out where they were.

"Over there." Kane pointed. "See the sign that says Frunter's Shoes?"

As she stood on tiptoe to try to see over the sea of heads in front of her, she heard a boom, a crack, a loud explosion or something. The earth shook, a rolling wave of sound and pressure. Somehow, she found herself on the ground, her ears ringing.

Dazed, she lay there, trying to make sense of what had just happened. Gradually, she realized there was smoke. Fire? People were screaming. Shouting, crying and wailing. As she tried to push to her elbows, she saw her hands were scraped and bleeding.

What had just happened? Had someone set off a bomb?

Another pop, almost like a gunshot, immediately followed. The billowing black smoke stung her eyes. Disoriented, she heard more screams of pain and terror, faint as if coming from a distance. Weakly, she pushed up onto her hands and knees, trying to stand. Finally, she managed to do so, shaky and confused, her mouth dry with shock and tasting of ashes.

Kane appeared in her wavering line of vision. "Lilly." He reached for her, gently pulling her close. "Are you okay?"

Before she could answer, she saw Kris, staggering toward them. "What happened?" she asked, her voice weak and shaky. "What on earth was that?"

"I don't know," Kane answered, grabbing for his brother with his other arm. "It sounded like an explosion."

"A bomb?" Kris moaned, wiping ineffectively a trickle of blood running from his forehead down his cheek. "Damn." He squinted, trying to see through the smoke. "Debi and the kids are out there. And Mom and Dad and Kyle and Sharon."

Jerking away from Kane, he staggered in the direction they'd initially been heading. "Come on. We've got to find them and make sure everyone is all right."

Without waiting for an answer, he lurched away, trying to get to the spot where, moments before, the entire McGraw family had been standing.

Kane started after him, then hauled Lilly against him, his gaze searching the crowd. "Are you hurt?"

Numb, she looked down at herself. While she might be bruised, she didn't see blood except on her hands and both her knees, where they'd hit the concrete. Minor stuff. "No," she croaked. "Please. Let's go check on your family."

"Not you. I need to leave you with one of the Protectors," he said, soot-stained expression grim and desperate. "I've got to go help Kris and make sure my family is safe."

In the distance, sirens sounded. As Kane looked around them, trying to locate one of the Protectors, just like that, Bronwyn materialized. Despite the ash in her hair and on her clothes, with her big floppy hat and denim overalls, she looked as if she'd just come into town directly from the farm. Her disguise was so at odds with her true personality that Lilly could only stare in dazed wonder.

"Bronwyn?"

"Yeah." She grimaced. "I was pretty close to where it detonated, but I think I'm okay."

"Where'd it go off?" Kane stared at her, unable to mask his desperation.

"Over there." Bronwyn pointed. "Kind of in between the shoe store and the ice-cream place."

In other words, close to where Kane's family had been standing. Kane blanched, going pale.

"Can you guard Lilly?" he asked, balancing on the balls of his feet as if about to take flight.

About to protest, Lilly bit her tongue. She'd do whatever was needed to help ensure Kane got his family to safety. She could only hope no one had been hurt.

Bronwyn glanced at her as if she expected her to object. When Lilly didn't, the other woman nodded.

"I've got her," she told Kane, low-voiced. "Sly and the others are helping set up a triage area for the wounded. Go!"

Kane nodded, planted a quick kiss on Lilly's mouth, and took off. Lilly watched him go, her entire body aching.

"Come with me," Bronwyn said, all business and appearing completely unruffled by the chaos around them. The wail of sirens had grown closer, and then stopped. People were still shouting, weeping and running in every direction. The keens of pain and grief were the worst, cutting Lilly to the bone.

Bronwyn took a step, and her knees almost buckled. She grabbed Lilly's arm to steady herself.

"I want to help the McGraws," Lilly rasped, staring as she realized a huge bloodstain was spreading on Bronwyn's side. "You're hurt."

"It's nothing," the other woman said, her face pale but determined. "Come with me. Remember what Kane said."

Watching as Bronwyn's bloodstain grew larger, Lilly started to protest, and then finally nodded and followed the Protector.

Weaving on her feet, Bronwyn led her around a corner, to an area where several police cars, ambulances and fire trucks were parked, lights flashing. "This is probably the safest spot right now," she said, using the brick wall at her back to support herself. "We'll wait here."

The instant she finished speaking, she slid to the ground in a crumpled heap, the bloodstain spreading from her to the concrete.

"Help," Lilly shouted, motioning to one of the ambulance workers. "We need help."

Two men came running over. Taking in the situation instantaneously, they lifted a now unconscious Bronwyn onto a stretcher and carried her off to one of the ambulances. A moment later, the lights started flashing. The siren whoop-whooped and the vehicle roared off, leaving Lilly alone.

Now what? The McGraws. She needed to make sure Kane's family was safe. Thankful for her disguise, Lilly turned and began staggering back the way she'd come. Though she didn't think she'd been hurt, she believed she might be in shock. It didn't matter. She needed to find Kane and his family.

As she rounded the corner, a third explosion went off. In the distance, flames roared toward the smoky sky. The acrid scent hurt Lilly's nose. The awful cries from the wounded hurt Lilly's heart.

"Help me," someone moaned, staggering out of the dusky cloud toward her. With a jolt of recognition, Lilly realized it was Anabel, holding her torn and bloody dress closed around her waist. Blood trickled from a deep gash on one arm, and part of her hat appeared to have been singed.

Forgetting her disguise, Lilly stepped toward her. "Anabel. Are you hurt?"

Raising her head, Anabel squinted at her with a bleary gaze. "You look familiar," she croaked. "Please, help me get away from here."

Thoroughly disoriented, nonetheless Lilly nodded. "Come on. Let's go find the McGraws."

Anabel stared. Covering her mouth with her hands, she began making a keening sound. "The entire McGraw family was there, right by where the bomb went off. I don't know if they made it."

As she looked at Anabel, Lilly felt bile rise in her throat. "No," she managed. "They have to be all right. Kane and Kris went to go check." She gasped, trying to catch her breath. "Come on, Anabel. Let's go find them. They'll know."

Anabel didn't move. Despite her obvious injuries, she stared at Lilly as if she thought her insane. "Who *are* you?" Anabel asked. "Are the McGraws friends of yours?"

"It's me, Lilly Green. I'm wearing this because…" She waved her hands, wincing as she saw spots. "Long story. Now come with me. We ought to be safe together."

Slowly, Anabel nodded. "I thought so. I know a short cut. It will help us get away from the crowd and the wounded." She pushed herself forward, clearly hurting. "Follow me."

Suddenly, misgivings gave Lilly pause. "Anabel, you're hurt. Let's go talk to the medics first. Then we'll go and find the McGraw family."

"I'm fine." With a jerk of her chin, Anabel squared her shoulders. "You have no idea what I've been through. I'm strong. I can handle this."

That said, she staggered off, not even looking back to see if Lilly followed.

Debating for the space of two heartbeats, Lilly hurried after the other woman. She caught up with her as Anabel grasped the door handle of what was clearly a back door leading into one of the shops. "There you are," Anabel huffed, brushing an ash-coated strand of her jet-black hair out of her face. "Help me get this door opened."

"Why?" Lilly hesitated. "It's probably locked. And if it's not, it seems a lot like breaking and entering to me."

Anabel shook her head. "Whatever. A friend of mine owns this shop and the next four, which are being used as a warehouse now. If we cut through it, we'll come up on the other side of where the bomb went off."

This raised another set of questions. Chief among them, Lilly wanted to know if it was safe. Logic dictated any structures near the point of detonation would be shaky, at best.

She started to tell Anabel this, but the other woman continued to pull on the door handle. Finally, with a grunt, she managed to yank the door open. "Are you coming?" Without waiting for an answer after casting a backward glance at Lilly, she disappeared inside.

Lilly debated for half a second. She wanted to check on the wounded. If Anabel truly knew a shortcut, then she was wasting time by waiting.

She took a deep breath, grabbed the door handle, and went after her.

Chapter 17

Following his brother into the smoke brought Kane back to a mission he'd once gone on overseas in a war zone. The smoke, the chaos and the smell of charred flesh was the same. Ditto the rubble still falling and the panic.

With an explosion that size, he knew people had been hurt and killed. He could only hope his family wasn't among them.

Ahead, Kris disappeared into a crowd of first responders. Ignoring the stitch in his side where a piece of metal had struck, Kane hurried after.

When they reached the area where the shoe store had been, Kris stopped and stared, causing Kane to nearly run into him. A huge hole had been blown in the front of the building. An emergency triage area had been hastily erected in the street, and here the people with the worst injuries were treated and made as stable as possible before transport to the hospital.

"Come on." Kane grabbed his brother's arm. "Let's check over here first."

The scope and severity of the injuries boggled the mind. Missing limbs, gaping wounds, the kind of things one expected to see in a war zone. Not at the Labor Day parade in Leaning Tree, New York.

Moving quietly, Kane and Kris searched through the victims, both relieved and worried when they didn't see anyone they recognized. "Where are they?" Kris muttered. "We've got to find them."

Once outside again, Kane stood facing the shoe store. He tried to breathe deeply, to keep his hopes high. He tried to focus on what he did know—his family wasn't in the triage area among the wounded—rather than what he didn't.

"Over there!" Kyle shouted, lurching toward a crowd of stunned survivors being shepherded away by uniformed police officers. "I think I saw Mom and Dad."

Kane rushed after him. When he caught sight of his father's shiny bald head and mother's long gray braid, the relief that blasted through him almost sent him to his knees.

The instant his mother saw him, she cried out and opened her plump arms. Her gardenia scent brought him comfort, even as he looked past her for the rest of his family.

Kris had already located Debi and his children. A little ways beyond him, Kane spotted Kyle and Sharon, huddled together with their brood. At first glance, everyone appeared uninjured.

The police continued to move the uninjured away from the blast zone. Kane went along with them, keeping one arm around his mother's rounded shoulders and the other around his father's waist. "Where's Kathy?" he asked, realizing he hadn't seen his sister.

"Kathy and Tom already left," she said, still sounding a bit shaky. "Tom was frantic that the shock and stress might make her lose the baby, so he hustled Kathy away." Her smile wavered a bit, but she continued. "He says he's going to make sure she gets an evening of pampering."

"Good. She needs that." Kane dragged his hand across his chin. "You should consider having one of those yourself, Mom."

"I just might," she said, even though they both knew good and well she wouldn't. "This was a close call."

"What happened?" Kane asked. "How did you all escape without being hurt? It looked like the blast went off near you."

"I can't imagine how we were spared," his mother said again. "It was a last-minute series of events actually. If little Anthony hadn't chased after that puppy, and Kyle and Sharon hadn't gone after him, and we all hadn't rushed over when he was nearly run over by that bicyclist, we would have been standing right next to where the bomb was detonated."

Kane didn't even want to think of how things might have turned out if not for blind luck. Or fate. Either way, no McGraws had been injured. Once they were outside the temporary police barricades, they stopped moving. His mother smiled at him, and then turned and watched misty-eyed as his two brothers shepherded their individual families toward the area where they'd parked their cars.

Chest tight, Kane did the same. Glancing around him at the damage and destruction, the barely organized chaos of the first responders and the numerous wounded, he struggled to understand.

"Do you think it was terrorists?" his father asked, apparently thinking the same thoughts.

"I don't know." Kane shook his head, his mood grim. "But what else could it have been?"

"Good thing we've already got Protectors on-site," the elder McGraw continued, wiping more soot off his bald head with his hand. "Though I imagine they'll be sending more."

"I'm sure they will. Pretty soon, this place will be crawling with FBI and ATF, not to mention the media." He couldn't help but think their planned attempt to capture the cultists was now doomed.

He hugged her again. "Now that I know the family is all safe, I've got to go check on Lilly."

"Lilly?" Wide-eyed, his mom did a quick search of the crowd. "What happened? How'd you two get separated?"

"It's okay." He gave her what he hoped was a reassuring smile. "I left her with Bronwyn. She's fine."

Exhaling, she fiddled with her braid. "Thank goodness. By all means, please go and find her. And then I want you to bring her to us, so we can all see that she's all right with our own eyes."

Kane hugged his mother again, and then his father. "I will." Then he turned and reversed direction, slipping past the police barricade and heading toward the ambulance area where he'd last seen Bronwyn and Lilly.

The instant she stepped inside the building, Lilly had to stop and allow her eyes a moment to adjust to the darkness.

"Anabel?" she called, coughing as she choked a little on the dust. "Anabel, where are you?"

"Almost to the door." Anabel's voice, faint and ghostly

sounding, drifted back. "When I reach it, I'll hold it open for you so you can see the way."

"Thanks," Lilly croaked, coughing again to clear her throat. While the interior was dark, the dim light coming from the front room was enough to guide her steps. "But I think I can find my way to you, if you'll only wait."

Anabel didn't answer.

Lilly's wolf chose that moment to raise a ruckus inside her, snarling and whining. She paused. Her other self felt something was amiss, and barked a warning. For the first time Lilly wondered if she'd made a mistake following Anabel. Kane and Kathy both had said the other woman wasn't right in the head.

"Lilly?" Anabel's voice, perfectly sweet. "I'm waiting for you. Are you lost?"

Remembering the pain in Anabel's eyes, Lilly took a deep breath but regretted it as she doubled over coughing.

"Lilly?" Anabel sounded concerned. "Are you all right? Do you want me to come back for you?"

"No." Lilly wiped her mouth and made up her mind. She ignored her wolf instincts and moved forward.

As she rounded a corner, someone jumped her from behind, twisting her arms behind her. Remembering Kane's lessons, she fought back. She kicked, high and swift, hard to the groin.

It worked. Whoever had grabbed her let go.

Not waiting around to see who or what had assaulted her, Lilly hurried toward Anabel. She couldn't leave Anabel alone, especially with this danger. She didn't know if the other woman knew how to fight, so Lilly might have to defend her. Plus two were always better than one.

As if her thoughts had brought double danger, two shapes materialized in the dusty light. Willing herself

to calm down, Lilly dropped into a battle crouch, ready
to deflect and defend until she could attack.

They both rushed her at once. At the same time as
the one she'd just fended off, jumped her from behind.

Lilly screamed. Not for help. No, to warn the other
woman. "Run Anabel, run. I'm being attacked. Run and
get help."

The man behind held her while the other two tied up
her feet and then her hands. They shoved her, still standing, into the cement wall. "No sense trying to get help
from that one. She's been paid to bring you here to us."

As if on cue, Anabel emerged from around the corner. Her mocking laugh seemed to echo in the empty
room. "I know you're being attacked, silly. I'm the one
who arranged this."

She came closer, letting Lilly see her wide, toothy
smile. She held up a shopping bag as if it was a trophy.
"It's been a pleasure doing business with you, gentlemen
and lady. I'll be taking off now."

"Not so fast." One of Lilly's captors, reached for Anabel. "You'll be staying with us. We can't have you leaving." And he snatched the shopping bag out of her hands
just as the other two grabbed her.

That voice. Lilly's heart thudded in her chest as her
blood turned to ice. She recognized that voice. He was
one of the doctors from Sanctuary, one of the ones who'd
held her prisoner and tortured her.

Anabel let out a snarl, the sound full of fury. "Don't
you touch me," she screamed. And just like that, she
began changing into her wolf self.

The instant Lilly recognized the brilliance of this, she
too dropped to the ground and began to shape-shift. Her
clothing ripped as her bones lengthened. As soon as the
change was complete, she crossed over to stand flank to

flank with the other wolf. Though Anabel had betrayed her, in this they were kin. She'd deal with the other later, if, no, *when* they got out of this.

The three humans, and now Lilly recognized them as Sanctuary doctors all, glanced at each other and began to slowly advance.

Both Lilly and Anabel crouched low, giving nearly identical warning growls. One of the men had rope, the same one that had earlier been used to bind Lilly's ankles.

The lone woman stood in between the two men, as if their larger size would protect her. Lilly exchanged a glance with Anabel, communicating silently that they should attack her first. In nature, the weakest always were the initial target.

Anabel rushed forward, powerful jaws snapping. The woman went down, screaming as Anabel tore at her flesh.

Taking advantage of the distraction, Lilly jumped the shorter of the two men, aiming her teeth for his crotch. She slashed, tearing at his clothing and ripping skin. He screamed, a high-pitched, terrible sound.

The third man raised his arm and metal glinted in the faint light. Lilly recognized his weapon, the same tranquilizer gun from Sanctuary that had been used on her too many times to count.

She twisted and went for his ankles. He shot her mid-stride, barely pausing as he pivoted and then shot Anabel, while the other two humans continued to scream.

As Lilly felt her consciousness ebbing, she struggled against it. She only hoped that the one who had the tranquilizers didn't remember how she'd built a gradual tolerance to the dosage, even as she prayed that was still the case.

While mentally struggling against the sedative, she let her entire body go slack and closed her eyes. Best if they thought she'd gone unconscious, like the slack-jawed Anabel on the floor close by.

As she watched through her lashes, Anabel's body shuddered and began to change back to human form. Lilly remembered how that had always happened to her as well, and that trying to stop this occurrence was one of the doctor's many experiments on her.

She realized she'd need to shape-shift back into a human, too, or they'd know she was faking. Taking care to keep her breathing deep and even, she initiated her own change.

The hard cement floor hurt her human skin and joints. She hated her nakedness, wishing she had a way to cover herself, but knew she could not. She thought of Kane, wondered if he even knew she was missing.

"Now we've just got to load them up and get them out of here," the female cultist, a Dr. Menger, if Lilly remembered right, spoke.

"You know, that's why we set off that bomb," one of the men said. "Creates a hell of a diversion. No one will even notice."

Lilly tried to swallow past the sudden lump in her throat. *They'd* caused the explosion, callously injuring and even killing who knew how many people, simply to create a distraction?

Worse, they'd done it because of *her*.

She thought of Kane and his Protectors and their now useless plan. The doctors from Sanctuary had managed to outsmart them without even trying. They'd take her somewhere and finish the experiments they'd started.

Experiments. Suddenly she remembered what had happened to Kane when she sang. Was there some way she could use that to her advantage without getting herself raped?

Since they'd used the tranquilizer on her, her captives hadn't bothered retying her bonds. She tried to picture the scenario, feeling that if she could get a clear vision as to how she might fight her way free, she'd have a better chance.

She knew she had to try. It was better than just going meekly to her fate, which would be a fate worse than hell.

Starting out low, she began singing the same song she'd made up that night with Kane. She'd never forgotten it, because every note had come from someplace deep inside of her.

As her voice soared, she pushed slowly to her feet, testing out her balance, the strength of her limbs. She was ready. More than ready.

Her two captors paused. The woman froze. They all stared at her as if she was a demon emerging from the bowels of the earth. Which, to them, she supposed she was.

Drawing strength from this, Lilly sang with all her heart. She had a mental image of the evasive moves she would take when the men tried to rut with her, and she knew she'd need to avoid the woman at all costs. Lilly had no idea what her voice would do to a female.

But instead of lust, pain contorted their features.

"Stop it," Dr. Menger shouted, hands over her ears. "Stop it right now!"

Ignoring her, Lilly stared at the men. One of them had dropped to his knees. He, too, had his hands covering his ears and appeared to be shaking with pain.

The other man screamed.

Seeing her opportunity, still singing, Lilly ran. Back the way she'd come, knowing once she made it into the alley, she could find help.

To her surprise, she wasn't followed.

Only when she'd pushed into the outside air, did she stop singing. Since she was naked, she grabbed a discarded black trash bag from the ground and used it to cover herself as best she could. Then, gasping, she rushed away, screaming for help, her cries mingling with those of the injured and panicked.

When Kane made it over to the area where he'd left Lilly, he spotted one of Sly's men. Hurrying up to the other Protector, he asked about Bronwyn.

"She was wounded," the man said, his expression grim. "They took her by ambulance to some hospital in Margaretville."

Kane cursed. "What about Lilly? She was with Bronwyn."

"I don't know. Maybe she rode in the ambulance with her."

Jaw clenched, Kane considered punching the guy, but knew it wasn't his fault. "Find Sly," he ordered. "Tell him the asset— No," he corrected himself, "tell him Lilly's gone missing. He needs to mobilize the team and help me find her."

He hurried off without waiting for an answer. He knew Sly would do his best to help, but most of the Protectors had joined the other first responders in helping the wounded. He couldn't, in all conscience, pull his men away when they were needed to help save lives.

He had to find Lilly.

Taking off at a slow jog, he circled the area where he'd last seen her. He considered her viewpoint, asked himself what would she do? Once she realized Bronwyn had been injured and needed help, he knew she'd get the other woman to the medics.

And then what?

She'd try to find him and Kris and the rest of his family. She'd have headed in the direction of the shoe store.

Turning, he jogged in that direction.

"Kane!"

That voice. Lilly. He spun around as she came barreling out of an alley, covered in soot and dirt and wearing a filthy black plastic trash bag.

He held her while she sobbed out her story. Sly came up with three of his team, and they followed Lilly to the back door of the deserted shop.

Weapons drawn, they entered. Kane made Lilly stay behind him. He planned to get her outside at the first sign of trouble.

But once they reached the room where Lilly had told him she'd sung, their footsteps were the only sound. At first, Kane feared they'd escaped, but once they rounded the corner he and the other Protectors stopped in shock.

The three cult members lay on the floor, immobile and unconscious, their frozen expressions still contorted in expressions of pain.

Next to them lay Anabel, still out from the tranquilizer. Kane found her torn clothes and gently covered her nakedness. The others were cuffed and prodded until they groggily came to.

As soon as they were able to stand, they were led away. Sly went to find a medic to tend to Anabel, hopefully to neutralize the tranquilizer or at least monitor her until she was back to normal.

"Come on," Kane told Lilly, gathering up her ruined sundress and taking her arm.

"Wait." She pointed to a shopping bag on the floor. "That's what they gave Anabel for helping them get me. I want to see what's inside."

He fetched it for her and they opened it together. Inside were neatly rubber-banded stacks of hundred-dollar bills. "There has to be several thousand dollars in here," Lilly said. "She sold me out for cash?"

"I guess she needed money," Kane answered, his heart aching at the bewildered and stunned shock darkening Lilly's expression. "Come on, let me get you home so you can clean up and rest."

Home. The last cabin on the lane at Wolf Hollow Motor Court Resort.

If Lilly noticed his slip of the tongue, she didn't comment. Instead, she simply nodded, slipping her hand into his.

Later, after Lilly had showered and he'd taken her up to the main house to let his family see she was safe and vice versa, he watched as she and Kathy, Debi and Sharon put their heads together over some magazine and then traipsed into the kitchen to attempt to make whatever recipe they'd found. With their hair all worn in ponytails of differing hair colors, brunette and blond and redhead, they looked like a hair-color advertisement straight from the pages of some glossy magazine.

Kane's brothers had taken Tom and the kids outside for a raucous game of tag football, leaving Kane alone with his parents.

"How'd she get away?" his mother asked, watching him closely, her light blue eyes worried. She fingered her braid as she caught him staring at the kitchen doorway through which Lilly had just gone.

He told her, not sure she'd believe the story.

"I've heard about that talent somewhere," his father mused. "I can't remember where, though. It sounds awfully familiar."

"The legends mentioned it," Kane's mother said, her voice rising with excitement.

"Really?" Kane scratched his head. "I don't remember ever hearing about anything like that. I remember learning about a Healer, but not any kind of singing skill."

"I do." Getting up, she pulled out her laptop and accessed the internet. "They call it being a Wolf Siren. Just one second. Here we are." She handed the computer to him.

"A Wolf Siren." he read out loud. "Every generation, a few selective females are born who can sing to determine which male is their mate. The sound of her voice beguiles and bewitches the wolf who is to be hers, but incapacitates any other male or female who hears her sing. In ancient times, these females were revered and became oracles, and their offspring were carefully monitored since it was likely one of their children would carry this gift."

Both his parents were smiling and nodding. At first, he didn't realize why, but then he understood.

"It only affected me." He swallowed hard, his throat tight. "That means I'm her mate."

"Yes, and once the mated pair acknowledge this fact to each other, the song no longer affects anyone in the same way." To his shock, his mother winked.

On top of that, next his father playfully punched his arm. "You're her mate. As if you didn't know."

Kane grimaced. He looked down, then at the kitchen doorway, before meeting their eyes. They'd all been through so much today, how could he be any less than honest now. "Yes. I know. I've known since the first moment I laid eyes on her."

"Then why haven't you talked to her?" his mother asked.

"I don't think Lilly is ready to hear anything about

that. She claims she doesn't want a relationship. She has this idea that she wants to go off and be on her own."

"What?" His mother sounded shocked. "That girl spent fifteen years in solitary confinement. If there's ever been someone who needs to be with someone, she does."

He shrugged, trying to appear casual, when in fact every word his mother said had hope flowing through his veins and energizing him.

"Doesn't she realize how difficult it is to find one's true mate?" his father groused, still smiling, still watching Kane closely. "To disregard such good fortune would be such a waste."

"You need to tell her, son," his mother put in. "At least give her the option. Have you ever mentioned how you feel?"

"No." Kane swallowed. "I didn't want her to feel she owed me anything, or that she had to be with me out of pity."

At this, his mother snorted. "Lilly? That girl's become a regular firecracker. She's really gained a lot of self-confidence since she's been here. Give her a chance."

Give her a chance? As Kane stared at his mother, wondering if she'd lost her mind, or he had, he realized she was right. He'd never actually told Lilly how he felt, and the only discussion they'd ever had about a future relationship, he'd had a sense she was telling him what she thought he wanted to hear.

At the time, he'd told himself that was wishful thinking. Now, he realized he'd never given her a chance to choose.

If she truly wanted to be alone once she knew he loved her, well then he had no choice but to let her go.

"You're right," he slowly told his parents. "And I know

exactly what I want to do and how I want to do it. I'll need your help. But first, I want to test something."

In the days after the remaining cultists from Sanctuary had been apprehended, Lilly felt a lightness to her spirit that she hadn't felt since she'd been fifteen, before Jacob Gideon had caught her and Lucas shape-shifting and labeled them demons.

Kathy had taken her under her wing and Lilly suspected they might have become best friends if she'd been able to stick around Leaning Tree longer. Still, for the time she had left here, Lilly accepted the offer of friendship. Debi and Sharon, who seemed to defer to Kathy, appeared to welcome Lilly into their new circle of four.

Today they were cooking desserts. Since the Labor Day celebration had turned into a disaster, none of the law enforcement personnel or first responders had gotten to celebrate the final summer holiday. The women of the McGraw family, led by Kathy, had decided to remedy that. They planned to bake as many cakes, pies and desserts as possible, and then deliver them to those police officers and firefighters and EMTs.

Though Lilly had never baked a single thing in her life, Kathy had laughingly promised to teach her. "Watch and learn," she said. Sharon and Debi echoed the sentiment. They'd banned the elder Mrs. McGraw from the kitchen, telling her to enjoy her rest, and planned to spend the next several hours baking.

Without the shadow of the cultists hanging over her, Lilly realized she was truly happy. Kane's family had accepted her as one of their own and sometimes she caught herself wishing she could stay at Wolf Hollow forever. With him.

The thought caused her shivers. Kane had taught her

so much, but more importantly, he'd shown her how to have faith in herself. She wondered if her irrational desire to be with him longer would invalidate all she'd learned.

Confused, she decided to take things day by day. Though Lilly had spoken to her brother, Lucas, about the cultists' capture, she hadn't yet told him of her tentative plans for the future. Of course she was going to have to stay somewhere until she could find a job. It might as well be with him and Blythe, but she needed to emphasize it would only be temporary. Again, even the thought of leaving Kane felt like ripping a hole in the center of her chest, where her heart was.

Kane hadn't yet given her a date when they'd be leaving Leaning Tree, but the darkening shadows in his amazing eyes told her he, too, had this on his mind.

Later, after all the baked goods had been delivered to their grateful recipients, Kathy dropped Lilly off at her cabin. Kane waited out on the front porch, his guitar on his lap.

Struck by the homey feel of the scene, Lilly got out of the car and waved goodbye, watching as Kathy smiled and drove off.

Feeling inordinately self-conscious, Lilly walked over to Kane. In the waning light, he watched her come, his silver eyes blazing with summer lightning. Her heart turned over in her chest as she drank in his masculine beauty.

"Hey," she said softly, stopping on the bottom step and looking up at him.

The slow smile he gave her made her feel warm all over. "Hey yourself. I'm playing around with a few songs. Remember that one we worked on together? I played the melody and you made up the lyrics."

Heart skipping a beat, she nodded. "That's when I sang and you..."

He nodded. "Yes. I want to try that again."

Chapter 18

Lilly recoiled, exactly as Kane had known she would. "You can't be serious," she said. "I know you don't remember what happened before, but—"

Setting his guitar down, he got up and crossed the distance to her. "You said you sang when you were captured and the sound of your voice incapacitated the cultists."

Slowly, she nodded.

"Yet when you sang to me, you said I wanted to jump your bones. I need to know if that's still the case."

She frowned. "Why would anything have changed?"

Giving her a deliberately casual shrug, he took her hand. "Come on, try it."

"Absolutely not." She jerked her hand away, gave him a look as if she suspected he'd lost his mind, and hurried past him into the cabin.

Dropping back into the rocking chair, he realized he'd gone about this all wrong. Deep inside, he believed she loved him. Getting her to realize this wouldn't be easy, but he thought he knew how he could go about it.

He had to go big or go home. With that in mind, he put down the guitar and walked a short way from the cabin. He needed to enlist help to pull off what he had in mind. He dug out his cell phone and called his mother.

Once the conversation was finished, he walked back inside. Lilly was still holed up in her room, avoiding him. Though every instinct inside of him wanted to go to her, take her in his arms and show her they belonged together, he forced himself to be patient.

Decision made, he turned and went back outside. He'd walk and clear his head, and then turn in early. Tomorrow would be another day.

The next morning when Lilly made her way into the kitchen, drawn by the mouthwatering smell of bacon frying, Kane smiled at her and handed her a cup of coffee. "Already made the way you like it," he said.

Relieved that he wasn't immediately going to rehash his crazy idea of having her sing, she accepted the mug and took a seat at the kitchen table.

"I've also made you breakfast," he continued, his silver eyes gleaming.

"Thanks." Should she be suspicious? No, this was Kane. He'd always been upfront with her. "So what's up?"

"What do you mean?" He set a plate in front of her. Scrambled eggs, toast and three slices of perfectly crisp bacon.

"This." She leaned over and inhaled the wonderful scents wafting from her plate. "Not that I don't appreciate it, because I do. But…"

His smile seemed a bit sad. "This is one of our last mornings here together. I wanted to make it special." He turned away, busying himself again with the stove and his own plate.

His words made her chest tighten. She let her gaze roam over the back of his head, his broad shoulders to his narrow waist, lingering on his amazing backside. Her entire body flushed as she remembered cupping her hands on his taut flesh when they'd made love.

Heart pounding, she forced herself to look away. Though her food had lost its appeal, she picked up her fork and dug in. She barely looked up as Kane carried his own plate over to the table and took the seat across from her.

"Do you like it?"

She nodded. "I do. Thank you very much."

To prove he hadn't wasted his efforts, she forced herself to clean her plate. When she looked up again, she realized Kane had done the same. He sat back, drinking his coffee and watching her. She shivered at the heat in his gaze.

"My mother wants to have a party," he said. "A going-away type of thing. She and Kathy are already deep into planning it."

Though Lilly could scarcely breathe, she took a deep breath and nodded. "That sounds lovely. When?"

"Tonight?"

Shocked, at first she couldn't react. "Are we leaving so soon?"

A shadow crossed his face. "Yes."

She knew she had to ask him when, even if she didn't really want to know.

As if he understood her dilemma, he told her. "I figured we'd pull out midday tomorrow. I know your brother is eager to see you."

"He is," she answered automatically, while mentally reeling at the short notice. "I...I suppose I'd better pack."

His hand covered hers. "No rush. You can do that in the morning. I want you to thoroughly enjoy today, so I've made plans. We're finally going to take that day trip to Woodstock."

Now, knowing her time at Wolf Hollow numbered hours, she shook her head. "That sounds lovely, but I'd rather spend time here, with your family."

"Mom wants us out of the way so she can plan this party," he told her. "She specifically asked me to find us both something to do away from here."

That hurt. She knew it shouldn't have and, while it made perfect sense, she'd rather have spent time with Kane and his family here, in the place she'd grown to love and would always miss.

But none of this was Kane's fault. Slowly, she nodded. "I understand."

"Good." Sounding satisfied, he checked his watch. "Why don't you get ready while I clean up in here? We'll head out as soon as you're ready."

She fought hard not to allow herself to sink into depression at the thought of leaving. She bit her lip and then pushed to her feet. "I just need a few minutes," she said.

Once she'd closed her bedroom door, she sank down on the edge of her bed and struggled not to cry. What on earth was wrong with her? She'd known this day was coming, longed for it, in fact. She'd thought she wanted to test her wings and learn to fly solo, but now she realized there was greater strength in learning to forge bonds with others.

Hell, who was she kidding? She wanted Kane. Not just for a day or a week or a month. But forever. Clearly, he didn't feel the same.

Trying to locate the numbness she'd once used to cloak her heart, she went to her closet, grabbed an old T-shirt and a pair of khaki shorts. She brushed her hair into a tight ponytail, slipped her feet into her most comfortable flip-flops, and sighed. Once, she'd thought she couldn't wait to get out of Wolf Hollow. Now, realizing how much these people and this place meant to her, she didn't want to leave.

Squaring her shoulders, she told herself to suck it up and be strong. And then she opened the bedroom door and walked into the den where Kane waited, car keys in hand.

On the drive, she kept her gaze focused on the scenery, afraid if she talked too much, she might let slip how she really felt. Torn apart, hurting and wondering why she couldn't seem to regain her equilibrium.

Kane appeared to have no such problems. One beautiful, long-fingered hand on the wheel, he drove with his usual self-assured confidence, making her love him more. It broke her heart that he acted as if this day was no different than any other, as if this wasn't one of the last times they'd spend together before beginning the journey to reunite her with her brother.

As Lilly battled to keep her inner turmoil hidden, Kane sang along with the radio, cheerfully pointing out places of interest as they drove past. She alternated between wanting to snarl at him and weep. Instead, she kept her head held high, feigning interest in the landscape, and wondering when she'd become such a fool.

Her inner wolf wanted out, and his apparently did, as well. Several times, as she tried to keep her inner beast leashed, she caught Kane struggling to do the same.

The town of Woodstock was crowded and quaint, as

though locked in an earlier time. They ate pizza in an out-door restaurant and wandered in and out of various shops.

She bought a lovely natural stone necklace and ear-ring set, the deep blue and green colors reminding her of a mountain stream. She thought it would always remind her of this place, and this man. The thought brought her melancholy back, though she managed to push it away.

Several hours passed. Attentive and solicitous, Kane also appeared nervous, judging from the numerous glances she caught him sneaking at his watch. He ap-peared in no hurry to go back home, despite the upcom-ing party.

Finally, after reading a text message on his phone, he asked Lilly if she was ready to go.

Relieved, she nodded.

As they got in his car, she again fought the urge to kiss him. Once again, she concentrated on the scenery while Kane drove.

As they approached the turnoff to Wolf Hollow, Kane pulled over. "I need you to do me a favor."

Crossing her arms, she waited.

"Mom has been decorating the backyard all day and she doesn't want you to see it yet. She wants it to be a surprise."

"I'll cover my face with my hands," she said.

He grimaced. "I promised her I'd tie this scarf over your eyes. Do you mind?"

Did she mind? Not really. What she minded was that there even was a necessity of a going-away party. If she was honest, she'd like to stay at Wolf Hollow, or at least in Leaning Tree, for the indefinite future. Maybe even… dare she think it? Maybe even forever.

"Fine," she said, holding perfectly still while he tied a silken scarf over her eyes.

Once he had it secure, she waited for him to put the car back in Drive. Instead, he kissed her, his lips touching hers like a whisper. Shocked, at first she couldn't respond, but then as he continued to sensually caress her with his mouth, she returned his kiss with reckless abandon. Surely now, he must understand how she felt about him. Surely now, he'd tell her he wasn't going to leave her.

Instead, his lips left hers, blazing a path down her neck, making her shiver. Finally, after one last kiss at the hollow of her throat, he moved away from her and the car began to go. She felt like he'd stolen her ability to breathe.

Luckily, she managed to get herself under control. The sensation of driving without her sight was disconcerting, to say the least. Even her inner wolf went quiet, as intrigued as her human half. She kept wondering if he'd touch her, even the slightest caress. The thought made goose bumps rise on her skin and her nipples pebble. But, to her disappointment, he must have kept his hands on the steering wheel.

She felt when they left the pavement for the gravel road, knew every turn and bend, and could tell when they'd passed the main house. Nevertheless, Kane didn't tell her she could remove her blindfold, and she couldn't help but picture what it would feel like to make love with it on. Judging just from the kiss, every other sense would be intensified, magnified to compensate for not being able to see.

She barely hid her disappointment when, as soon as Kane parked and cut the engine, he took the silken cloth off. She blinked, dazed and disoriented, and glanced his way to find him smiling at her.

Again, he looked as if he hadn't a care in the world. No, more than that, she thought as she climbed out of the car. His entire body practically vibrated with excitement, his eyes bright and full of half promises. She didn't understand this and even considered asking him, but knew whatever he might reply would most likely decimate her pride.

Still, it really was a struggle not to let this put her in a bad mood. And right before the big going-away party.

Once they were inside the cabin, he stretched and grinned. "I'll let you have the first shower."

She nodded, fisting her hands to keep from crossing the room to him, grabbing him by the shirt and making him kiss her again. What the hell had that been? Another form of torture? His way of saying goodbye, by letting her know exactly what she'd be missing?

"You've got a little over an hour to get ready," he continued, the warmth of his smile echoing in his voice. "Mom said we need to dress what she calls resort casual, whatever that means." He shrugged. "It makes me think of Hawaiian shirts and swim trunks, even though I know that's not what she means at all."

Puzzled, Lilly knew she'd better ask. "So what does she mean?"

"I think she wants you to wear something like you'd wear on vacation, like a cruise or at some beach resort. You know, like that sundress you wore the last time we were going to visit Woodstock."

Nodding her thanks, she hurried into the bathroom, glad to escape the constant temptation.

After a nice long shower, she felt a lot better. Confident even, certainly able to deal with the myriad of emotions she was sure to experience that night.

Back in her bedroom, she ignored the carnal images dancing through her mind as she heard the sound of the shower start up. The thought of Kane, naked and wet… Shaking her head at herself, she went to her closet, wanting to dress carefully for the party. Instead of the flirty little sundress Kane had mentioned, she chose the only maxi dress she'd brought with her. The slinky material clung to her figure lovingly, and the green and navy diagonal slashes of color went perfectly with the necklace and earrings she'd bought in Woodstock.

She even applied a little makeup, her mood improving as she laughed at herself for her ineptitude—it had been too long since she'd used cosmetics.

By the time she'd finished, she felt much better. Confident even. Surveying herself in the mirror, she thought she looked good, maybe even pretty. Her hair, usually the bane of her existence, fell in natural waves past her shoulders.

When she emerged from her room to find Kane waiting, she even managed to smile at him.

Staring at her, he slowly stood, his gaze traveling over her, as intimate as a caress. Her pulse leaped, but miraculously she kept her expression merely pleasant.

"Are you ready?" she asked, her voice cool.

"You look…amazing," he said.

"Thank you." Deliberately, she surveyed him in much the same way he'd done her, praying her rapid increase in pulse didn't show. Kane wore khakis and a short-sleeved, button-down shirt, along with deck shoes. As always, he carried himself with a masculine air of self-confidence. His stance emphasized the force of his muscular legs, and the well-fitting white shirt did little to hide his broad shoulders.

Her mouth went dry as she stared at him.

Smile widening, he held out his hand. "Let's go."

She slid her fingers through his and, at the contact, her entire body felt energized, as though his touch had delivered a powerful jolt of electricity.

Marveling at this, she wanted to ask him if he'd felt it, too, but she chickened out.

Dusk darkened to night as they walked outside. Kane drove the short distance slowly, and she gasped as they rounded the curve and she caught sight of the hundreds or thousands of tiny white lights decorating the trees and patio in back of the main house.

"It's beautiful," she said, stunned. "Simply amazing."

When they pulled up in front, all the other vehicles parked there told her everyone else had already arrived.

Inhaling deeply, she smoothed down her dress as she climbed out of the car.

"Nervous?" Kane asked.

"Maybe a little." But she wasn't, not now that the moment had actually arrived. She owed these people so much, and the fact that they cared enough to throw a party to say goodbye was humbling.

"Come on." Again, Kane took her hand, leading her in through the front door instead of their usual way out back.

The front room was completely devoid of people.

"Where is everyone?" she asked.

"Out back," he told her, with a gentle smile. "This way."

Feeling like a fairy-tale princess, she let him lead her through the kitchen, out the back door, and into the transformed backyard.

Everyone waited, smiling at her. A little girl broke away from a group of children and ran to her, shouting her name.

"Hailey?" Stunned, Lilly caught her niece midjump. "What are you doing here?"

Beyond excited, the five-year-old grinned and pointed. "Mommy and Lucas are here, too!"

To Lilly's amazement, her brother and his new bride appeared, gathering her close. Blythe wore white flowers in her hair, and a long champagne colored dress that appeared to be made entirely of lace. Lucas was still growing out his dark hair, giving him a slightly dangerous air. They both glowed with happiness.

Hugging them, Lilly struggled not to cry. She blotted at her eyes, glad she'd chosen waterproof mascara. "What on earth are you two doing here?"

Lucas grinned. "Kane invited us. He wanted us to see where you've been living, and to meet his family."

Still perplexed, she smiled back. She nearly gasped out loud as she realized what this most likely meant. She'd be going home with Lucas. This, then, would be her last night with Kane.

She wished he would have warned her.

As she tried to keep smiling, the rest of Kane's family surrounded them. Kris and Debi, Kyle and Sharon, Kathy and Tom. Not to mention their combined brood of children. Someone put on music, everyone talked at once, and Kane's mother began bringing out the food as Kane's father manned the grill.

There was steak and chicken and fish, every kind of protein a carnivore could desire. Head swimming, Lilly found herself being pulled here and there, as Kane's family all had brought her small gifts. Sharon and Debi gifted her with a bottle of their favorite tequila and margarita mix, Kathy with a box of homemade cupcakes.

She didn't think she could eat, but to her surprise as the meal was set out buffet-style, she found herself with a heaping paper plate. Kane sat next to her, his thigh touching hers. She tried not to let it affect her while she ate.

The celebratory air of the party made her wonder, but she put it down to the fact that the escaped cultists had finally been caught. Still she couldn't help but question all the smiling glances everyone cast their way. As if they all knew some big secret to which she was not privy.

Once everyone finished eating, the tables were moved away. Kathy's husband, Tom, set up a drum set on a brick area to the side of the large patio, and Kane's brothers appeared with guitars. To Lilly's surprise, Kathy joined them, carrying a guitar of her own.

"What is this?" Lilly asked Kane. "Are you going to play, too?"

Never taking his gaze from her face, he slowly shook his head. "Nope. They're making music so you and I can dance."

Stunned, she looked around. "I don't know how."

He laughed, lightly touching her chin. "It's instinctual. I'll guide you and all you have to do is follow my lead."

Still she balked. "In front of everyone else? I don't think so."

"Lilly, I'm sure Lucas and Blythe will dance, too. Even my parents will probably take a spin around the floor. It'll be fun, I promise."

"But—"

He silenced her with a quick kiss, right there for anyone to see. She felt her face turn to fire, but his tactic worked. "I'll try," she finally said.

Kane's mother appeared, carrying drinks. A beer for Kane and some orange concoction for Lilly. "It's a mai tai," she explained. "Try it. You'll like it."

Lilly took a tentative sip. Fruity and sweet, it tasted a bit like punch. "It's good."

Both Kane and his mother laughed. "Enjoy yourselves," Mrs. McGraw said, patting Lilly on the shoulder. "This is a special night." She waved to a teenager who was watching the children play on another part of the back lawn, and bustled off.

The band started playing, leading off with a catchy song that had Lilly inadvertently tapping her feet. She stood next to Kane, watching as her brother and Blythe began dancing.

"Do you want to?" Kane asked.

She shook her head and sipped her drink. "Not yet."

The next song was slower. Lilly couldn't get over the feeling that everyone was watching her as if they expected something to happen. But what?

Lucas and Blythe swayed to the music. A moment later, Kane's parents joined them.

"Come on." Kane took Lilly's arm. "Let's give it a try."

She couldn't say no to the beseeching look in his eyes. Setting her drink down on one of the small tables that had been set up with chairs on the perimeter of the dance area, she walked with him out to the center.

Lucas smiled with approval as Kane took her into his arms. Then he began to dance and she forgot all about her brother and everyone else.

There was only Kane.

Slow dancing, body to body, he moved and she moved with him, stunned by the way they seemed to flow together. It was sensual and more. Gazing up at Kane's chiseled profile, her heart swelled, her throat ached, and she realized she'd never been as happy as she was at that exact moment.

This man…this wonderful, beautiful, rugged man. Dancing with him, she craved him. She ached to have him desire her, just this once, without any siren song compelling him.

The song ended and they stepped back to the side.

Stepping to the mic, Kathy announced they'd be taking a short break.

Kane led her away from the others, to a little stone bench in between two towering oak trees.

They sat. Suddenly she found herself close to tears.

"Lilly?" Hand cupping her chin, Kane raised her face. "What's wrong?"

He needed to know the truth.

"I don't know how to seduce you," she said, her low voice vibrating with need. "I have no idea how to make you crave me the same way I do you."

"Make me?" Incredulous, he kissed the tip of her nose. "Lilly, don't you realize you merely have to be in the same room as me and I'm on fire?"

Gaping at him, she couldn't find words. Then, to her complete and utter shock, Kane stood and dropped to one knee in front of her. He took out a small box and opened it.

"Lilly Gideon, I've loved you since the first moment our eyes met, there in that horrible cell at Sanctuary." The tinge of wonder in his raspy voice made her smile. "I grew to love you even more in the time we've spent together. If I know anything, it's this. I don't want to go on living without you."

A warm glow began spreading through her, she tried to speak, and found her throat too clogged with emotion.

"You are my mate," he continued, his voice breaking with emotion. "Do you realize this, too?"

Raising her head, she took a deep breath and pushed aside the last lingering shred of fear. Her strength, deep within her, would never be lessened if she shared her life with Kane. Instead, she knew it would only be enhanced.

"Yes," she whispered. "I definitely do."

For an instant he closed his eyes, as though her words

overwhelmed him. When he opened them again, the silver had become molten. "Since you know we're mates, will you marry me?"

Cocking her head, she decided to pay him back a little for his earlier torture. "Only because we're mates? Not for any other reason?"

He groaned. "Because I love you. You know that. Marry me, please, and let me love you for the rest of our lives?"

Joy bubbled from her heart. Blissfully happy, she nodded, finding words of her own. "I will, if you'll let me love you, too. For the rest of our lives."

He gave a glad shout, slipping the ring on her finger. As he rose, he pulled her up with him. He kissed her, a kiss of possession and promise, before tugging her along with him, back to where his and her entire families waited expectantly.

"She said yes!" he told them, holding up her hand so everyone could see the ring that sparkled on her third finger.

At once, everyone cheered.

Kane swung her around in his arms, kissing her cheek, her neck, before muttering in her ear the things he planned to do to her the instant they got back into their cabin.

She gasped, and then laughed, her entire body growing hot as Kane caressed her with his eyes. More laughter and clapping from the others, made her see where she was, and that there were others watching. And then she realized she didn't really care. She reached for him, feeling completely and utterly naked even though she still was fully clothed.

He met her halfway, claiming her mouth with his, the heat emanating from him making her melt against him. "Will you sing for me now?" he rasped. "Please, sing to me."

"Here?" she gasped, looking around at his assembled family, all of whom watched them with a combination of love and amusement and joy. "I can't."

"You can."

When she hesitated, he kissed her again, his mouth lingering over hers. "Do you trust me?"

Bemused, she nodded.

"You're what's known as a Wolf Siren," he told her, his handsome face full of a fierce, possessive love. "*My* Wolf Siren. And legend has it that once we've committed to each other, your songs no longer have any kind of power. Over anyone."

At his words, a quiet knowing filled her. "So it wasn't because of any of the experiments they did on me at Sanctuary."

Slowly, he shook his head. "No. Now please, will you sing?"

"Only if you'll accompany me with your guitar."

When he nodded, she took his hand. Completely without fear, she walked with him to the area where the band had been playing and stepped up to the microphone.

As if they sensed something momentous was about to happen, everyone drifted back to stand in front of them. They grew silent as Kane began to play the melody.

Lilly began to sing. She remembered the words, even though she'd only made them up that one day. Unknowingly, even then she'd sung their song, a song of love and finding the one who could complete her. Her voice rose and soared and she caught more than one of the women wiping a tear from their eyes.

No one fell to the ground and Kane continued playing, no longer driven by the compelling and immediate need to possess her.

Because, she realized, he already did and he always would.

* * * * *

BONNIE VANAK

fell in love with romance novels during childhood. After years of newspaper reporting, Bonnie became a writer for a major international charity, which has taken her to destitute countries to write about issues affecting the poor. When the emotional strain of her job demanded a diversion, she turned to writing romance novels. Bonnie lives in Florida with her husband and two dogs, and happily writes books amid an ever-growing population of dust bunnies. She loves to hear from readers. Visit her website, www.bonnievanak.com, or email her at bonnievanak@aol.com.

DEMON WOLF

Bonnie Vanak

To Robyn Lees.
Strong, courageous and spunky, you fought
the good fight to the end and inspired us all.
You'll live forever in our hearts.

Prologue

Nicaragua, 1990

The Contra war was over, except no one had told these guys.

The crack of bullets and rattle of machine-gun fire echoed through the mountains of northern Nicaragua. Lieutenant Junior Grade Dale "Curt" Curtis crouched down behind a scarred oak tree and signaled to his men to wait. Heavy green and black greasepaint disguised their faces and the green camouflage uniforms blended in with the surrounding scrub.

Intel said nothing about fighting in this region. Could be a local turf war, but the sounds of that artillery to his seasoned ears warned this was a heavier engagement. Dale pulled his boonie hat low, scanned the terrain and cursed the godforsaken ass who'd assured them this area was safe to cross. But they were SEALs and accustomed to shifting gears.

He and his team of six operators had finished a successful op near the border. Now Dale had to figure out how the hell to get his men out of what was supposed to be uninhabited, safe terrain.

Motioning to his men to stay back, Dale crept through the jungle, making no noise. Four of his operators were norms. Then there was himself, a Primary Elemental Mage whose powers could blast through this jungle like a firebomb. And Etienne "Wolf" Robichaux, a Cajun from Louisiana, who was also a Draicon werewolf. Like him, Etienne used his powers sparingly around others.

The sickeningly sweet stench of decay assaulted his senses. Dale belly-crawled up a small rise, to a ravine and peered over. Revulsion and horror punched him.

Flies buzzed around a dozen naked bodies lying atop each other amid the dirt, grass and leaves. Women. Men. His stomach threatened to spill out the MRE he'd eaten.

In his five years as a navy SEAL, he'd seen his share of horrors. But this… The way the little group clung to each other, as if providing comfort in their last terrified moments, made him sick with anger.

A small whimper caught his attention. Dale raised his weapon and crawled down.

A black puppy, barely alive, hidden by the corpses. Dale's throat tightened. The little guy hadn't wanted to leave his mistress.

Or maybe it wasn't a dog. He called for Wolf on the radio. When Etienne arrived, the werewolf studied the dog, his eyes furious.

"It's a wolf, sir. Not a dog."

Stunned, Dale glanced at the corpses. "Your people?"

"Not Draicon. Our young don't shift until they reach puberty. I've never seen this species before."

Like Mages, there were different classes of were-wolves.

"Who are they?"

"I don't know." Etienne wiped a trickle of sweat from his face, smearing the green and black greasepaint. "These carry a deeper, richer scent."

"This place smells of darkness. No wonder the intel was screwed up."

The sounds of battle ceased. Dale glanced around and made a decision. "Take the pup, head west and lead the men out of here. Use that nose of yours and flush out the smells of gunpowder, avoid the fighting at all costs."

"Curt…"

"It's not human. Whoever did this isn't human."

Etienne's jaw tightened. "All the more reason for me to stay with you, sir."

"I'm right behind you. I'm not leaving this area for some naive civilian to stumble into and get killed."

"If you ward it with magick, you'll drain your powers," Etienne warned.

Dale gave a cold smile. "You have no idea of the extent of my powers. Now go."

As soon as his men had passed, Dale lifted his hands, closed his eyes and began a low chant. The magick shield would prevent humans from entering the area, and save them from meeting the same fate as the wolves.

Slightly drained, he opened his eyes, and turned to leave. A low growl rumbled behind him.

The wolf was as large as a small Shetland pony. Sleek black fur stood on edge. Dale remained motionless, his gaze never leaving the creature.

Not even when the wolf opened its mouth, showing fangs as sharp as dinner knives....

Her world had shattered. Nothing mattered anymore. Her parents, her pack, they were all dead.

Simon, her little brother, whom the demons promised to spare in exchange for her slavery to them...dead, as well. The demons had lied.

She was only eleven, but already experienced in her powers as wolf. In wolf form, Keira stumbled through the undergrowth. Rage and anguish blinded her to everything. Soon the demons would return and force her to do their bidding.

Magick skimmed her fur, pinged off her muzzle. Light, good magick. She shook her head and growled and loped toward the source.

A tall man lifted his hands to the sky and chanted. He was clad in uniform, his face disguised, and the metallic scent of weaponry clung to him. Rage engulfed her. How dare he violate her people's final resting ground?

Blinded to everything except the red haze to hurt as she hurt, she stalked forward and growled.

The man fingered the gray metal weapon and she charged.

Knocking him down, she leaped on him and raked a sharp claw over his arm. But the man made no move to fire the weapon.

Confused, she backed off, watching warily as he stood. Their gazes met and she felt an odd connection, as if this powerful man of magick understood.

He regarded her quietly, sadness in his gray eyes. "I won't hurt you. I will not return evil for evil, for whatever was done to your people is making you react."

A giggle sounded nearby. Keira tilted her head, fear

curling in her stomach. The demons were returning for her. Pure evil had infiltrated the region and it would never die. But this man who'd refused to hurt back, he was good. She sensed it.

She lowered her head, pawed at the ground and hit him with her muzzle, urging him to leave. The man's mouth narrowed.

"I won't leave you here alone."

Keira growled and head-butted him again. The man seemed torn, and glanced toward the west. She knew if the demons found him here, they'd enslave him, as well. He must not remember her, or he'd return. She sensed it.

So she bit him. He yelled and looked down at the wound, blood trickling with her saliva, saliva that carried the memory spell the demons infused into her. By the time he looked up, she was gone, fleeing into the forest toward her captors, vanishing from the man's sight and memory.

Giving him time to escape to safety.

While she charged forward straight into hell.

Chapter 1

If he discovered her true identity, the powerful Mage would kill her.

From across the bar, Keira Solomon studied her quarry. The glass of white wine gripped in her trembling hand rattled against the polished wood counter. She ignored the flirting drunk to her right and riveted her gaze to Lt. Commander Dale Curtis.

The navy SEAL commander of Team 21 sat by himself, his expression as lonely as she felt. Keira's heart went out to him, knowing she was the reason for his turmoil.

Careful, she warned herself. *If you let him get under your skin, you're a dead woman.* She concentrated on the man instead of her feelings, gauging how to approach him.

Though he looked no more than thirty-eight, the Mage was hundreds of years old. The commander had taut, angular cheekbones, a chin carved from granite, tempered by a full, wide mouth. His thick black hair, silvered at the temples, did not touch his starched collar. He looked like a powerful man of strong character, unaccustomed to compromise. But his most striking feature was his piercing gray eyes, shaded by thick, dark brows. Those eyes could become hard and unyielding, coaxing a confession out of the most tight-lipped prisoner, or turn seductive with promise, charming a woman into his bed.

She'd discovered all this about the man from listening to gossip in public haunts like this bar.

A severe khaki uniform hid a body firm with muscle that was now layered with deep scars. Keira knew the depth and width of each mark, knew how he'd endured, tight-lipped, as each one lashed his skin. And she knew the depth of his screams when the agony she inflicted became too much to bear when the Centurion demons forced her to hurt him.

No other man had survived such torture. Past victims had died from the force of her claws. Centurion demons had enslaved her to torture others. Now she had a rare chance to break free, because the man she'd tortured was strong enough to vanquish the demons for eternity.

"Hey, sweetie." Obviously determined to get her attention, the big, barrel-chested drunk put a paw on her arm. "Lemme buy you another drink."

Giving him a look of utter disdain, she pushed her glass aside. "No, thanks. I don't accept favors from gorillas."

The man narrowed his eyes as his companions chortled with laughter. "Ain't no ape."

"Okay, then. Chimp shifter." She gave him a singularly sweet smile. "I can't quite tell, but you all smell the same."

"Bitch." The shifter scowled. "I should drag you out to the parking lot, show you the meaning of respect. Flat on your back, your legs spread."

Demon blood surged. Keira held up a hand. Like flicking a switchblade, her claws emerged, each a razor-sharp talon. Ape Boy's eyes widened as she gouged the bar's surface. "Care to try?"

The men pushed away from the bar and fled. She sighed.

"I hate having to do that," she muttered to no one.

One day, she wouldn't have to worry about the demon blood inside her. The key to her freedom lingered temptingly close, but it wouldn't be easy to fool him. Curtis's piercing gray eyes could see straight inside her, and discover who she really was.

And if that happened, no point fearing the demons capturing and enslaving her once more.

Because Curtis would have at her first.

Ladies' night at the paranormal Dive Bar.

Once a month, Tom dropped the magick shield blinding humans to the bar's presence. He announced two-for-one drinks and the human women streamed inside as if he'd offered marriage proposals to millionaires.

The custom was for regulars, who liked human women warming their beds once in a while. Tom's bar was a short distance from Little Creek, home to SEAL Team 21's elite Phoenix Force in Virginia. When in town, the secret force of paranormal SEALs crowded the seats.

Dale ignored the chatter around him. He sipped his beer, waited for his burger.

Scar tissue pulled and stretched uncomfortably, reminding him of a body no woman wanted to see naked. While in the hospital, his sometime girlfriend had visited. Melissa had taken one look at the blood and bandages and left.

No Mage female wanted him. No human, either, even if she didn't sense he was a powerful Primary Elemental Mage who could fry her to ashes with a single flick of his finger.

Dale knew he was better off alone.

"You okay, Commander?"

Tom always called him by his title. Dale nodded. It had been the ultimate bitch of a day, back at work only ten days after two long months of mandatory medical leave. Paperwork piled to his nose, submerged in long meetings, most of his team deployed to dispatch a last-minute threat overseas. Only Ensign Grant "Sully" Sullivan remained at base. Chief Petty Officer Sam "Shay" Shaymore was in North Carolina, training in close-quarters combat with SEAL norms—human navy SEALs. He'd taken his new wife with him.

Dale relaxed into a smile as he thought of the much younger Shay. Last month the SEAL had married his girlfriend. Dale had proudly escorted the fatherless Kelly down the aisle. A wedding he'd never forget, as he was glad to see the two Mages declare their love in a lifelong bond. Those two had rescued him from the dark, dank basement where he had only memories of pain and blood.

And the scent of a woman…he could never forget.

Across the bar, Sully flirted with a pretty, slightly tipsy blonde. The woman rested her hand on the SEAL's arm, giving him a suggestive look. Someone was getting something-something tonight.

Dale hoped Sully remembered to glove before love. A half-human bastard faced a lot of hardship in the real world.

Children. Setting down his beer, he closed his eyes.

One regret he'd had in his eleven-year marriage. Kathy hadn't wanted any. The Mage had used one excuse after another and finally, she just left, but not before admitting she'd been sleeping in another man's bed.

You're a good man, Dale. But you're never around, not when I really need you.

Deep inside, he still craved a home life, a wife and a family. But what woman would want him now, his body looking like a road map to hell?

Someday, maybe, he'd find someone else. But first, he'd find the demon wolf responsible for scarring his body and when he did, that shape-shifter would pay. Such evil must be eradicated before innocents got hurt. Dale would do so gladly, sending the SOB straight to hell.

Tom slid a steaming burger, with fries piled high, before him. "Here you go, Commander. My treat."

"Thanks, Tom," Dale said, surprised.

"No, thank you, sir. If not for you…" Emotion shadowed the man's face. "What you did to free those kids, sacrificing yourself, hell, we're all grateful to you. I've got five kids and the thought of them enduring what you did…"

The cougar shifter's spine stiffened. "I'm proud to call you a friend. You're more than a SEAL. You're a damn fine officer and gentleman."

Holy hellfire, the man actually saluted him. Uncomfortable with the praise, Dale nodded. "No thanks necessary."

A few of the bar's regulars studied him like a moth pinned to a corkboard. Damn, all he wanted was a burger, not this scrutiny. Dale began to eat.

The brunette next to him spoke. "Come here often?"

Once in a while, against the ladies' room wall, pushing deep and hard, a woman's long legs wrapped around his thrusting hips. Dale nodded.

She gave a sultry smile, red lips moist and pursed. The tight blue dress clung to a body that had caught quite a few glances from the bar's male occupants.

"You're a SEAL."

Wonderful. Human frog hog. He swallowed a bite, shrugged.

"My second cousin's best friend is a navy SEAL." Now she slid over, her long red nails on his forearm. "I adore you guys. I can't thank you enough for what you do for our country, to keep us safe. You're so brave and strong, and I'd love to demonstrate my appreciation."

Hollow words, spoken by a woman who just wanted to bang a SEAL. Maybe one time he'd accept her offer, follow her home and show her the alternative meaning of *hooyah*. Not tonight. Tonight he felt every single one of his 420 years.

The woman's nose wrinkled as she studied his right arm. Dale automatically moved to hide the jagged gash. "That's a nasty scar. Did you get it in combat?"

No, I got it, and a rash of others, when I was tied up in a basement and tortured by a wolf's claws. Care to know more?

Appetite turned to dust, Dale slid his plate back. "Thanks, Tom."

Clear disappointment showed on the woman's face as he pushed back his stool. She turned to her right, engaged a member of ST 21's support staff, the vampire enthralled with the woman's long neck.

Nice night for a quick bite, Dale thought in sour amusement. Like every human here, she would recall only a pleasurable buzz the next day, assume it was alcohol-induced.

As he went to leave, a familiar scent hit him. Not the floral perfume of the human women, nor the heavy cologne of the males pursuing them. Something deeper, richer, more fragrant.

It reminded him of crushed autumn leaves, the burning richness of smoke on a hearth, the musky scent of pure…sex.

Dale whipped his head up, a memory pinging.

Her.

There, across the bar. An ebony-haired woman, a wineglass before her. Eyes blazing with fire and life glanced up. His gaze fell to her right hand.

Each finger was a sharp black talon.

Shock slammed into him. And pain. Distant memories…knives over raw flesh, biting back the screams that rose in his throat. Salt water dripping onto the fresh gouges, searing his skin with her tears.

He'd been tortured and left for dead, and recalled only flashes of memory. But that scent, it wound around him in an erotic ribbon, and pulled tight. His body hardened, blood pulsing to his groin.

Bleeding from a thousand cuts, the pain so deep he couldn't breathe, and that scent filtering through the agony, turning his cock to steel. Forgetting the pain, wanting nothing more than to roll her beneath him, spread her wide and drive hard into her soft, wet flesh.

He hadn't been merely tortured, but humiliated and debased, getting turned on, and then feeling something raking cold claws over his warm flesh….

This woman had something to do with those long, dark hours in the basement.

Dale went preternaturally still. The woman stared at him, wide red mouth parted in apparent shock. Then she slipped off the stool and fled.

Not so fast, he thought grimly. Dale raced after her. In the parking lot, against a parked SUV he caught her. Dale grabbed her arms, pinned her against the vehicle. The scent faded, leaving only the exotic smell of expensive perfume. But he hadn't imagined it. Wasn't going crazy.

"Who the hell are you?" he roughly demanded.

Fear clouded her gaze. "Not hurt, not hurt," she whimpered.

Gentling his voice, he loosened his grip. "Who are you? I remember only darkness, pain and your scent."

The woman wriggled away, lifted a hand to his face. The velvet of her voice stroked across his senses. Sexual energy jumped between them at the mere brush of her fingers. "Strong and courageous is your heart, yet lonely and hurting…so much pain."

Dale lost all sense. He lowered his head and did what he'd lusted to do all those long, anguished hours in the dark after he'd been turned into a pitiful, whimpering shell of a man.

Crushing her against him, he fisted a hand into her hair and kissed her hard. She responded back with a moan, her tongue tangling with his in a fury of erotic heat.

And then she began to struggle and nipped him on his lip, hard enough to draw blood. Dale jerked away in shock. Son of a…

His mind fogged. Closing his eyes, he fell into a dizzying vortex, where memory was once more a clouded dream. When he opened his eyes, he was alone.

The woman, if there had been a woman, vanished into the shadows. Just like before, he could not recall her, making him wonder if she were a dream.

Or his worst nightmare.

Chapter 2

The moon hung like a silver nickel in the sky.

Hovering in the woods, Keira waited for Dale to arrive home the next night.

Other houses on the street showed signs of life. Lights flicked on. Children ran around their backyards, and then ran inside as their mothers called them in for supper.

Or their mothers threatened to zap them inside. It was a paranormal neighborhood, after all.

Hiding in the shadows, she felt a pinch of deep melancholy. She'd adjusted to loneliness during the infrequent intervals when the demons gave her brief freedom so she could find new men for them to torture. Keira had beaten the demons. She'd refused to associate with anyone, refused to give them new victims, but stalled them by promising them new ones.

They found one on their own. This last time had sliced off a piece of her heart. Dale Curtis had taken her spirit and turned it inside out. She'd almost killed him. And then, a miracle happened.

The commander's friend had arrived in the house where Curtis was being held prisoner and chanted a cleansing spell to vanquish evil. The spell had sent the demons temporarily to the netherworld and freed her, as well. But in a few weeks, as they always did, the Centurions would use their bolt-hole to this world and break back in.

Then the real fun would start. They would find her, find Curtis and force her to torture the SEAL once more, maybe until he died. The demons would steal all his strength and courage and become solid entities, able to taste the pleasures of the flesh once more.

Keira touched the valise containing the silver armband, which enslaved her to the Centurions. When the demons had vanished unexpectedly, the bracelet unlocked, freeing her from their spell. Only by enslaving herself to another could she escape them.

And Lt. Commander Dale Curtis was the only living person with enough power and courage to destroy the Centurions. She had to overcome her personal fear of seeing him again if she wanted to achieve her goal.

For twenty-three years she'd lived under the demons' control. No more. Emotion clogged her throat. Dale Curtis looked thin and haggard. The demons had sapped his strength, his vitality. If she didn't help him recover soon he'd weaken and die.

She needed him strong, needed his resources to find and destroy the demons' bolt-hole and imprison them forever in the netherworld.

Crouching down, Keira watched the commander's house. Beneath the light of the nearly full moon, she waited hopefully, and wondered if this brave man would be the one to kill her captors and finally set her free.

Another day of keeping the world free of paranormal terrors. At least free of the terror of paperwork.

Hell, he was so tired, he could barely function. Dale looked forward to a cold beer, a quick sandwich, a little light reading and then crashing. It was a lonely life, but right now, he preferred it that way. No complications or interference.

Yet as he drove home from the ST 21 compound on the base, Dale imagined a loving woman greeting him at the day's end. Someone who rushed to the door, eyes lighting up as he walked inside, the good smell of a delicious dinner cooking in the oven.

Instead of always coming home to an empty, silent house.

Dale snorted. He cherished his privacy. He didn't need a woman in his home, rearranging his life, turning things upside down.

Especially now, he needed to be alone to recharge and recover.

As he turned onto his street, he saw a white Lincoln parked in his driveway. He parked next to it, cut the truck's engine. His front door was locked. Once inside, he tossed his keys into the antique candy dish on the hallway table and relocked the door.

Someone was home to greet him, after all.

A light glowed down the hall. Mage instincts went on alert. He narrowed his eyes, took a deep breath and headed into his study.

"Nice of you to break in," he told the gray-haired man sitting in shadow.

"You're late."

Vice Admiral Keegan Byrne, pillar of support for SEAL Team 21 and a powerful Primary Mage, toasted him with a whiskey glass filled with amber liquid. Dale glanced at the built-in wood bar against the wall. The bottle of twenty-year-old smooth Scotch malt had been full until tonight.

"Had to finish up paperwork. I'm not asking how you gained access to my home without permission."

"You need a better security system, Dale. An infant could bypass that alarm."

"An infant armed with electromagnetic current. Did you fry the panel again?"

Byrne grinned. Dale sighed. Another visit from the electrician.

"Help yourself to more Scotch. Just don't take my beer."

Running upstairs in a light jog, he headed to his bedroom, removed the trident, the fruit salad and the insignias from his khaki shirt. Then he stripped and tossed the uniform and undershirt into a white wicker hamper. As he walked toward the closet, the dresser mirror showed the image he'd tried to avoid.

Dale approached, staring at his body for the first time in two months.

Reddened scar tissue raked over his chest, muscled torso, arms and long legs. Razor-sharp claw marks began just below his throat, continued down his belly, ending at his groin, and dwindled out at his thighs and calves.

A remembrance of white-hot pain surged through him. Dale braced his hands on the dresser, hissing through his teeth.

Jerking open a drawer, he sorted through folded shirts and found an old, frayed Virginia Tech T-shirt. Another drawer held gray fleece pants.

When he returned to the study, Byrne remained motionless, the glass of Scotch untouched. He steeled himself. If the old man wasn't here to socialize, it meant one thing. But he'd let the admiral set the pace.

Dale fished a beer from the minifridge, tossed the cap into the trash and took a seat in front of the fireplace. He knew Byrne would take his time.

Finally Dale gave him a pointed look. "Why are you here?"

"Have you used your powers since leaving the hospital?"

Stretching out a hand, he summoned the current simmering inside. Dale flung it at the fireplace, igniting the logs. "Happy now?"

Understanding and something deeper, and wiser, filled Byrne's gaze. "I wasn't talking about toasting marshmallows, Dale. I meant on assignment."

Surprised, he sipped his beer. "I joined my men on that op to extract Dakota and Kelly. I'm a paper pusher now, not an operator."

"Maybe it's time you took off with your boys, joined a mission to evaluate their tactics and skills in the field. Spend quality time, jaw with them, get to know them again."

Suspicion filled him. "What's the deal, Keegan? You lost faith in me ever since I got carved like a Thanksgiving turkey?"

Silence.

Anger slowly rose. "That's it, isn't it? You think if I were deployed more, I'd have fried my attackers' asses? Never mind the nine innocent children's lives at stake. You think I wasn't strong enough to beat the demons."

"Were you?"

Dale set down the beer, his hands shaking. "Screw you, Keegan."

"I'll leave that for the wife." The admiral set down his barely touched glass. "Dale, we've known each other for a long time and I have to say this. I'm concerned about you, son."

He hissed out a breath. "I'm not your son. I'm CO of the finest SEAL team in the United States Navy and a 420-year-old Mage."

"And I have enough years to make you look like a baby sucking on his momma's tit. Dale, you're losing touch. I've had reports of you being distracted, short-tempered and restless. I don't know if it's a residual effect of what happened to you in that basement, or something else."

"Reports from whom?"

"Your team."

"Renegade? A sulky SEAL denied leave because Shay was on his honeymoon and I couldn't afford another man out?"

"No," Bryne said. "All of them. The entire team. Even Robyn Lees, the new ensign who thinks you can do no wrong."

Dale sat back, trying to hide his shock. "Nice of them to tell me."

"They're worried about you. You've changed."

Almost afraid to ask, he groped for his lost composure. "You said it was my time in the basement or something else that's affected me. What's the something else you think is wrong?"

"A woman."

Dale raked a hand through his short, dark hair and laughed. "No woman's gotten to me." Or would want him, the way he looked. "I'm trying to catch up after being out so long. I had a difficult time healing in the hospital."

"You were almost dead when Shay and Kelly found you."

Temper rising, Dale straightened up. "Are you lecturing me on how I should have been smarter, knowing the waiting children were a trap? Maybe you should shake the demon's hand, pin a medal on his chest for catching me off guard."

Admiral Byrne gave him a long, level look. "If I found the son of a bitch who did this to you, I'd tear him apart with my bare hands. And then toss him to your team to deal with the remains."

The quiet—but strong—statement made Dale sit back.

"The boys worship you, Dale. They don't want another commander. They need you, but they're reluctant to say anything to your face because lately, you've been difficult to talk to. You're a damn good leader, a smart operator, a fine Mage and a close friend. So I'm saying it for them."

Byrne leaned forward, hands on his knees. "Get your shit straightened out, Dale. Get help from a private psychiatrist or a navy one. Or I'll assign a mind-melder to you."

Holy hellfire. A mind-melder, diving into his deepest memories, turning him into a whimpering mess when he barely managed to hold it together now? He didn't trust the shrinks, either.

"I don't need a witch doctor," he said, taking a long pull of beer, ignoring Byrne's scrutinizing look.

"You're too thin and haggard. Take a vacation, go see some sights…get laid and then come back and get help."

Nearly spitting out his sip of beer, he sputtered. "You came all the way from D.C. to tell me to have sex?"

A faint memory surfaced. Sitting in Tom's bar, a beautiful, mysterious woman staring at him. The memory became fog on glass. Damn it.

Lazily swirling the amber liquid, Byrne snorted. "Sure as hell didn't come here for this. Damn, twenty-year-old Scotch doesn't taste the same when you're 1,500 years old."

Then the admiral gave him one of his paternal, but knowing, looks. "What happened in the basement, Dale? You never talked about it. Who was that woman found with you, the wolf who vanished?"

Emotion squeezed his throat. He sucked in a deep breath. Byrne was right. He had changed, and denied it. His men deserved better. For two months, he'd hidden the truth, refusing to talk about what the demons had done to him.

"I don't remember. Everything's a blur. All I remember are smells and pain. The smell of a Roman orgy, this delicate, delicious female scent…and waking up to see Shay and Kelly standing over me."

And screams tearing from his throat, until he'd fallen unconscious.

"The Roman orgy was the Centurion demons who tied you up to torture you. Shay banished them with a spell. But the woman found with you, you don't recall her face? Or a black wolf?"

Dale shook his head, the knot in his stomach tightening. "She must be the demon wolf that tortured me. When I find her, she'll pay. She'll lead me to the others and I'll send them all back to hell."

"Remembering would help, but sounds like they infused you with a classic demon memory spell. Clouds the victim's brain in case he survives, he can't recall specific details." Byrne's expression sharpened. "So the demons can come at you again, and catch you off guard."

Right. Like I'd ever let that happen again. "I don't

need you to watch my six. I'm not rushing headfirst into a sitch without knowing all the intel. Got it?"

Byrne's look remained steady. "I'm not watching your six anymore, my friend. But I am serious. Get help this week or I'm placing you on mandatory medical leave for another two months and it's going in your record that you're mentally unstable. Your team needs you."

The barbed wire knotted tighter in his stomach. Dale squeezed his beer bottle and felt it crack beneath his palm. He set it down, trying to regain his composure. Couldn't let Byrne see how rattled he truly was. He didn't trust him anymore.

Hell, he trusted no one. Not even himself.

The doorbell rang. He glanced at Byrne. "What is this? Another well-meaning friend?"

"Maybe a home invader," the admiral suggested.

Dale headed down the hallway. The double doors were warded with magick, but anything could be lurking outside. A Girl Scout selling cookies or a demon. Or a very human home invader.

After what happened two months ago, he never took chances.

Gathering his powers, he felt the current hum through his body. And pulled open the door

Not a Girl Scout or a demon, but a petite, ebony-haired woman clad entirely in black leather, except for a powder-blue T-shirt with some kind of business logo.

Chaos.

He gave an appreciative visual sweep of his visitor. Very curvy, with long, curly hair spilling down to her waist. She had a delicate, innocent face. Wide, full lips pulled down slightly at the corners, giving her mouth a cute pout. She looked no more than eighteen.

But deep in her green eyes swirled ancient knowledge, and a weariness he'd seen in the mirror these past two months.

Parked beneath a streetlamp was a motorcycle with a very flat tire.

The girl pushed back a lock of hair. "I'm sorry to disturb you, but do you happen to have an air pump? I've got a flat."

Neither the statement nor the soft, pleading words stopped him. It was the look of faint despair in those lovely, but sorrowful, sea-green eyes.

Dale glanced over his shoulder as the admiral strolled down the hallway. "She doesn't look like a home invader."

The girl glanced at the very intrigued and curious Admiral Byrne. Panic flared in her gaze and then her expression smoothed out. She ignored the admiral and stuck out her palm to Dale.

"I'm not. My name's Keira Solomon. I was visiting one of your neighbors two blocks away and my bike went kaput on your street."

He took her hand and shook it. Memories tugged… the fog temporarily lifting. Pain, so much pain, agony in each muscle, pulling off bone, shredded flesh…and a large black wolf panting in the corner, sorrow flaring in her green eyes, a long, low howl echoing his screams…

The memory died, leaving him grappling for it like a sleeper groping for wisps of a dream. Keegan looked at him, laid a hand on his shoulder.

"Dale? You okay?"

"Fine." He shook off his hand.

The admiral gave him a thoughtful look. "Have to get home. The wife is expecting me."

The woman politely stepped aside to let him pass. Suddenly he pushed her against the wall, his palm splayed over her forehead. Eyes opened wide, she stared at Byrne.

Dale remained motionless, watching with interest. The old man hadn't done a mind-meld in years.

When he pulled away two minutes later, the admiral didn't look worried or pleased. Just thoughtful. He glanced at Dale.

"She's a paranorm. Trust her." Something very old and sorrowful flickered in the other man's gaze. "She'll do you more good than you'll ever anticipate. You both need each other."

Keira's wide mouth wobbled precariously. Seeming to gather her composure, she shot the admiral a scathing look as he pushed past her and went down the steps to his car.

Turning to Dale she asked, "Do you have an air pump? Because it's getting late and I need to hit the road. If you can't help me, I'll knock on someone else's door."

The knight in rusty armor, he thought. *Can't help you with anything simpler than an air pump.* "Come with me."

He walked to the garage, where he opened a cabinet door and retrieved the pump and a can of instant flat-tire repair. Keira studied his garage. "Very organized. Everything labeled. Military man. I bet you're the type who irons your underwear and folds it neatly in the drawer."

He shot her a look, but she smiled at him, mischief dancing in her green eyes. That look turned him upside down. No one had dared to tease him in a long time.

As they walked back onto the street to her bike, and he set about fixing her flat, she plopped down on the pavement beside him. "I know this is a paranormal neighborhood. I'm a Luminaire."

Dale plugged the flat and reached for the air pump. "Witch doctor."

Keira laughed. "That's what some call me. I'm a psi therapist who helps paranorms restore their energy balance. Perfectly legit. Your neighbor, Mrs. Henderson, asked me to cleanse her home. Had a little issue with dark energy. And you are…?"

Although the admiral vetted her, Dale still didn't trust the girl. She looked like a pixie with her wide eyes and petite body, but pixies could be trouble.

"Dale Curtis. Don't know what you're talking about." He filled the tire and checked the pressure. Perfect.

She gave him a knowing look. "You should. I can feel the power emanating from you. I know you're a Mage, but can't tell what type. I have power, as well. I'll show you mine if you show me yours."

Her teasing, melodious voice almost coaxed a smile from him. Damn, how long had it been since he'd flirted with a pretty woman?

"You first," he told her.

Uncurling her fist, she displayed a tiny ball of white energy. The ball danced in the air and then slowly drifted upward, exploding into a shower of silver sparks. Dale went still. He hadn't shown his powers to anyone but Keegan in a long time. Truth was, his powers had gone south since the demons kicked his ass. No telekinesis. All he could do was shift into a wolf and toss a current of power strong enough only to light dry kindling.

"Not bad."

He focused all his energy and summoned a large ball of energy, which danced in his open palm. Bouncing it like a baseball, he sent it drifting upward, and it exploded in a much larger shower of sparks. Blood drained from her face, but she stood her ground.

"Yours is bigger than mine."

Dale's mouth quirked at the joke.

"You're a Mage—what kind?" she asked.

"Primary Elemental."

"Very powerful. But your aura is pulsing with dark energy. You need deep cleansing." She studied her hands. "Speaking of cleansing, may I wash up? I took a bit of a spill back there."

Mistrust flickered inside him, but he stood and nodded. She was such a tiny sprite, what harm could she do? Still, he took her hand and turned it over, his hand practically swallowing hers. Dale felt no darkness or negativity flaring from her, only a deeper, sexual spark igniting between them. Curious, he circled the scrape on her palm.

"You hurt yourself," he murmured. "Come inside, and I'll find antiseptic."

He picked up the air pump and can, put them back in the garage and let her into the house through the laundry room. Dale fished out a brown bottle of peroxide and bandages from a white cabinet. Keira winced slightly as he ran warm water over her hand, then treated it with peroxide.

"You're very good with your hands, but wow, the dark energy I feel from you, it's not you. Not normally you."

Dale glanced at her as he finished bandaging her hand.

"I use psi therapy, light and massage techniques to eradicate negative energy. High-frequency healing energy, using the natural elements. Harmonic meditation to calm the mind and soothe the spirit."

"Natural elements?"

"The power of the sun, wind, earth, even fire."

"I don't believe in any of that 'woo-woo' stuff." He replaced the bottle of peroxide.

"Of course. Because even though you're a Mage, you're very much a military man who believes in what he can see. You're a natural leader, a colonel or a captain.

No, not army, not with the navy base so close." Keira wiggled her bandaged fingers. "Thanks."

His gaze narrowed. "Lieutenant commander. How did you know?"

"Simple deduction. The flag out front, this is a military neighborhood, although a paranormal one, and…"

Silently, she pointed to the uniforms hanging on the door, still covered with dry-cleaning plastic. "I'm really quite psychic. I have ESPN."

As she winked at him, Dale cracked a reluctant smile.

"Seriously, I can tell you need cleansing. You've been in contact with some pretty nasty demons."

His smile dropped. He gestured to the mounds of dirty laundry piled high in the overflowing hamper. "That's the cleansing I need. My housekeeper quit."

Sally had quit with the excuse to move closer to her grandchildren. They both knew the truth. Dale's nightly screams had fractured her nerves.

She traced a pattern in the air. "There's thick tendrils of blackness in your aura, blackness pulsing with the other colors."

"What other colors?" He didn't believe in Luminaires, but he knew about auras.

"Deep red, indicating you're a strong-willed and realistic person and a bright, vibrant red that says you're a powerful and extremely competitive individual."

"Bright, vibrant red also means someone who's very sexual," he said, enjoying the hint of pink spreading across her cheeks.

"Yes, that, too. And you have other colors as well, but they're so obscured by the blackness, I can't tell them apart. You've come into contact with great evil, evil that touched you deeply."

This was too close for his comfort zone. He folded his arms across his chest.

"Hire me and I'll give you a big discount. Only three thousand dollars in cash."

"That's all?" he asked drily.

Keira shrugged. "Work is slow right now."

"And what do I get from you for three thousand dollars?" He pushed close to her, getting in her face, crowding her. "And for how long do I get it?"

His brazen, suggestive words brought an attractive flush to her face. To her credit, Keira refused to back off or drop her gaze. "You get me, for however long you need me. A week. Or a month, or more, if you desire. I need a place to stay while I'm in the area."

Dale caught a faint whiff of an enticing scent that wound around his body and yanked hard. Oh, yeah…he desired. His body tightened, blood running hot and thick.

Their gazes met, connected. Something long dead inside him stirred to life. He reached out and with calloused fingers, touched her cheek.

Keira's eyes widened and darkened. Her lush mouth trembled.

Just as suddenly the connection broke. Dale stepped back.

"And why are you in the area?"

"I travel a lot across country. Never been to Virginia before. I like the beach."

She looked innocent. Guileless.

"What exactly are we talking about? What methods?"

"I combine aromatherapy massage and meditation with crystals to restore harmonic energy and fight evil. Light therapy, massage and reflexology." At his questioning look, she added, "I work with your feet on certain pressure points."

"Interesting," he murmured. He liked the idea of the massages. Maybe this could prove to be worth his time. How long had it been since a woman had grabbed his interest?

"I'll need you to sign a contract, of course. To protect us both," she said. Her gaze whipped around the house, so fast he could almost see her mind recalculating like a GPS. It was fascinating and disturbing, because he knew she was pushing him hard to go where he didn't want to venture.

Hiring Keira would get Keegan off his back. Keegan already voiced his approval of her. She was better than a navy shrink and ten times safer than a damn mind-melder. And much sexier. The surge of sexual interest flared again.

But he'd be damned if he let her try any of her woo-woo techniques. She could clean the house instead, cook his meals.

"I need a live-in housekeeper. You'd have your own room downstairs by the kitchen and I'll pay you the three thousand and you stay for the month. Come back tomorrow at oh-five-hundred with your contract before I leave for the base."

A tentative smile. "You sure?"

The hesitant words contrasted sharply with her earlier confidence. She almost sounded like a child hopeful for acceptance. Dale's curiosity was piqued.

He gave a rueful glance at his feet. "I'm not into all that New Age crap, but my feet could use some pampering."

"It's not massage. It's a technique to free the energy."

"You're not going to nibble at my toes? Damn."

Her mouth wobbled in a tentative smile. Dale chuckled, the sound rusty and grating. Hell, had it been that long since he laughed? "I'm teasing you. I'm not into having my toes nibbled."

At her widening smile, he added, "There are exceptions, if the mouth happens to be wide, and lush…and a tad crooked."

The most intriguing blush ignited her cheeks. Keira put her hands to her reddened cheeks as that lovely, wide and crooked mouth parted. "Oh-five-hundred sharp. I'll be here. I'll even treat you to coffee."

She leaped down the steps, marched to her motorbike and with a kick start it coughed to life, and she took off into the night.

For a few moments Dale stood in the doorway, staring after her, feeling something tighten in his chest.

He shut the door and called his neighbor to see if Keira's story was true. After talking a few minutes, he hung up and then dialed Keegan's number. "Spill it. Tell me what you saw in her mind."

"Dale, it's late…."

"Tell me."

"I couldn't get a fix on her memories and who she is, but I'll say this, you need her. Trust me on this. Do yourself a favor. Let go and don't question, just go with your gut."

Right. Last time he did that, his guts almost ended up spilling out on the table where he'd been tortured. Damn, he hated coyness.

"Keegan…level with me."

"Already have, son. Find yourself help and get straightened out. I don't give a damn who straightens you out, as long as it's done. Hire a witch doctor if you must."

"Already did." He told the admiral about Keira. "You satisfied now? You'll get off my back?"

"You're doing the right thing, Dale."

He snorted. "We'll see. I don't believe in any of that woo-woo shit."

"Maybe you should. Maybe that's the only thing that can free you."

The admiral hung up, leaving Dale to ponder his cryptic words.

He went to the window and stared at the full moon, feeling the itch and pull of scar tissue. Or maybe it was the itch and pull of something deeper.

That wolf that hurt him, if he got his hands on the beast…

Dale went into the kitchen, opened the sliding glass doors and stepped onto his deck. A cool, refreshing breeze caressed his cheeks. He was a powerful Primary Mage, a Mage who could shape-shift into any life form. Right now the wolf called to him, the urge to run wild and free in fur. Closing his eyes, he stretched out his hands and called upon his magick, and shifted into a large gray timber wolf. He ran into his backyard, and leaped over the wood fence, giving a joyful yip as he raced through the woods. Senses filled with the night air, the sights and smells of the land.

Freeing and exhilarating, he relished the feel of leaves and earth beneath his paws. The wolf had no responsibilities, didn't have to visit a shrink to keep his job. The wolf had no scars, only thick fur. The wolf would never be tied down and helpless and vulnerable.

His wolf had power.

And if his wolf ever got his big paws on the demon wolf that tortured him as a man, that SOB would pay with Dale's claws.

The wolf grinned as he ran with the night.

Chapter 3

A gentle breeze stirred the American flag hanging next to the front door. Everything about this house, from the bright white paint to the neat black shutters and the truck in the drive, seemed normal.

But nothing was normal, especially not the man living inside.

Keira took a deep breath and steadied her nerves. When the door opened, she gave a bright smile.

"I hope you like your coffee black. Because I took you for a black-coffee guy."

She thrust a steaming coffee cup at the man in the doorway. Dale Curtis stood military straight in a starched khaki uniform, looking crisp and fresh and undeniably more handsome than a man should look at 0500 hours.

Those scrutinizing gray eyes showed a hint of a smile. "Thanks. Come in."

Carrying her valise, Keira followed him to the kitchen.

Tension knotted her stomach. His older friend, clearly a superior, had done some kind of odd mojo on her last night. She remembered nothing except that his smile had been kind.

Still, she couldn't trust that the older man wasn't setting her up, even though he whispered into her mind that she was safe now. Right. Nothing was safe anymore. Not since the Centurions had torn her world apart.

This arrangement troubled her. Living with him wasn't on her agenda, but she needed to buck up his powers so he could destroy the Centurion demons. Keira suspected he hired her only to fulfill an obligation.

The commander set down the coffee, then sat on a wood stool at the breakfast nook. His penetrating gray gaze seemed to bore into her. For too long, she'd operated alone, avoiding others, especially men. This close proximity unnerved her. Dale Curtis studied her, as if puzzling out her real identity. Her hand trembled as she fumbled in her case. Not this soon. She needed time, needed to gain his trust. But instinct warned that was something this man did not easily give.

He glanced at his watch. "Let's see the contract. You have thirty minutes before I leave for base."

Tempted to take the watch and throw it into the trash, Keira plopped the contract on the table. "In conveniently large type, unlike most legal contracts. You can actually read this." She glanced up at the clock. "Of course, I'm sure you'll have to be at work soon."

Dale slid the papers closer and began to read, his brows drawing together. Holding her breath, she tapped her fingers. But he was a fast read and finally came to the last page.

"Sign here."

Keira handed him an old-fashioned quill. When he

scratched his name in bold, strong letters, she took the quill and pricked her thumb. A droplet of blood spilled over his signature. She licked her thumb and gestured to the contract.

"I'll give you a copy. The contract states you are free to break the agreement at any time by declaring verbally to me, 'I renounce you. I renounce our agreement.'"

She'd seen him pour over the rambling legalese in the document, but wanted to ensure that Lt. Commander Dale Curtis knew exactly what he was getting into.

Without telling him every single, small detail.

But cooperation was essential. No man could be bound to her against his will.

At his nod, she snapped open her case and withdrew a velvet box. Inside the red velvet bed was a shimmering wide silver armband. A large blue sapphire was in the center amid intricate runes studded with smaller sapphires.

"Please slide this on me, above the elbow."

She held out her bare right arm.

"This is a slave armband."

Suspicion flared in his eyes. Keira held her breath. So close, would he balk now? A man of reason, she realized. A man who questioned all because he left nothing to chance.

She shrugged. "Is it? The armband provides me protection while I cleanse your house, and assures you that as long as it remains on me, I'm bonded to you as your contractor."

And as long as you put it on me, I'm protected from demons. They can't touch me.

"Then if it protects you, why don't you wear it all the time?"

Smart. She wasn't accustomed to dealing with a man who had both valor and a piercing intellect.

Keira pointed to the gleaming sapphire. "Why would I wear it when there are more human thieves who'd harm me to steal the jewels, not knowing the armband's real value?"

Dale's full mouth pursed, but his eyes twinkled. "You have an answer for everything. Rehearse much?"

But he gently slid the armband in place. Feeling the warmth of her skin, the metal settled against her arm, not uncomfortable, more reassuring than restricting. She was bound to him. Her wolf could not attack him as long as the band remained in place.

He didn't remove his hand. Instead, his fingers brushed against her skin. Heat curled inside her body.

For a wild moment, she wondered what he'd be like as a lover. What would it feel like to at last surrender her innocence, give everything to a man as magnificent and powerful as him?

And surrender your heart, give total power over you, a small voice mocked. *After twenty-three years of guarding what little you have left?*

Dale stroked the skin under her arm along the band, and she bit her lip. Feelings surged, along with a delicious heat that made her toes curl. "This band bonds you to me. So it means you must do anything I tell you."

Keira fisted her hands to hide their trembling. "Not exactly. I'm no pushover, Lieutenant Commander."

With forefinger and thumb, he lightly clasped her chin. The spicy scent of his cologne swam in her nostrils. She became lost in the intense grayness of his eyes. Dale's mouth parted as he lowered his head.

But instead of a kiss, he nuzzled her neck, inhaling deeply. Dread filled her.

Mages couldn't scent the demon blood inside her. But he was a Primary, and much more powerful than an ordinary Mage.

"What are you, Keira Solomon? Why do I crave you? Every time I draw close, I think of sex," he whispered.

"They have support groups for that."

She backed away until her backside connected with the sliding glass doors. The commander advanced, a determined look on his face.

He would have answers, would wring them out of her.

"I thought you said you had to go to work." She mustered a smile and tapped his watch. "Better get going."

Please, let him be the kind of guy who's never late.

"The base can wait for once. This is more important."

Closer still he came, until his tall body overshadowed hers. He could overcome her with weight and sheer physical strength.

Inside, the demon blood surged, but her claws did not emerge. Because her wolf could no longer hurt him. Good for him, not so wonderful for her if he wanted to overpower her. Could he find out who she was?

Keira cringed and squeezed against the glass doors. He slowly stalked toward her.

"The admiral sensed something about you. I sense something about you. Something in my blood is calling to you. You're not who you appear to be."

She wriggled away as he reached for her. "Blood is for vamps. I don't like vamps. They like to sleep in and they never appreciate my cooking when I make garlic sauce."

He clasped her chin in one strong hand, his grip gentle, but firm. "I will have answers, Keira. You'd better hope and pray I don't find out anything I don't like."

Tightness constricted her chest, but she gave a small laugh. "Why? You'll feed me to the wolves?"

A slow smile touched his mouth. "Not quite."

"Too bad. Because I always liked to play Little Red Riding Hood, only with a big knife and some nunchakus. I don't fight fair."

"Neither do I." He pushed a strand of hair away from her face and tucked it behind her ear. "Not when it comes to chasing down something I want very, very badly. I can be quite ruthless. Like a wolf."

"And here I thought you were a puppy dog, Lieutenant Commander. A seemingly nice guy with too much starch in your collar." She tried to duck beneath his embrace, but he caught her and pinned her against the door.

"You don't want to know what I'm capable of, Keira. And you'd better pray you can handle what I deliver, because I guarantee by the time I finish with you, you'll be in no shape to fight me. I'll know every cell of you, every inch of you. And there will be no secrets between us."

He lowered his head toward her. "None. I'll cull every last one from you. So start now by telling me the truth."

She bit back a moan as he traced her lower lip with his thumb. Oh, gods, this was a risk Keira knew she'd have to undertake, but she didn't reckon with the magnetic power of Dale Curtis's personality.

The force of his will.

Keira felt herself begin to crumble as the commander stroked her bottom lip, his touch gentle and erotic. His piercing gaze seared into her. *Please, don't ask the question, please. I don't know if I can withhold the truth....*

The commander would kill her. She knew it. Keira tensed as he whispered.

"You're bound to me. The contract states it. Now, tell me the truth. You must. Who the hell are you and why the hell are you really here?"

Chapter 4

"I'm a Luminaire...."

"I know what you are. Who are you?"

His aura pulsed bright red, spiked with black. Sexual energy, as well as negative forces. Keira shoved lightly at his chest, breaking the physical contact.

"I'm your new housekeeper, a woman who needs a job, okay? I've been roving from town to town."

"Why?"

The man was relentless. "I like helping people. I search for individuals that need enlightenment and then help them heal. Ask your neighbor if you need a reference."

"I did. Odd how you showed up just when she needed you." He lightly clasped her wrist. Sexual current sizzled between them.

Keira closed her eyes and breathed deeply, channeling every bit of white light she could to fight the temptation to lift her face to his and kiss him. "I heard her crying. Psychic cries, not real cries. I'm a healer and it compelled me."

"Right."

"There's enough darkness and negative energy in this world. What's wrong with trying to eradicate it and make people feel better?"

"Maybe there's no hope for them." He dropped her hand.

Keira watched a shadow drape across his expression, then his face smoothed out. Dale Curtis was hiding deep pain, pain she knew well, because she'd caused it.

Suddenly he went still. Keira's heart dropped to her stomach as she caught the small, scampering sounds.

"Damn mice," he said. "One reason why my house-keeper quit."

"That's not a mouse," she said and bolted down the hallway, hooked a right and ran into a locked door. Keira jiggled the knob. "Open this," she told him as he pulled up short behind her.

A fierce scowl tightened his face. "That's private."

"If you want to get rid of your pests, open it. Now."

He looked shocked, as if no one ever talked to him that way.

Dale clicked a series of buttons on a brass plate and opened the door. She burst inside, barely noting that it was an office, with stacks of papers piled on the desk. Her sense of smell overtook everything. Those little, nasty creatures, smelling like a bad combination of bad breath and rotting cabbage…

"My report to the admiral…"

Ignoring Dale's mutterings as he sifted through papers on his desk, she dived to the floor by the credenza. Keira groped beneath the furniture and felt slicing pain scrape her hand. She peered down. The imp had affixed razor blades to the credenza's bottom, effectively making a protective nest for itself.

Two red, beady eyes glared at her. It started to lash out with its tiny claws and then backed away, obeying the hidden compulsion in the slave armband. Keira stretched out her fingers and summoned the power deep inside.

The creature squealed as it slid into her hand. She wriggled from under the credenza, clutching it tight.

"Jar," she gasped.

Dale stared at the creature as it wriggled in her hand. Blood seeped down her clenched fist. "What the hell…"

"Jar, hello, could use a little help here, get a jar, something to hold it. Please hurry."

He seized a heavy metal pencil holder from the desk, dumped out the contents.

Keira squatted down. "Be quick, they're really, really fast… I'll let go and you trap him. On three… One, two, three!"

As she released the creature, Dale slammed the pencil holder down. Damn, the man was fast.

He picked up a scrap of paper and tossed it down with a disgusted sound. "My report to the admiral… It's chewed to pieces."

"Uh, of course. They adore paper. Almost as tasty as flour." Keira examined her injured hand with a rueful sigh. "If he'd have gotten to your computer, your hard drive would be royally screwed."

To her surprise, he gave a small, wry smile. "Never did like anything royally screwed, especially my hard drive. I prefer the commoner's touch."

It took her a minute to realize the joke. And then to her enormous chagrin, she blushed. He gave his rusty, deep laugh again. And then he looked at her injured hand and stopped laughing. Dale took her hand very gently and examined it. His touch was absolutely gentle. Fishing out a clean, white square from his pocket, he wrapped it around her bleeding palm.

"Remind me to be careful dusting under there. It fastened razor blades to the credenza's bottom to keep anyone from going after him."

Dale focused his attention on bandaging her hand. "Even without a contract, you'd have to stay now. Can't have you leaving here wounded."

"It's not much. It'll heal."

"I always take care of my own." He looked slightly dangerous as he stared at the floor. The pencil holder trembled, but the creature was effectively trapped.

"What the hell is that thing?"

"Imp." Keira wrapped her hand tighter to slow the bleeding. Blood was bad, attracted bad things, and this house already had enough darkness. She couldn't risk drawing out more.

"A demon," he said slowly.

"A very minor one. Imps are drawn to negativity and darkness. They feed on it."

That and residual demon energy left on a victim, she thought.

Dale frowned. "That thing invaded my home because I've been in a bad mood?"

"Not exactly. You've been expelling dark energy. Something must have happened to you to suck out your white light."

He shot her an incredulous look.

"Imps tend to make a person bad-tempered and irritable. They make a bad situation worse. They're hard to kill because they're so fast. They can outrun almost anything."

He raised a dark brow. The commander opened a desk

drawer and withdrew a pistol. Keira's jaw dropped as he chambered a round and pointed the gun at the pencil jar and fired. Shards of plastic exploded, along with a nasty splatter of gray demon blood. The stench stung her nostrils.

"Not a 9 mm," he said with satisfaction.

Sweat trickled down her spine. "Um, you're not very forgiving, are you?"

"No."

"I'd hate to be on your bad side."

"You would." His expression darkened. "Good thing you're not a demon."

Keira swallowed hard. "Yeah. Sounds like you've run up against them. It's the source of your dark energy."

"I'm only interested in one." A hard smile touched his mouth, making him look dangerous. "No matter how long I must wait. I will find her and make her pay for what she did to me."

The coffee soured in her stomach as she remembered how skillfully he'd wielded the pistol. Keira didn't relish him discovering her true identity. Holding back her nausea, she pointed to the mess on the floor. "If you'll show me where I'm sleeping and then where your cleaning supplies are, I'll get started on my first assignment."

He gently clasped her injured hand. "After I clean your wounds. Those are some nasty cuts."

"I can do it."

"I told you, I always take care of my own."

She was almost afraid to ask. "And those you consider your enemies? You take care of them, as well?"

Dale gave a slow smile. "The same way I did to the imp."

Keira didn't look at the splattered remains on the floor as they left his study.

* * *

After Dale left, Keira brought the saddlebags containing her possessions inside and set them on the floor. Then she sat on the bed of her new room, stroking the ecru duvet.

A real bed, with feather pillows instead of a thin blanket on the cold concrete floor. A brass reading lamp with a comfortable chair by a window that overlooked the wide backyard instead of a windowless basement. Her own bathroom, not a foul bucket in the corner.

Freedom, for the first time in years, not fearing that at any moment the demons would yank her back to captivity and imprison her once more.

Oh, how she longed to sit in the chair, crack open one of the books on his shelves and read. But she had a job to do.

Keira unpacked her kit and set about cleansing the house the way a regular housekeeper would not.

First, his office. Two wide computer screens took up most of a desk. Papers that had been neatly stacked and organized were scattered about the surface.

A map of the world was mounted to one wall, with several colored pushpins inserted into various countries.

She cleansed the remains of the dead imp and burned them in the stone hearth fireplace. Blood called to blood, and even imp blood attracted dark forces.

Keira then took a small box, opened it and arranged the crystals around Dale's office in a pattern. Then she closed her eyes and began the sacred chant. The crystals began to vibrate and hum, the music of elemental energy creating a harmonic vibration.

White light suffused the room, ribbons of light beaming out from each of the four crystals. Soothing and melodious, the light singing its own song of purity, drawing out the negative forces.

A dark cloud arose from the corner near Dale's computer. Ribbons of white light attacked the cloud, overcoming it, and the darkness evaporated. Keira watched, her chest tight. She lowered her hands. Why could she cleanse rooms and people and not herself?

Because of the demon blood inside me, she reminded herself. Until the Centurions were permanently vanquished to the netherworld, part of her would always remain in darkness. Lately it got more difficult to regain her inner light. Each time the demons returned her to captivity, her inner light shrank. Eventually it would go out all together, leaving her in the abyss.

Each time the Centurions allowed her freedom, Keira used the time to refresh herself with positive energy, using elements from the earth and her crystals. White light held the demons' darkness at bay for a little while, until the Centurions forced her wolf to torture a new victim.

Refreshed, she set about cleansing the other rooms, until reaching Dale's bedroom.

Keira hesitated at the door. She drew in a deep breath and stepped into the room, feeling the despondency and grief. The master bedroom had an attached bath. Large, with a glassed-in shower and a Roman tub big enough to fit four, it was sleek tile and slick chrome.

The darkness of horrible pain slammed into her temples.

Holding a hand to her head, she opened the medicine cabinet above the sink. Lined in a neat row were several prescription-pill bottles. All of them recently issued, most for pain, some for sleeping.

The bottles held a layer of dust.

Dale Curtis had not touched a single pill. Instead, he'd suffered.

Keira cleansed both rooms, feeling the light chase away the thick layers of suffering. With a much lighter spirit, she started on her housekeeping duties.

She worked steadily, leaving the basement for last. It still needed cleansing with her crystals, as well. Dread curled in her stomach as she finally gathered her courage and climbed down the stairs, clutching her most powerful crystal. Sweat dripped down her temples and she wiped it away with the back of her hand, the dust rag gripped in her fist.

You can do this, you can do this....

The basement ran the length of the house and was enormous, divided into two sections. The smaller section was unfinished, with a utility room, wood workbench and neatly arranged tools, the furnace and storage cubicles.

This section was separated by a wall with a solid door. She opened the door and went into the larger section. It was a comfortable living room covered with beige carpeting, a small, tiled kitchen with shining stainless-steel appliances, a dining table and chairs and a sectional sofa set before a flat-screen television mounted above a fireplace. Next to the stairs were eight bunk beds. She opened a door and found a bathroom with a tiled shower.

A shiver snaked down her spine as she gazed around the room. Another door was near the bunk beds. She opened it and found a small, windowless room with a narrow bed. No light switch. Nothing to chase away the darkness...

A sly, rollicking laugh echoed in her mind. *You will never escape us....*

Whimpering, Keira slammed the door and leaned

against it, the crystal in her left fist squeezed tight. She raced up the stairs.

Maybe she'd tackle that room tomorrow.

Dale arrived home after seven. When he walked into the kitchen, Keira noticed the shadows beneath his gray eyes were pronounced and dark.

He flipped the light switch, flooding the room with overhead lighting. The man was thin and haggard, and looking worse each day. If he didn't regain strength soon, he'd lose the fight to darkness. Keira glanced up from the pot of stew she stirred on the stove. He brightened as he sniffed the air.

"Smells great, but you don't have to cook. I usually grab a sandwich at the commissary."

"I like cooking and making new dishes."

And you need more than sandwiches to get your health back.

He eyed the dining-room table, set with the china she'd found in the elegant cabinet. "I just eat in the kitchen."

"This is nicer, though, don't you think?" He had such nice things. Keira wanted to relish and experience every good thing she could while she was free.

He sighed deeply, as if something hurt him. "It's been a long time since I sat down at a dining-room table."

Dale looked down at his uniform. "You went to a lot of trouble. Mind if I change first?"

"The stew will keep warm. Unless you decide on a hot bubble bath."

"I never take bubble baths alone, only with company. Saves on water."

He gave a real smile, showing white, even teeth. The smile lit up his face and chased away all the dark shadows.

Keira stared out the kitchen window as he went upstairs. Her pulse raced. First time alone all night with the man she'd tortured, a man of honor and integrity and tremendous power. She didn't underestimate his rough appearance. If he wanted, Dale Curtis could turn her to ashes with one flick of his hand.

A few minutes later, Dale returned to the kitchen, clad in khaki trousers and a navy blue polo shirt. Deck shoes covered his feet. He went into the dining room and returned with a sparkling crystal wineglass.

"What do you think?" he asked. He went for the built-in wine rack among the cabinets. "Red or white?"

She hadn't drunk spirits in ages and placed the glasses on the table more as pretty decor. It was dangerous to imbibe around him, dangerous to lower her guard. But he was acting more animated and she didn't want to spoil the mood. "Red, I think. You select it."

Dale opened a bottle and poured a small amount. "I haven't had wine since I got home from the hospital. Just beer, and I rarely finish the bottle."

Her heart skipped a beat. She watched him sample the vintage and nod. "Excellent."

"How long were you in the hospital?"

"Long enough."

As he carried the bottle and glass into the dining room, she ladled the stew into two bowls. He turned on the crystal chandelier hanging over the table. A lump rose in Keira's throat.

She had been forced to torture him in the dark. He never knew when she'd attack, never saw her coming, only felt the burning agony of her sharp claws.

Dale filled her glass with wine as they sat. Keira tried not to think of what she'd done to this man, but the stew tasted like cardboard as she ate.

He looked up, his brows arched. "It's very good. I taste thyme. Did you season the stew with it?"

Keira flushed under the praise. "Thyme and other spices."

Dale smiled, the sharp angles and plains of his face softening. "You're a good cook. I thought New Agers ate only wheat sprouts and fruit."

Keira thought quickly. "In all my travels, I had to adapt to various lifestyles, so I learned to enjoy their foods, as well."

He toyed with the stem of his wineglass. "You're a gypsy."

"With a Harley instead of a caravan. I like to travel and see the country."

"Why?"

"Because there's so much to this life to see, and experience." Keira spooned up more stew. "I want to relish every single moment I've been given and find the good in people, the good I know exists."

"It doesn't always exist. There is much evil."

"And good."

"That's not my job. My job is to find the evil and eradicate it, to keep the American people safe."

Keira's heart pounded like an excited dog's tail against the floor. She set down her spoon. "You're too young to be so cynical."

"Old enough. Seen enough." Dale sipped his wine. "My family was insular. I chose against it."

"Why?"

"Because they cared only about money and status. When I chose to join the navy and become a SEAL, they were not happy. But serving my country, and keeping civilians safe, meant more to me than making millions, like my father wanted me to do."

"Who is your family?"

Dale raised a brow. "In all your travels, you've never heard of Curtis Mark Industries? The software empire, second only to Bill Gates and Steven Jobs? That's my father's company."

"You wanted to rebel against your father so you didn't work for him?"

"I wanted to do something with my life other than remain a part of a society that cared only for being seen and flaunting their power. There's an evil I wanted to eliminate to keep others safe. I have much power and what good is power if you don't use it to help others?"

Keira was touched at his dedication and selflessness. The Mage could have had a very comfortable, and very safe, lifestyle. She tilted her head, studying him. Why did she have the feeling she'd met him somewhere before, around the time the demons killed her pack?

But all those memories from Nicaragua were scrambled. The demons had seen to it by infusing her with four drops of their blood when they became temporarily corporeal.

"You sacrificed a lot to keep others safe. Your parents would be proud. I would be."

"They didn't understand. Neither did my wife. Ex-wife. Kathy was cut from the same bolt of social-excess cloth." He seemed to catch himself and stared at his meal. "Damn. Sorry. Didn't mean to go there."

"Let me guess. She didn't like being the wife of a military officer."

He nodded. "We've been divorced a long time now. No children. Enough of me. What about you? Where's your family?"

The familiar lump rose in her throat. Keira struggled to swallow a mouthful of stew. She set down her spoon.

"They were killed in a demon invasion while we were living in another country. I was able to escape."

His expression softened. "I'm sorry."

She shrugged to hide the tears welling in her throat. "It happened a long, long time ago. My pac—parents liked to rove around the globe, see the world and experience new cultures. Guess that's one reason I'm a gypsy. I don't have a real home."

Goodness, she'd almost revealed she once had a pack.

Dale ate with zest. "This is terrific. I haven't had a hot meal in weeks. Never bother cooking. No time, too much trouble."

She studied his lean frame. He'd lost weight since she'd last seen him. If he kept this up, Dale Curtis would resemble a walking skeleton, his powers useless, his body prime for takeover by other demons.

"You need more protein, real meals, not grabbing sandwiches. Now that I'm here, I'll cook dinner for you every night." Keira smiled, trying to lighten her mood. "I promise if I find another imp, I won't throw him in the stew pot. Besides, those little buggers can take the heat."

"How do you normally kill them?"

"Not with guns, though yours did the trick."

Dale smiled, looking less severe.

"Usually it's best to blast them with white light. They're so small, it's easier than trying to kill a demon with white light. With demons, you need the big guns."

Those startlingly gray eyes met hers. Beneath the mild look was an exacting scrutiny. Uncomfortable, she realized he was sizing her up, digging beneath the surface to find out what her deal was. Not a good idea.

"How do you know so much about imps and demons?" he asked.

"I studied them."

"Most women wouldn't want to get near a demon, even an imp, if they lost loved ones to dark forces. Yet you knew exactly what was in my office, and where it would be hiding."

Guilt surged through her. "I studied demons and their minions. Wanted to know what my enemies were capable of doing."

"I do the same, only I'm trained in combat and weaponry."

"Did you know imps love to invade kitchens, food supplies, even liquor? Once I found a dozen of them in a liquor cabinet. They'd managed to break open a bottle of brandy. Have you ever seen a drunk imp? Not a pretty sight."

She set down her spoon. "And I'm rambling. If you want, I can eat in the kitchen, leave you in peace to digest your meal."

"Stay," he said quietly. "It's nice to share a meal with someone. I get tired of eating alone."

"Me, too." The words slipped out before she could catch herself.

Warmth shone in his eyes. For a moment, she indulged in the fantasy that this was her real home, and she could cook here every night. A real home, with someone to belong to.

The lump returned to her throat. Keira gripped her spoon. If she allowed melancholy to consume her, she'd dim her white light. Think positive. "Tell me about the piano. Do you play?"

He nodded. "Not for a long time, though."

"Classical or contemporary?"

"Only the classics. I once wanted to be a concert pianist, but wanted to fight our nation's enemies more."

He gave a crooked smile. "You can't kill the bad guys with music."

"You've never heard me play."

Dale gave his deep, husky chuckle. "And you've never heard me sing."

They were deep into a discussion of classical music versus rock when a clear thud sounded downstairs.

"Something's in the basement." The spoon rattled against the table as she set it down.

Dale wiped his mouth with the linen napkin. He stood, his expression shuttered. "Or someone. I have quarters down there for my men when they run into trouble. But they always ring the front doorbell."

"I don't like your basement. It's a bit spooky," she admitted.

His gaze turned troubled. "I haven't been down there...in a while."

Keira didn't want to go down those stairs. Not now, as shadows draped the house and the darkness pushed away the sunlight. Her pulse raced. And then she looked at Dale and thought about how he must feel about basements.

He dragged in a deep breath and went into the hall-way. When he returned, he carried the same pistol he'd used to shoot the imp. Dale slid the chamber back, the racking sound echoing in the room.

"Stay here."

Something vulnerable flashed in his gaze. Keira's heart kicked. As much as she loathed and feared what lay below, she couldn't let him go there alone.

"I'm coming with you."

"No."

"Bullets won't stop a demon."

"My powers can."

"You'll need extra help. White light can aid and enhance your powers." She fished her white quartz crystal from her jeans pocket.

Dale narrowed his eyes. "Fine. But you stay behind me at least five steps, and if I order you to run back upstairs, run."

She followed him. He opened the door to the basement as she squeezed the crystal tight.

Keira swallowed hard, seeing the steep, gray steps swallowed by inky blackness. Anything could be down there. She'd failed to cleanse the room with white light. Her breathing ragged, she prepared to descend with him into the darkness.

Chapter 5

Dale hadn't been in his own basement since before the incident. Cupping his gun, he crept down the stairs. Sweat trickled down his temples. This was his home, damn it, and he'd tolerate no intruders. But his pulse rate tripled and he struggled to swallow past the panic rising in his throat.

Memories assaulted him. The terrified little boy held in a demon's cruel grip. "His life for yours," the demon had cackled.

And then Dale had willingly become the Centurion's captive, as they tied him down and tortured him until his voice grew hoarse from the screams....

A soft whimper sounded behind him. Keira was just as terrified. Dale straightened and motioned for her to stay back. Damn it, he was a navy SEAL, not some wimpy ass scared of entering his own damn basement.

He flipped on the light switch. Soft white light illuminated the downstairs. When he reached the bottom step he heard singing.

"I don't think demons sing," Keira whispered.

He lowered the gun, relief making his knees weak. "That's no demon, but an imp from hell. What his mother calls him, anyway."

Dale rounded the corner to the section he'd built as quarters to house his men when the Phoenix Force needed to discuss ops in private. He flipped the safety on his weapon and shoved it into the waistband of his shorts.

Grant "Sully" Sullivan lay on the carpet, singing a bawdy song. Dale inhaled and recoiled.

"Jesus, Sully, what the hell?"

The ensign struggled to sit up, and fell back, the odor of whiskey clinging to him like cheap perfume. "Sorry, Curt. I'm a little…little drunk."

"And you came here to sleep it off? Or escape from a lover?" Dale squatted down beside the young SEAL.

Keira entered the room and looked at Sully. Dale sighed. "Keira, meet Ensign Sullivan, one of my men. Sully, this is Keira, my new housekeeper."

Sully opened one eye and held out a hand. "Pleased to meet you, ma'am."

Her mouth quirked. "It's a pleasure since you're not a demon." Her gaze whipped to Dale. "Although I've heard you're an imp."

"That's what Mom says. Of all her eight kids, I was the worse. Worst."

Dale wiped his clammy palms on his shorts to hide them from Sully. Even drunk, the man was sharp. Of course. He'd trained the SEAL himself. "Why did you teleport here?"

"My sis. Cassandra's worried about you. Made me promise to warn you in person, Curt."

"Who's Curt?" Keira asked.

"It's my team nickname." Dale glanced at the kitchen. "Could you get him a glass of water?"

As Keira headed for the sink, Dale sat beside Sully and lowered his voice. "I told you, I'm fine."

The last thing he needed was Sully's well-meaning but nosy older sister fretting about him. Did the whole world have to fuss over him?

"Cassandra saw a vision in her crystal ball."

Keira handed the glass to Sully, who gulped down the water. "Your sister has a crystal ball?"

"Just for fun. Doesn't need it." Sully set the glass down and looked slightly more alert. "She sees her visions in her mind. She came to my place and yelled at me for drinking too much. Jeez, I hate when she yells at me. Like I'm eight again and she's my bossy older sister nagging me. Well, I was a mess, but damn, I didn't expect company, sorry for swearing, ma'am...."

Trying to follow a line of conversation with Sully when he was soused was like trying to read Latin backward. Dale pointed two fingers at his eyes. "Focus, Sully. Why was your sister at your apartment?"

"Cassandra was worried about you. Came to tell me. Saw a vision in her crystal ball of you dancing with a demon. Not your ex-wife, either."

Dale's mouth quirked. He glanced at Keira to see if she absorbed the joke, and saw blood drain from her face.

He wondered what it meant. Then she smiled, but it seemed strained.

"What kind of demon?"

Sully frowned. "She started bitching... Sorry, ma'am, I mean, complaining, about how messy my place was and how I drank all the whiskey."

"The demon?" Dale asked.

"My sis."

"Why did you drink so much?" he asked gently, already knowing the reason.

"Ever since Miranda broke up with me, my life's been a wreck. I loved her and no one will ever be as sweet." He sighed. "'Cept maybe Paulina. She was amazing...."

Keira gave him a questioning look. "How did you break in?"

"Teleported. Never break in."

She gave Dale a questioning look. "He teleported over. Sully's a Light Mystic."

"Which is Curt's polite way of saying I'm the bastard son of a Mystic Witch and a psychic human. Unlike Cassandra, who's a pure-blood Mystic." Sully rubbed at his face.

She tensed visibly. "Mystic Witches have visions of the future."

"Cassandra's are usually spot-on, which is why I need to know more about this one." Dale turned back to Sully. "What did your sister see?"

"Oh, Dale, let the poor man sober up. He looks hungry." She smiled at Sully. "Have you eaten?"

Sully ran a hand through his thick hair. "No, ma'am. Was gonna grab leftovers or something out of a can."

"I made stew. There's plenty. Would you like dinner?"

Dale shot her an incredulous look, but she ignored him and focused on Sully, who brightened, his boyish face lighting up like a Christmas tree. "Gee, thanks. I love real home cooking."

He didn't like the idea of Sully dining with them. Dale ruminated over this. It wasn't the thought of Sully treating him with kid gloves or asking him again and again how he was healing.

Dale disliked the idea of sharing Keira's company with another man.

Interesting. He rubbed a spot on his chest, his scars itching suddenly. Or was the itch much deeper, the burning wish to enjoy a quiet conversation with a woman who didn't look at him with either fear or desire in her eyes?

Sully scrambled to his feet, swayed a moment and then caught himself. Dale stood as well, wondering about Cassandra Sullivan's cryptic message. Her visions in the past had proved correct. But no way in hell would he ever dance with demons.

Dale headed for his study and locked his weapon in the safe. When he returned to the dining room and re-took his seat, Keira had set a bowl of stew on the table before Sully.

The SEAL began to eat. "Wow, this is terrific," he said around a mouthful of stew. "Maybe if Curt fires you, you can cook for me."

She sat, looking amused at Dale's scowl. "I just got hired. Why would he fire me?"

"You're not his type. Too nice." Sully waved his spoon. "He likes tall, model types with sharp tongues."

"Ensign," Dale warned. "Tell me about your sister's vision. What did this demon look like?"

Keira choked on her wine. Dale glanced at her. "You okay?"

"Fine." She coughed. "Drank too fast."

"Sis said the demon's face was blurred, but she had pretty hair. Silky." Sully squinted at Keira. "Kinda like yours, ma'am. No offense. Didn't mean to compare you to a demon."

"No prob," she said quickly. "Care for some wine?"

"Think I've had enough to drink. Wouldn't wash down well with the finest whiskey this side of—"

"Ensign," Dale interrupted. "The vision?"

"Cassandra said that the demon is closer to you than you'd ever realize…a demon in disguise—"

"More stew?" Keira persisted.

Sully shook his head. "Could use coffee, though, if you have any. Need to sober up."

Her smile was bright. "Sure. Would you like dessert? I made chocolate cake."

"From scratch?"

Keira had already vanished into the kitchen. "Dale, would you help me? I can't carry this by myself."

He went into the kitchen and carried out the cake as she set up the coffeemaker. Keira scurried after him into the dining room.

As she began to cut slices of the thick cake, Dale shook his head. "I'm full. I'll save it for later."

He aimed a stern look at the ensign. "Sully, your sister's vision."

"A sad demon. Weird. A demon who liked to dance and invaded your house to get close to you, the devil in disguise. She said your future depends on vanquishing the demon." Sully dug into his slice of cake. "This is great. Thank you, ma'am."

"Keira," she said. "Dale, I think the coffee is ready. I couldn't find anything to serve it in. Do you mind?"

Dale bit back his impatience as he returned to the kitchen. Damn it, why couldn't Cassandra have clear-cut visions instead of sounding like a Chinese fortune cookie? What demon? Why would he allow a demon into his own home?

Then again, he'd changed since the time in the basement. Dale pressed a hand to his temple. Things that were normally clear before had grown muddied in his mind. He needed to get his act together.

When he returned, carrying a silver service and three cups, Keira was eating her slice of cake. Sully snapped his fingers.

"That's what Cassandra said. I forgot. She said the devil you dance with is the devil in your house, the demon you'll fall hard and fast for, the devil you'll bring to your bed...."

"Oh, my God," Keira cried out.

They both turned. She was licking frosting off her fork, her tongue slowly stroking the tines. Dale's jaw dropped. Holy crap, the woman turned eating cake into carnal art.

"Oh, my God, this is so good! Chocolate," she breathed. "I haven't had any in months. You must try this. I used dark *and* milk chocolate."

Keira took another bite. Eyes closed, expression ecstatic, she looked like a woman in the throes of orgasm.

He forgot all about Cassandra's vision. Forgot about why Sullivan came to his house. All his focus centered on the woman eating a slice of chocolate cake with such sensuality, his blood thickened.

Dale hungered to see her looking this way again, only naked beneath him, her pleasure visible to his eyes only.

Sully stared at her with wide eyes, a pulse beating wildly in his throat. The man was clearly turned on. She licked the fork slowly, and Dale had the oddest feeling she was truly savoring the meal, but also distracting them.

Why? Did she see Mystic Witches as a threat?

Keira flicked her tongue over the tines and slowly slid the utensil into her mouth. Out. Then in again. Sweat trickled down Dale's back. He gulped down his wine, his gaze riveted. Beneath his shorts, his cock hardened.

Stunned, Dale set down his wine. He hadn't experienced arousal since his torture. Now his new housekeeper, with her innocent air and pouting, full mouth, had given him an erection. He narrowed his eyes at Sully.

Leave us alone. Now.

The SEAL wasn't stupid. Sully suddenly pushed back his plate. "I'll be going. Thanks for the meal."

He stood and stretched out his arms as if to teleport, but began to sway. Dale bolted out of his chair. Damn it, he was so tuned into Keira's little display, he'd forgotten his first responsibility—to his men.

"Downstairs, Ensign. You're not headed anywhere. Either I get you a taxi to your apartment or you stay here. Last time you teleported someplace drunk, you ended up inside the lingerie department of a department store."

"I do love the ladies in silk." Sully sighed.

Dale helped him down the steps and watched him collapse onto a bunk bed, covered him with a blanket. Then, as an afterthought, he left a lamp burning.

No one should be left alone in a basement with the lights off.

No one should be left alone in a basement with the lights off and the sound of his own blood slowly dripping onto the cold concrete floor.

His erection deflated. Dale climbed up the stairs, needing to return to the brightly lit kitchen.

A soft, sweet voice hummed a tune he recognized from the sixties. Keira's arms were plunged into a sink filled with soap suds. Disappointed, Dale cocked a brow. He wanted to watch her eat more cake, with him as her only audience. He wanted to slide chocolate frosting over her mouth and slowly lick it off, then trail his tongue down her neck and lower...

What the hell was wrong with him? All he could think about was sex. This was the woman he'd hired to clean his house and keep Keegan Byrne the hell out of his personal life. Dale drew in a deep breath, then another, and folded his arms.

"I have a dishwasher," he told her.

At her questioning look, he pulled open the stainless-steel door and slid out a rack. A most becoming blush tinted her round cheeks.

"Runs on electricity, saves time," he added.

"Some things are done best the old-fashioned way. Save the planet."

His irritation grew. "Hope you're not into only candlelight and battery power like most New Agers and I'm going to wake up to find organic sprouts for breakfast instead of bacon and eggs. I don't eat sprouts and I'm not into peace and love." Dale fetched a clean dish towel and began to dry the plates she stacked on the drainer.

Keira's lovely mouth wobbled. "Are you making fun of me?"

His stomach churned at her woebegone expression. He set down a plate. Damn it, had he lost all his manners? Since when had he been so rude?

He took another deep breath, wrestling for control, feeling his life was spinning away from him again.

"I'm sorry. I'm rather bad-tempered these days."

Especially when facing a woman who really turned him on, and made him feel even more out of sorts because each time he was around her, all he could think about was getting her naked.

Her peaches-and-cream complexion looked creamy and smooth, like fresh milk. The pink-and-green-flowered frock floated around her calves, hugging every inch of her curves. With her huge green eyes and the dark curls tumbling down her backside, Keira looked more like a forest nymph than a housekeeper.

"Why?"

That voice, it stroked over his clammy skin like velvet. So lush and melodious. Seductive and yet without the artifice of his sometime girlfriend, Melissa, who knew how to use her feminine skills to get her own way.

Keira was his housekeeper. It was none of her business why he was bad-tempered. She was his employee, nothing more.

Dale braced his hands on the counter and looked her in the eye.

"I told you before that I was in the hospital. It's only been two weeks since I returned to active duty. I'm still trying to find my feet again and learn to be civil." His mouth twisted. "Hard to be social and polite when you spend days and nights bare-assed, needles and tubes snaking out of your body, nurses waking you up every hour to check and see if you're still breathing."

Sympathy shone in her green eyes. "Why were you in the hospital?"

He dragged in a deep breath. Sooner or later, she'd hear the rumors. "I was tortured by demons."

She flinched.

"But I made it, and thanks to one of my men and his girlfriend, who saved my ass and got me airlifted to a hospital in time, I'm going to be fine. Great. Terrific."

"Do you remember anything?"

"Not much." Dale picked up the dish towel and began folding it into thirds.

"The man and his girlfriend who saved you, do they remember anything?"

He frowned. "Shay and Kelly told me there was a girl in the basement, but she vanished. His memory and Kelly's both got fogged. But he'll never forget the girl's face."

She drew in a deep breath. "Where is this Shay and his girlfriend? Maybe they can help you."

"They got married. Shay's away on training, took Kelly with him to live near the base. They won't be back for a few weeks."

Keira's expression remained shuttered. He stared at the counter, willing the memories to become stronger.

"I remember the little boy the demons threatened to torture and kill and how they said they'd make him die slowly if I didn't take his place. I'll never forget his name. Joshua."

"Josh," she murmured.

Dale studied her and Keira flushed again. "Most boys with that name are nicknamed Josh. What else do you remember?"

"There was a wolf there, a black wolf. And a woman. I think. I remember her scent." He rubbed an aching spot behind his throbbing temples. "Citrus and wood chips. No, maybe it was lilies and honey. It's a blur now."

Keira rummaged in the freezer, found a bag of frozen peas and handed it to him. "Here. This will help your headache."

"Thanks." He pressed it against his pounding skull. "How did you know my head hurt?"

"Your face is all compressed."

The cold bag felt good against his throbbing head. "I thought you were going to say my aura is red and black."

"It is." Keira dried her hands. "But I know you're not into that woo-woo stuff."

He had the grace to feel ashamed.

Dale tossed the peas back into the freezer and stuck out a palm. "Let's start over. I'm Dale Curtis, lieutenant commander of the best team of SEALs in the U.S. Navy, sometime classical pianist and foot-in-the-mouth jerk."

A tentative, sweet smile touched her mouth as she offered her hand. "Keira Solomon. Roving gypsy, Luminaire and quirky New Ager. Oh, and I happen to detest bean sprouts."

Her palm felt soft, the bones delicate beneath his big hand. Dale caressed it very gently, feeling the bandage he'd placed there, feeling loath to release her. The delicious scent of cookies, vanilla and almonds drifted from her, tendrils wrapping around him and invading his senses. She smelled like freshness and innocence.

She smelled like home.

Dale hadn't been home in a long, long time.

His guts clenched as he dropped her hand. She did not move but moistened her mouth, staring at him.

Riveting his gaze on her mouth, he moved closer. Closer still, his own lips parting. Hungering to sample her, see if she tasted as delicious as she smelled.

Dale reached for her, ready to cup her cheek and lower his mouth to hers.

A sharp scream cut through the air. Keira blinked, and paled.

Downstairs. Sully.

The SEAL never had nightmares. Ever.

"Oh, God, get it off me! Please! Someone help me!"

Chapter 6

Keira's gaze widened. "I never cleansed the basement with white light."

"I have to get down there." Dale ran into his study and removed his SIG Sauer 9 mm from the safe. Adrenaline pumping through his veins, he grabbed a flashlight and then bolted for the stairs. Keira raced behind him, two large white crystals clutched in her shaking hands.

More terrified screams. Sully was a stalwart SEAL. He'd faced down terrorists and fire demons. What the hell was down there? Dale toggled the light switch, but nothing happened. The basement remained dark.

Dark as the night the demons had tied him down and giggled, and then the hot, razorlike claws had gouged his torso…

Loaded pistol in one hand, flashlight in the other, he climbed down the first step.

Another haunting scream cut through the air. Fear slicked his throat. Immobilized by it, he could not move.

And then he heard Keira's ragged breathing behind him. With every ounce of his strength, he started down the stairs, pointing his flashlight at the steep steps. One of his men needed him.

Soothing white light suddenly cut through the darkness from behind him. He stopped and turned.

White light pulsed from the crystals Keira held. She bit her lip and handed him a crystal. "Take this. It will amplify your powers."

Another bloodcurdling cry cut through the air. Dale tucked the crystal into his pocket. He believed in his powers as a Mage and the gun's bullets, not magick stones.

Sweat beaded his forehead as he advanced toward the bunk beds.

The stench of sulfur and rotting flesh assaulted his nostrils. Dale gagged and forced himself to push on.

He swept the flashlights beam over the room. The lamp he'd left burning so Sully wouldn't be alone in the dark lay shattered on the floor. Dale ran to the wall. While in the hospital, he'd hired an electrician to install floodlights on a separate circuit breaker, in case of emergencies.

So the basement would always have plenty of light.... He flipped the switch, turning on the lights, revealing a nightmare.

Dale dropped his flashlight and stared.

Still lying on the bunk bed, Sully thrashed wildly, fighting with a gray, scaly thing atop him, yellowed fangs sinking into the ensign's neck. Blood slicked his gray T-shirt.

"Get it off me!" Sully screamed.

The ensign's cry was a sharp slap to his terrified mind.

Dale pointed his gun, feeling helpless all over again. His SEAL was being shredded by a demon and he could only stand there with a gun in hand, looking for the best shot.

"No!" Keira cried out. "I'll place the crystal on the demon's back and that will break its hold. Then you grab it and throw it to the floor."

Grab it. He pocketed the pistol, stretched out his hands and reached for his powers of telekinesis. Nothing. Drier than the Sahara, damn it.

As Keira advanced toward the demon, memories flashed. Fangs sinking into his side, the burning agony searing his flesh, his voice hoarse from screaming…

"Curt, please!"

The ensign's voice snapped him from immobility. He ran forward as Keira touched the demon's thick, sinewy tail with the crystal. The demon pulled his fangs from Sully and released a high-pitched screech like glass grinding in a blender.

Dale seized the demon, ignoring the stinging lash of its razor-thin tail whipping against his arms, and threw it on the ground. He withdrew his SIG and fired.

The bullets vaporized in midair. Damn! He spotted the poker by the fireplace and grabbed it.

The demon turned and hissed. Sully's blood covered its mouth, making it a red oval. Dale brought the poker down, slamming it on the triangular head.

Another banshee shriek. Dale hit it again. And again. Grayish blood splattered his bare legs, but he barely noticed. Hands wet with sweat, he kept a death grip on the weapon. The poker descended over and over. Had to kill it, make sure it would never hurt again.

"Dale! It's dead."

Keira's soft voice sliced through his frenzy. Dale stared at the floor. Quarter-size dents gouged the carpet. The demon had vanished, leaving behind a pile of gray goo. The poker clattered to the floor and he wiped his hands on his once-clean polo shirt, turning to Sully.

Keira had taken strips of the white sheet and was pressing them against the ragged gash on the ensign's throat. She also held the crystal against his neck, the stone's white glow fading.

Sully gripped the makeshift bandage, his gaze wide. "Thanks, Curt. Thought that thing was going to rip my throat out. What the hell was it? One minute I was passed out, the next this foul breath was in my face, and something burning my skin in the dark."

"It's an espy," Keira said. "Minor demon that sucks on its victim's blood. Prefers dark, damp places to hide and lie and wait like a spider. Goes after those who are helpless, likes to take from drunks." She gave Sully an apologetic glance. "Favorite prey."

Dale wiped his hands on his shirt again, wondering how she knew so much about this demon.

Sully shook his head. "Screaming like a baby. Feel stupid."

He dropped to the bunk bed and clapped a hand on the SEAL's shoulder. "You had a demon gnawing on you like a dinner bone. Nothing to be ashamed of."

Dale had screamed plenty in the dark, dank basement when the demons came after him…. He focused on Keira, who was staring at the mess on the carpet.

When her wide-eyed gaze met his, he gave a rueful smile. "Don't worry. Not going to ask you to clean that. I'll cut out the section and replace it. I doubt my carpet cleaner can remove demon blood."

Sully removed the stained makeshift bandage. The jagged gashes on his neck had knit together. "Amazing," Dale murmured. "The crystal heals."

"White-light therapy."

He still didn't embrace all this crazy stuff about crystals and energy, but the evidence was daunting.

Dozens of questions raced through his mind, but he tucked them away for later. "Can you walk?" he asked his friend.

Sully snorted. "No demon's gonna best me. I'm not a girl to be carried out of here on a stretcher from a puny demon attack." Then he colored deeply. "I'm sorry, sir. I didn't mean to imply…"

"Imply what, Sullivan?"

At his rough tone, Sully paled and looked at the floor. Silence descended, broken only by the tapping of Dale's foot on the floor. "Get upstairs, Sullivan."

The young SEAL sat up straight. "Yes, sir."

Once they were all back up in the kitchen, Dale went to phone for a cab, but Sully stopped him. "I'm sober now, sir. Nothing like a demon attack to chase away a good drunk. I'll see you tomorrow on base, sir."

Sir, not Curt. The formality had returned. All because Dale had once more lost his temper. Guilt pinched him, but he brushed it away.

He had demons to deal with.

Sully vanished in an eye blink. Dale pulled out a chair in the kitchen, gestured for Keira to sit by him. Interrogation time. But he had to be subtle. He shoved aside the niggling feeling of guilt. Had he his powers of telekinesis, he could have beaten the demon more easily.

"Tell me about this demon. How could it have gotten into my basement?"

"Demons are attracted to emotional darkness. It's my fault. I neglected to cleanse the basement today. It must have been lying in wait and when Sully slept, got hungry." Her lovely mouth wobbled. "I'm so sorry. I'll clean the basement now."

Dale gently clasped her wrist. "You weren't at fault. It's my house and I'm responsible for what happens here."

She looked up, her expression troubled. "I don't know if a regular cleansing with white light and crystals can help. Because there's bigger demons to worry about. And when they get here, all you can do is run screaming because they'll do worse than suck a little of your blood. They'll steal your soul and seal you screaming in hell. And no one can free you."

He gazed into her eyes, deeply concerned. What the hell had Keira Solomon run into?

"My team, the Phoenix Force, can handle demons. For now, why don't you get some sleep? It's been a long day."

"I have to cleanse the basement or more will arrive." Her eyes grew huge. "Maybe they're already down there."

Dale didn't want to return to that basement, but no way in hell was he going there alone. He followed her to her room, helping to unpack the bags of crystals and then carry them to the basement. He watched as she set several in each corner of the room and more on the steps, murmuring chants the whole time.

"If any are hiding, for now this should hold them at bay and prevent them from coming upstairs."

When they returned to the kitchen, she headed for the sink, but he stopped her.

"The dishes…"

"Told you. I have a dishwasher for that. I'll finish cleaning up. You get some rest."

And then, because he could not resist touching his lips to her soft skin, Dale brushed a gentle kiss against her knuckles. He watched as she headed toward her room, her hips gently swaying in a seductive dance. For the sec-

ond time that night, he found himself wondering about
Cassandra Sullivan's warning.

Her room felt icy cold. Keira lay beneath the blankets
and shivered.

Although it was summer in Virginia, she could not
escape the chill of knowing a demon had invaded the
sanctuary of Dale's home.

After Dale had finally trudged upstairs, his heavy
tread indicating his exhaustion, she'd gone down into
the basement and cleaned up the mess. It had taken all
her courage and strength.

She knew, more than Dale did, exactly how vulnerable this house was to dark forces.

Demons could still break through the frail barrier of
white light and creep in through cracks between the win-
dowsills, wiggle their way into the basement.

She'd dozed off for a couple of hours. Now, the blue
lights of the small clock radio glowed three o'clock, the
hour of demons.

The thick band around her upper arm felt reassuring
and did not cut into her skin. The reminder of her tie to
Dale Curtis would protect her against the Centurions.
But what would protect Dale? Her crystals were drained
and needed replenishing.

How much more evil was hiding below in the dark?

Keira threw back the covers and went to the dresser.
Her meager possessions were in the top drawer, including the last crystal that held pure white light. Every time
the demons allowed her freedom, she used her spare time
to learn the healing arts of Luminaires, and used some
of the money they gave her to lure fresh victims to purchase crystals.

She cupped it in her hands, relishing the purity and

soothing peace, then placed it on the nightstand by the bed. As she started to drift back to sleep, something rattled in the kitchen.

Trembling, she gripped the bedcovers. Perspiration soaked the clean bed sheets. *Calm down, demons don't invade the kitchen late at night....*

But restless men tortured by them did.

Keira threw back the sheets and shrugged into her white terry-cloth robe. She slipped out of her bedroom and stood at the kitchen door.

Wearing a robe of his own, Lt. Commander Dale Curtis stood at the opened refrigerator door, staring at the contents.

Keira cleared her throat. "See anything good?"

Fork held out like a weapon, he whirled around. Dale relaxed when he saw her. "Couldn't sleep. Sorry I woke you."

"I was awake, as well." She turned on the overhead lights, dimming them.

Dale looked haggard beneath the soft illumination. She wanted to go to him, assure him all would be well and he could safely sleep again in his own house. But she knew it would be a lie.

Because nothing was safe until the Centurions were put in hell for good. The demons, once Roman soldiers in their time, were condemned to the netherworld for their cowardice, never to walk in flesh until they acquired the courage they lacked in battle.

When they'd found a way to escape hell, they found a shortcut to becoming corporeal. By torturing good, brave men, and stealing their strength, they became solid form and were able to enjoy the pleasures they had in Roman times.

They had found the bravest man of all in Dale Curtis.

He poured a glass of milk, offered her one. She shook her head. Her stomach was too queasy. Dale lifted the top of the glass cake holder and cut a slice. Her gaze wandered to the robe's hem, stopping just above his knees, showing his strong calves.

She joined him at the table.

"Amazing. Absolutely delicious."

He licked the tines of his fork, and a tingle shot through her body as she watched his tongue slowly stroke the utensil. Dale closed his eyes, long, black lashes lying against his stark cheeks. His face was all angles and planes, but his eyes, laser-sharp, were his most arresting feature.

Dale's mouth, usually pinched and compressed, now relaxed. He licked his lips and she sensed he did so on purpose. Fascinated, she watched, wondering what it would feel like to have Dale Curtis's mouth pressed over hers, his tongue tasting her with the same pleasure he now exhibited tasting her cake.

His eyes flew open and he looked at her with amusement as heat filled her cheeks.

"It's very good cake." He pushed away his barely touched slice.

"You're not having more?"

"Just a taste. I have to work back slowly to getting my strength. Too many calories and I'll go to fat." He drained the milk.

Keira swiped a finger through the frosting and licked her finger. "Indulging yourself once in a while is permitted."

"Not for me."

"Why are you so rigid?"

"I'm navy. It's part of my life. Discipline and training, that's what makes a SEAL. And endurance and strength."

"You're not a SEAL or a commander here in your home. So kick off your shoes and relax. Have a slice of cake. A whole slice." Keira sighed with renewed pleasure at the enticing taste of the chocolate. "Life is short and you never know what tomorrow brings, so enjoy every moment. That's my philosophy."

"And never letting down my guard is mine." Dale reached over and stroked a corner of her lip, wiping off frosting with a finger.

He brought it to his mouth. Keira's heart kicked hard as he licked his finger. Her body felt loose and wanting.

Dale's gray gaze burned like fire. He looked hungry, but not for food. She drew back. She couldn't risk liking this man. Or lowering her guard and trusting him.

"After we work together, you'll get to relax and sleep," she told him.

"I haven't slept through the night in a long time."

"When we start working on fine-tuning your inner frequencies, you'll have to relax and let down your guard."

Dale stiffened. "Impossible. The moment I let down my guard, look what happens. I get a damn demon in my basement attacking one of my men. I should have brought Sully up here, let him sleep in the guest room."

"It's not your fault."

"Maybe. But there is plenty of evil out there in the world and I'm not allowing it to ruin the lives of innocents."

Keira sighed. "Stop focusing on the bad guys. There will always be the bad guys out there. You have to channel positive energy to beat back the darkness inside you."

"Evil must be punished. There's no gray area about it. You saw the demon attacking Sully. You think that should be pardoned?" Dale threw out the rest of the cake, went to the sink and washed his plate.

"No. But if you consistently look for the bad, you'll find only the bad. You have to look for the good in people, as well."

He needed to heal and recover. Instead, the man held himself as rigidly as a ruler and refused to indulge in an entire slice of cake.

"Discipline and training helped me to become a SEAL and it'll help me regain my strength."

"I heard SEALs are the best of the best. But you can't focus all your time on searching for evil. There is good in the world."

Keira had to believe it, had to find the good each time the Centurions released her. The day her inner white light died, she would want to die, as well.

"That's not my job, to look for the good—it's to search out the evil and eliminate it so other Americans can sleep through the night." He traced a line on the tablecloth.

Her heart ached for the man. He risked his life so others could experience peace, but he enjoyed none himself. She went to the refrigerator to get some juice and paused, remembering what she'd seen earlier. Tacked to the refrigerator door was a child's crayon drawing of a man next to an American flag. There was also a photo of a little boy blowing out candles on a cake, flanked by an adoring couple.

A note was pinned to the refrigerator. She read it aloud.

"'We can't thank you enough for what you did for our son. Because of you, Josh is celebrating his seventh birthday. You are a true hero. Josh drew this picture of you and we thought you'd like to have it.'"

She turned and saw him quietly watching her.

"You keep this on your fridge. So you must believe in

some good in people. Helping people isn't wrong. Look at how you saved this little boy."

Dale's mouth tightened. "For every Josh I manage to save, or my team manages to save, there's four more the monsters get to first. That's what keeps me up at night."

This brave man, who'd sacrificed himself to save children, had suffered greatly, still suffered. *All my fault,* she thought, the hollow ache in her chest intensifying.

She must make amends.

Keira went into her bedroom and cupped the small white crystal in her palms. Dale had given so much for others. This was one small act she could do for him.

When she returned, he was standing at the sink, looking out the window, into the dark. She placed the stone in his hands.

"Put this by your bedside, near your head. The crystal's white light will chase away bad energy and help you sleep. I promise it. It's worked for me."

Her fingers brushed against his strong, calloused ones. Dale's masculine scent of citrus and pine teased her nostrils.

"What about you?"

She shrugged. "Cake. And if that doesn't work, at least I'll enjoy the remedy."

Dale smiled. "Thanks. Good night."

Keira watched him walk away, the stone clutched tight in his palm.

Upstairs, Dale placed Keira's stone on his nightstand.

He cracked open a book, but could not concentrate. There was no peace at night. He would power up the laptop and surf the internet, check emails, read reports or sometimes would read one of the well-worn books he loved.

The bottles of prescription sleep aids sat untouched in his medicine chest. He refused to take them. Sinking into a deep sleep meant risking vulnerability, slowing his reaction time if he were attacked.

Always, there was a bedside lamp burning.

Some nights, he would lie down and close his eyes and breathe deeply, and drift into a peaceful sleep. And then the nightmares would begin.

They were varied, but threaded through all was a common theme. He was strapped down with heavy chains in the dark basement, listening to the sound of his blood dripping on the floor, wanting to submit to death. And then he'd heard screams, a child's screams. Little Josh, crying for his dad as the demons giggled and took him to the basement. Then a terrible silence. More footsteps and another child's screams as the demons hauled them, one by one, to the basement to die. And he struggled in the grip of the chains, helpless to stop their deaths, their shrill screams punctuating the air over and over....

And Keira wanted to practice her New Age mojo on him? He was beyond magick stones and chants, especially if it meant giving up control.

Drowsiness engulfed him, but this time he did not fight it.

Dale closed his eyes and surrendered. And dreamed.

Not of dark basements and crying, terrified children, but a white room filled with white light, and an eggshell-white bed, soft as lamb's wool.

Keira lay upon the bed, her long dark curls spread across a bank of downy pillows.

She wore a sheer white nightgown that clung to her generous curves and rode up nearly to her thigh, showing the shapely angle of her calf. Soft as the bed itself, and the pure light pulsing through the room, chasing away every single dark shadow.

No demons here.

Eyes of green sparkled with seductive promise. So sweet and pretty.

"I want you," she whispered. "I shouldn't, but I can't resist."

"Take off your gown."

He barely recognized his rough voice, harsh with command. Dale gripped the bedpost, watching as she tugged the fabric over her head and tossed it aside.

Her breasts were round and full, tipped with coral nipples. His gaze tracked down her belly to the small indent of her naval. Blood rushed to his groin, causing his slight erection to harden to stone.

Stretching out her slender arms, she beckoned to him. "Let me heal you."

His body tightened. This was a dream, but her scent of vanilla and lilies pulled at him. He did not want to awaken. Dale shrugged out of his robe. Gathering her in his arms, he kissed her deeply. She tasted like blackberry wine and sweet chocolate, like sin and innocence.

Keira tasted like all his tomorrows.

Groaning, he fisted a hand in her long hair and drew her closer, against the hardness of his body. Her softness molded against him as he kissed her hard and deep.

He felt like a teenager with his first woman. Dale mapped her body with his trembling hands, tracing each square inch of her skin. Fingertips trailed over her round, slender shoulders, caressed the knobby points of her collarbone. Her body was rounded and supple, giving and pliant. He kissed the juncture of shoulder and neck, tasting the salt of her body. A shudder coursed through her as she shifted beneath him.

He continued kissing her warm flesh, tensing his own body for better control, to keep from ruthlessly plunging into her. His mouth trailed a line to the top of one firm breast. When he encased her hardened nipple with his mouth, she gave a startled cry and arched.

But it had been too long since he'd had sex, and he could no longer wait. Dale mounted her naked body and guided his rigid penis to her soft wetness.

His heart wanted to explode when he sank into her.

Never had he felt such astounding bliss.

She was a hot, wet, silky fist around his cock. So tight and warm he wanted to die with shuddering pleasure. He thrust hard and deep and, with a strangled groan, came hard and fast, pumping his seed deep inside her. For a wild moment, knowing it was a dream, he imagined she was his wife and they were creating a child. A family of his own at last.

Coming home to Keira each night, children chattering at the dinner table, helping her clean up after dinner and then once the kids were asleep, taking her by the hand into their bedroom and making love to her long into the night.

Dazed with erotic pleasure and drunk on hope, he gazed down lovingly at the woman lying naked beneath him.

And looked straight into the face of a grinning Centurion demon.

Chapter 7

Dale avoided Keira for the next two days. Every morning, he was gone before she woke. At night, he'd return late, leaving her a polite note thanking her for the meal she'd cooked for him and left in the refrigerator.

But each night the strains of opera or classical music floated upstairs. The man did not like silence.

He was postponing their session. Dark forces were at work and Keira didn't know how long she had before the Centurions broke free and found her.

If she didn't help him to cleanse away the dark energy and become stronger, the demons would make fast work of him. Dale was her only hope for vanquishing the Centurions.

Two nights ago, his screams had awakened her. Running to his room, she'd seen him caught in the throes of a nightmare, thrashing in the damp sheets of his bed. Horrified, she picked up the crystal on the nightstand, only to realize she'd given him the wrong one.

Not a crystal for peace, but clarity.

Keira had replaced the crystal with an amethyst and run it over his perspiring forehead. She smoothed back his damp hair and watched him finally ease into a deep, dreamless sleep. Such an honorable, courageous man of great strength. A man of discipline and tremendous power, and loyalty. Something inside her had turned to restless yearning as she watched him sleep. Then finally, she'd snapped off the light and left his bedroom.

Her own sleep remained restless and edgy.

Nights brought on erotic dreams of Dale making love to her in a pure white bed, his big body moving over hers. She woke trembling, perspiration covering her skin, her heart thudding in erratic beats and her body tight with longing.

With the money he'd given her, Keira bought a massage table and new equipment. She paid extra to have the table delivered by late afternoon to an empty upstairs bedroom.

The bedroom was big, with two large windows and a western exposure to catch lots of sunlight. The walls were painted a lemon yellow, except for one mirrored wall. The mirror would reflect the white light and aid in the sessions, she decided.

The room had no furniture, which was very odd. But perhaps he'd planned to renovate.

She opened the walk-in closet and saw several boxes. Curious, she knelt down and opened one.

Baby clothes. Chest tight, she combed through them, removing an adorable little pink dress. A lump rose in her throat. Had Dale planned this room as a nursery? Had he lost a child?

With great reverence, she closed the box, then shut

the door and smudged the room with sage to cleanse it of sadness.

That night when he arrived home, she was fixing dinner. The front door slammed and the sounds of opera filled the air. Like each night, as soon as he came home, he turned on the CD player in the living room.

Dale entered the kitchen, carrying a bouquet of fresh yellow daisies. Wearing a hat and a stiff-looking uniform, he looked quite handsome and very military. Even his shoes were mirror bright.

Cellophane crackled as Dale handed her the bouquet. "I've been buried in meetings with brass the past two days and it's been nice to come home to a real meal."

Keira buried her nose in the daisies to hide her smile. No one had ever given her flowers before.

"Thank you," she said.

He shrugged. "It's a small gesture to show my appreciation." He did not smile. The rigid navy commander returned.

Remnants of a price tag were still on the clear wrapping. The flowers were a gesture, a meaningless one. Keira pushed aside her small disappointment. It would not ruin her joy of the moment. She tore off the cellophane, found a vase in the cabinet and filled it with water, then put the daisies inside and placed the vase on the table. "After dinner, we'll start on your first session."

Dale shook his head. "I have a report to write. I'll eat in my study."

"The work can wait. This can't."

His brows drew together as his mouth thinned. The navy commander didn't like being ordered around. Tough.

"Unless you'd like more imps in your office, chewing on your report and your computer cables and who knows what else."

"You cleansed my house."

"But you're the conduit, the reason why they're attracted here. This—" she spread her arms wide "—is only a house."

He broached the distance between them, his eyes steely gray. "You're accusing me of being a magnet for demons."

Keira didn't back off, even as he got close enough to kiss her. "Yes."

He closed his eyes, his shoulders going rigid. Guilt washed over her. Dale Curtis had a normal life before she'd dug her claws into him, literally. He could work all night and never have to worry about an imp tearing apart his papers.

"I'll offer you a compromise. I'll serve your dinner in your study, and you can work and then at ten, you come upstairs for your first session."

Dale's eyes flew open. "I don't compromise."

"Fine. Then I'll leave, you can be overcome by demons and you won't have to worry about paperwork anymore."

Holding her breath, she watched to see if her bluff worked. His jaw tightened so hard, she could have used it to pound nails. Finally he nodded. "I'll be in my study."

As she exhaled a shaky breath, he warned, "I don't believe in magick stones and herbs and all that feel-good stuff. This isn't going to work."

Keira gave him a serene smile. "Don't worry. I'll use some of my magick relaxing potion on you and you'll be skipping down the hall and tossing flowers everywhere. Works like a charm."

"What are you, a witch?"

"I've been called much worse."

Chapter 8

Her client was not very cooperative.

At first, he'd refused to change into more comfortable clothing. When he finally did and entered the room she'd set up for therapy, he frowned.

"Not this room. It's off-limits."

"There are no other empty rooms." She tilted her head. "Unless you wish to do this in your study?"

He looked at her as if she'd suggested painting his man-cave pink and decorating it with stuffed animals.

Scented candles burned on a table she'd lugged up the stairs. Colorful crystals were arranged around the ring of glowing candles and the slow, steady beat of a drumming circle played on the portable CD player. Keira had brought the daisies into the room as well, and turned off the harsh overhead lights.

Dale took one look at the massage table and shook his head.

"If I lie down on that, I'll fall asleep. I have to finish that report after you finish your New Age mojo crap."

Keira refused to let his gruff insult sway her. She knew he was scared, and hiding it.

"Falling asleep is good. I want you to relax. Take off your shoes and lie down."

He climbed onto the table and stretched out, stiff as a wood casket. *No, don't think of coffins and death.* She cleared her mind of negativity, thought of a field filled with sunflowers lifting their heads to the sun's caress, a cloudless blue sky and walking barefoot through a lush field of soft grass.

She glanced at her patient. Dale folded his arms across his chest.

"It smells like a flower bed in here," he grumbled.

"Lavender and rose. Aromatherapy."

He gave a derisive snort.

"Why are you so opposed to this? You're a Primary Mage. Magick runs in your veins. You need to stop and smell the roses once in a while."

"I'm a SEAL commander first. I don't stop to smell the roses because the enemy probably planted an IED in the flower bed."

"IED." She experimented with the unfamiliar word.

"Improvised explosive device. One caught one of my SEALs off guard in Afghanistan. He was killed."

Her heart wrenched again. Dale had dealt with the worst of humanity as well as demons. "The bomb blew him up."

Dale sat up, his gaze suddenly guarded. "No, a fire demon burned him to death."

And suddenly she made the connection. Dale wasn't an ordinary navy SEAL and neither was his team. They were fighting both human and paranormal enemies.

He watched her carefully. "You're not supposed to know that, but if we're going to work closely together, there is no way of avoiding it. I'll have to scrub your memories when you leave my employment."

If I live long enough, she thought.

"I'll start with a session of reflexology." She started to remove his socks and he bolted upright.

"Leave them on."

"It works better on bare feet."

"I never go barefoot."

Then she remembered. He'd been barefoot in the basement and the demons whispered to him that his feet were next—her claws would gouge his soles so deep, he'd be crippled for life.

"Forget the reflexology. We can work on that later. Let's try aligning your energy centers. Lie down. All I'm going to do is use the crystals."

Keira selected a large lavender crystal and started to wave the stone over his body, but he remained tense, his aura so dark she could barely see it flickering in the dimmed light. She set the stones back on the table. "I'm going to leave the room for a minute. I want you to remove your shirt and lie on your stomach."

Dale raised himself up on his elbows. "Why? More woo-woo crap?"

Irritation surged, but she kept her voice calm and even. "Woo-woo massages. Can't be beat for getting those stiff upper lips in the navy to relax. You'll enjoy it. Trust me."

The look on his face told her this man had not trusted anyone in a long time. She knew his scars, knew the length and depth of each one. They were all on his torso and belly and arms and legs. Not his back.

She walked out of the room, doing some deep breathing herself. Dale was one stubborn man.

When she returned, he was lying on his stomach, head cradled in his folded arms. His shirt lay folded neatly on a nearby chair.

She hesitated. The last time she'd faced this man on a table, she'd been a wolf, her sharp claws gouging out his flesh. Quivering, she stared at him.

Calm down. You're in control. Think calming, peaceful thoughts.

A field of sunflowers, lush grass against her bare feet…

She stared at the strong muscles of his back and something stirred inside her. A grass field…lying in the grass, Dale's strong, naked body covering hers as they made love…

Okay. Not so peaceful or calming. Summoning all her discipline, she focused on her task. He needed healing. She held the thought in her mind.

Keira changed the CD on the player.

Dale raised his head, his brows drawn together. "You like classical music?"

"No, but I know you do. You play it every night when you return home. This is to help you relax."

She removed a bottle of lavender lotion from her woven basket and poured a small amount into her palms, rubbing them briskly.

Hovering just above the strong muscles of his back, she hesitated. So masculine and rugged, Dale Curtis was chiseled marble. The rich scent of lavender permeated the air, slicing through the thick vanilla, cloves and cinnamon.

Dale's eyes began to close.

"Just relax," she whispered. "Don't think. Don't talk. Breathe. And relax. Let me remove all your cares."

Her fingers smoothed the lotion over his skin. The

man was a little thin, but his back was ridged with muscle and sinew. Keira's hands quivered as she stroked over his back, working the lotion into his thirsty skin.

The camouflage pants hugged his taut buttocks. She worked the lotion into his skin, kneading stiffened muscles and sighing with pleasure as she touched him. He reminded her of a marble sculpture, masculine beauty at its finest. Every time she stroked over his skin, shivers of pleasure coursed through her.

Then he turned his head and opened his eyes, looking at her.

"You're all flushed," he said drowsily.

She put her hands to her burning cheeks. "It's hot in here."

His gaze dropped to her breasts, where her nipples stood out like exclamation points against the loose, flowing print dress.

This time, Keira was the one folding her arms across her chest.

Interest flared in his expression as his eyes darkened. Dale's gaze swept down the length of her dress to the hemline ending above her knee.

"You have very nice legs," he murmured.

"I think that's enough for tonight. It's getting late and I have to get up early."

"It's not late."

She thought rapidly. "I have a lot to do tomorrow. Need to get an early start, find a local greenhouse and buy pants. I mean, plants. Herbs. Rosemary, stuff like that."

"You don't need to fear me," he said softly. "Keira. Lovely name. Lovely legs."

Dale started to raise himself up, then glanced down at his torso. A dark flush covered his cheeks and he dropped back to the table.

"I'd like to be alone."

Her heart dropped to her stomach. He did not want her seeing his scars. A lump rose in her throat. *I'm sorry. I'm so sorry.*

"Tomorrow night, we'll start on the real work with the aromatherapy and crystals," she told him.

"Tomorrow night I'm busy. I don't have time for this crap."

Gone was the camaraderie and the progress she'd made. He'd turned back into himself, shutting her out.

It's your fault. Do you really think healing sessions with white light would make up for all you've done?

She closed the door gently behind her on the way out, and then went into her bedroom. All the crystals arranged in a pretty pattern on the nightstand turned dull and lifeless, reflecting her inner misery.

Chapter 9

It had been a bitch of a morning.

First, he'd awakened late and when he'd come down-stairs, dressed and ready to grab a cup of Keira's excel-lent coffee, he found no coffee. No breakfast, and the dinner dishes still piled in the sink.

Dale hated disorganization. And in his house, his ref-uge, the sole place he could exert a little control in a cha-otic world?

Unacceptable.

He knew she was playing hardball. Ever since the massage five days ago, he kept putting off another ther-apy session. Blaming the intense training sessions in the new firestorm chamber now that most of his team had returned from deployment, Dale dodged her, returning home late each night and leaving early for the base every morning. Much as he hated to admit it, he did enjoy the homey touches she'd brought into his life, from the delicious coffee to the dinners, to knowing there was someone waiting for him when he walked through the door.

Even if the someone was nagging him to do things he firmly resisted.

His housekeeper sat at the breakfast bar, reading a book. She did not glance up.

"Miss Solomon, I hired you to keep house and make coffee, not read books."

She finally glanced up. "You hired me as your personal psi therapist. When you give me an exact time for the second session, I'll start making coffee again."

Infuriated, he snatched the book from her hands and set it on the counter. "Coffee. Now. That's an order."

She plucked at her colorful skirt. "Does this look like a regulation navy uniform? Ah, think not. You're not my commanding officer."

"I am your employer. Get to work."

"Are you willing to do a second session tonight?"

"No."

"Then make it yourself."

Keira picked the book up and resumed reading.

Dumbstruck, he stared at her, feeling everything slip out of his control once more. No way was he consenting to her New Age crap, opening himself up and becoming vulnerable. Hell, every time he glanced in the mirror at his messed-up body, it was a reminder of how helpless he'd been.

He looked at his watch. Damn it, no time to argue. Today they started training with real flames and he needed his men alert and ready.

"This kitchen had better be spotless when I return. I expect dinner promptly at seven. As for your unorthodox, unregulated session…" He struggled with his temper. "You can kiss my navy-regulation trouser-covered ass."

Keira did not glance up as he slammed the door behind him.

The drive to the base took forever. He barely muttered greetings to his staff and concentrated on PT, a six-mile run with his men. Dale pushed himself for another mile, determined to prove he was back on top.

Even though he felt lower than the dirt on his running shoes.

After a quick shower, he headed for his office, snapping at several staff members who kept asking if he was all right. Would they ever leave him alone?

He *was* in a bad mood. Dreams of hot, intense sex with Keira had plagued him all night, leaving him frustrated and edgy. Then he'd woken up to find his house in complete disorder, and a battle of wills waged on the front lines of his kitchen.

Once ensconced in his office, Dale sat at his desk and stared at the stacks of paperwork. Lt. Ted Morrison, his executive officer, was on mandatory training, something he'd put off while Dale was recovering. Ted had been in charge while Dale was on medical leave.

ST 21's new firestorm chamber cost the government a chunk of change and now he had to justify it with form after form. Keegan was right. He was losing his touch with his men, and needed to get back into the field with them.

He also needed coffee.

There was a tapping sound on his door.

"Come in," he barked.

Ensign Robyn Lees entered, a mug filled with steaming coffee on a tray. "Your coffee, sir," she said.

Dale gestured to the desk. She set it down and hovered.

He took a sip and choked. "Sailor, what the hell is this sludge?"

Ensign Lees raised her brows. "I'm sorry, sir, I usually make the coffee but today Artie made it and…"

"I don't need excuses, I need a fresh cup of coffee that doesn't taste like sewer water. Now!"

"Are you all right, sir? You're not acting yourself lately." Concern etched her pretty, freckled face.

Damn it, if another person on his staff asked that question, he'd hang them out to dry. Growling low in his throat, Dale flung out a hand. A ball of dark gray energy shot out of his palm, missing the ensign by inches, and smashed into a table, shattering a vase.

Her eyes widened, and then she hissed at him and vanished.

Dale stared at his hands. Darkness. Demon darkness, just like Keira had warned.

He pushed back his chair and stood in time to see a gray tail vanish beneath the credenza.

Dale got on his knees and peered under the credenza and saw a small gray cat curled in the corner, claws extended, eyes glaring at him.

All of ST 21's support staff were paranormals. Robyn was a Halfling, a cat shifter. "Robyn, come out. Please. I'm sorry."

More hissing. The cat refused to budge.

Dale grappled for control. Great start to the day. He was losing control of his temper and had nearly hurt an ensign whose biggest sin was serving lousy coffee.

Now he had to deal with an angry cat who refused to shift back into her human form. Hell, the way he acted lately, he was lucky his entire staff didn't start using their powers for protection.

"Darling, what are you doing on the floor?"

Startled, he reared up and banged his head on the credenza. Biting back a curse, he crawled backward and stood, brushing at his trousers. A tall, slim blonde stood in the doorway. She closed the door.

"Melissa. Why are you here?"

The last thing he needed was a visit from his some-time girlfriend.

"Everyone's talking about the admiral's birthday ball next week. All the top D.C. politicians will be there. I thought I'd shop for a new gown and came to see if you needed your dress whites dry-cleaned."

Silence hung in the air.

"Of course you received an invitation," she prompted.

"Yes." It was somewhere in the pile of mail he'd tossed aside.

Relief flickered on her face. "Then you'll need a proper escort. Someone experienced in political and military protocol."

Of course. Melissa was skilled in navigating through those murky waters. She enjoyed rubbing shoulders with powerful movers and shakers.

Today she wore a dress that accented her slender fig-ure and thin shoulders. At his silence, she sidled up to him, and ran a hand up his chest. "Darling, I haven't seen you in forever. I miss you."

"You saw me in the hospital. For about five minutes." Dale removed her hand.

She actually pouted. "And you so ill, not able to stand company. What was I to do?"

Stay with me, he thought. Keira would have. Keira, with her stubbornness, refusing to let his gruffness drive her off.

Melissa trailed her manicured hand down his chest. "I was a bad girl for running off and leaving you alone. Let me make it up to you, Dale."

Melissa liked parties and money and wearing designer

dresses. Keira wore wild lime prints with pink-and-orange flowers, gauzy material that floated around her long legs. Keira didn't pin her hair up in a tight bun and fasten it with jeweled clips like Melissa, but let it flow wild and free, like a horse's mane.

A soft meow sounded beneath the credenza.

Robyn. He'd forgotten about her. Dale turned to the credenza. "Kitty, please come out. It's okay now."

Finally, Robyn, still in cat form, crawled out. Dale scooped her into his arms and she began to purr.

"You don't own a cat." Melissa looked more bewildered.

The ensign looked at her and hissed.

"Melissa, I'm busy. I'll call you later."

Then, because she was right, he did need an escort to the ball, he gave her a quick kiss on her cheek.

When Melissa left his office, he set Robyn down on the floor. "Ensign Robyn Lees, shift back now. That's an order."

When she did, clothing herself through magick, he aimed her a stern look. "Shape-shifting on the compound without permission or in nonemergency cases is expressly prohibited. I need every man and woman on this team alert and aware. We cannot allow norms to know what we are. From now on, there will be no shifting. Understood?"

"Yes, sir."

He gave a rueful smile. "And that goes for myself, as well. No displays of power. I apologize for that."

"It probably was the coffee, sir. Does taste like bilge water."

He nodded. "Call my house and tell my housekeeper to bring over the manila envelope I left on the kitchen counter. You may meet her at the gate. She doesn't have security clearance. I need those forms ASAP."

Robyn left, returning a while later with another cup of coffee. He sipped and sighed with relief. Finally.

The ensign lingered before his desk, her blue eyes sparking with mischief.

"What is it?"

"I called your house, sir, and asked your housekeeper to bring the envelope, exactly as you instructed."

Dale set the mug down on his cluttered desk. "And?"

"I'd rather not say what she told me."

"Tell me exactly what Miss Solomon said."

"She said she's not driving to the base. As for your report, you can kiss her floral-print nonregulation ass."

Leather creaked as Dale leaned back in his chair. An unfamiliar tickle began in his throat, and spread. He threw back his head and released a loud bark of laughter.

Gods, it felt so good to laugh again!

Ensign Lees smiled. "She was very nice and asked if anything happened. And I told her you got a little short-tempered."

Dale stopped laughing. Damn.

"She said you were in a bad mood and if I made the hazelnut coffee with the pinch of ginseng she sent with you a few days ago, you wouldn't be such a bear. The ginseng gives you balance. It's in the coffee she makes for you each morning. When she makes it."

Dale stopped laughing and sniffed his coffee. "I'll be damned," he murmured.

"Do you want me to drive to your house and get the envelope, sir?"

"I'll get it myself at lunch. Go round up my men. Training session at oh-eight-hundred."

As she started to leave, he saluted her with the mug. "Thank you, Ensign Lees."

Without batting an eyelash, the ensign meowed. "You're welcome, sir."

The morning training session with the portable, dry, chem-fire packs hadn't gone well. He'd pushed and pushed his SEALs, but only Sully, with his powers of teleportation, had successfully defeated the flames in the chamber. Dakota, Dallas and Renegade, all Draicon werewolves, sustained minor burns and even J.T., with his powers of telekinesis, had failed.

Greg, the new guy, had shifted into a tiger and actually charged the flames in a foolhardy show of bravado. Greg was still trying to prove himself to the team and Dale had to reel in his leash.

The half-bred demon training them had extensive knowledge of fire demons. Thad was patient. But Dale was not. He needed his men ready to deploy. All SEALs on the Phoenix Force had to become expert in defeating the flames before the other SEALs under his command could use the chamber.

After losing a SEAL to a fire demon in Afghanistan, he never wanted the team to be caught off guard. Adam was still an aching spot in his gut.

Exhausted, Dale drove home for lunch, intending to pick up his forms and then head back to base for a stale sandwich. Part of him itched to see if Keira had continued to defy him. He longed to have her banter with him, drive away the thick darkness clogging his emotions.

The house was quiet when he walked in and slammed the door behind him. Dale entered the kitchen and found Keira pulling a roast from the oven.

The savory smells of beef and wine sauce teased his nostrils. His stomach issued an approving growl.

She turned, face flushed from the heat. "Great timing. Lunch is almost ready."

Dale narrowed his eyes. "I'm only here to pick up my report."

"And why waste a good meal as long as you're here?" She gestured to a place setting on the table. "Sit down. This won't take long."

Because he was starved, and it smelled good, he sat. Dale looked around the sparkling kitchen. "You did as I asked. Good."

He was partly disappointed she'd not defied him. For some reason, he liked sparring with her. It invigorated him and he enjoyed seeing the spark in her eyes.

"Don't look in the guest bathroom." With an impish grin, she began slicing the beef.

Dale went into the guest bathroom down the hall. All seemed normal. He pushed back the shower curtain.

All the dishes from the kitchen sink were neatly piled in the bathtub.

Laughter tickled his throat. He snorted and then shut the curtain, assuming his most severe look as he returned to the kitchen and began to eat.

"Like your new bathroom decor?" Keira winked as she spooned vegetables onto his plate.

Damn, this woman was going to get the best of him yet.

He cut the meat, marveling at the luxury of having a hot lunch. It was tender and flavored with spices. Suddenly famished, he ate in a hurry. Keira brought him a cup of hot tea and joined him.

Wiping his mouth with the linen napkin, he nodded. "Thanks. I haven't had such a delicious lunch in ages."

She gestured to the white bandage on his left arm. "What happened?"

"Small burn. Training session."

"I'd hate to see what happens when you're out of training."

He sipped his tea. "It's why we train. We're SEALs. If my men slack on their training, they become ineffective. The more training, the better they're equipped and less likely they are to die."

Her gaze grew troubled. "Have you ever lost a SEAL?"

Dale set down the teacup. "Yes. Remember I told you about this."

"I'm sorry. What was his name?"

Under the rules of ST 21, they were not to mention those who'd passed. Their team was top secret and the public could not know details. But a hollow ache settled in his chest as he thought of Adam.

Keira touched his arm gently. "You said you're going to scrub my memories when I leave your employ, so why not talk about him now?"

And so he found himself talking about Adam and the shifter's incredible bravery, his wit and how important he'd been to the team. She listened, not interrupting, and her gaze didn't wander in boredom as Melissa's would have.

He put their dirty dishes in the clean sink and washed them by hand. Keira left, returning with a first-aid kit. She gestured for him to sit at the table, took out bandages and ointment and then removed the hastily applied bandage he'd slapped on his arm.

"This is a real nasty burn."

"I've had worse." He didn't want medics fussing over him, not now, when he was trying to prove to his team he was strong.

She uncapped the tube of antibiotic ointment and spread it over the burn. "I'm guessing that your body has an increased capacity to heal, since you're a Primary Mage. But if you're undernourished and your powers aren't up to par, that will take longer, as well."

As she finished bandaging his arm, he flexed his fingers. "Thanks. I had planned to bandage it better later, when my men weren't around."

"Why didn't you want them to see you were hurt?"

"We all had a few minor burns. I'm their leader, and have to set an example."

"You should think of yourself for a change. There's nothing wrong with being a little selfish," she said.

Dale shook his head. "Self-centered people have no place in the teams. SEALs function as a team, and we're tighter than family. Brothers to the end." He paused and thought of Adam. "I would die for my men, and they'd die the same for me. I rely on them."

Keira rolled the bandages. "I believe the only person you can really rely on is yourself. People will let you down. I've always found it better to be self-sufficient."

"You don't believe in teamwork?"

"I believe in myself and my abilities. I've seen the results of teamwork when the team isn't working to benefit anyone but themselves. Some use teamwork as an excuse to manipulate others."

Then her expression tightened, something so unusual for her, Dale wondered what caused it. Who had hurt her so badly she didn't want to get involved with anyone else?

"Who manipulated you?"

She shrugged. "Doesn't matter. I'm not into teamwork. I fly solo. I'd rather fend for myself and watch my back."

"My men watch my six, and I do the same for them. We're tighter than family."

Scowling, she packed the bandages back into the first-aid kit. "Very nice. Sounds like you're all machines in the military. I'd rather be freethinking and individualist than a cog in a wheel like you are."

Dale's temper slipped a few notches. He kept his voice even. "SEALs learn to think for themselves, adapt and survive. My team is extremely flexible. They must be, to survive in terrain from the Arctic to the jungles of South America. Rules and discipline enable us to function as a unit and work together to defeat evil."

Keira turned away, but not before he caught a glimpse of despair in her eyes. "Some evil is tougher to defeat than others. Sometimes I wonder if it can ever be defeated."

He didn't know where this was coming from. Dale touched her arm, wanting to offer reassurance and chase away her sadness. "Trust me, it can. That's why my team exists, to do all we can to protect the innocent from being hurt."

"Doesn't always work, does it? Because the innocent sometimes get hurt along with the guilty. That's life."

His guts wrenched as he thought of Adam. "That's why we have to be the best."

She pushed away from the table and began to dry the dishes in the rack. "Go back to your team. But I'm warning you, if you don't agree to the second session tonight, you're going to be the cog in the wheel that breaks them."

"I'm fine." He pushed back his chair and stood behind her at the sink. The delicate scent of her floral shampoo filled his nostrils. He glanced down at her bare feet, with the toes painted a wild blue color.

So unconventional and free-spirited.

Keira turned, her green eyes narrowed. "You're fine. So fine that your body can't heal from a burn that should have healed by now. Your aura is filled with darkness and if you care so much about your almighty team, then you'll work with me. Because the more time you spend avoiding me, and don't deny you've been doing exactly that, the less time you'll have to save yourself and them from a darkness you can't even imagine. And then who's going to save the world if you're all dead?"

Dale went still. "My team has dealt with evil before."

"Not like this." She picked up the dish towel and began to wring it in her hands, her gaze focused on the sprigs of rosemary she'd placed on a crystal dish.

His instincts went to full alert. "What are you talking about? What kind of demons have you dealt with? Who killed your family, Keira?"

"The worst kind. The kind that keep you alive when you beg to die." Then her mouth compressed and she set down the dish towel. "Tonight. After dinner. Because the longer the darkness resides in you, the weaker you'll become, and the more vulnerable."

Dale clenched his teeth and released a breath slowly. "All right."

He grabbed the manila envelope and started for the door. Damn it, he agreed only because he never wanted to put his men in jeopardy. Keira was right. He was endangering his team.

But now he had more questions than answers because this woman with her pixie smile and troubled eyes and sparkling blue toes was turning out to be more of an enigma than he bargained for.

He would do her healing session tonight.

And then a little grilling of his own, and have one of his men investigate her.

Keira Solomon was hiding a very large secret. And he'd find out exactly what it was.

Chapter 10

Six feet four inches of pure male sat on the massage table, his body rigid as steel.

Keira lined up the crystals on the side table, centering her own energy. Not only was she dealing with a stubborn man who blocked off all positive energy, but now her own feelings also came into play. Dale Curtis was a magnificent specimen of pure masculinity. Rugged and tough, yet compassionate and courageous. Long-dead female senses sparked to life around him.

Very dangerous. Every time she got feelings for a man, the man ended up becoming demon bait. Most died.

Others had been horribly wounded, and turned into shells of themselves.

She'd learned to shut down her emotions.

Every time the Centurions released her into the world, giving her money and the means to lure new men into their trap, Keira become more despondent. They wanted her to attract strong, courageous men they would force her to torture and then they'd steal their essence and become corporeal for a few days. A few days when they would roam the earth as men once more, only men with demonic powers. They stole vast amounts of money to live a lavish lifestyle, found women to either seduce or rape, and ate and drank in an orgy of gluttony.

So she refused, staying alone, never even talking with men in desperate hopes the Centurions would finally weaken enough for her to break free of their enslavement. Didn't work. On their own, they captured new victims for her to torment.

Keira couldn't fight them when they triggered her wolf to attack, but she could fight them in human form by refusing their orders. She would not lure another innocent man into their grasp.

She learned to switch off desire like a spigot.

But now, faced with Dale Curtis, everything dormant charged back to life, like a drought-ridden meadow after a spring rain.

A tight black T-shirt hugged his muscular torso and arms. Faded jeans covered his long legs. His face was chiseled granite, carved by a master artisan, the cheekbones boasting of an aristocratic lineage, his startling gray eyes keen and yet soulful. He even smelled delicious, clean and outdoorsy, with a sprinkle of spices.

Dale had the sharp, intense focus that made her wonder what he'd be like, centering all that intensity on her in bed....

Touching him... Oh, yeah, she wanted to touch him. But she had to be professional and concentrate on her work.

"You can leave your shirt on as I do this."

She turned on the portable CD player. Soothing piano music filled the room.

"What's that?"

"A special playlist of music I made. Guaranteed to soothe scared dogs and cats, and scowling navy commanders."

"I'm not scowling."

She pointed to the mirrored wall. Dale looked at himself. "Okay, you made your point."

"You can probably play all these songs. Maybe sometime you can play the piano for me."

He folded his arms. "I haven't played in a long time."

Silently she made it a goal to coax him into opening the piano lid once more.

Keira lit a bundle of sage and smudged the room. Then she set down the sage onto a plate and picked up a crystal.

"The clear quartz crystal is ancient and sacred, and it makes the hidden transparent. Crystals have a natural vibration attuned to the earth, harmonizing with it, but also act as prisms, channeling white light from the sun's rays. Elemental energy is very powerful."

Her subject stared at the ceiling as if readying himself for more pain. Guilt squeezed her chest. She breathed in the sage and reminded herself of all the good things life had to offer and focused her energy on the pulsing clear quartz crystal.

"Once we achieve the right energy flow, I can work on pouring white light into your spirit and chase away the negative energy and vibrations."

Keira passed the crystal over his body, hovering just above his torso. His gaze tracked her as she held the clear quartz over his heart. The crystal grew black. Alarm raced through her. This had never happened. There was more darkness in him than she'd realized.

"You're filled with negative energy," she murmured. "I have to infuse you with positive energy first. Concentrate on something soothing and healing. Relax."

But he remained rigid. Keira set the stone on the windowsill.

"What do you do for fun?" she asked.

Dale looked bewildered.

She tried again. "Isn't there anything you enjoy doing that gives you a lot of pleasure?"

He raised himself up on his elbows and gave her a slow smile. "Yes. But usually it involves a bed, and getting naked."

Heat filled her cheeks. She looked away as he softly laughed.

"I didn't mean sex."

"It's how I relax and unwind. You should try it instead of playing with magick stones and energy fields."

Mischief twinkled in his gray eyes. She didn't want to think about it—Dale's strong body, naked and mounting her as they writhed together in ecstatic...

Don't go there. Be professional.

"Sex is overrated," she muttered. The demons had wanted her to lose her virginity and use sex to lure men to her side. Keira refused and even when they beat her, didn't cave in.

"Maybe you've never had the right man to show you how it's done."

Keira shook her head. "Sex without love and emotion is as pointless as fighting evil with bullets and guns."

"Bullets and guns protect people against the bad guys. You're very innocent."

The remark stung. "I'm no innocent." She'd seen things that would send strong men screaming into the night.

"Naive, then. Thinking evil can be fought with herbs and crystals." Dale lay on his side, watching her, propping up his head on one hand. "Wanting only to see the good in people."

"I hope I never lose my ability to find the good in people. Because that's what keeps me functioning from one day to the next. If someone could tell me how to find joy another way, and shove away the bad stuff, I'd sell my magick stones and follow him."

His expression softened. "No one can tell you the true way to joy and how to avoid evil. All I know is you have to stand on your feet and take in life as much as you can, and face it with courage."

For all his stubborn resistance, Dale Curtis was a good man and had a compassionate heart. He camouflaged it with gruffness, but once in a while, it peeked through.

"Thank you." Then she gave him a gentle push. "Now lie down and let me work with my magick stones."

Dale closed his eyes. She chanted sacred words as she passed the crystals over his body.

When she stopped, he sat up, alert and aware. Already she felt his aura pulsing stronger bands of red and blue.

"We're finished for now, and I'd like you to rest for a while, then we can do another session in two hours. I need time for the crystals to drain of negative energy."

"Can't we do this tomorrow night?"

"The faster we work, the better. You can take a break tomorrow night."

She needed to investigate his aura more clearly. Keira suspected the Centurion demons had implanted something in Dale, but she hadn't been able to find it yet.

He jumped off the table as she walked to the mirror.

"I've cleansed this room, but it still has very faint traces of residual energy. Not sad or negative, just hopeful. What was in here?" She paused. "I'm sorry, I don't mean to be nosy, but I've never experienced anything like it."

Dale's gaze turned haunted. "A nursery. I started painting it the day Kathy told me she was pregnant. I was overjoyed, always wanted children and we'd been trying, or so I thought. I mirrored one wall to reflect the light because I wanted our child to have a bedroom filled with sunshine. Went out and bought baby clothing. Friends gave me their baby clothing they didn't need anymore."

He gave a derisive snort. "Fool I was. The paint was barely dry when she came home and said she was leaving me. She was pregnant, but with another man's child. Her lover."

Then he touched the mirror. "I wanted to feel angry at her leaving, but realized we'd grown apart a long time ago. Never wished it to come to that. Odd, how empty I felt. As if I ached more over losing a child than losing my wife."

Keira's eyes filled with tears. She turned to hide them. So much emotional and physical pain, yet he'd remained staunch and solid.

When they left the room, she closed the door, wanting to keep the stones and herbs protected within the sanctuary. Any negative emotions Dale experienced would remain outside the room.

He glanced at her. "If we have two hours to kill, how about watching an old fifties movie? Want to join me?"

Silly of her heart to beat so fast, for that flutter of excitement to spread through her body. "Only if you let me make popcorn."

Dale grinned. "Only if you let me put extra butter on it."

"Calories."

"I'll work them off tomorrow." He stopped, braced an arm on the wall, effectively trapping her. "Some things in life are meant to be savored."

He had the most extraordinary eyes, gray as morning mist, gray that could turn hard as cold steel. Dale Curtis was a man who looked you straight in the eye and did not shy away. But his voice was deep and husky, stroking over her like the brush of warm velvet. She wanted to wrap herself in his voice to ease the constant yearning and longing for what she could not have.

They would never be lovers.

They would never be friends.

And yet this was a man of deep integrity and courage, who represented everything good and decent she wanted to see in the world.

He drew near, his warm breath feathering against her cheek. Close enough to kiss her. Close enough to coax all her dead dreams into life. Such a firm, sensual mouth, contrasting with his masculine chin and hard, lean cheeks.

Keira put a palm on his hard chest, but not to push him away.

Dale regarded her beneath his hooded gaze. Then his nostrils flared as if he'd scented something. He turned his head sharply.

Keira's heart stopped as she looked toward the stairs.

She hadn't effectively warded his house against all the demons, after all. One materialized and now stood at the stairs, cackling with glee. Dale stared.

"What the hell…"

"It's a Geldsen." Keira backed away, recoiling in disgust. "A minor demon, drawn to nobility and strength, because it lacks any of its own. It was a human woman, and traded its soul for power."

"How did it get in here?"

"I think you brought it here." This was worse than she'd thought. If Dale were a demon conduit, how many other ugly creatures would come chasing after him?

"The Geldsen is drawn to your strength and courage and honor." She breathed deep, pushing down panic. If only she had enough power and white light to ward the house, this creature could not have entered. But it was here now, and they were hard to vanquish because they had to be weakened first.

The Geldsen cackled and raked a claw down the wall, shredding the elegant gold-and-white-striped wallpaper. Dale's expression tightened. He pushed Keira behind him in a protective move.

The Geldsen advanced, pointed spikes shooting from what were once wispy strands of red hair. With its slit of a nose, and slash of a mouth, it looked hideous, though it once was pretty, she guessed.

Stepping from behind Dale, Keira threw a crystal at the Geldsen, but the crystal cracked and shattered before touching the demon. Stunned, she reeled back, summoned a small energy ball and tossed it at the demon.

The Geldsen laughed and batted it away like a child's toy. She simply wasn't strong enough to fight demons. Then the demon ignored her and fixed its gaze on Dale.

"How the hell do we get rid of this thing?" Dale asked.

And then insight slammed into her. "Let's lure her into the therapy chamber."

The Geldsen advanced, her glittering yellow eyes fixated on Dale. "You're a handsome one," the demon cackled. "I'll eat your insides for lunch and save your man parts for dessert."

Dale grabbed Keira's hand and tugged her down the hallway. He threw open the door to the chamber. The Geldsen followed, screeching like an enraged banshee.

"In the corner by the mirror," she told him.

She prayed this would work. Hatred and envy fed the Geldsen's demon strength. Both were powerful sources. But Dale was a courageous navy SEAL and a Primary Elemental Mage.

Dale crouched in attack position as the Geldsen advanced. "Die, bitch," he snarled and threw her against the mirror.

Keira raced for the light switch. Harsh overhead lights flooded the room.

The Geldsen looked stunned for a minute. Then it snarled and reached out with red talons for Dale.

"See yourself for what you are, demon." With a hard kick, Keira sent the Geldsen reeling.

The Geldsen caught its reflection in the shiny glass and staggered back, screaming.

White light glowed in Dale's right palm, the energy ball dancing in his outstretched hand like a child's toy.

"Do it," Keira choked out. "Send her straight back to hell."

He threw the ball. It hit the Geldsen's chest, where a human heart once resided, and exploded. The banshee scream turned into a pathetic whimper as the Geldsen shattered into thousands of dust particles and then was no more.

Keira gulped down several breaths, more shaken than she wanted to let on. The Geldsen was an unwelcome surprise. She'd warded the house with as much powerful white light as she could muster, but her feeble powers weren't enough. She needed Dale stronger.

She went down the hallway and cringed at the shredded wallpaper. "Sorry about that," she told him as he joined her.

Dale's grin made him look boyish. "Never did like that wallpaper. Was planning to remodel, and that bitch just gave me a head start."

"Guess this is a good lesson." She flexed her fingers, thinking of her meager, diminishing power.

"Hoo, yeah. Don't mess with a navy SEAL." He gave another lopsided smile. "Or a pretty Luminaire. That was some kick."

"You didn't do so bad yourself, sailor."

His smiled faded and he got an intense, dangerous look. Keira sucked in a breath. This was no man to trifle with, and a powerful Mage who could fry demons even when not at full strength.

Intelligent man he was, if Dale figured out the Geldsen had not attacked her, and started asking questions why…

Let's really not go there.

"Forget the movie for now." He turned and folded his muscled arms over his chest. "Tell me why you know so much about demons. I want to know everything. Starting now."

Chapter 11

For the next two hours, Keira told Dale most of what she knew about demons, how she'd made it her business to go to libraries on her travels and consult with books.

By the time they returned to the therapy room, she felt drained and numb. Keira lit several fragrant candles and breathed in their scent, then took the largest crystal and poured all her white light into it. She placed the glowing stone gently on his chest.

Trying to keep her emotions even wasn't easy in this room filled with past pain and her own inner guilt. Keira studied the crystal and his aura and concentrated.

She needed to see the inner striations of his aura for a hidden demon signature.

Continuing with the chanting, she finally was rewarded with sparks of yellow and red that formed a pattern she knew well.

Sucking in a deep breath, she removed the now dull crystal.

Dale opened his eyes and regarded her with his usual intense focus. "What is it?"

"Demons implanted a signature pattern in your body. I didn't see it before because it's hidden deep in your aura. The crystal has brought it into sight."

"What kind of demons?"

"Centurion demons. Basically, it acts like a homing beacon so the demons can find you, no matter where you go."

He looked stricken. "Get rid of it."

"I can't, not without your help. I need to cleanse all the darkness from you to do it."

"Terrific. I'm a walking demon target." He sat up, looking alert. "Wait. Maybe I can use this to my advantage. Lure the bastards here, including that demon wolf, and then break their necks. I've made it my goal to find that bitch."

You won't have to look that far, she thought.

Keira bit her lip and rubbed her sweating palms against her dress. "I wouldn't do that. You're the target, but the demons will use you to get to others. Maybe even your men."

Dale would use himself as a target, but refused to endanger others. "Too risky. How can I trap them for good? Tell me what you know."

Must tread carefully here. If she revealed too much, he'd get suspicious. "Centurion demons are not corporeal when they roam the earth. They're not easy to vanquish. How did your SEAL banish them?"

"He chanted a powerful Mage spell."

"Probably only strong enough to vanquish them for a

little while, until they can access their bolt-hole here in this world. Once they do, they'll head straight for you."

His jaw tensed. "How do I kill them?"

She had pondered that question many times over the past twenty-three years. "Probably the only surefire way is vanquishing them and then sealing the bolt-hole they use to access this world. That way they can never return here."

"Bolt-hole. I'll get one of my men on it ASAP."

"It won't be easy to find."

She knew, because she'd sacrificed some of her free time searching for it herself.

"What would be the sig pattern of this demon bolt-hole?"

At her surprised look, he added, "I have some experience with them. My team sealed a few."

Hope filled her. If his team had sealed bolt-holes, then they had a fighting chance.

"It's not like anything you've encountered before. It has to be in the earth, connected to the earth and the elements. You won't find it in an urban environment, but it will be surrounded by an area of past violence."

He looked thoughtful. "Not Iraq or Afghanistan?"

"No. The violence isn't controllable." She struggled to explain it. "Terrorist violence is sudden, unexpected and destructive. This bolt-hole is like a rift to the underworld. It opens and shuts like a door. Enough dark energy opens it, and terrorist violence is too random to give it adequate strength to stay open long enough for the demons to use it."

She hesitated. If she gave an approximate location, it would speed up the search. But she couldn't risk Dale finding out too much about her past.

"The violence keeping it open is probably induced

by the demons and not by humans. In my travels, I've come across residual dark energy from past wars, and extremely violent campaigns in Central America. Civil wars there were brutal, especially in Nicaragua. The bolt-hole may be there, in an area where villagers whisper of ghosts from the war."

He jumped off the table and headed for the door. "I've got work and I'll be in my study. Feel free to borrow any DVDs and watch a movie in the living room."

"I have work, as well." She needed to set more protective measures around the house. Keira had once felt safe and secure here, but now the house felt filled with demon land mines. She rubbed her palms against her skirt. "Tomorrow's Saturday. I need you to drive me into town with your truck to pick up some plants."

As he arched an eyebrow, she added, "Herbs and plants to ward the house. Might help."

Dale's eyes grew hard and cold. "Not as much as finding that bolt-hole. And the woman who put me in this mess in the first place. The woman in the basement who tortured me. When I find her, she won't have to worry about a bolt-hole to hell. I'll send her straight there myself."

He headed for the stairs as she sank against the wall, shivering and afraid.

Two hours later, Dale sat in his leather easy chair in the study across from a tall vampire with shoulder-length chestnut curls. Stephen was ST 21's best asset, a good friend and the best man for finding the demon bolt-hole.

The vampire had been in D.C. visiting with friends. He not only changed his plans at Dale's request, but also brought a bottle of 200-year-old French Hennessy cognac. As they drank snifters of the amber liquid, Dale filled in Stephen on the details of the demon visits and Keira's attempts to heal him with light therapy.

"A demon bolt-hole, probably in Nicaragua, surrounded by violence. Shouldn't be too difficult for me to find." Stephen sampled the cognac. "Demon sig patterns are fairly consistent, with overlays of crimson and black striations. It's how they recognize each other, even disguised as humans. They can even use the patterns as a calling card."

"The same sig Keira saw in my aura. She's trying to cleanse away the demon traces and negative energy."

The vampire looked thoughtful. "It's a time-consuming and draining process that takes a lot of power, more than a Luminaire usually has. Their methods are too fruity for me. Unconventional and feel-good. I like to kick demon ass, not bathe it in white light."

"Oh, she can kick ass all right."

Dale inhaled the cognac's fragrance of spices, flowers and nutmeg. Rich and heady, it suddenly reminded him of Keira. She seemed as delicate as oak-barrel-aged brandy, but that leg kick to the demon... He grinned and swallowed a sip.

"You're looking much better than you did in the hospital, my friend. You look alive again."

Dale roughly nodded in agreement. In the hospital, his eyes were cold and dead, blank and devoid of emotion. He'd look into the mirror and see nothing, feel nothing, except a frozen emptiness.

He wasn't a man.

He had become nothing.

When he came home, he learned to regain his life. Little things like shaving on his own with a steady hand. Sleeping with only one pistol under his pillow instead of two.

Turning off the downstairs lights when he went to bed, not leaving them blazing to chase away every shadow.

Little by little, his routine returned, with small changes. Now, instead of the basement, he kept the iron in the kitchen to press his shirts and get the crease in his pants perfect. He turned on the radio to SiriusXM's classical-music station and let the soothing tones fill the air to tune out memories of his blood dripping on the basement floor.

And then there was Keira, with her unevenness, disorganization, crystals and spontaneity, turning his ordered life upside down all over again. Keira with her shining white light and big green eyes and air of innocence amid a world-weariness he'd seen so many times in his mirror.

Keira, who was bringing light back into the dark corners of his life.

He wanted to kiss her, draw her into his arms and hold her tightly against him. Jesus, it had been too long since he'd had sex. Melissa was often his bed partner, safe and predictable, and always combing her hair after, checking her makeup and teeth. She always seemed to worry about ruining her hair.

Orgasms, yeah, she'd had a few. Dale knew he was a good lover. Staying with Melissa had been the easy way. She never complained when his work took him overseas, never hinted about marriage or commitment. There was no real passion, no fire.

With a start he realized his relationship with Melissa was tepid as cold tea. But Keira…

Keira would probably love it if he fisted a hand in her hair and kissed her hard and deep. She wouldn't complain about getting hot and sweaty if he coaxed her to scream and beg. She'd cling to him tightly as they tangled together, two lost souls reaching for pleasure to chase away the cloying darkness....

Where the hell had that come from? He shook his head, trying to clear his mind.

"I wonder if it has to do with your new Luminaire, Keira," Stephen mused.

"She's definitely improved my life since I got out of the hospital. I'd have introduced you, but she went to bed early."

"Have you done a background check on her?"

Dale nodded and told him about the admiral's mind-meld. "She's clean, seldom stays in one place, usually takes odd jobs here and there, probably to bulk up her income. No known relationships or associations with any groups."

"Bring her to the base and have Thad check her out."

He swallowed his surprise with the brandy. "Planned to bring her to the base, but not to have my half-demon petty officer examine her. Why?"

"Most Luminaires lack sufficient power to tackle demons. Just being cautious. Especially since she's so closely connected to you. Call me a concerned friend." Stephen stretched out his fingers. "Tell me about her."

Dale did. For the next few minutes, he told Stephen how she'd invaded his life, turned it upside down. A wide grin touched his mouth as he relayed the story of the coffee.

"She sounds quite spirited." Stephen studied him. "You like her. A lot."

His shrug hid his feelings. "I like how she cleans my house."

"You like more than that, I sense it. If that's the case, don't screw it up, Curt, or you'll lose her the way you lost Kathy."

The brandy soured in his stomach. "My wife left because she cheated on me with a goddamn yoga instructor named Larry. They're probably eating macrobiotic food and living in a hut somewhere while they commune with nature."

"Your wife left because you couldn't give her an emotionally satisfying relationship. You neglected her."

"Bull. I gave her everything she wanted. There was no reason for her to leave our bed." He tossed back his drink. *When I was around to please her.* But the life of a SEAL meant deployment and down range took precedence over the home range.

Stephen leaned back and swirled the brandy in his snifter. "I'm not talking about sex. For women, it has to be more than great sex if you want a relationship to outlast the tough times. When was the last time you told Kathy she was pretty? Brought her flowers, ones you picked out yourself, not had one of your staff buy? Took a day or two off to spend in bed with her, feed her chocolate and strawberries?"

The vampire set down the glass and leaned forward, hands braced on his knees. "Told her all your dreams and hopes? Shared your fears about the job, shared yourself?"

Dale's scowl faded. Had he been so caught up in the job that he'd neglected Kathy's needs?

"I know a thing or two about women, Curt. And I know you SEALs. You're so busy jumping out of planes and blowing things up that even when you spend time at home, your mind is still on the job."

Stephen glanced at the doorway. "That Luminaire is the first woman to make you this animated in the past ten years since Kathy left. She's the best chance you have at happiness. Don't blow it. Give her an emotionally satisfying relationship, not just the ten orgasms a night you give the other ladies who've wandered through your life."

"Twelve," he said absently. Far easier to please Keira in bed and keep her so enthralled with sex than to share himself. He couldn't risk handing over his heart because no way in hell would he risk having that particular organ sliced and diced again like his ex had done to it.

He rubbed a hand over his face. "That pretty Luminaire is my housekeeper, vamp. I have no intentions of forming any kind of relationship with her."

"Oh." Stephen ran his tongue over the tip of one fang. "Then you won't mind me indulging. I've never had a Luminaire in my bed. I bet she likes her sex with a bit of bite."

Dale grew enraged at the thought of Stephen nibbling his way down Keira's long neck, getting her naked and tumbling her into bed. He fixed a cold stare at the vampire. "She's in my house, under my protection. You touch her, and I'll snap off both your fangs and break your fingers, one by one."

A low laugh rumbled from Stephen. "A little much, Curt. See? I knew she was more than just a housekeeper and your therapist."

Then the vampire drained his brandy in a single gulp. "Be careful, Curt. Soon as you can, bring her to the base and have Thad check her out."

"She's not a demon," Dale countered.

"Maybe not. But there is something about her you like," Stephen said darkly. "And if she's hiding something, you could be in danger, my friend."

"My heart or my life?"

"Quite possibly both."

Chapter 12

Sunrise was the best time of day.

After filling a mug with coffee, Keira opened the sliding glass doors and stepped onto the wooden deck. Pink streaked the leaden sky, chasing away the ghosts of night. Behind her, Dale stepped out, looking crisp and refreshed in dark trousers and a powder-blue polo shirt.

"You don't have to get up this early. It's Saturday," he told her.

"I like watching the sunrise and greeting the day."

Dale braced his hands on the railing. "It's just another sunrise. I've seen plenty."

"There's no such thing as just another sunrise. When you've spent a long time in darkness, you learn to appreciate every single time the sun rises, because it means a new day filled with possibilities and fresh hope."

He turned and studied her. She cradled her coffee cup, holding her hands around it protectively.

"Is that what happened to you, Keira? Is that why you travel around the country, doing your feel-good routine? Because you want to chase away the darkness? What kind of darkness are you talking about? The darkness of demons?"

How astute of him. How well he'd pegged her. But she wasn't one of the problem countries on his map. Stick a pushpin into it, categorize it and file it away. And suddenly, she needed him to know that, needed him to realize she wasn't a problem easily solved and soon forgotten.

Because for years, she had remained forgotten, a dusty pushpin tucked away in a drawer, never taken out into the light, no one ever knowing of her existence. Anyone who would have remembered her, family or friends, was dead.

Keira needed this man, who'd call her his enemy if he knew who she was. But being remembered, even as an enemy, seemed much less painful than having her life wink out into permanent darkness. Once she left Dale Curtis, that was it. She wasn't aiding the demons again. If Dale failed to vanquish the Centurions, Keira would never return to hurting others.

Even if she lost her own life.

"Everyone has demons. Some are larger than others." She sipped her coffee and lifted her face to the dawn.

"True. I have my own."

Dale crossed the distance between them, his gaze intense as he studied her. She became aware of the way the peacock-blue and green satin kimono clung to her body, how the cool morning air touched her skin and made her nipples stand erect. Oh, how she adored pretty things. They fed her soul.

But the way he gazed at her now, as if she were more lovely than the satin or the sunrise, filled her heart.

Silly heart, she thought, feeling it pound harder as he

stroked a finger over her satin-covered arm. *Don't you know that hearts are made for breaking?*

Dale Curtis could steal inside hers, crush it beneath his military boots.

But she'd been lonely for so many years. Keira yearned for closeness and connection. All those horrific hours in the basement when the demons forced her into wolf form, and made her angry, pain-ridden beast rake claws over Dale's exposed body, the small part of her humanity had registered his bravery, and his sacrifice.

This was a man worth saving.

This was a man she could fall in love with.

"There's all kind of darkness. I've seen my share. It's why I cherish the light, and try to find the good in people."

Dale gave a wry smile. "I've seen my share as well, and why I try my damnedest to vanquish it."

His mouth was firm and yet looked soft, soft enough to kiss. He had a rock-hard body, and suddenly she wondered what it would feel like to hold him against her. Casual sex for once, now that she was free to make her own choices.

For a little while.

His gaze was warm and as the sun touched the horizon, his admiring look made her toes curl.

You're not good enough for him, a small voice whispered inside her. *He deserves better.*

She pushed aside the whispers, knowing they stemmed from the dark thoughts the demons had planted in her mind. Instead, Keira imagined herself looking at the monkeys at the zoo, sitting on the shore by the ocean, and eating a hot-fudge sundae in her flannel pj's while watching old movies, all the things she'd taken a little time to enjoy when the demons granted her freedom.

"You're so pretty when you smile like that," he murmured, and brushed a lock of hair away from her face.

The bare touch against her cheek sent shivers of need curling up her spine. What would it be like waking up with this man in her bed, curling her naked body against him as they greeted the dawn?

Dale didn't release her hair, but rubbed it between his fingers. "So soft," he murmured.

She slowly inched away, forcing him to release the strand. "And it's a mess. Bedhead. Shower time. Hang out here a few and I'll make you breakfast when I'm finished."

Keeping the smile in place, she saluted him with her coffee cup and ducked back into the house.

She took a hasty shower, combed her hair and pinned it in a severe bun, then selected an old pair of jeans and a candy-cane-striped shirt. Left untucked, the tails dangling past her bottom, the loose shirt looked definitely unsexy. Then she prepared a hot breakfast of eggs and sausages.

After breakfast, she rode shotgun in his truck to a local nursery. Dale switched on the radio and the droning sounds of classical music filled the cab. Keira shook her head and gave him a mock smile.

"No wonder you're filled with negative energy. This music is boring."

He threw her a look. "It's classical."

"Dirge music."

"I suppose you'd tune in to a station that featured love songs."

"Actually I prefer rock and roll. Or bluegrass."

She punched a few buttons, brought up a satellite-radio bluegrass station and began humming the music. "Classic. Listen to that fiddle."

"I prefer violin."

"Snob. Live music is best. Always wanted to attend a big music festival, like Bonnaroo in Tennessee."

Dale shook his head. "I think sealing my eardrums with hot wax would be more pleasant."

"Expand your horizons and maybe you'll learn to like it."

She opened her purse and withdrew the checklist of what to purchase. Fennel and holly repelled evil. Burning mistletoe fended off negativity. Keira already made bay-leaf sachets, soaking the leaves in water for three days and then straining them, sprinkling the dried leaves around the house.

"Rosemary and heather, lavender against bad dreams and negative energy," she murmured. "We may not find everything at one nursery. This could take a while."

"There you go again, focusing on the negative," he teased.

"I'm not negative, just practical. This is a war. In war, don't you use every weapon in your arsenal against the enemy?"

At his nod, she continued. "My arsenal consists of plants and herbs and crystals, and what white light I can coax from elemental energy."

"Not as effective as an M16."

"No. But some demons eat M16s for dinner before gnawing on your bones as their dessert."

A long silence stretched between them. She noticed how tightly he gripped the steering wheel, his gaze haunted. "I know."

He fiddled with the radio knob, punching buttons. The lively sounds of an orchestra blared from the speakers. "Georges Bizet's opera, *Carmen*. Not melancholy or sad."

She began humming along. "This sounds like marching music."

"It is. I learned to drill in the navy to this music. Learned to take my first steps as a baby to it. Got diaper-trained to it."

Keira turned her head and saw him wink. "Tease."

As she'd expected, the first nursery they visited didn't stock all the plants she needed. They spent the morning combing through several Virginia Beach nurseries. He surprised her, this navy commander who liked classical music and teasing her. He asked several questions of the staff about landscaping and colors, and fertilizers. Like everything else he did, he did nothing by half measures.

When the truck's bed was full, Dale consulted his watch.

"Since it's Saturday, and I don't have to be at the base, let's take a leisurely ride back and stop for a late lunch."

"We should get back and start planting."

Dale took her hand and turned it over. "You've been cooking for me all this time and it's about time someone cooked for you. Let me treat you."

His calloused thumb stroked over her palm, making small circles. Keira shivered again, wondering what it would feel like to have his hands roving all over her body.

They pulled into the parking lot of an Italian restaurant surrounded by tall trees. Dale escorted her to a booth by a wide window overlooking a garden. The natural rocks and plants soothed her. Sitting across the table from him, she almost felt like they were on a date.

The slave armband around her arm was a constant reminder this man was not a potential lover, but her employer and her protector from the Centurions.

Since she'd had so few pleasures, Keira indulged her

imagination. The restaurant, with its mauve leather banquettes and music softly playing in the background, was charming and romantic.

A waitress in a starched white shirt and crisp black pants took their drink orders and handed them thick menus.

Dale scanned the selections. "Lots of garlic. So no vamps here."

"Any recommendations?"

"The lasagna and the spaghetti. Food here is excellent and they have good wine."

The waitress came with a beer for Dale and a glass of ice water for Keira and took their orders. They started discussing places where they'd traveled, his favorite destinations and places she longed to visit. Enthralled, she watched him begin an animated discourse about volcano boarding in Guatemala.

The way he paid attention to her, how he kept asking her opinion and listened to her, really listened, made her feel special.

Only one other table was occupied. A man and woman on the restaurant's other side sat across from each other, accompanied by a baby in a high chair and a little boy about four years old.

Keira sipped her water. "This is a nice restaurant. Isolated, though. How did you find it?"

"My team comes here for dinner. We like it because it's hard to find for starstruck tourists wanting to see a real navy SEAL. The owners only recently started serving lunch and opening earlier. Word probably hasn't gotten out yet."

He glanced toward the restaurant's other patrons and his expression lit up. "I'll be a son of a bitch…"

Grabbing his bottle of beer, he slid out of the booth

and went to the couple. "Blake the snake, how the hell are you?"

The man looked up and grinned. He jumped out of his chair and embraced Dale in a bear hug. "Curt! You bastard."

They pounded each other on the back as the woman gave an indulgent smile. Dale grabbed an empty seat and pulled it up to the table.

"Dale, this is my wife, Jessica. Jess, meet Dale Curtis. Went through BUD/S together. Ex-swim buddies until I had to drop out, wuss that I was."

"Wuss? You broke your left femur in two places." Dale stuck out his palm. "Pleased to meet you."

The woman smiled. "Hi. Honey, I'm taking Michael over to see the fish tank while you two catch up. Keep an eye on the baby."

Dale politely stood as the woman did. Then he and Blake started talking. The waitress brought over two plates and placed them on Keira's table. She glanced over at Dale, but he seemed oblivious.

"You here alone? Want to join us?" Blake asked.

Dale shook his head. "No. I'm here with…a friend."

Keira had excellent hearing, even when she wasn't in wolf form.

He didn't even glance her way. Keira drank more water, feeling invisible.

"Friend, right. Is that what you call them these days?" Blake laughed and clapped him on the shoulder.

Dale shook his head and sipped his beer. "She works for me. Nothing more. We were buying plants for landscaping."

"Speaking of nurseries, when are you going to start growing one of these?" He jerked a thumb at the cooing toddler.

Dale's expression slipped. "One day."

The baby began to cry. Blake started to get up and Dale shook his head. "I'll get her. Sit and finish your lunch before it gets cold."

His own lunch sat, untouched, across from Keira.

She watched as Dale picked up the little girl, then sat down with her, rubbing her back. He looked so peaceful and content, a lump rose in her throat.

What would it be like, to have a family? A real home and a husband and children?

Keira's throat closed up. She was Dale's employee. Nothing more. Her job was to restore his health and get him into fighting form. She inhaled the scent of her meal. Pasta wasn't her favorite, but this had a zesty, homemade smell with a bite of oregano. Food was a real pleasure.

Under the demons' enslavement, when they had a new victim for her to torture, she'd been given bread and water and only enough thin, stringy meat to keep her alive. The starvation diet made her wolf meaner, hungrier, more vicious.

As she picked up her fork, the door leading to the kitchen opened. A man in a chef's hat, dressed in a white uniform stained with spaghetti sauce, stood in the doorway.

Sloppy cook, she thought absently. The sauce had splattered over the lower half of his shirt, like a large bloodstain. She looked down at her lasagna.

The bowl filled with pasta was filled with wriggling worms swimming in sauce. Her fork clattered to the table.

Heart racing, she looked at the chef again. His face bulged and changed, the nose flattening, the eyes bulging out and yellowing, the mouth a red slash.

Demon.

Chapter 13

Keira's thoughts spun crazily in her mind as she struggled against rising panic.

My team comes here for dinner.... The owners recently started serving lunch and opening earlier....

Wildly, she signaled to Dale, who, though he had set the baby back into the high chair, was as oblivious of her as the demon chef. Of course. She was one of the few who could see through any demon's human disguise.

She had to let Dale know without alerting the demon. Keira beckoned to the waitress, who she could see now had a long, forked tongue snaking out of her thin mouth, and beady, red eyes.

"Something wrong with your meal?" she sneered.

"It's delicious. But I'm afraid my companion's lunch is getting cold. Would you mind returning it to the kitchen and reheating it?" She forced a smile. "He and his buddy got to talking. You know men when they catch up. Oh, and please bring me more garlic rolls."

The demon waitress removed Dale's plate and went into the kitchen, followed by the demon chef. That should keep them preoccupied for a few minutes.

She slid out of the booth and approached Dale, trying to appear casual and not raise suspicion. To her relief, the food on his friend's table all looked normal.

No, the demons saved the good stuff for me, she thought. Keira squeezed Dale's muscled shoulder. "Time to leave. Don't bother with a carryout box. The meal's not all that great, after all." She looked at Blake. "Get your wife and kids out of here. Now."

Dale stared at her as if she'd grown two heads. Blake's eyes narrowed. She couldn't blurt out that the special of the day was live worms and the restaurant was run by demons. For all she knew, Blake was human, not a paranorm.

"There's a gas leak in the kitchen," she whispered. "I overheard them talking about trying to plug it."

Blake and Dale both pushed back their chairs at the same time and stood. But Dale, thank the gods, looked in the direction of the kitchen and his eyes narrowed. He knew. He saw.

His friend only looked concerned.

The woman and the little boy had finished looking at the fish tank. The brightly colored coral fish and blue-gills were all floating at the top. A sinister air fouled the restaurant, as cloying as cheap perfume. Why hadn't she noticed it before?

Because it wasn't until Blake called Dale's name, she realized. Names had power and once the demons heard the name, and saw the taint of darkness clinging to Dale's aura, they dropped the guise.

The powerful guise.

Immobilized, she watched a demon exit the kitchen and head right for the woman and the little boy. Clutched in the demon's hand was a meat cleaver.

Keira didn't wait to see if the demon planned to use it. The stones in her pocket glowed hot and fierce. She removed a crystal and called to the demon.

"The food here sucks!"

The demon turned as Dale made a strangled sound. The woman gasped and clutched her son. Damn it, still too close. She couldn't risk hurting them.

"Blake, call your wife over here. Right now," Dale ordered.

Fortunately, Dale's friend did so. Lifting the boy in her arms, the woman ran to join her husband.

"Get out of here, Blake. I'll handle this. You've got your family," Dale told him.

The man hesitated, as if he wanted to help Dale, but hustled his family out of the restaurant.

Keira threw the crystal. It hit the demon in the chest and sank deep. Gray blood splattered the clean granite counter.

Her focus centered on the dying demon, and the others now entering the dining room. Three, five… Oh, damn. Ten demons.

One she could defeat. But ten? Odds were not too good.

"Keira!"

She turned and caught the salt shaker Dale tossed to her. "Throw it on them!"

She pelted the first demon with the salt, watched its skin dissolve. The demon clawed at its chest and howled. But they couldn't vanquish them all with salt. Dale threw another salt shaker and it landed at the demon's head. It exploded in grayish mess.

"Behind me," he growled, and removed a pistol from his back pocket. Before she had time to tell him bullets wouldn't kill these demons, the navy commander fired several shots.

Not at the demons, but at the bottles overhead on the shelves. Glass exploded, showering vinegar and pickled vegetables down on the demons, who clawed at the shards.

Dale shoved the pistol back into his jeans, grabbed her hand and they ran out of the restaurant, slamming the door behind them as the demons rushed forward. They leaned their weight against the heavy wood door as Blake stood by his SUV, his family secure in the car.

"Curt! You need my help?" the man called out.

"Stay where you are," Dale yelled back. He looked at Keira. "Cell phone, right pocket. Dial pound-three and then hold the phone up to my ear. Those are ectoplasmic demons. Shape-shifters who imitate human form. Had some acquaintance with them on a mission a few years ago by the Red Sea. What the hell are they doing here?"

Dale braced his weight against the door, fighting to hold the demons back as they scratched and pounded on the door. The frame shook.

"They didn't materialize until your friend called your name. They're after you, and everything and everyone associated with you."

She fumbled with his phone, pressed pound-three. When a male voice answered, she held the phone to Dale's mouth.

"Red zone warding, Taste of Naples restaurant ASAP! Bring all you have," Dale barked out.

She clicked off the phone and leaned against the door.

Horrified, she saw a forked tongue flick between the frame and the wall, licking her ankle.

"Oh, gross," she cried out and stomped on it.

A car filled with men in navy uniforms pulled into the parking lot and the sailors climbed out. They stared at Dale and Keira.

"Sorry, restaurant's closed," Keira called out, struggling to keep the door shut. "Health-department orders. Rats inside. Big ones. Really big."

Desperate, she looked at Dale. "Use your powers. You're the only one who can dispatch them."

The door kept shaking and trembling as the demons screeched and wailed. "You'll have to hold the door."

"I can do it. Just be quick. On the count of three, when they rush outside, hurl a ball of energy at them."

"I don't have enough power for all of them. One or two, yes." Dale clenched his fists. "If only I wasn't so damn weak."

"Pull strength from the sun. Elemental energy for an Elemental Primary Mage. Hurry!"

Dale stepped away from the door and into the sun as she struggled to hold the door closed. Stretching his hands upward, he closed his eyes. Sunbeams streamed down toward him like the rays of a rainbow, pouring into his body. As he looked at her, his gray eyes glowing with fiery power, she felt her feet slip and skid.

The door opened a few inches and a claw lashed out. Biting her lip, she used all her strength to push it shut again.

"Keira, on three! One, two…"

"Three," she whispered and let go, ducking and rolling to the ground.

Dale blasted the demons with energy balls. They

screamed and exploded into grayish muck, splattering the sidewalk.

Keira lay on the ground.

Gray gaze steady, Dale helped her up.

The carload of sailors stared at them, their mouths hanging open, as a shiny black SUV screeched to a halt before the restaurant. On the back of the SUV was a bumper sticker that read Orgasm Donor. Doors opened and four muscled men jumped out and raced over. She recognized Ensign Sully. The other three must be Dale's SEALs, as well. Tight-faced, they ran over to their commanding officer.

"A little late," Dale said drily. "You missed all the fun and games."

"Curt! You okay?" the tallest one asked.

He gave a rough nod. "We're fine. Need a mind cleanse on the lookie-loos over there ASAP. I'll handle Lieutenant Blake and his family. Implant the memory the restaurant was evacuated due to a propane-gas leak."

The tall SEAL grabbed a bag from the SUV and handed a penlike instrument to Dale, then took two others. The men rounded up the bystanders and used the cylinder to flash light into their faces.

Dale did the same to Blake and his family, then shook the lieutenant's hand before they headed to their car. He jogged back to her and scrutinized her face.

"You okay?"

She nodded, drawing in several deep breaths. "I had to figure out how to warn you without alerting your friend and his family. I knew what was going on as soon as the food was delivered."

His jaw tightened. "I didn't mean to ignore you. Blake and I go way back and I hadn't seen him in months."

"No prob. Not like we were on a date. Good thing,

too, because if this were a date and you took me to a place where demons served bowls of worms disguised as spaghetti, I'd have to end our relationship. I prefer my worms dead and sautéed, not swimming in marinara."

He smiled and touched her hand. "Live worms and demons are deal breakers, huh? I'll remember that next time we go out."

Her insides clenched at the power of his smile, and the simple caress of his hand against hers. She didn't want this attraction, didn't want to get close to Dale.

Keira pulled away. "Not necessary. Going out to eat is overrated, anyway."

Dale gave her a speculative look as if he read her mind and knew she deliberately lowered her expectations because she didn't want to face disappointment. So much disappointment in the past.

Changing the subject, she gestured to the four men finally approaching them. "Your team?"

Dale introduced her. The tall one with the quiet air who wore a shiny gold wedding ring was Matt Parker. Dallas and J.T. were the other two, and she already knew Sully.

"Keira Solomon. She's a Luminaire psi therapist and healer, and I hired her as my housekeeper."

She kept a smile firmly in place, knowing Dale didn't want his men knowing her real purpose, though he probably wouldn't even admit it to himself.

"Luminaire psi therapist?" Matt asked.

"Yeah, but don't let that fool you. She makes a great chocolate cake and not all that wheat-germ organic stuff that other Luminaires love," Sully said.

"Luminaires. New Age hippies. Peace, love and all that bullcrap. What a waste," Dallas murmured.

He exchanged a look with J.T. Irritation gnawed at her.

Why did everyone always look as if she were about to break into a chorus of "The Age of Aquarius"?

"Nice truck," she told Dallas. "Yours?"

At his proud nod, she added, "Nice bumper sticker, too. Does your mother know about it?"

The three other SEALs laughed at Dallas's red face. Keira cautioned herself. She treaded on dangerous turf. Shay, the SEAL in training, had seen her face, although he couldn't remember her name, thanks to the demon spell. But she couldn't be certain he had not told the other SEALs what little he remembered.

The best defense was a good offense. She smiled and stuck out a palm to the scowling Dallas.

"Let's start over. I'm Keira Solomon, Luminaire, psi therapist and healer, and all-around snarky woman when I've been tangling with a restaurant filled with demons. Didn't mean to poke fun at you, but when your spaghetti lunch turns into a bowl filled with worms, one does tend to get a little testy."

As he shook her hand, his eyes still narrowed, so she added, "So glad you guys did show up. We can't be certain there aren't other demons lurking inside the restaurant, demons who didn't come out." Her smile dropped as she thought of the innocents who may already have died. "Or that they killed the real owners and staff."

The scowl finally faded from Dallas's handsome face. He looked at the restaurant, his expression thoughtful. J.T. cleared his throat. "They've been opening a new restaurant in Maine. Mark and Tina took their staff with them and turned this restaurant over to their 'cousins' while they are gone."

"We didn't think any relatives would have the same home cooking as Tina makes, so most of us shunned the place." Matt gave Dale a steady look. "We were going to tell you, but it slipped our minds. You were in the hospital still."

"Right," Dale said. "Check out the rest of the restaurant. I want a full report in fifteen."

"Yes, sir. We're glad you're okay," Matt said.

"We freaked when we got your message. Not that you couldn't handle it," he added, as a scowl darkened Dale's face.

"But we worried something big was going down. After I told the others about that demon gnawing on my neck, we needed to make sure you were okay, Curt," Sully added.

J.T. and Dallas nodded.

"Don't want to lose you, Curt. After what happened to you…" Dallas stopped.

"I'm fine," Dale told him. "Now go do your job and I'll feel even better. We'll be out here."

Keira's chest felt hollow. Dale had people who cared about him.

She did not.

He escorted her over to an outdoor table while the SEALs investigated. Keira sat down, grateful to rest her shaky legs.

She drew circles on the tabletop with her forefinger. Gently, he clasped her wrist. "You sure you're all right?"

"Not really. I'm a little queasy."

"Nearly eating worms does that to you." He stroked a thumb over her thudding pulse. "Not many women could hold it together as well as you did back there. You're a strong one, Keira Solomon. Not your typical New Age hippie."

At his wink, she laughed. "Your men are like you. Very pragmatic."

"A little. But they're all individuals, each with their

own talents and personalities. It's what makes the team strong, like a family."

"You're proud of them," she said, not wanting to hear more about teams and family and all the things she'd never have.

"They're good men, all of them. We've been through a lot together."

He frowned. "Why were the demons here? What did they want?"

You, she almost said.

"It's the dark energy you have inside you," she told him. "I told you, you're a demon magnet. They must have been attracted to your energy pattern, knowing you have frequented this place."

The SEALs emerged from the restaurant. Matt held up a large rice sack. "Not all of them are dead, Curt. Found this one in the freezer, trying to hide, but the temperature killed it."

Icy cold slammed into her as he set down the bag and opened it. Dread curled down her spine as she peered at the creature inside. Oh gods, oh gods. It was the size of a small woman, but with pale, hairless skin, a bald head, pointed ears, long talons and the nubs of breasts. Pointed teeth showed through its parted lips.

"Jimali," she breathed. "Oh, Jimali."

"What's a Jimali?" Dale demanded.

Not answering, Keira sagged onto the chair, trying to collect her reeling thoughts. Jimali was another Centurion slave she'd met while the woman was still human. Jimali started to enjoy tormenting men after doing it for decades, but as a result, lost all her inner white light, and eventually, her soul, becoming a shriveled, ugly shell of her former self.

This is what I'll become if I don't defeat the Centurions.

Glancing at his men, she gave a tight smile. "It's a toy for demons. Kind of like a dog toy, without the squeak. And it's not dead. The cold just paralyzed it. Keep it locked up tight because when it comes back to consciousness, it's going to be in a real bad mood."

All five men studied her with narrowed gazes. Ignoring the others, she turned to Dale. "Can I talk with you alone?"

Taking her by the elbow, he escorted her to his truck while the men continued examining the creature in the sack. Dale folded his arms across his chest. "Details. Now."

She clenched her fists and gulped down a deep breath. "I didn't want to share this in front of your men."

"What I know, they know. They're the best and most highly trained at hunting demons. Go on."

"Jimali is not a what, but a she. She's a minion, a scout sent by specific demons to find the target they're searching for. Easily sacrificed if necessary, very expendable."

"It looks almost human."

"She was human. Not anymore." Keira locked her gaze to his. "This is what I didn't want your men to know. She must have been sent by Centurion demons. They're sending out scouts to search for you, and they're narrowing in. Unless you regain your powers and eradicate the darkness inside you, they will find you, and when they do, they'll kill you."

Chapter 14

Dale didn't scare easily.

As a commander of the finest SEAL team in the U.S. Navy, he prided himself on being a levelheaded, confident leader.

Hearing that Centurion demons were on his heels didn't frighten him.

But the news sure as hell scared Keira.

Sweat trickled down her brow. He could pick up threads of her increasing heartbeat and even if his hearing wasn't ultrasensitive, the way her hands shook clearly indicated fear.

He wanted to bring on the Centurions, lead them straight to his house and he'd be waiting, not with guns and bullets, but everything he had. She was right. He needed all his powers at top performing levels.

And he needed to know why these particular demons scared her so much. The woman had calmly confronted

imps, Geldsens and ectoplasmic demons, evil creatures
that would send a strong man into shrieking hysterics.
And now, with the news about the Centurions, she broke
a sweat.

Why?

"If you eradicate the darkness tainting me, will all
my powers return? What must I do to regain all my lost
magick?"

Keira scrubbed her palms against her skirt. "The healing sessions will help. I'll have to ramp up the intensity
and work faster, because it's usually a slow process."

"Let's do it. Right now."

Dale lay on the table in the spare bedroom, watching
Keira arrange her crystals in a row. Downstairs in the
basement, his men guarded Jimali, now imprisoned in
a steel cage as Keira had instructed. If she succeeded in
restoring Dale's powers and ridding him of the demon
sig, Jimali would grow confused, like a hound that lost
the fox's scent.

Right now, the creature was snarling and snapping to
be free. It had Dale's scent and wanted at him, to mark
him for her masters and then share in the prize of slowly
torturing him to death.

He wondered if Jimali were the demon wolf he sought.
Keira had been evasive when he'd asked if the demon
could also be a wolf. But the thing's scent was too foul.
No way in hell would he find himself attracted to it.

Unlike the demon wolf that had shifted into a lovely
human woman, whose scent made his cock grow rigid
even as his blood dripped to the floor.

"Like humans, paranorms have chakras, entry doors
to the person's aura. But unlike humans, the more powerful the paranorm, the more protected the chakra. It's

tougher to heal a paranorm than a human, and you're a Primary Elemental Mage. Your body naturally protects itself against anyone tampering with your aura and your powers."

"Then how did the Centurions strip away my powers and invade my aura?" he asked.

"They targeted specific areas by testing you to see your greatest fears and then used those fears against you, ramping them to extreme levels and opening you up to being invaded. Like an enemy army striking down all a country's defenses first before taking the offense."

She gave him a serious look. "I thought couching it in military terms might help offset your suspicion of woo-woo crap. Because if this is going to work fast, you're going to have to trust me, and believe it can work."

Keira picked up a clear crystal, the glowing stone emitting a low hum. "Luminaires use a crystal infused with their own natural white light, combined with elemental energy, to divine what chakras need cleansing."

She passed the stone over his body. At his scalp, throat and heart, the crystal's serene white glow faded, becoming cloudy and pulsing weakly. "Your crown, throat and heart chakras are unbalanced, but not that weakened."

Next, she passed the stone over his solar plexus and it glowed white, the hum becoming louder and the light more strident. "Your sacral chakra is fully functional. It's tied to your creativity and sexuality." Again, the charming blush. "No problems there."

Dale agreed. He never had trouble in either of those areas, just not enough time to indulge them.

She passed the crystal over his body and hovered at his groin. Her perfume teased his senses and his cock gave an appreciative twitch. Dale tried to concentrate on something else, anything else. Baseball. Home runs.

Sliding into home plate…sliding into a woman's soft, wet core. Score.

Then he imagined the Centurions, their thick, eerie giggles each time the demon wolf shredded his already raw flesh and he screamed….

Dale breathed deeply and looked down. The crystal had turned jet-black.

"Your root chakra. The sig pattern is here. This is the gateway they used. Root chakras affect fear and can be weakened from several things. Being tired, career troubles…"

He sat up. "When the demons lured me into the trap, I was exhausted, two days without sleep, worried about my men and that damn mission in Honduras. Kept thinking I should have gone with them instead of staying in the office, dealing with bureaucratic bull."

"That's it. You were restless, anxious and your guard was let down, and the demons only had to prey on your fears to slip their mark inside your aura. This is why you've been irritable and tired, and resisting any kind of change."

She went to the table and selected three vials of oils and poured them into three separate dishes. The pleasing scents of cedarwood, sandalwood and patchouli filled the air. Keira brought over a flat, round black onyx stone with runes carved into it. She placed it on his groin.

"Now for the hard part," she murmured.

"Actually, it's soft right now," he joked.

She looked sympathetic. "I know this is difficult for you, because it goes against what you're conditioned to believe. I know you're scared, too, because it is different. Trust me. Remember your origins, and remember a time when you weren't in the military, when your life was taken up more with music and creativity and you opened yourself up to other belief systems, to trusting others and yourself."

Keira picked up his hand and stroked her fingers gently across the back. "You were trained as a classical pianist and became a military man because your heart suffered to see such evil in the world. Your musical talent was set aside to focus on the physical because while your playing brought joy to others, it didn't bring you joy. Not while there were bad men out there who wanted to silence the joy for others forever."

So true. He'd traded his Steinway for a pistol.

"When we're finished, you'll be able to play again, because you'll have balance. You'll remember how to center yourself with both work and leisure. Now close your eyes and breathe deeply, as if you're getting ready to dive into a deep, warm pool."

He didn't know what to say. Dale closed his eyes and breathed deeply.

"We're going to use music to help you focus. Think of a time when you were happiest playing the piano."

He did, remembering concertos and notes and the joy of losing himself in the music.

The low, lyrical sound of her chanting voice drummed a soothing vibration in his ears. Her notes corresponded with each inhale and exhale. Harmony and melody, he thought, concentrating on holding the image of himself sitting at the keyboard, stroking the keys to coax the music into life once more. Mozart's Piano Concerto No. 20. As he imagined the final movement, working up to the final cadenza, her chanting became louder and more urgent as he played faster and faster.

The chords of the concerto became more frantic and resonated with energy.

At the crescendo, a thrilling D-major finish, the music

in his mind became loud and brilliant and fierce. He heard Keira grunt, felt something yank, hard, out of him and then an odd but fulfilling emptiness, as if a heavy weight had lifted from him. He felt energized and filled with vitality, stronger than he'd been in weeks. Hell, no. Months. A low, vibrating frequency hummed in his body. His powers.

And then a loud, shrill scream split the silence. Dale opened his eyes and sat up, staring in dumbstruck disbelief.

Keira lay on the ground, tussling with a large, white-and-black-striped snake about seven feet long. Not a snake, not with those segments and the blind, searching head.

A worm.

Keira screamed. "Help me! I can't fight it off any longer."

Jumping off the table, he went to seize the worm, and remembered. Dale stretched out his hands. "Let go," he commanded.

Releasing the worm, she rolled away. Using his telekinesis, he yanked the wriggling creature away from her, flinging it against the mirror. It hit the mirror with a mighty crack, shattering a glass pane, and slithered downward. Still alive. Still writhing and hissing.

Dale gave a cold smile. "Come and get it, bastard."

Gathering his powers, he sent a current of pure white light singing through the air, aimed at the worm now sliding toward Keira, who was gasping for breath as she crawled on her elbows away from the creature.

The energy ball hit the creature, sizzling along its scaly skin, and the worm screeched from its gaping mouth filled with rows of sharp teeth. Then it burst into a froth of white goo. Even as it burst, he sent another energy current toward it, burning the white gelatinous mess into ash.

Particles settled over the floor, lightly dusting the hem of Keira's dress.

He ran to her side, smoothed a hand over her sweating forehead. "You okay?"

She nodded.

He glanced at the ash-strewn floor. "That thing, that worm, it was inside me?" His guts churned at the thought.

She nodded again.

"It's what made me bad-tempered and out of balance, draining my powers," he offered.

"Worms tend to do that to people." Keira gave a shaky smile. "But it's gone now. You did it. You got rid of the demon sig. You're on your way to healing now. It will take a little while to get all your powers back, but now you're no longer blocked. And I bet you'll have better control over them, too."

"We did it. Together. We make a good team." Dale, now filled with a wild energy and joy, helped her to her feet.

Unable to resist the softness of her skin or how lovely she looked, despite her tousled curls and a smudge of ash on her cheek, he drew her into his arms and kissed her.

She stiffened and planted her palms against his chest, but then made a small whimper he knew was pleasure, as her body relaxed and her arms wound around his neck. She tasted like ripe berries and sharp wine, and her mouth was soft and warm and pliant.

His cock gave an eager jerk upward in response. Never had he been aroused this quickly or wanted a woman this badly. Even making love with Kathy hadn't been like this, searing and intense, a kiss that struck a deep chord inside him, leaving him hungering for more.

Too long the joy had vanished from his life. Dale intended to make up for lost time, and Keira would play a part. His accompanist, who had returned his life to him.

When she sighed into his mouth, and her tongue darted out to meet with his, he nibbled at her lower lip. With tremendous reluctance, he broke the kiss. Dale smiled down at her.

Such a brave, strong soul, this Keira Solomon. Never had he imagined an unorthodox Luminaire, with her unconventional magick, would cure his soul.

"Now all we need to do is find those Centurions and that damn demon wolf." He rubbed a thumb along her cheek. "And fry her to ashes, too."

Dale wanted to fry her to ashes. Keira sucked down a breath, and put a trembling finger over her kiss-swollen mouth. He was filled with energy, his powers almost fully restored.

Hers were nearly diminished. After pouring everything she had into the crystal, and then yanking away the psi worm from his spirit, she had nothing left. Vulnerable, weakened, she didn't dare say anything because in this state, she could very well spill her secret.

His sexual energy thrummed and sent vibrations of pleasure echoing in her feminine core. Drained of all energy and power, her female self responded to his pure masculine force, aching to be filled. If she didn't balance her own chakras and restore some semblance of internal harmony, she'd surrender to desire and tumble into bed with him.

Bad idea.

Dale rubbed a thumb along her lower lip. "You look like you've been kissed and kissed well. Let's take a minute before going downstairs?"

Keira tried to gather her scrambled thoughts. "Downstairs?"

"The basement. My men are there, watching Jimali. Remember?" He kissed the corner of her mouth again. "You smell like honey and fresh lavender."

"Maybe I should meditate, try to restore myself first. I'm a bit shaky."

"Meditate later. I'll even light the candles for you." Dale tugged her hand. "I don't want to spend another minute with a damn demon in my house. Right now I feel I could fry an army of them."

When they reached the basement, all four SEALs stood around an empty cage, a circle of wary, frowning men. Keira's heart pounded harder.

"Curt! It vanished. Poof!" Sully snapped his fingers.

"More like a slow fade-out," Dallas amended. "First it stopped snarling, and looked confused and then this black slit appeared in the air and Jimali was yanked inside."

"Because it lost the scent, and whoever is holding its leash recalled it before anyone could poke and prod and discover who sent it." Keira flexed her sore fingers. Holding onto the worm that she'd pulled from Dale's aura had drained her.

He told them about the worm, and his men's faces tightened. "That thing was inside you all this time? What do you want us to do, Curt?" Dallas asked.

"I want a full search of every restaurant, bar, cathouse, doghouse, any house either I've been in, or any of you have visited in the past two months. Need a full electromagnetic scan for dark energy forces, specifically demon."

"Stephen can help us. He can scent demon blood a yard off. Vamp's a real hound dog about demons," Dallas stated.

"I've assigned Stephen to finding the bolt-hole used by the Centurions and that hellhound wolf."

"That demon wolf. When you find her, let us have at her, Curt. We'll all take turns doing to her what she did to you." Dallas growled and extended his long fingers. Claws erupted from the tips.

Draicon werewolf. Shifters who held the power of changing and other psi powers. All the SEALs nodded grimly.

Oh, gods. They'd kill her. Simply kill her. Show her no mercy. Keira pasted a smile on her face, hoping no one heard her rapidly pounding heart.

Dale paused and glanced at Sully. "We may need to bring your sister in on this."

Blood drained from the young SEAL's face as the others chuckled. "Ah, hell, Curt, don't do this to me."

"Cassandra's a pure Mystic Witch. She's got years of skill flushing out demon energy."

Dallas elbowed Sully. "Your sister's going to have a good time, looking through all those nasty places you've been to, Sul. All those skanky beds—"

"Enough," Dale interrupted. "Sully, you team with Cassandra and search all the restaurants. The family ones."

Sully looked relieved.

"The rest of you, cover the others."

But before leaving, the SEALs nodded at Keira. "Thanks, Miss Solomon, for saving our Curt's hide from that thing. We owe you one," Dallas said.

A shaky smile touched her mouth. *Remember that when you find out what I really am, okay, fellows?*

When the men left, Dale turned and lightly gripped her upper arms. "You okay? You're pale and sweating."

"I hate basements. And violence."

His thumbs slowly stroked over her bare skin, streaking the thin layer of ash left by the exploding worm. "I know. But this is a necessary violence that can save lives."

"Got it. Listen, it's been quite a day. Think I'll shower this gunk off."

Gray gaze searing into her, he stood a breath away. She wondered what it would feel like, to be subjected to his intense focus in bed, his hands stroking over her bare skin. Dale had a smoldering male sexuality she found irresistible, a promise of molten pleasure. Images flared: a naked Dale covering her, all slick, hot maleness as he pushed slowly into her untried body.

"Now you're blushing," he said softly.

Keira put her trembling hands to her face. "All these demons, zinging straight out of hell, no wonder. It's too hot. I can't stand the heat."

Dale picked up her hand and thumbed her knuckles. "There's also a good kind of heat, the type stemming from passion. The flush of a woman's skin, indicating her desire."

"Best remedy for that is a cold shower. Real cold." Keira smiled and stepped back, breaking the connection. She did not want to bond with this man, emotionally or physically.

"Don't be afraid of me, Keira. You restored me. I'm in your debt."

"I take credit cards," she said lightly.

He laughed, but as she turned and fled up the stairs, she felt the heat of his burning gaze watch every move.

She'd removed the demon sig from his aura and saved him from turning into demon prey. And now felt like a deer stalked by a hungry wolf. Not demon prey.

His prey.

Chapter 15

Sunday, Keira awoke early and donned her oldest clothing, and tackled the yard. Planting gave her great pleasure. Feeling the dirt slip between her fingers grounded her to the earth.

Her people were of the earth, and being outdoors in the fresh air and sunshine gave her fleeting peace.

Dale didn't come outside once. Keira didn't see him at all. When she took a break and went into the kitchen for a drink of water, she saw a note in his crisp, flowing handwriting.

Went to the base for a meeting. Will be back for dinner. Save your appetite. I've got a surprise for later. My treat.

He signed it with a bold, slashing *Dale*.

When he returned home, carrying two large sacks of

groceries, she was dressed in a nice dress, waiting. And deeply curious. She'd had so few surprises in life and those had not been very pleasant.

He dumped the sacks on the granite counter. "I'm cooking dinner for you."

At her crestfallen expression, Dale laughed. "Cheer up. I may not be a gourmet chef, but I make mean Maryland crab cakes."

"How mean? Do the crabs bite?"

"Very mean. Enough to tempt your palate." He playfully tapped her nose and then guided her to the high stool by the breakfast bar. "Sit, and watch the master at work."

"Should I get the first-aid kit handy, in case you slice your finger?"

He laughed, such a deep, hearty and unrestricted sound, it made her heart leap. Keira suspected this was the real Dale Curtis, the man who'd been lost inside his own soul.

As he mixed ingredients for a pie, they talked about their favorite desserts. Then he slipped the pie into the oven.

He started preparing dinner as she watched. "It's nice having someone cook for me for a change. Although this is a great kitchen to work in."

"I redid it after Kathy left. Remodeled the whole house." Dale added crab to a bowl and began to beat in eggs. "She seldom spent time in the kitchen, but I needed a fresh start."

"Who taught you to cook?"

"I did. Read books, watched television shows until I got it right. Since Kathy didn't like to cook, I learned."

She reached for the platter of cheese and fruit he'd set out and sipped the white wine he'd poured into her glass.

"Cooking is like yoga. You get into the rhythm of things, it becomes like a mantra."

Dale held up the bowl and gave her a solemn look. "Ooooom."

Keira giggled.

"Not everything relates to positive and negative energy," he added. "Sometimes you have to let go, have fun for the sake of fun."

"I believe that, too. Embrace life with both hands because you never know how long you have."

Dale set the bowl down and looked at her. "What are you afraid of, Keira?"

"I'm afraid your delicious dessert is going to burn if you don't watch that oven," she said lightly.

He turned and pulled the pie from the oven. Smoke curled in the air, and instead of crisp, brown crust, the pie looked burnt.

"Ah, well. Dessert is ruined." He glanced up, his gray gaze twinkling with good humor. "But there are alternatives. Much better options."

Heat spiraled through her at the sexual suggestiveness of that look. Keira hoped he meant more fruit and cheese, because she didn't know if she could handle Dale Curtis in bed.

How could she have sex with this man? Surrender everything, engage her emotions, when they were so different?

Guilt suffused her. And what of him, and how badly she had hurt him?

He served dinner in the dining room, lighting two elegant tapers and turning off the lights. "I'm trying to be energy-efficient," he said, smiling.

The crab was excellent, served with fresh green beans, the salad crisp, and Dale put her at ease with amusing stories of growing up during a time period when "children were seen and not heard, except if they had magick powers and made their wishes known."

When he saw her glass was empty, he waved a hand, and the wine bottle rose into the air and refilled it. Keira jerked back, startled. She'd forgotten this particular power.

Dale watched her. "I'm sorry. I didn't mean to show off. Just that it's been so long since I had my powers that I want to fully experience them."

"No prob," she said lightly, sipping the wine. "As long as you don't use telekinesis to lift up my dress hem."

He grinned. "I promise if I lift up your dress hem, it will be with my hands."

His glance was warm and teasing. Keira polished off the wine, feeling more nervous than when she'd first come to his house to gain access.

Then, she'd been the one in control. But clearly he was now.

And clearly flirting with her, as well.

"You're very pretty in a dress."

Whoa, boy. "I like pants, as well."

Dale's expression turned serious. "I know I haven't been easy on you, or nice. I still don't believe in all this woo-woo crap...."

At her arched eyebrows, he sighed. "Well, not all of it. But you did something extraordinary yesterday, Keira. Thank you. Thanks for putting up with my bad moods and snarly attitude."

"I'll forgive you, if you cook dinner for me again. This was delicious." She pushed back her plate and feigned a yawn. "But it's getting late."

Now his dark brows arched as he glanced at the grandfather clock ticking in the corner. "It's nineteen-hundred."

Only seven o'clock. Too early to plead sleep. But this was dangerous, growing close to Dale.

"I've had a long weekend," she said, twisting her hands in her lap. His scent, delicious spices and wine, teased her wolf senses, awakening feelings she wanted to remain buried. Dale gave her a crooked smile, and she melted.

"Watch a movie with me. I'll make the popcorn, and I promise not to burn it."

Keira hesitated. Further involvement aside from professional interactions was a bad idea. But the idea of spending a cozy night, munching on popcorn and indulging in old movies, tempted her badly. She'd had so few treats.

I can resist him.

Then she looked into his gray eyes and saw the sexual chemistry flare.

"Only if you let me pick the movie."

"Deal." He stretched out a hand. "Let's shake on it."

His palm was strong, warm and calloused, the hand of a man accustomed to hard work, not pushing papers. Dale rested his hand a moment in her grip and then drew back. "Go into the den, pick out a movie and let me clean up."

She'd chosen *Breakfast at Tiffany's*. Total chick flick. Keira shook her head when he'd suggested *Lawrence of Arabia*. So he'd let her have her way. Big green eyes wide, she'd sighed happily as they settled on the sofa.

And then, halfway through, Keira fell asleep.

Dale regarded his housekeeper with tenderness. Should have been more considerate. She'd expended all her energy fighting his demons, and needed recharging, not movies and popcorn.

He'd let his libido and interest carry him away, thinking of his needs, not hers.

Removing the bowl of popcorn from her lap, he placed it on the table, switched off the flat screen. Then he lifted her into his arms, burying his nose into her hair. Fresh citrus and sunshine invaded his senses. She felt soft and warm.

Hunger bit him. Keira was wholesome and innocent, uncomplicated and assertive.

Yearning for Keira filled him. She smelled like citrus and sunshine, not old cigarette smoke and lost hopes, or money and ambition like Melissa.

Yearning for a house filled with laughter instead of silence, and munching on crisp popcorn on a Sunday night instead of a barstool and a burger.

Determination filled him. He was a navy SEAL and never quit. Not when he wanted something badly, and he wanted Keira.

Dale carried her into her room. He pulled off her shoes, tucked her between the sheets and kissed her forehead. "Sweet dreams," he whispered.

He knew what his dreams would be of, and anticipated the night when they would turn real, Keira naked in his arms, reaching out to him in trust as they made love.

For the next five nights, Dale pursued her with gentle persistence. Not overtly, always a gentleman, but his male interest remained keen.

He took her out to dinner at a restaurant his team assured him was clean of demons. He brought her fresh flowers, ones he picked up himself at a florist. And he insisted on spending every night after dinner either watching old movies or taking long walks around the neighborhood.

Keira kept him at arm's length. She brought him to the basement and they set up an exercise studio where he lifted weights and she mediated. And each night, she did a short session on him with the crystals.

The other night, he took an amethyst she'd placed on his neck and spun it lazily in the air, using his telekinesis. Delighted, she watched and clapped like a child.

"Always like doing this with my marbles when I was a kid," he'd told her, grinning.

Keira suspected he seldom showed his light, playful side to his men. The serious navy commander had a quirky sense of humor and charm.

I could fall in love with you, she'd thought, feeling despair chase away her joy.

When Saturday arrived, he apologized.

"I've got a black-tie ball to attend. I'll have to take a rain check on our movie tonight."

Keira sat on his bed, watching him adjust the tie. "I need a favor from you," he told her. "The admiral is inspecting the new firestorm chamber on Tuesday. I want you to visit the compound, meet with him and assure him I'm cured."

"It'll cost you. An entire night of watching *Doctor Zhivago.*"

He shot her an inscrutable look. "How about a massage?"

"I've given you enough massages."

"I was referring to you," he murmured.

Warmth surged through her. Keira pushed aside rising desire. "You're not cured," she warned.

"I feel terrific."

In his formal dress uniform, he looked distinguished and handsome. As he turned for inspection, her heart did another little flip-flop.

"You look amazing," she told him.

His mouth curled in a wry smile. "It's the uniform. Covers all the shortcomings."

Keira went and straightened his tie. "You don't have shortcomings."

"Tell that to Melissa. She didn't think so when she saw me in the hospital." He snorted and shook his head. "Tonight, in this uniform, she'll find me acceptable."

"Is she a Mage, like you?"

"Melissa is a normal, ordinary human woman who knows nothing about the paranormal world." He gave her an apologetic look. "I'd arranged earlier to take her to the ball because I needed an escort. It's a formal obligation. Nothing more. There's nothing between us."

Cheered by this admission, she trailed her fingers over the gold buttons. "Does she know you feel this way?"

His gaze hardened. "Melissa cares about appearances. When she found out it was the premiere social event of the month, she sped over to the base to ask me. Much faster than when she visited at the hospital. After all the nights we spent together, I thought I meant more to her than an invitation into military social circles."

Jealousy nipped her heels. This Melissa had known Dale intimately, had shared his bed, his life and everything normal in it. Melissa didn't worry about demons pursuing her or spending endless days locked in a cold, dark cage. This Melissa never looked over her shoulder, wondering when everything would come crashing down.

"You should probably leave soon to pick her up, if you don't want to be late."

Dale seemed distracted. "She's arriving here in a limo she hired for the night."

"A limo? Like the prom? Should I get out the camera and take your photo?" she said lightly.

"Melissa insists on making a grand entrance. Appearances are important to her."

"Sounds like she uses you to climb the social ladder."

Their gazes caught in the mirror and met. Connection flared between them. Dale cupped her cheek. Keira shivered, relishing his palm upon her skin. Strong, capable, and yet tender.

"I'd rather stay home with you and watch *Lawrence of Arabia,* but this is a necessary social obligation."

"Silly," she whispered. "*Lawrence of Arabia* is about guys draped in sheets and sand. I prefer *Gone with the Wind.*"

Warmth curled through her veins as he stroked a thumb across her cheek. "Women in big skirts waving fans. Chick flick."

"It's a military classic. Typical macho film. Guys smoking cigars, battles and guns."

Chuckling, he released her. "You're very persuasive when you're trying to get your own way."

Only with you, she thought. *With you, I'd do anything to get my way because then I could finally be free. Live a normal life. Maybe even find a way for us to make this something more.*

Dale Curtis was honorable and strong, and had all the values she cherished. He had a playful side she found endearing. But his rigid code of honor did not easily forgive. Dale viewed life in shades of black and white, while she clung to the gray areas, struggling to find the light amid the darkness.

The doorbell chimed, and his expression hardened, a reflection of the military commander with duties and obligations.

Her chest felt tight as she followed him into the hallway. Brimming with curiosity about this mysterious Melissa, Keira hovered at the upstairs landing, peeking through the stairway rails like a child peering down at her parents' party.

A tall, thin woman swept inside. Blond hair pinned in an elaborate arrangement of curls, she was pretty, with bright red lipstick accenting a full, sensual mouth, but beneath the glittering beauty lurked something cold, like a hard diamond. Gold sparkled on her dress like shiny coins. Keira squinted.

Melissa put a possessive hand on Dale's chest. "Like my gown, darling? I bought it especially for you, to match your uniform."

She spun around, the shiny fabric floating outward.

Dale nodded, his expression remote and shuttered. He barely said a word. Too busy prattling about the ball and checking out her appearance in the hall mirror, Melissa didn't notice. Anger stabbed Keira. The man deserved a nice night out, with good company. He deserved normalcy and a woman who pried her attention away from herself long enough to pay him a compliment about how handsome he looked, ask him how he was doing.

Maybe the woman needed a good reminder. Or a kick in the shins. Keira bounded down the stairs and stopped short, smiling at Melissa.

She stuck out a palm. "Hi, I'm Keira, Lieutenant Commander Curtis's housekeeper. I'm glad he's finally getting out to a party. He's been working too hard lately and deserves a nice night out."

The woman stared at her hand as if she held out a live cockroach. "It's not a party. It's a military ball. Not that a servant would understand the difference."

Unfazed, Keira regarded her shark's-tooth smile. "Sure, I get it. A ball. That's why you need such a sparkly dress. Very shiny. You match the buttons on his uniform. Wow, so bright, everyone's going to need sunglasses."

The other woman sized her up like a prizefighter studying an opponent. The briefest amusement crossed Dale's face.

"We should be going, Melissa," he murmured.

As they turned to leave, a faint, but familiar scent drifted into Keira's nostrils. Interesting. The same scent from the bar where she'd first seen Dale...

And Dale had no idea.

Then again, the cloying stench of Melissa's perfume would fool most. *Except a pure-blood wolf like me,* she thought.

"Normal, ordinary woman, huh? She never told you what she was?"

A frown touched his face as he turned. "Keira..."

The woman rolled her eyes. "Really, Dale, we don't have time for games. We'll be late."

"Sure hope they have bananas flambé at your little party. Or just plain bananas. That'll make your date hoot with glee, Dale." She gave a small, knowing smile.

Melissa's mouth pinched as she glared at Keira. "Watch your mouth, you impudent maid. You're nothing but a lowly servant."

She got in her face. "Actually, I'm a Luminaire. And you're nothing more than a throwback to Charles Darwin's origin of species. Except you smell better. Then again, all that perfume..."

Dale's eyes widened as his nostrils flared. "Son of a..."

Turning to Melissa, he narrowed his eyes. "You're a shifter."

An uneasy smile touched the woman's mouth. "I have a titch of cougar shifter. On my mother's side."

"And monkey on her father's side." Keira laced her hands around the newel post. "Chimpanzee, actually."

"You know what I am," Dale said slowly.

Melissa rolled her eyes. "Of course. You're Lieutenant Commander Dale Curtis, commander of SEAL Team 21. You're from upstate New York and your father founded Curtis Mark Industries. Your mother is known in all of New York society, all the Newport and Palm Beach social circles and all the Mage…"

The woman's mouth dropped. "I mean, Maine. I meant to say Maine."

"Mage," he corrected quietly. "Primary Elemental Mage, to be exact."

A haunted, almost sad look entered his eyes. Keira's heart twisted. Dale valued honesty and all this time his girlfriend had been living a lie, trying to use him to gain access not to military social circles, but his family's power.

Sympathy and guilt coiled in her stomach. She wanted Dale to have a good time and she'd wrecked his night. The woman had not meant Dale harm, only wanted to hide a secret from him.

How well she understood that need…

Dale checked his watch. "Forget it. Let's go."

Keira cleared her throat. "Actually, I could be wrong. There is more cougar there than I'd thought. Good for you for concealing your shifter abilities all this time, Melissa. That takes skill, and you blend so well with human society."

But the woman didn't take the peace offering. Her gaze hardened. "I don't need compliments from you. A cheap, peace-loving hippie Luminaire who has no more power than a psi human."

She raised her brows. "Wow, you are more cougar than

I'd thought. Meow much? Want to get into a catfight? No dice, sweetie. Just take Dale out and show him a good time. He deserves a nice night out."

Melissa smirked. "I plan to show him a very good time. Just like all the other nights we've spent together, when we woke to greet the dawn."

"Melissa, let's roll. Now!"

Breath caught in Keira's throat as he escorted her to the door. He was so…handsome and charming. Couldn't that twit see beyond the scars to the stunning man who bore them? Dale did deserve better. Much better than a gold-draped phony who only wanted to use him to clamber up the Mage social ladder.

Melissa scurried down the steps to the waiting limo. At the door, he turned and gave Keira a stern look. "Behave."

As he started out the door, Keira called out. "Dale!"

He turned and she made hooting sounds, scratching at her chest.

His face scrunched up into such a boyish, carefree grin, her heart leaped. Then the polite mask dropped again. "Don't wait up for me," he murmured. "And don't eat all the popcorn."

The door softly closed behind him.

Formal balls were never his forte, but he usually enjoyed the chance to socialize and mingle. And dance. Not tonight. Tonight his thoughts constantly drifted home to Keira.

Dale sat at his table, watching the tableau, as Melissa danced with the admiral. An orchestra played on a raised dais as couples swirled on the dance floor. Sparkling crystal chandeliers reflected the brilliant jewels worn by the women. Candles adorned tables holding silver fountains of the finest champagne.

The ballroom glowed like fairy lights, he thought whimsically, wondering where that thought came from.

Then he smiled. Keira. She'd turned on his imagination like a spigot.

Most of the people who knew him commented how well he looked. Even cagey old Byrne remarked he was putting on weight, looked much more relaxed and fit.

All thanks to Keira. None to Melissa.

For two years, he'd shared Melissa's life and her bed. They'd been intimate and he'd introduced her to his family. And she knew what he was, probably targeted him because he hailed from an old, established and powerful Mage family, yet never told him she was a shifter. Oh, he'd sensed something slightly different about her, but he'd dismissed it, always too much focused on other matters like work to pay attention to his private life.

Dale understood Melissa's reasons for never telling him. Wishing to discreetly blend into the human world, many paranorms hid their identities, even from other paranorms.

He could forgive the omission.

But he couldn't ever trust her again.

Honesty was a value Dale cherished with those in his life, because as a SEAL and a paranorm, lies were necessary to protect lives.

Those under his command knew his strict rules about honesty. *Be honest with me. If you mess up, admit it.* Better an admission than trying to cover up the truth because he would find out and the consequences were not pleasant.

He needed a woman in his life who held those same

values. A woman without secrets, a woman who told him the truth and left nothing hidden.

Suddenly he grew weary of duplicity and false smiles and social climbing. Dale longed for home, his sweatpants and faded T-shirt and beer, not champagne and starched uniforms.

He made his apologies to the admiral and other dignitaries. Melissa was stiff as he kissed her cheek goodnight, but upon leaving he saw her flirting openly with an attentive, politically influential lieutenant.

A very human lieutenant.

Dale watched them, an amused smile quirking his mouth. "Good luck, buddy," he murmured.

Thoughts of Keira's monkey sounds kept the smile on his face.

It was past midnight when the cab pulled in front of his house. Light shone from the den halfway down the hall.

Curled up on the leather sofa, Keira ate popcorn, a dreamy expression on her face.

Dale tugged his tie loose and dropped beside her. She glanced up. "Home so early? You okay? They didn't wear you out, did they?"

"Never been one for stiff, formal events. Besides the company's much better at home."

She gave a shy smile.

"I told you not to eat all the popcorn."

"And when did I ever listen to you?"

Dale shrugged out of the jacket, tossing it over a chair. Keira raised an eyebrow.

"What's this? Mr. Starched Shirt Meticulous, actually throwing his clothing around? Hope you don't expect me to hang it up for you. What do you think I am, the housekeeper?"

Grinning, he kicked off the polished dress shoes. He

slid close, grabbed a fistful from the bowl. She looked startled, but did not move away.

"What's this?" He pointed to the screen.

"Black Swan."

He gave her an incredulous look. "You like romance movies and chick flicks. This is a dark drama about a ballerina who takes on the role of Odile from *Swan Lake* and how it twists her mind. It makes *Psycho* look like a comedy."

"It's a musical. Has music in it."

Giving an amused look, he munched on the popcorn.

Keira was fun and carefree. She made him feel comfortable, relaxed and, hell, he was enjoying himself for the first time in months. Then she gave a small sigh as the strains of *Swan Lake* played. "What was the ball like? Was there lots of dancing?"

Dale ate another kernel. "I didn't dance much."

"Afraid to show your two left feet in their very polished, shiny shoes?"

"Actually, I'm a good dancer with the right partner." He finished his handful of popcorn. "Didn't see one there tonight."

She sighed again. "I love watching dancers. Just wish I had…"

Keira fell silent.

He wiped his fingers on a paper towel. "Tell me."

"It's stupid."

"Try me."

Glancing up through her long, dark lashes, she set down the bowl and wiped her hands. "No one ever taught me to dance. Not the formal, elegant dances like the waltz. Always imagined what it would feel like to sweep across the floor. I thought it must feel like flying."

She looked so dreamy and wistful, his heart gave an

unexpected tug. Dale stood, pushed back the coffee table and chairs, clearing a space. Then he pulled her to her feet. "Come."

At her puzzled look, he added, "I'm going to teach you to dance."

She felt good in his arms. A perfect height, the top of her head reaching his nose. Scents of citrus and sunshine filled his senses, chasing away memories of Melissa's heavy perfume.

Keira gazed upward, uncertainty in her eyes.

He gave his first real smile of the night. "Trust me."

Slowly, he showed her the steps. She matched his pace and they swept around the den. Laughing, she followed his lead, matching his stride perfectly. As the music ended, she gazed upward in sheer adoration.

Dale stood still, amusement shifting to a stronger, deeper emotion.

"You're staring at my mouth," she breathed.

"Because I keep wondering what you'll taste like. I've been wanting to do this for some time now." He cupped the back of her head with a strong hand. "Slow and easy. Relax, sweetheart. I'll take it slow and easy."

Lowering his head, he kissed her. His mouth gently covered hers. Keira's lips felt soft and warm beneath the pressure of his own. Slowly he teased her mouth to open to his, toying and nibbling with her lower lip until she finally yielded.

She stiffened against him, her breathing ragged, her heartbeat erratic and pulsing as he pulled her closer. Then she sighed beneath his mouth and wound her arms around his neck. She felt warm and soft in his arms, her mouth pliant beneath his. She tasted like sweet raspberries and buttery popcorn, and her mouth was hot silk. Dale deepened the kiss, his erection pulsing. Never had he been this swiftly attracted to a woman, never had he felt such exhilarating bliss in a mere kiss.

He wanted more, needed more, his body aching and demanding. But he sensed her innocence and confusion twining with blossoming desire. When she pulled back a little, he abruptly released her.

Hunger washed through him as he studied her mouth, swollen from his possessive kisses.

He wanted her badly and, judging from her delicate flush of passion and darkened pupils, she wanted him, as well.

"I think I'll call it a night," she whispered, eyes huge in her heart-shaped face.

Dale tapped her pert nose. "Sweet dreams, Luminaire."

As she left, he collapsed on the sofa, rubbing a hand across his face, filled with desire and dismay. He was falling fast for Keira Solomon, the most unlikely woman he'd ever met.

And he still knew little about her.

But soon, he'd find out. Because the rules had changed. He'd let Melissa onto the base, never dreaming she was a shifter. The woman held more interest in his family's power than the team. But what if she did want something much more dangerous?

What if Melissa had been a snake, lying in wait to prey upon his staff, his SEALs, hoping to destroy them by using Dale to gain close access?

He couldn't endanger his team. Dale fished his cell from his trouser pocket and dialed Stephen, who answered on the first ring.

"Report, vamp. And don't tell me it's past your bedtime or you're too busy having breakfast in bed with a blonde."

"Actually, I was dining on a blonde in bed," the vampire deadpanned. Then he drew in a deep breath. "I have intel for you."

"Report."

"Not over the phone. This needs to be delivered in person. Tomorrow morning. I'm in New Orleans, but I'll catch the red-eye. Be at your house around noon. Long as you don't have any demons lurking in the corners. Had my fill here in Naw'leans." The vamp's Southern accent came across strong and thick.

Stephen hated demons and had tangled with a few nasty ones.

Dale smiled. "No. No demons here. Not a hint of one."

"Actually, I was dining on a blonde in bed," the vampire deadpanned. Then he drew in a deep breath. "I have intel for you."

"Report."

"Not over the phone. This needs to be delivered in person. Tomorrow morning. I'm in New Orleans, but I'll catch the red-eye. Be at your house around noon. Long as you don't have any demons lurking in the corners. Had my fill here in Naw'leans." The vamp's Southern accent came across strong and thick.

Stephen hated demons and had tangled with a few nasty ones.

Dale smiled. "No. No demons here. Not a hint of one."

slid close, grabbed a fistful from the bowl. She looked startled, but did not move away.

"What's this?" He pointed to the screen.

"Black Swan."

He gave her an incredulous look. "You like romance movies and chick flicks. This is a dark drama about a ballerina who takes on the role of Odile from *Swan Lake* and how it twists her mind. It makes *Psycho* look like a comedy."

"It's a musical. Has music in it."

Giving an amused look, he munched on the popcorn.

Keira was fun and carefree. She made him feel comfortable, relaxed and, hell, he was enjoying himself for the first time in months. Then she gave a small sigh as the strains of *Swan Lake* played. "What was the ball like? Was there lots of dancing?"

Dale ate another kernel. "I didn't dance much."

"Afraid to show your two left feet in their very polished, shiny shoes?"

"Actually, I'm a good dancer with the right partner." He finished his handful of popcorn. "Didn't see one there tonight."

She sighed again. "I love watching dancers. Just wish I had…"

Keira fell silent.

He wiped his fingers on a paper towel. "Tell me."

"It's stupid."

"Try me."

Glancing up through her long, dark lashes, she set down the bowl and wiped her hands. "No one ever taught me to dance. Not the formal, elegant dances like the waltz. Always imagined what it would feel like to sweep across the floor. I thought it must feel like flying."

She looked so dreamy and wistful, his heart gave an

unexpected tug. Dale stood, pushed back the coffee table and chairs, clearing a space. Then he pulled her to her feet. "Come."

At her puzzled look, he added, "I'm going to teach you to dance."

She felt good in his arms. A perfect height, the top of her head reaching his nose. Scents of citrus and sunshine filled his senses, chasing away memories of Melissa's heavy perfume.

Keira gazed upward, uncertainty in her eyes.

He gave his first real smile of the night. "Trust me."

Slowly, he showed her the steps. She matched his pace and they swept around the den. Laughing, she followed his lead, matching his stride perfectly. As the music ended, she gazed upward in sheer adoration.

Dale stood still, amusement shifting to a stronger, deeper emotion.

"You're staring at my mouth," she breathed.

"Because I keep wondering what you'll taste like. I've been wanting to do this for some time now." He cupped the back of her head with a strong hand. "Slow and easy. Relax, sweetheart. I'll take it slow and easy."

Lowering his head, he kissed her. His mouth gently covered hers. Keira's lips felt soft and warm beneath the pressure of his own. Slowly he teased her mouth to open to his, toying and nibbling with her lower lip until she finally yielded.

She stiffened against him, her breathing ragged, her heartbeat erratic and pulsing as he pulled her closer. Then she sighed beneath his mouth and wound her arms around his neck. She felt warm and soft in his arms, her mouth pliant beneath his. She tasted like sweet raspberries and buttery popcorn, and her mouth was hot silk. Dale deepened the kiss, his erection pulsing. Never had he been

this swiftly attracted to a woman, never had he exhilarating bliss in a mere kiss.

He wanted more, needed more, his body achi demanding. But he sensed her innocence and conf twining with blossoming desire. When she pulled a little, he abruptly released her.

Hunger washed through him as he studied her mout swollen from his possessive kisses.

He wanted her badly and, judging from her delicate flush of passion and darkened pupils, she wanted him, as well.

"I think I'll call it a night," she whispered, eyes huge in her heart-shaped face.

Dale tapped her pert nose. "Sweet dreams, Luminaire."

As she left, he collapsed on the sofa, rubbing a hand across his face, filled with desire and dismay. He was falling fast for Keira Solomon, the most unlikely woman he'd ever met.

And he still knew little about her.

But soon, he'd find out. Because the rules had changed. He'd let Melissa onto the base, never dreaming she was a shifter. The woman held more interest in his family's power than the team. But what if she did want something much more dangerous?

What if Melissa had been a snake, lying in wait to prey upon his staff, his SEALs, hoping to destroy them by using Dale to gain close access?

He couldn't endanger his team. Dale fished his cell from his trouser pocket and dialed Stephen, who answered on the first ring.

"Report, vamp. And don't tell me it's past your bedtime or you're too busy having breakfast in bed with blonde."

Chapter 16

Keira could not sleep, thinking about that kiss.

Tender and yet passionate, it cranked all her hormones into overdrive. Temptation had called her to fist her hands in his dress shirt, pull him closer and then see where the night led them. Worldly when it came to life's evils, she was totally innocent in bed. She wanted Dale, wanted to finally taste passion.

But she couldn't make love to this man she'd nearly killed.

Not until he knew the truth. Keira had dealt with too many lies and too much deception to save her skin. If she were finally to be intimate with a man, she wanted Dale. And she wanted nothing but honesty between them.

Somehow, she had to tell him who she really was....

Finally she drifted off. And dreamed.

Vermilion. The color of death was vermilion, sharp and biting. Vermilion, dripping from a platform in the room's center, cold and dank.

She put a hand against the wall to steady herself, but the room kept swaying.

"Admit it. You ripped him open."

"Not me. I did not…"

"You—"

"I am innocent…."

"Are you saying you did not torture those young men? You have done worse, much worse, with your claws." Behind Dale, the demon giggled and clapped.

"Please…"

"You let them bleed to death. You watched them scream and writhe in pain. You did it. You tore them open. The demons were bystanders. You did it all." His voice became deadly calm. "You tortured me. You left me to die in the dark, alone. In agony."

"Never kill. Never. I care, I care about you, Dale." Her voice dropped to a bare whisper.

He said nothing, only studied her with his cold, dead gaze. Members of his team formed a horseshoe around him, a tight little group. All the SEALs were clad in battle gear, their expressions hard and cruel.

They wanted a pound of her flesh for the torment she'd inflicted on their beloved leader.

Dakota, the Draicon werewolf with the deep blue eyes, spoke in a loud, booming voice. "Keira Solomon, I find you guilty of the deaths of all your past victims. Guilty of attempted murder of a U.S. Navy lieutenant commander."

"Guilty," each SEAL echoed.

"Sentence?" Dale asked them. He looked at Keira, his full, sensual mouth turning hard with resolve. "There can be only one sentence for such evil. Death."

* * *

Keira stared into the mirror as she combed through her damp hair. Showering failed to rinse away lingering wisps of last night's horrible nightmares.

She still felt slick with sweat, a film of guilt coating her. Maybe today, she'd work up the courage to somehow tell Dale and have nothing stand between them.

Nothing to prohibit them from becoming lovers.

The comb stopped halfway through her hair.

How could she tell him? Dale needed her to find the demons and needed her guidance in vanquishing them. Telling him the truth risked expulsion from his life, or worse.

Male voices sounded in the kitchen. They sounded serious, official. Deeply worried, she twisted her long, damp hair into a bun. She dressed in a pair of black trousers, strappy sandals and a long-sleeved blue shirt.

In the kitchen, she saw that Dale stood near the sink, gazing out the window, a mug in his hand. The delicious scent of hazelnut coffee filled her nostrils. Amusement mingled with apprehension. Finally, he knew how to make his own coffee and make it right.

He turned and offered a warm smile. "Good morning."

Then she noticed a man sitting at the breakfast bar, a glass of clear liquid before him. Chestnut curls tumbled down to his slim shoulders. He wore a rumpled gray shirt and dark circles were under his intense green eyes, as if he'd gone without a night's sleep.

Mingling with the strong smell of coffee, and Dale's delicious scent of fresh air and pine, was the new smell. The bite of whiskey, the burn of hot passion and a metallic scent she instantly recognized.

Keira stiffened.

Blood.

Vampire.

The man also went still, his gaze tracking her like a predator. Dale, oblivious to the sudden tension, waved at the stranger. "Keira, this is Stephen. He works with my team. Came over the other night, but you were already asleep. Stephen, this is Keira, Luminaire extraordinaire, and my housekeeper. She cleansed the house of demons. And she makes a damn fine cup of coffee."

Warmth filled his gaze, but she felt icy cold. Vampire. She'd encountered a group of them while imprisoned by the Centurions.

Heard them tearing into the victim she'd refused to torture, and he'd died a horrible death, his shrieks stabbing her ears like icy spikes.

After the vampires, she never fought the demons' compulsion again. Instead, she'd devised a new method of trying to save their victims.

"Hello." Stephen's gaze narrowed. "You're the Luminaire."

His nostrils twitched. Fear rolled through her. Vampires had exquisitely sensitive olfactory senses. They could smell a wounded person more than one hundred yards away. Some could even detect the slightest defect in a person's...

Blood.

Perspiration beaded her temples, trickled down her back. Panic rose in her throat, sharp and biting. She started to back away. Too late. The vampire stood and rounded the breakfast counter. Sharp white fangs flashed as he hissed.

"Stephen," Dale snapped. "Watch it."

"She's no Luminaire. Get her out of my sight." The vampire's talons elongated, along with his fangs. His eyes turned bloodred.

Keira turned and ran into her room, slamming the door shut. She flung herself on the bed and buried her head beneath a pillow, trying to shut out the sounds.

Shrill screams of agony, sounds of tearing, wet flesh, cackling laughter.

Sobs wrenched her shoulders as she cried. Would she ever find redemption?

Dale stared after his housekeeper and then turned to his friend and colleague. "You bastard, what the hell did you do to her?"

Ashen, the vampire collapsed back on the stool. "Demon blood. She has demon blood, Mage. I can smell it a mile away. The stench…it turns my stomach, burns my nostrils."

He picked up the glass of water and gulped it down, wiping his mouth.

Dread shot through Dale. He set down his mug very carefully. "You're wrong."

"Not about this. Ever. You know how much I loathe demons. Ever since that San Fran episode…"

"She can't be a demon. She killed an imp in my house, fought demons with me…." Dale staggered back against the counter, leaning against it for support.

Stephen stared at the hallway where Keira had fled. "I'm not saying she's a demon. But she has the blood. Maybe she's a hybrid."

Mind spinning, Dale grappled for explanations. "Like Thad, the petty officer who's been training my SEALs in the firestorm chamber."

"And you know how I can't stand to be near him, either." Stephen's mouth thinned. "But this one, your Luminaire, she's hiding something big. And the blood inside her, it's powerful. Dark and evil. Thad's a puppy dog compared to her. Keira, she's much worse, a…wolf."

Demon wolf.

The words flashed through his mind. Pain pulsed in his skull, behind his eyelids. Dale pressed a hand to his head. Damn headaches.

Frustration tensed his muscles. He'd acknowledged the feeling, dealt with it. Sexually, he found Keira desirable, wanted her in his bed. She'd aided him and helped him recover. But his position as ST 21's commander put him at risk for infiltration by enemies, both human and nonhuman.

Keira couldn't remain in his life until he knew exactly what she was….

"What are you going to do?" the vampire asked.

"Bring her to base. And have her thoroughly examined."

After she heard Stephen leave, Dale knocked softly on her door. Keira hastily splashed cold water on her face, dabbed a wet washcloth over her puffy eyelids.

"Let's talk," he said quietly and she followed him to the kitchen.

He poured a fresh mug of coffee and handed it to her. "Black, right?"

Keira nodded and leaned against the counter.

"First, let me apologize for my friend. Stephen's not very social in the morning. He's more of a night owl." His expression shuttered. She couldn't tell what he thought.

He could want to kiss her again.

Or kill her.

Acid churned in her throat at the suspense. She set the mug down. "Spill it, Dale. What did he tell you?"

"He says you have demon blood inside you. A strong strain of evil demon blood."

Oh, damn, this was worse than she'd thought. Everything inside her screamed to tell him the truth. But the cold look on his face and her fears kept her from doing so. She couldn't face his rejection or worse if he knew the truth now.

I'll level with him. Just not now, she thought.

"I must ask you some questions." He walked over to the kitchen table, pulled out a chair. "Please sit."

Keira sought refuge in a defensive attitude. "Interrogation time? After everything I've done, you've decided to treat me like a suspect? Or are you simply going to assume I'm guilty?" Bristling, she sat, fisting her hands beneath the table to hide their trembling.

Dale sat across from her, his expression neutral, but his posture commanding and powerful. "I don't assume. But I want honest answers."

Warily, she looked at him. "Go on."

"Are you demon?"

"No."

"Was either your father or your mother a demon?"

"No."

"Have you ever been possessed by a demon?"

"No."

"Have you ever held an evil thought about killing another and acted upon it?"

She considered. "I wanted to kill that ass who ran me off the road when I was driving to Virginia."

"I'm serious."

"So am I. You should have seen how I nearly wrecked my bike."

"Keira, do you have demon blood inside you?"

Sharp, concise and commanding, Dale had turned

from friend to a powerful military commander. The scrutiny made her squirm, lashed her with guilt and despair. Not now, she thought. Please, not now.

The best defense was offense, she remembered him saying while they'd watched a war movie the other night. Keira sprang to her feet and slapped the table, making the vase with fresh roses rattle.

"Damn it, Dale! I told you my parents were killed by demons and I've been hunting demons all this time, risking my hide to eradicate them. That vampire smelled demon blood, of course he'd smell it, after all the contact I've had with them!"

He didn't flinch. Didn't move a muscle. Dale remained still, his gaze penetrating and assessing. No emotion. The Mage was rock-solid.

While she was rapidly turning into an emotional mess.

"I want you to take a blood test." He drew in a deep breath. Okay, maybe not such a rock. Hope filled her.

"A complex blood test that analyzes your paranormal abilities and determines exactly what you are."

Keira stilled. "A test that will tell you if those abilities include demonic powers."

"Yes."

"No." She shook her head, strands of hair tumbling down from her loosely pinned bun. "You talked of trust with your men, trusting them and how you created this bond. And you won't share that trust with me, after we've worked together, fought together! Is your loyalty only to your team because they're SEALs?"

"My loyalty is to the men and women under my command," he said quietly, but a shadow crossed his expression.

"And I'm not on the team, not good enough to claim your loyalty and trust. Just good enough for making you dinner, a few fun nights out and movies shared with pop-corn. That's all."

"Keira…"

The roses he'd presented to her with such a flourish seemed to mock her with their bright crimson and sweet fragrance. Crimson like blood…

With a strangled cry, she swept the vase off the table, sending it crashing to the floor.

Dale sprang up and ran to her, placed a hand gently on her shoulder. "Did you cut yourself?"

Why? Hoping to get a blood sample to analyze?

But she shook her head and wrapped her arms around her chest. "I'm going to my room now. Please, leave me alone," she said dully.

He did not respond as she sped down the hallway.

She couldn't hide forever.

Nor could she avoid him.

An hour later, she headed into the backyard. Picking up her spade, she dug in a frenzy and planted the remain-der of the hydrangea bushes. Keira touched a leaf. Living things, those would ward off demon magick.

If only they could ward off other things, like distrust and suspicion.

He had a right to be suspicious, she reminded herself.

The sliding doors opened. Dale climbed down the deck steps and knelt beside her.

"I'm sorry I upset you," he told her. "Allow me to make up for it with lunch?"

Suspicion filled her. Dale Curtis was a single-minded man.

"Why? Are you dining at a blood bank?"

"No. I do wish you'd level with me, though."

"I leveled with you as best as I could." True enough. "And now you want to take me to lunch?"

"I'd like to get to know you better." Gray gaze steady, he studied her.

"More interrogation? As a navy SEAL commander questions a suspect?"

Dale sighed. "I want honesty from you and I'll be honest with you in return. I like you, Keira. A lot. I like spending time with you, as a man does with a woman. It's my day off. Let's abandon our roles. No more SEAL commander, no more Luminaire."

Understanding filled her. "And if I am a demon, the more time you spend with me, the more you'll be able to tell what I am."

"I know you don't like worms in your food, so that's a good start." He smiled, then sobered. "No talk of blood, tests or demons. It's Sunday, my day off, and it's a beautiful day. I'd like to spend the afternoon with you. Thought we'd eat out and then bike ride at the beach."

Tempting. She sighed. "I never learned to ride a bike."

"You ride a motorcycle. Not much difference. I'll teach you. You can learn this afternoon."

"How hard is it?"

Impish light glinted his eyes. "They say it's like sex. Once you do it, you never forget how."

Chuckling at her blush, he touched her hand. "Come on. When you're finished, have lunch with me. Let's spend the afternoon having fun."

"As long as there's no demons in the restaurant."

Dale chose a crowded diner by the beach. The diner's other patrons were mostly navy personnel, some uniformed, crammed into the mulberry-colored booths near the window, or sitting on stools at the counter. The air was warm, and smelled of grease and fried food.

In a forest-green polo shirt that hugged his wide shoulders and khaki shorts that displayed long, muscled legs, Dale looked handsome and athletic. Every hormone within her sat up and saluted.

"It's safe here. Nothing to worry about except clogging your arteries," he assured her. "My men checked it out. Just burgers and sandwiches, though."

Keira dipped a French fry into a lake of ketchup. "Good. I've lost my appetite for Italian. I'll take a heart attack any day over meeting another demon."

She wanted to tell him the truth. Maybe here, in the open where he couldn't risk a meltdown. Or take out his gun and shoot her.

Two sailors perched on stools at the counter kept glancing at them and whispering. Dale's jaw tightened. She caught the words *commander* and *injured badly* and *back on duty*.

Anger stirred inside her. Couldn't he enjoy an outing without everyone looking at him as if he were a specimen on display?

Keira pivoted and fixed a cold stare on the sailors. "Yo, Popeye and Bluto, want to quit ogling me? I know I'm cute, but this obsession of yours has to stop. I'm with this guy. Go chase Olive Oyl."

Red-faced, they turned back to their meals. Dale gave her a brief smile. "You don't let much faze you."

"Just demon worms in my meal. Forget them. Tell me about being a SEAL. What kind of training does it require?"

He told her about BUD/S, the intense program all recruits entered to qualify as SEALs.

"Drown-proofing," she murmured. "Sounds difficult."

"It's actually a good skill to learn for anyone who lives near water."

"Do you dive a lot with your team?"

Dale's expression shuttered. "Not me. I'm a commander, and I usually don't accompany my men on missions."

"Your missions require a lot from you."

"Honor is our code. Death before dishonor, like many military branches. We believe it and live it."

Keira gulped down her iced tea. "It also sounds very rigid and unforgiving. Mistakes are made. Can you ever forgive a big mistake?"

Dale looked surprised. "Of course. Mistakes are how we learn."

"What about from someone who isn't a team member? Could you forgive a betrayal from your family?"

"My team is my family."

"Someone not your family, a friend perhaps."

His mouth compressed into a firm slash. "Doubtful."

Her own resolve wavered. She couldn't tell him the truth, not now. Later, she promised herself. Dale would know the full truth.

They left the restaurant, drove to a public beach and parked. Dale retrieved the two shiny bikes he'd placed in the truck's bed. After walking their bikes to the sand, they stopped at the shoreline.

"The sand, not the boardwalk?" she asked.

"Too crowded. You need space. These are mountain bikes, with wide tires. They'll suffice."

Keira looked down at the bright blue bicycle he'd borrowed from a neighbor and made a moue of distaste. "I don't know about this…."

"The only way to learn is to get on. And if you fall,

you fall on sand. Less injury." Dale held out a hand. "Just like I showed you back home. You can do it."

Keira depressed the ringer on the silver bell adorning the handlebars. Dale lifted his dark brows.

"Stop stalling."

"I'm not stalling. Bells keep demons away."

"You expect them to come racing along and knock you off your bike?"

"Nope. Figure I can do that all on my own."

"Get on and start pedaling. I'll be right beside you."

Dale rode nice and slow, although he itched to speed down the beach at breakneck speed. Beside him, Keira wobbled precariously. Suddenly she hit a patch of loose sand and toppled over, crashing onto the sand. He stopped, concerned. Churning waves washed over her legs. "You okay?"

Sitting on the wet sand, she grinned. "I wanted to fall. Because I needed to know what it feels like."

His heart kicked up a notch. Damn, she was so cute. His gaze dropped to those terrific legs, the sexy curve of calf and thigh. He wondered what it would feel like having those legs wrapped around his hips as he thrust deep and hard inside her....

Then she splashed the waves curling around her body. "Wow, this is great. Forget the bike ride. Let's swim!"

After unfastening her sandals, she ran into the ocean and dived straight in.

Retrieving her bike, he parked it. Transfixed, he watched her frolic in the ocean as if this, too, were a new experience. Never had he met such a fascinating woman who embraced life and didn't shy away from the unknown. Keira had a sense of adventure that refreshed his jaded soul.

Desire pumped through his blood as he watched her splash in the ocean, chortling with delight. Such energy and passion. Would she be like this in bed, tumbling with him in unbridled sensuality? Melissa had been cold and stiff, lukewarm at best.

With Keira, it would not be screwing, but making love. Slow and tender, and other times, hot and abandoned.

His hands tightened on the bike's handlebars. And then he realized she had dived into the waves and had not emerged.

Panic clawed at him. Dale kicked off his shoes and ran into the water. He dived down, ignoring the stinging salt in his eyes, searching for her with all his senses. Then he spotted her hovering on the bottom. He wrapped an arm around her waist, and tugged her to the surface. The current turned wicked, wanting to drag them out, but he used all his strength, swimming parallel for a while, then aiming for shore in deep, strong strokes. When he hit bottom, he stood, righting her.

Like a mermaid, Keira twisted her long, dark hair and wrung out seawater. She looked as insouciant as if she'd emerged from a bathtub.

All the water made the white shirt transparent. He could see the outline of her breasts and the darkness of her nipples through the fabric.

Sexual frustration and anger bit him. He put his palms on her slender shoulders, feeling fragile bones beneath her skin. "What the hell were you doing down there?"

Wide green eyes stared at him. "Drown-proofing. You said it was a good idea for everyone who gets near water."

His mouth dropped open, and then he began to laugh. Dale cupped the back of her head and lowered his forehead to hers. "You nutcase. You'll be the death of me, scaring me like that."

He lifted his head and studied her. Droplets clung to her long, dark eyelashes. Her emerald eyes glimmered like wet jewels. So sweet, and oddly naive and yet savvy, Keira was food for his jaded appetite. He couldn't resist that mouth, warm, soft and glistening.

Dale kissed her, losing himself in the sensations, not caring that he was a navy commander on a public beach. Not caring that she'd waltzed into his life and spun him out of control.

Not caring about anything except the sweetness of her mouth, the hesitant flicks of her tongue against his, the richness of her fragrance.

Not caring about the demon blood surging through her veins…

Damn it. Breaking the kiss, he drew in a deep breath, noting the flush of passion tinting her cheeks, the confusion and desire shading her eyes. "Let's get back to riding."

This time, he remained behind her as she pedaled, her movements assured and confident now, her wet hair trailing behind her in the breeze. Dale concentrated on shoving aside burgeoning feelings for this pretty Luminaire. He was a navy commander first. His duty to his team came before romance and relationships.

But deep inside pinged a familiar ache. He was falling hard and fast for this woman.

And if she were a demon, he didn't know if he could stand it.…

He would find a way to test her blood. Somehow.

Chapter 17

Tuesday dawned sharp and clear. Keira rolled out of bed and jumped into the shower. Dale had already left for work. But when she came into the kitchen to grab coffee and a croissant, she spotted his neat, crisp handwriting.

> Be at the base at 1100. The admiral will be finished with his tour by then and I'll arrange a personal meeting.

He signed it *Dale*. And added a small smiley face. The smiley face eased her nervousness.

In the mirror, she studied her appearance. The sleeveless floral dress was light and breezy, and the green and yellow contrasted well with her dark hair. A matching green sweater made her look more presentable for a visit to the navy base.

Dale left the keys to his Jag sitting on the breakfast

nook. She adored driving the car, listening to its smooth purr as she accelerated. Heart beating hard, she drove to the base and at the gate, presented her ID.

The base was huge, intimidating, with hulking buildings that screamed military power. Keira tried to calm her racing pulse. She followed the directions Dale gave her and pulled up to the fenced compound housing ST 21. The sentry checked her ID, glanced at her with curiosity and waved her through.

After she parked, Keira left the Jag, keys jangling in her hand. The weight of several eyes rested upon her.

Electronic eyes. Cameras were posted around the compound's entrance.

A concrete walkway, flanked by bushes, wound up to a steel-door entryway. Keira took a closer glance at the bushes and saw more cameras planted in the middle.

She waved at one.

At the door, a uniformed guard opened it before she could press the buzzer. Keira glanced at her watch. "You're late. I expected someone to come out the moment I left the car."

The man grinned, looking less severe and more boyish. "Sorry, miss. Would have, but the commander gave express orders to meet you at the door and not strong-arm you."

"I'll bet he did," she murmured as he escorted her inside.

They passed through three locked doors and a series of security checks, including a metal detector. As the sailor escorted her down a hallway to yet another steel door, she joked, "Didn't think you needed a metal detector here, with all the X-ray eyes under Dale's command."

The sailor flashed another grin. "The stuff up front is all show-and-tell for brass. Don't need it."

After they cleared the last steel doorway, they met with Dallas, one of Dale's SEALs. Dressed in green battle fatigues, he looked harder and more lethal than the good-natured man who'd helped trap a demon inside the Italian restaurant.

Her escort bid her goodbye.

"Commander Curtis asked me to take you on a tour of the compound," Dallas said.

"He's not joining us? Too busy trying to make coffee?" she teased.

"Commander Curtis is on a conference call with brass in D.C., ma'am."

Ma'am. Not Keira. The SEAL did not crack a smile. The man who'd jested in Dale's basement had vanished, replaced with a military-erect professional. Keira swallowed hard. So different from the casual, friendly jesting she'd experienced.

Down a long hallway they walked as Dallas explained about the compound's importance to the team.

"We train daily, on-site and off, when we're not deployed. Air, close-quarters combat, diving, marksmanship and more. Training is essential to our survival."

At the hallway's end, he opened a door and they walked outside into the sunshine. The yard resembled a bizarre jungle gym, with rope climbs, towers and equipment. A few men were fighting in hand-to-hand combat.

"Over there is the shoot house where we conduct live-fire training."

She walked over to the monkey bars. Dallas gently clasped her wrist as she went to touch it.

"It's electrified. Oh, not enough to kill," he added, seeing her stunned expression. "Just enough to give you a good jolt."

"You train with live current?"

"Every SEAL on ST 21 has to be prepared to encounter the unexpected. Both paranormal and normal human traps. Training with live-current conditions us to become impervious to it, but we have SEALs who can absorb the current into their bodies and use it to maximize their powers."

Fascinating. In the distance, gunfire cracked and popped, making her jump. Dallas gestured to a target range. "Today we're using regular ammo. Tomorrow is when we train with the heavy stuff."

She didn't want to ask about his idea of heavy.

They walked to a small concrete building. Dallas punched a few numbers on a keypad and opened the door.

There was a small area, like a holding cell, and a large door. Dallas flicked on a switch and opened the door to a large, concrete-lined room.

"Our new firestorm chamber." Pride was evident in the junior lieutenant's voice.

"May I?"

Keira walked inside the room. Senses tingling, she looked around. The walls were thick concrete, with blackened marks scorching the sides. She placed a palm on one wall and shuddered.

She turned to Dallas, who was standing with his hands folded behind his back.

"You use real fire?"

Admiration filled his voice. "Curt insists. He says just like we train with live ammo because the enemy won't use blanks, we need to use real flames because demons won't use stimulated ones."

A shudder raced down her spine. "What kind of demons fight with flames?"

"Mostly pyrokinetic demons." A shadow crossed his face. "But we sealed all of them in the netherworld. Bastards won't be coming out anytime soon. Biggest threats are from minor demons or hybrids. Worst are the Iginus demons. They shift into inanimate objects, furniture, tables, even photos on your wall, and then attack when your back is turned."

They continued the tour. In a gymnasium, men fought with various weapons. Dallas showed her the weapons the SEALs trained with. Not only regular navy issue, but also strange objects like pentagrams, throwing stars, spears and even a whip tipped with tiny sharp triangles.

"Looks like a torture chamber." She laughed lightly.

Dallas picked up the whip. "We confiscated this from a rogue wizard using it to torture his apprentice."

Keira touched one of the triangles, shuddering as she imagined the inflicted damage. Muscles knotted in her back as she thought of the pain the young apprentice suffered.

Seeing her expression, he added, "The boy suffered more emotional trauma than injury. The wizard would crack it behind his back as a threat."

"So cruel."

Dallas's face tightened. "We've witnessed much worse."

He nodded at a nearby dummy holding out a silver wand. He flicked his wrist and cracked the whip, slicing the wand in half.

"The wizard invented the whip to destroy his enemies, good magicians who threatened to expose him. We turned it into a weapon to disarm him without causing injury."

"Works good if your target is standing still," she murmured.

He gave her an amused look. "The dummy is for practice shots. We train on each other as active targets. It's necessary because any rogue wizard holding the wand will be moving against us. And probably tossing energy bolts at us, as well."

Revulsion coiled low in her stomach. "What if you miss?"

"We don't, because we're working as a team and we always watch each others' sixes."

Must be nice. She never had anyone working with her, or watching her back.

"What if one of you is having a bad day?" She thought of how nasty the Centurions could be, and when they got impatient, poured on the pressure, making her life even more hellish.

At his blank look, she explained. "What if you're working with someone you dislike, or someone who has a problem with you? How can you trust him not to miss and hit your face?"

"We're SEALs first, ma'am. We have to trust each other in training and down range."

"Down range?"

"Deployment. I don't get along with all the men on this team, but I sure do rely on them to do their job, and they rely on me to do mine." He set the weapon neatly back on its peg.

"Gives a whole new meaning to whipping you guys into shape."

Dallas did not smile. "Curt insists on our regular training as SEALs, and extra training as paranorms. Double duty, but we do it gladly because we know what we're up against. The Phoenix Force is often a last resort, protection for civilians against the darkest evil."

She felt deep awe at what these men did. And Dale commanded them all. Keira wistfully wondered what it would feel like to have the respect and devotion of a team that worked closely to protect others, instead of forming alliances to hurt them.

They concluded the tour at a small cafeteria with long tables and folding chairs. Dallas nodded. "I'll leave you here, ma'am. Ensign Robyn Lees will be here soon to escort you to your next meeting. May I fetch you coffee?"

"Only if it's hazelnut."

The barest smile touched his mouth. "I do enjoy your special coffee, ma'am. We're fresh out. But we do have regular."

"I'll make sure to send more over. Thanks, but I'm fine."

She went to the counter and brushed a finger against it. So much responsibility and so many lives under Dale's command. Keira began to understand his rigid need for order and discipline.

If he blinked wrong, or made a bad decision, not only did he put his men in jeopardy, but lives could also be lost. Many lives.

She thought of the blood spilled by the Centurions and imagined it multiplied by several hundred...no, several thousand.

Keira shuddered.

"Good morning, Miss Solomon."

She startled and whirled to see a petite, freckle-faced woman clad in the standard khaki, short-sleeved uniform. "Whoa. I didn't hear you come in. You're quiet as a cat."

"You could say. I'm Ensign Robyn Lees, here to escort you. Commander Curtis asked me to relay to you his wishes that you report to the infirmary before meeting with the admiral. He requests you take a blood test."

"He does?" Anger spiked. "Still hasn't given up on that one. You can tell him to kiss my...never mind. I'll tell him myself."

The ensign's blue eyes twinkled. "Thought you'd say that. If you refuse, I'm requested to escort you to the conference room."

They went back into the hallway. At the end, the ensign opened the door to a narrow room with a long, polished table and leather chairs. A large-screen television was at one end.

"Please wait here, ma'am."

Catching her unique scent Keira smiled. "You're the ensign who spoke to me on the phone the other day. Cat shifter."

The ensign grinned. "Your recipe for coffee's real good. Although I prefer milk to get started at oh-five-hundred."

Keira laughed as the woman closed the door behind her. She sat at the elegant, polished conference table, tapping her fingers.

This was too easy. Dale was not the type to give up. *Don't want to take a blood test? No prob, just go to the conference room and await the admiral.*

When the door opened, she half expected Dale to storm inside, a scowl on his face, demanding she hold out her arm.

Instead, a short, stocky man entered. Like the others, he wore a khaki uniform, but instead of close-cropped hair, his fell below his collar.

Keira stood and pushed back her chair. "Where's Dale? And the admiral?"

"Commander Curtis will be here soon." The man smiled, but it didn't meet his dark eyes. "I'm Petty Officer Thad Lennox."

The scent of darkness and rich crimson slammed into her. "You're a demon," she said, backing up against the table.

He pushed back a lock of hair, exposing pointed ears. "Half demon and half Fae. But the good half of me is committed to serving my country, and fighting people like my father. He was a real piece of work." Thad picked up a small, cylindrical object. It looked like a wand.

Or a probe.

Keira's frantic gaze darted to the conference table. It had elongated, turning into a narrow metal slab, covered with disposable paper. Suddenly she realized shelves lined the walls, holding a variety of instruments and equipment.

Illusion. They used illusion to lure me inside, fooling me into thinking this was a meeting room.

Thad politely gestured to the exam table. "If you'll please sit, this will only take a moment. It won't hurt, I promise. But I must run some scans and examine you."

"Why are you doing this to me?" she cried out.

"Just relax," he murmured. "All I'm going to do is touch you, right here on the forehead...."

Panic surged, bright and hot. He'd know. And Dale would know, and in this compound, surrounded by paranormals trained to kill, she'd be dead in seconds. Self-preservation kicked in. Keira's claws emerged and a snarl ripped from her throat. Lashing out, she caught the petty officer by surprise. Cloth tore and blood bubbled up from the furrows she'd carved into his upper right arm.

He didn't even cry out, or glance at the wound, only stalked toward her with a determined look. Dimly she heard a door behind her open.

"Sir," Thad said quietly. "Do it."

Something stung her buttocks, sharp and piercing. Keira staggered, and looked back.

Dale stood behind her, pity tightening his expression. He plucked free the dart and tossed it aside.

Gray clouded the edges of her vision. She started to collapse and fell into his strong arms.

The last thing she saw before losing consciousness was his handsome face, and the coldness of his gray eyes.

Chapter 18

Thwock. Thwock.

The tennis ball banged against the far wall. Dale caught it in one hand.

At the hospital, they showed him tricks to cool down his anger and deal with frustration and strengthen the left hand, which had been weakened during the attack. Squeeze the tennis ball.

Instead, he'd tossed it at the wall and practiced catching it left-handed. The mindless routine soothed him.

Not today.

The ball landed in his sweating palm as a knock sounded on the door. "Come," he said.

Thad entered, bearing several sheets of paper. He placed them in front of Dale and perched in a chair before his desk.

"She's not a demon. But she has demon blood inside her."

Thwock. The ball burst in Dale's grip. He tossed it aside. "How?"

"I don't know. It's very dark and powerful. But it's muted, as if she's struggled to contain it." Thad's faced tightened. "Whoever she is, Curt, she's not evil. But she's tangled with some nasty creatures. My guess is they used her, and injected her with their blood to bend her to their will."

"I don't need guesses, Petty Officer. I need facts. Deal in facts." Dale pushed aside the report and rubbed his face. "Is she a Luminaire?"

"Oh, hell, yeah. But Luminaires, anyone can claim to be one. A Luminaire is more a title than a species. Mostly Fae. They're into white light and chanting and healing with crystals. But their magick is weak and usually ineffective unless combined with others. This one…"

"Her name is Keira."

"Keira, she's putting out powerful vibes. And claws." He ruefully examined three jagged tears in his shirt-sleeve. "Caught me by surprise. She could have gone for my throat, but I sensed she deliberately avoided it because she only wanted to defend herself. Animal instinct."

Claws. Animal instinct.

Wolf.

Another memory pinged, sending a searing ache through his head. If only those damn Centurions hadn't put a memory spell on him. Every time he thought he was getting close to answers, the memories became like mist. He needed to focus on the present and stay sharp.

"Answer my question, Petty Officer. To the best of your knowledge, what is she?"

"I honestly don't know. But she's very strong and there's a deep well of courage running through her. Whatever she's endured, she's fought it hard and long and it hasn't overtaken her." A small smile touched his thin mouth. "Make a hell of a SEAL, sir."

"How is Keira?"

"Still unconscious, but resting comfortably in the infirmary. Do you want to see her?"

Dale shook his head. "When she wakes, have her escorted to my office by Ensign Sully."

Surprise flared on the half demon's face. "Yes, sir."

When the man left, Dale leaned back in his leather chair. Had to handle this with the utmost sensitivity and diplomacy. Rushing to sick bay to offer comfort would put him on the defensive, and weaken his position before his men. Here on base, he must maintain command.

The man in him wanted to comfort her with assurances and seek understanding.

The military commander knew he must maintain a rigid posture to keep his people protected.

He'd done the unforgivable. Broken her trust.

Dale rubbed a hand over his face. He hoped she would understand, and eventually forgive him.

But even if she did, he knew it would be a long time before he forgave himself.

Cold and darkness surrounded her. Keira moaned, thrusting out with her hands to survey her surroundings. The cell was damp and noxious, filled with the stench of dried blood. A pencil-thin shaft of sunshine speared the gloom, falling on the concrete floor. Crab-crawling over to it, she huddled in the tiny beam, desperate for light, for warmth. And then she saw her hands and realized the stench came from her—her hands were covered in someone else's blood.

A startled scream tore from her throat. She bolted upright.

Only to find herself lying on a narrow, but comfortable bed, a warm blanket covering her. A counter filled with instruments and a small sink was across from the bed.

She put a hand to her pounding skull. A sick room.

The door opened and cheerful, impulsive Sully walked in. But no wide grin touched his face. He looked as rigid and stiff as his teammate, Dallas.

"Are you all right, ma'am?" Sully had morphed into a stranger. Ensign Sully, whose loyalty came first to his commanding officer.

His rat-bastard, sneaky commanding officer.

Grief clogged her throat. Keira tossed aside the blanket and stood on wobbly legs, pushing aside his hand as he sprang to help. "I'm fantastic. Get me the hell out of here."

The barest emotion flicked in his eyes, then vanished. "I apologize, ma'am, but Commander Curtis has requested your presence in his office."

"Oh?" She smoothed down her floral skirt with a trembling hand. "You can tell your Commander Curtis he can go to hell. I'll give him a first-class ticket."

Now his lips did quirk. "Can't do that, ma'am. Please, come with me."

No prob. She knew her way out.

As they entered the hallway, she bolted, running for the thick steel door standing between her and freedom. She didn't want Dale's explanations or having him poke her with needles or probes.

The door was in sight, so close, the handle near.

Two strong hands pulled her back. Whipping her head around, she saw Dallas on one side, Sully on the other.

"Miss Solomon, please come with us," Dallas said tersely.

Screw this. Summoning all her wolf strength, she

flung them off and ran for the door. The handle was in her grasp. Keira jiggled it. It did not move. Panic surged, bright and hot. She was trapped, caught in an endless nightmare where they'd force her to do nasty things, force her to their will....

Two hands caught her upper arms and started to pull her back. Keira screamed and held on to the door handle. Solid steel splintered, and snapped off.

"Stop it, you morons."

The men let go. Keira whirled, holding the door handle like a weapon.

Ensign Robyn Lees stood in the hallway, scowling at the SEALs. "Is this any way to treat the commander's guest?"

"He ordered us to bring her to his office ASAP. And not let her escape." But Sully looked shamefaced.

"She broke the door handle. The goddamn door handle." Wonder and respect flared on Dallas's face, turning him from a military robot into something human.

"And you're lucky she didn't break your neck or claw you like she did Thad, the way you two have been manhandling her. Have you ever heard of finesse? No, you're too busy blowing stuff up and jumping out of planes. Stand down, both of you."

As Dallas and Sully stepped back, Ensign Lees held out a freckled hand. "Miss Solomon? Please, will you come with me? It's okay. I promise you'll be fine."

The warm assurance in the woman's voice eased Keira's fears. Swallowing hard, she took the ensign's hand.

The woman removed the door handle from Keira's death grip and slapped it into Dallas's hand. "Get maintenance here ASAP to fix that door."

As they walked down the hallway, the ensign squeezed her hand. "Don't mind them. They're good men, just overbearing at times when Commander Curtis issues a strict order."

"They listen to you."

"Have to. I'm the team's communications expert. When they're down range, I coordinate getting all the supplies the team needs to do their job."

The officer glanced at Keira's right arm, where the sweater had ridden up, exposing her upper arm. "That's a slave armband."

Keira's guts squeezed. "How did you know, Ensign?"

"Call me Robyn. My sister had one. She was enslaved in Egypt, but I freed her."

"Recently?" Maybe this woman could help her.

"About 2,500 years ago. Slave to a cruel Egyptian noble." At Keira's startled look, she grinned. "I'm much older than I look."

"How did you free her?"

"I used my influence. Cats were worshipped by the Egyptians so I had a little chat with the pharaoh. He freed her."

No pharaohs could free Keira from her demons. Despair set in as they reached a closed door with a shiny brass nameplate that read Lieutenant Commander Dale Curtis.

Robyn squeezed her hand again. "Go on. He can be a bear at times, but he does things for the right reasons. He's a good, honorable leader. We need him back the way he was. I've seen the changes in him because of you. Help him."

A tremendous balloon of anger and resentment deflated. This wasn't merely about her and how he'd mistreated her.

Mouth wobbling, she nodded. "Thanks."

Keira went inside and shut the door behind her.

The office was large, with a conference table and ten chairs to her left, and an enormous hand-carved wood desk to her right. A matching credenza lined with papers, books and a few photos sat beneath a window behind the desk.

A long leather sofa and two matching chairs made up a sitting area in the back, with a polished table in front of the furniture. Behind the sitting area was a door.

Dale was perched on the sofa, a silver tea service and two delicate china cups before him. He stood. "Keira, please join me."

So civilized for a brutal beast, she thought. Arms wrapped around her waist, she sat at the sofa's head, watching him through narrowed eyes.

"Are you all right?" he quietly asked.

Nodding, she watched him pour amber liquid into a china cup. Dale handed her a saucer. "Chamomile tea laced with honey. Nothing else, I promise."

Keira took it and sipped, feeling the warmth slide down her throat. Silence hung between them for a moment. Gradually the tension squeezing her chest eased.

He set down his teacup. Legs spread wide, Dale braced his hands on his knees and looked at her straight in the eye.

"I owe you an explanation."

She tensed, and the armband around her biceps gently squeezed, a reminder of her predicament. *Can't leave, as much as I want to. I put myself in this man's hands and until he releases me from our agreement, I'm trapped, just as I was with the Centurions. Except they didn't break my heart....*

She glanced at his face and the brief sorrow in his eyes gave her pause.

"I did not mean for you to get hurt, but what was done was necessary, and I take full blame."

"Go on."

He picked up his cup and took a sip. "I have nearly two hundred men and women under me, and I'm responsible for their welfare and protection on this base. If one so much as sneezes, I know. It's my duty as commander to protect the safety of the men and women on this compound."

"You thought I was a demon and wanted my blood."

"I didn't know what you were, and that unknown factor risked the lives of my staff." He set down the cup, his gaze serious. "I felt myself drawing close to you. You're an integral part of my life and a potential threat to this team because of that relationship."

A shadow drew over his expression. "When you pointed out Melissa's true origins, I realized what kind of threat existed. Melissa was thoroughly checked out because of my position, but not for…dangerous paranormal powers."

"She's a chimp, not a demon."

"A moot point. I failed to thoroughly investigate her background and vowed never to fail again. That's why I brought you here for an examination."

"Thanks a lot. Had a real swell time. It was better than a day at Disney."

Unsmiling, he regarded her. "If you were a demon, and gained access to this base because of me, you held the power to destroy lives and relay secrets."

She rubbed the armband. "Your goons would have stopped me."

"SEALs," he corrected. "They were under my orders to keep you guarded, and prevent you from leaving. I apologize if they acted rough."

"I've had worse."

"So I understand." Sympathy filled his gaze. Tensing, she wondered what the hell he'd discovered.

I'm still sitting here, in one piece so he can't know I'm the demon wolf he wants....

"Thad informed me you have traces of powerful demon blood in your system, but you have an equally strong will and have been fighting it. He informed me you attacked him, in self-defense and could have easily killed him. I understand you've suffered greatly."

The atmosphere grew thick with tension. Keira shrugged to diffuse it.

"I believe you were infused with this demon blood by the same ones who killed your parents."

A huge knot unwound in her stomach. True enough. She nodded.

"It takes a strong woman to survive a demon attack," he said softly. "I remember, I met such a female...once... long ago...."

He pressed fingers to his temple. "Never mind. What I am telling you, Keira, is that I know my actions were hurtful to you. I am sorry for upsetting you, but I won't apologize for doing it because the safety and welfare of my team will always come first. No matter how important a woman is to me."

Dale stared at a small, burnt hole in the wall behind the sofa. "Because of you, I've begun to heal. I can't thank you enough. I've broken the trust you put in me, but hope to regain it."

Jaw set like granite, he looked as if he'd been carved from ice. Suddenly she realized there was a bigger issue here. Much bigger, one he refused to share.

"Dale, what aren't you telling me?"

He rubbed a hand over his face.

"You say you want to regain my trust. Then tell me what's really wrong."

His big shoulders turned rigid and he shook his head. "I'm fine."

"You're not fine. I'm not one of your staff. You don't have to pretend or keep up appearances with me. Damn it, I helped you heal, saw the darkness inside you." Keira struggled with a tangle of emotions. "I would never betray your confidence. I want to help."

Silence hovered in the air a moment. She waited.

When he spoke his voice dropped to a bare whisper. "I'm losing control."

"No…"

"Yes." The shuttered look dropped from his expression and he looked stark and haunted. "I've had doubts about leading my team. Doubts that haven't left, doubts I never had until my captivity in the basement. I've been a SEAL for years. Learned to push past the pain and endure, but the torture in the basement… It left me a damnable, whimpering mess, a shell of a man."

Ice coated her veins. She waited.

"My greatest concern isn't me, it's my men and my ability to lead them. Every morning I push my physical limits to show them I'm strong, while inside, I still feel like an empty shell. Weak and ineffective. They know it, too."

He glanced at the hole in the wall. "That damage is from my powers. I lost my temper with Ensign Lees and nearly hit her with an energy bolt."

Stunned, she looked at the neat, round hole. "Well, you didn't. And after meeting her in person, I daresay she can take care of herself."

"Yes. But my staff continues treating me as if I'm the battered, beaten man Shay and Kelly found in the basement. When they get overly solicitous, it's frustrating. You're the only one who doesn't treat me like a helpless victim, as if I'll fall apart any moment." He paused. "Until I find the damn demons who imprisoned me, I'll never fully be able to move forward and be the man I once was, the commander they respected and need to guide them."

Breath caught in her throat. Dale was strong, but it took an even stronger man to admit to vulnerability.

Maybe she healed the darkness in his soul, but he still needed to heal from the trauma in the basement.

All along, she'd been selfish, only calculating how she could wrench free from the Centurions and finally gain freedom. Bigger issues were at stake.

She'd been so imprisoned by her own pain that she'd failed to see the bigger picture. Dale wasn't self-centered. He worried because everything he did directly impacted others under his command. The man could not even have a relationship without wondering if the woman was going to turn into a chimp…or a demon wolf, and endanger his men.

Keira chose her words with care. "You're a good and honorable man, even if your methods are questionable. I don't like what you did, but I do understand your motives. You're doing this for your team."

Maybe the concept of teamwork had benefits. She'd only seen the negatives.

She looked him straight in the eye. "You're not weak. Far from it. You're enormously strong and courageous. An ordinary man would have surrendered and let the demon darkness defeat him. You didn't." She took a deep breath. "I'll help you continue to recover."

Dale did not speak for a moment, only continued to

study her. Finally his shoulders eased slightly. "Thank you."

"It will cost you." The ghost of a smile touched her mouth. "More sessions with the crystals and two entire nights of watching any chick flick I want."

"Deal. I'm a SEAL. I can take such torment." He smiled and walked over to her, dropping beside her on the sofa.

The tantalizing scent of him wound around her senses. So close. She leaned away.

"Don't be afraid of me, Keira. I won't harm you."

I'm not afraid of what you'll do. More scared of what I'll do.

"I've begun to care for you, Keira. Not as a patient for a healer, but as a man cares for a woman." He took her hand. "You're beginning to mean a great deal to me. That's one reason why I needed you thoroughly checked out by Thad."

He stroked a thumb over the tips of her fingers. "You had claws."

Her stomach roiled. "They come out when I feel threatened. I shift sometimes."

Dale frowned. "Into a wolf?"

She looked at him and shrugged, hoping he couldn't hear her pounding heart. "Not a wolf like you think. I'll tell you more later."

He frowned and pressed a finger to his temple.

"You okay?"

"Damn headaches. I get them when a memory starts to return."

"Then don't think about the past," she told him, clutching his hand. "You're strong. We will find those Centurions and you'll be able to move on."

A tremor raced down her spine as he slowly stroked

a thumb across her knuckles. Erudite Dale enjoyed classical music, but also commanded an equally powerful military force. Never had she encountered such strength.

She'd wanted to siphon that strength and use it to break the chains of her captivity. How utterly selfish. Keira thought of the shining hope in Robyn's eyes, the solemn pride of Dale's SEALs and the trust they put in him.

You will heal from the trauma, she silently promised. *If it takes the last ounce of my white light, you'll become the man your team needs.*

"Oh, he thoroughly checked me out," she added when she remembered what he'd said earlier. "Must admit, when he came toward me with that probe thingie, I thought I was being abducted by aliens for secret experiments. But then you hit me in the butt with that needle and everything turned nice and dark and forgetful."

A rueful look crossed his face. "It was a regrettable choice. I've been wanting close contact with your pretty little bottom for a while, but not with a dart gun."

Flushing at the implication she lowered her gaze. Dale tipped her chin up with a finger. "Look at me, Keira. From now on, no more secrets between us. Nothing but honesty."

So close. His full mouth hovered near hers. Slowly, she closed her eyes and felt his lips soft upon hers. Such a gentle, sweet kiss. Her mouth parted and he pressed closer, not pressuring, a subtle invitation to a closer dance.

So patient. SEALs were quite patient, she remembered reading. And persistent.

Dale waited for a cue.

She needed to touch him, needed this connection, a physical touch to anchor her to a future filled with possibilities instead of a bleak past. Keira's tongue darted out and traced his lower lip.

Groaning, he cupped the back of her head and drew her closer. His mouth moved over hers, teasing and coaxing. Oh, she never guessed the sweet power of a kiss, how it could turn her into a melting puddle of sheer want.

When they pulled apart, her ragged pants filled the air. His pupils darkened, nearly overcoming the slate-gray irises. His hot, hungry look equaled the frantic racing of her heart.

That look promised they would be lovers....

"We'd better stop before the admiral gets here and accuses me of testing out a new kind of therapy."

Keira touched her flushed cheeks. "Oh, damn. Is there a way I can cool down? Have a bucket of ice handy, or a walk-in freezer?"

Dale looked amused. "The bathroom's through that door. Go freshen up."

As she started off the sofa, he pulled her down for another, lingering kiss. But this time, his hand reached around and gave a gentle squeeze to her bottom.

She playfully slapped his hand away. "Not so fast, sailor."

"Just checking to make sure I didn't hurt you too badly with the dart gun." His sheepish grin melted her all over again, making him look adorably contrite, like a boy caught stealing cookies from the jar.

"I barely felt it," she told him, and then went into the bathroom, closing the door behind her.

But as she splashed her face with cold water and then stared at the mirror, she had the sinking feeling Dale could hurt her much worse if he accidentally discovered the truth.

She would tell him tonight.

No matter what.

Chapter 19

All during dinner, Keira wrestled with one burning question. How could she confess her secret to this man?

The lamb chops were tender and succulent, the vegetables tasty and crisp. With his help, she'd prepared a perfect meal. They'd laughed and talked about everything that didn't matter, from reality television shows to her weakness for chocolate.

They'd talked about everything except her origins and his torture.

Together, they cleared the table and loaded the dishwasher. Then Keira glanced into the dark backyard.

"Let's go outside. I need to tell you something."

An inscrutable look crossed his face. "I need to show you something."

A cool breeze caressed her neck and teased her dress hem as they stood on the deck. Keira looked up at the cloudless night sky studded with tiny stars. Fairy lights, she thought dimly, and a pang of sharp sorrow pierced her.

Gripping the railing she stared at the grassy yard, the forest stretching beyond the wood fence protecting his property. "You asked about my origins. I'm a Celestial Hunter. A wolf."

She felt him join her, felt his intense focus upon her. "I've never heard of that type of wolf."

"My people are…" *Extinct.* "Quite rare. We live in packs that rove from country to country, seeking privacy so we can shift and run wild."

"Why didn't you tell me before, sweetheart?"

Gentleness laced his voice, the endearment causing her throat to clog with emotion. "Because I am a wolf, but not any wolf."

Hands clammy, she rubbed them against her skirt. Sweat beaded her forehead, trickled down her back, gathering in the waistband of the pretty mint-green panties she'd chosen out of pure desperation, a feminine defense for this night.

The night when he'd surely take his revenge.

Images flashed before her… Dale, chained to the platform, begging her to stop, screaming at her to stop. But she could not, her claws gouging into flesh, cutting deep into muscle and sinew…the stench of his blood making her beast grow wilder and more feral….

Keira squeezed her eyes shut and dug her nails into her palms. "I'm the woman who hurt you so badly."

A heartbeat of silence. Another. *Breathe, just breathe.*

She opened her eyes, only to see confusion clouding his eyes. He winced, and pressed a hand to his forehead. "Damn. Another headache. Where the hell are these coming from?"

From the mind spell the Centurions implanted deep

inside your brain. Somehow, she must cajole him into pushing past the pain and remembering.

"When you were tortured by a demon wolf who shifted into a woman…" She choked back a sob. "That woman was me."

Would he remember and react? Or was the memory too deeply buried? Torn between wanting his memory to return and keeping her secret, she reached out and ran her nails down his strong left biceps.

The biceps she'd carved into ribbons…

But he didn't even flinch. Dale simply kept studying her, as if she were a long-lost acquaintance he couldn't quite place.

Frowning, he pressed his fingers to his head. "There was a woman, a tall blonde woman, thin, she wore bright red lipstick." Dale's mouth flattened. "That's the woman who tortured me."

Stricken, she stared. He'd just described Melissa, his ex-girlfriend. The memory spell planted in his mind by the Centurions was extrapolating the image of his girl-friend and substituting it for whatever memories Dale had of Keira in the basement.

For nearly three weeks she'd worked up the courage for this moment. And it proved fruitless.

The only way he'd remember was the Celestial pen-dant. Back in the basement when she'd been in human form after torturing him as a wolf, when the demons left Dale alone to regain consciousness, she had sewn it into his flesh as protection, the sacred pendant among her people being the only item capable of avoiding her killing bite.

Once Dale touched the pendant, it would trigger all lost memories, demon spell or not.

"You're not the demon wolf who hurt me, Keira. You're the woman who saved me," he said quietly.

She opened her mouth to protest, but he pressed a finger against her lips. "Please. Let me speak now. I have something to show you. And damn, it's taking all my nerve to do this."

Lights flooded the yard and the pool as he flipped a switch on the wall. Then he stepped back, and before her eyes, the tall, handsome Mage with the scars and the serious air seemed to melt into the air.

In his place was a muscled, gray timber wolf. The wolf raised its head to the moon and howled, then bounded down the steps and raced through the yard.

Throat dry, she watched, her own wolf longing to join him and run free. Every cell pulsed with yearning, the beast inside clawing to get out, but unable to be free. Her female responding to the strong male wolf now running through the yard, leaping over the serene rock arrangement by the garden she'd planted.

Mesmerized, she descended the steps, watching from the pool's concrete deck, her hand resting on a lounge chair.

The wolf trotted over to the bushes and sniffed. Eyes gleaming like gray flashlights, he lifted a back leg and marked one she'd planted.

Marking his territory.

She recognized the primal gesture. To warn other males away, and a promise to her to later claim her in the flesh and make her his own.

Female hormones stirred and arousal pulsed. He loped toward the pool. The wolf leaped in, water splashing over the deck, baptizing her in a cascade of droplets.

A wolf had jumped into the pool.

A naked man emerged from it.

He rose from the water like Poseidon, lacking only a trident and beard. Water cascaded down his sleek flanks, his muscular, scarred abdomen.

Powerful thigh muscles rippled beneath his skin as he mounted the steps.

Keira took a step back. Another, as he left the pool and advanced, his black hair slick and wet. Her gaze traveled from the twist and tangle of scar tissue marking his chest and torso, to his strong, powerful thighs and the curve of muscle of calves, back to the apex of his legs and the water beading in the thick, dark hair of his groin.

His thick, long phallus. At rest, it was impressive.

She looked up into his face, tense with anticipation.

"You see what I am," he said quietly. He spread out his arms, reminding her of Darwin's celestial man. "What happened to me. This is me, Keira."

Deep, jagged scars lined his torso and chest, silvery gouges bisecting every plane of muscle and sinew. More scars flared on his thick thighs, ending just above his knees.

She'd gone for the thickest muscles to do the least damage.

He waited quietly, watching her face. Melissa had not seen him naked, only the bandages covering the injuries. But her horrified gasp and avoidance afterward had been enough warning.

The SEALs on his team knew his injuries, saw them each day when he swam laps with them. But no woman had seen him naked since a wolf had carved his torso like a roast.

Exposing himself like this was a gamble, but necessary. Dale had sworn to be honest with her after the exam at the base.

He would not keep secrets from her any longer.

No pity etched her expression. He saw a flicker of wonder and, as she glanced downward, frank female appreciation.

His sex stirred.

"So strong. Such a strong, courageous male to take such a brutal torture."

A dim memory flickered. Soft voice and sweet scent winding around his body like velvet ropes, a lick of passion teasing his groin, desire and pain mingling together until he wanted to scream and never stop....

Spikes of pain slammed into his temples. Dale pressed a hand to his aching head.

"Are you okay?" she asked.

He nodded, struggling more with pride than pain. Damn, getting naked in front of a woman usually meant pleasure.

Now it meant possible rejection. Gathering all his strength, he plunged ahead.

"I'm beginning to care for you, Keira. And I want no secrets between us. Especially...this." He pointed to his maimed torso.

Dale watched her reaction, his heart beating fast. Never had he felt this vulnerable and exposed. Not even when he'd been tied to the platform in the basement, helpless against the wolf's claws. He'd fought the chains, resisted the compulsion to scream with his last breath, until the pain became a hot, living agony scraping over bone and flesh. Even then, the hoarse cries torn from his throat were shrieks of rage and promises of revenge.

Now, all he faced was silence, and Keira. Waiting for judgment.

Or redemption.

Melissa had not wanted to see him naked. On the way

to the ball, she'd whispered how they could spend the night together. When he'd informed her, with overt sarcasm, it would require him to remove his clothing, she'd only replied, "Darling, we can always turn off the lights."

Tonight, Dale had flooded the backyard with lights, flipping on every lamppost, the pool lights, hell, even the motion-detector lights.

Leaving nothing to Keira's imagination, letting her see every single ugly groove and hollow marking him.

Her lovely mouth wobbled as her large eyes grew luminous. Then she stepped forward, and placed her hand on his chest, over his heart. Her palm was soft and warm against his chilled flesh.

"They couldn't scar this. Your heart. No matter what they did to you, they could never take away the courageous, noble man who stepped forward to save a child's life. Your scars are medals, a testament to your honor."

Tears shimmered in her eyes. "You are the bravest man I've had the privilege to know. Thank you for sharing this with me."

Something inside him eased. Dale cupped her cheek, thumbing aside a tear.

"Don't cry, sweetheart."

"It hurts to know how you suffered," she whimpered. "How you were in so much pain. I wish…oh, how I wish I could have stopped it."

Distressed, he bent his head and kissed the corner of her mouth. "It doesn't hurt. Not anymore."

A cry tore from her throat, a wrenching sob. She wrapped her arms around his neck and kissed him. He tasted her, and the salty tears running down her cheeks. Dale deepened the kiss, joy tumbling through him. She moaned beneath his mouth, and drew closer. His sex stirred fully, eager for more.

Dale nipped at her lower lip and broke the kiss. He gazed down at her, all thoughts of vulnerability gone, wanting only one thing.

"Make love with me."

He needed to be a man again, needed to feel whole. He needed her in his arms, her soothing touch stroking over bare flesh, healing him.

Keira slid a palm up to caress his jaw. "Yes," she whispered. "Tonight."

"Now."

He swung her into his arms and she gave a startled, but happy yelp. Legs dangling over his arms, Keira hooked her hands around his neck. "You don't do anything by half measure, do you, Commander."

"Never." His grin faded. "Not when it comes to you. I'm not a romantic, Keira. Just a man who's been to hell and back and needs you, desperately."

He hooked a strand of hair behind her ear. "I want you so much, I'm trembling inside."

Dale leaned his forehead against hers, needing to touch her, hold her, keep her close. "I want to wrap myself around you like a vine, entwining myself so deeply we become one. I want to make love to you until we become so close, we flow into each other like water. Push myself so deep into you that I become an unquenchable fire, burning you with passion. Give yourself to me, Keira, and I promise you I'll give you pleasure to remember for a thousand nights."

And then she pulled away, her gaze soft and shining, and touched his cheek, her soft hand a redeeming caress. "Yes. A thousand times, yes."

As Dale kissed her she wrapped her arms around him, losing herself in sensation.

For years, her heart had been guarded by walls as thick as her cell, encaged in a protective layer. Never had she wanted to share herself, give her heart away to a man and hand him the power to hurt her.

For the first time since those awful days in the Nicaraguan jungle when the Centurions killed everyone she loved, Keira wanted to open her heart. Dale could hurt her, badly. But she'd lived too long in the darkness.

Only the light would suffice.

Warmth suffused her as he kept kissing her, his wet body pressed close, the hardness of his erection digging into her lower belly. Keira moaned, wanting to sink into him, wrap herself around him and forget the world. Draw in his inner light and blend it with hers, bond with him in the flesh as their spirits would surely entwine.

Let him chase away the emptiness for a while longer.

Dale kept inching backward, toward the deep end. Oh, she was going off the deep end, losing herself in the sharp sweetness of his mouth....

He stepped back and they fell into the water together. Coldness washed over her. Keira emerged, sputtering, as he laughed and playfully splashed her.

"My dress!"

"Take it off and let it dry out."

She swam until she could stand, and wrung out her long hair. Fierce hunger glinted his gray gaze as he approached, eyes level with the water, like an alligator. Keira looked at the burning lights. He had the courage to get naked before her.

The dress clung to her like shrink wrap, but she wriggled out of it. Dale's warm gaze caressed her as she reached for the clasps of her bra and finally set it aside, then pulled down the matching green panties and tossed them onto the pool deck. Shyly she stood before him, feeling suddenly vulnerable.

He framed her face with his warm, strong hands. "You're so beautiful."

He kissed his way down her neck, while palming her breasts. Each stroke of her turgid nipples brought flaming warmth, oh, such lovely warmth it felt like she'd never be cold again. Squirming, she kissed him back, rubbing against him, not knowing exactly what to do, but eager to explore.

Dale nuzzled her neck and spread a palm over her belly, then slid his hand lower, between her legs. Fresh heat flared as he slid a finger between her slick, wet cleft. "Oh, man, I want you so much, so much…" he muttered against her neck. "Sweetheart, if we continue this, we're in trouble because we need to get upstairs…."

Deftly he slid a finger into her tight channel. Keira winced slightly. "Upstairs where the condoms…"

He stopped and raised his head with an expression of shock. "You're a virgin."

"Uh-huh." A little embarrassed, she ducked her head.

"Look at me, sweetheart."

Finally she did.

"You're thirty years old?"

"Thirty-four."

"And never had sex."

"I never met a man I wanted," she whispered, suddenly embarrassed and feeling awkward. "Not until you. Are you sorry?"

He gave her such a tender look, her heart melted. "Never. We'll just take things nice and slow."

Upstairs, he pulled her into his bedroom, tore off the covers with one hand and tumbled her backward to the mattress, droplets of water from their bodies dampening the sheets. She explored his body, every scar, each curve of muscle. Tattooed on his right biceps was the small insignia of an eagle with outstretched wings behind an anchor, a trident and a pistol gripped in its claws. Keira leaned on an elbow and examined it.

"Budweiser, what they call the SEAL pendant," he told her.

"It means a lot to you, being a SEAL."

He nodded. "Toughest, and best, life I've ever had."

"So much you marked yourself with it."

"Not the first mark. When you become a SEAL, they give you the pendant, place it over your chest and pound the pin into your skin." Dale grinned at her stunned look.

"That's barbaric."

"It's brotherhood."

"Macho, overrated, he-man ritual…"

He kissed her, and the warmth of his mouth made her forget her next thought. He'd seduced her with pleasure and promises of more, stroking her skin and baring her to his hungry gaze.

His hands slowly caressed her hips, then he left her mouth and nuzzled her neck, gave it a slow lick. Pain, sharp and brief, laced her as he nipped her skin. His tongue caressed the wound, replacing pain with erotic pleasure.

Dale cupped her hips and kissed his way down her quivering torso. Then he slipped his hands between her legs, drew them apart and put his mouth on her. Shocked pleasure shot through her.

He suckled her intimate feminine flesh, his wicked tongue stroking and teasing. Stretched out like a sacrifice, Keira released a frustrated whimper as the pleasured tension built higher and higher. Then, with his tongue he stroked the one place aching for his touch. Quick, powerful flicks that drew her taut, made her moan as she clutched at his silky hair, gasping until she threatened to fall apart, building the pleasure higher and higher.

With a shrill shriek, she climaxed, crying out his name. Tremors spilled through her, leaving her in a sensual haze. Dale stayed with her, tenderly kissing her intimate flesh as he cupped her bare bottom.

He sat back, his heavy phallus bobbing from the apex of his muscled thighs, and slid a hand across his wet mouth.

He moved his palm over one breast and gently squeezed, then lowered his mouth to sample her rigid nipple. Dale pushed a sleek thigh between her legs, rubbing against her sensitive, quivering flesh. She squirmed, then fisted a hand in his hair as he tasted and suckled her breast.

This Mage possessed a dark magick and turned her into a slave, shuddering with need. She would do anything he asked.

As she arched upward to the stroke of his thigh and the flick of his tongue, Keira shattered again in an explosion of hot, wet heat. Moisture gushed between her legs, bathing his strong thigh.

Her chest rising and falling with each ragged breath she stared into his darkened gray eyes, watching the steely coldness turn to tender warmth.

He smiled. "We're not quite done yet. Not for a long while."

She thirsted to see his control shatter, his passion shatter as she had shattered in his arms. Sexual pleasure washed through her, the little aftershocks of orgasm rippling along every nerve.

Keira sat up, and with a strength that surprised her, pushed him backward. Dale looked surprised, then amused, and she began exploring his body. She kissed a narrow hip, ran a hand over his taut belly and traced the groves and indentations her wolf had carved into his flesh. She felt a pang of pure sorrow, then focused on bringing him pleasure, delighting as his muscles quivered beneath her touch. Keira kissed his collarbone, then traced a line over his broad shoulder with her mouth. She licked smooth skin stretched over hard muscle and sinew, tasting the slight salt of his skin. Awe spilled through her at the vast differences between male and female. His was a warrior's body, thick with muscle, while her body was softer and pliant.

"Turn over," she ordered.

"Aye, aye, sir," he murmured with a twinkle in his gray gaze.

Dale turned onto his stomach as she straddled his thick, muscled thighs and ran her palms over the silky hair on his legs, marveling at the strength in his limbs. She slid her hands up to the smooth tautness of his bottom and squeezed, smiling as he groaned with pleasure. Keira trailed hot, wet kisses up from his bottom, along the smooth muscles bisecting his back, to his nape, loving the groans she culled from him. Then as easily as she'd pushed him back, he slid from beneath her and flipped her onto her back. Dale reached into the nightstand and removed a foil packet, tore it open and sheathed his erection.

Intensity radiated in his gaze as he settled his muscled body between her opened legs. Bracing himself on his hands, he stared down at her. She felt his rigid length probe at her wet, tight opening. Keira stiffened in real alarm.

"Shhh." He stroked her hair. "It's all right, Keira. Don't resist me. Relax."

It wasn't going to work. She was too tense and too small. But she wanted this.

Dale laced his fingers through hers, locking their hands together. He pushed forward, his penis like a thick steel bar invading her softness. She gritted her teeth. As the burning pressure turned into real pain, Keira gripped his fingers as if he were an anchor amid a stormy sea. His heavy weight pinned her to the mattress.

"Mine," he whispered. "All mine."

He pushed hard and deep inside her. Caught by the sudden shock of pain, she cried out, but Dale caught her cry with his mouth, kissing her deeply. As he raised his head, a single tear trickled down her cheek. He tore his mouth from hers, chased it away with his tongue.

"I'm sorry for hurting you," he said quietly.

I'm sorry I hurt you, she longed to say. Instead, she pulled him down for another deep kiss.

Locked deep inside her, Dale remained still. The burning pressure between her legs eased, replaced with a curious, delightful friction. He began moving, as her inner muscles clasped the male intruder eagerly, caressing him. Dale tensed and groaned. A bead of sweat rolled off his forehead and spilled onto her breasts like a teardrop. Tentatively, he began to move, groaning as he threw his head back and closed his eyes.

"So good, you feel so good," he muttered.

Emotions raged through her, a maelstrom of joy and intimacy so intense, she could barely stand it. She, who had delivered nothing but pain and suffering to this man, was now giving him this intense pleasure.

His face alight with fierce desire, Dale spread her legs open wide. Keira braced herself as he thrust deeply, their bodies, slick with sweat, rubbing over each other. He stiffened, then his body shook as he shouted her name.

Stroking his damp hair, Keira welcomed his heavy weight as he collapsed atop her, his head pillowed beside hers. After a minute, he slid off, disposed of the condom. Then he joined her in bed and gathered her tightly against him.

"You okay?" he asked softly, stroking her hair.

Tenderness shone in his eyes as she nodded. She felt complete and satisfied and filled with awed wonder. Something had happened, and more than making love. Something wonderful, and frightening. Her heart, Keira realized with dismay. She'd done more than give her body to his powerful Mage. She had opened her heart to him.

They lay in drowsy contentment as Keira curled against him, her head pillowed on his broad shoulder. Her fingers slid through the damp hairs on his chest, tracing the scars she'd placed there, wondering when Dale would remember she was the demon wolf he hated.

Wondering what he'd do when he finally remembered…

She had made love with this man, let him into her body, bared her emotions before him. They'd tangled together in hot passion last night. Dale was an excellent lover, tender and considerate.

Now, in the soft light of dawn, he looked official and commanding, a stranger capable of breaking her arm.

Or her heart.

She watched him dress in his navy blue double-breasted jacket with the thin gold stripes on the sleeves. Layers of medals decorated his left breast, along with a shiny gold pin, an exact duplicate of his inked arm.

So handsome and distinguished.

She jumped up and helped him adjust the navy blue tie around his crisply ironed dress shirt. Her fingers rested on the navy SEAL pin, a symbol of his dedication and honor.

"Fancy duds, sailor. Got a date?"

"With brass in D.C. I'll be back late."

Gray eyes twinkling, he caressed her cheek. "I've never had a naked woman help me dress."

Glancing down, she blushed and covered herself. Dale pulled her hands away. "Don't. You're such a beautiful sight in the morning. You make my blood race."

He kissed her, making *her* blood race. Dale leaned his forehead against hers. "If I stay here, all your hard work will go to hell because I'm going to rip off all my clothing and get naked with you in bed."

With a final kiss, he donned his white hat and left the room.

Keira sat on the bed, hugging herself. They were closer than ever, and nothing seemed to threaten her bliss. No Centurions banging on her door, invading the house. Keira touched the slave armband on her biceps.

Under Dale's protection. As long as he never renounced their agreement verbally, she remained safe.

But for how long?

Chapter 20

Her first dinner party ever. Keira felt more nervous than a new bride entertaining her husband's business partners.

Dale wanted to fully incorporate her into his life. All the Phoenix Force SEALs and their wives and girlfriends were invited. And, at Keira's insistence, Ensign Lees. She needed a familiar face, female company who could set her at ease.

Because being around Dale's team at an intimate dinner party scared the hell out of her. What if one of them had been in the basement along with Shay? What if she were recognized?

And Shay himself, his presence was left as a question mark. He might make it. Probably not.

Leaving Dale to finish preparations, Keira went onto the back deck and stared at the sun sinking behind the trees. Pink streaked the sky. Dale had family. He had his team, who would die for him.

She had no one.

Suddenly she felt unbearably lonely, missing her people, though it had been years. She thought of her little brother, his bravery and kindness.

How the Centurions, too, had brutally slaughtered him.

A sob rose in her throat.

The sliding glass door slid open. Two warm arms encircled her waist. "Sweetheart, what's wrong?" He pressed a soft kiss to her nape as she gathered her composure.

"I'm worried about dinner. All those big bad SEALs and we're serving a wussy fondue to start. Can't imagine them eating fondue."

Dale turned her around. "Honesty, Keira. Remember?"

I remember, but you don't.

"I was missing my family," she admitted. "Missing them, oh, so much. You have parents, two sisters and nieces and nephews. And your team, who are your brothers in blood. I have…no one."

He kissed the corner of her mouth.

"You have me."

Dale kept kissing her mouth, little brushes of his firm lips. "And once the guys really get to know you, they'll adore you. They'll have to, because if they don't, I'll assign them to deploy to the nearest ice cap to target-shoot penguins."

Horrified, she drew back. "Penguins?"

He grinned, the gesture impish and boyish. "Well, maybe just the ice floes."

A steady beat of gnawing trepidation pounded through her veins. "I made enough for the entire navy. You're not expecting anyone else to drop by?"

"Ensign Lees and her boyfriend. Shay's on the road. Won't be joining us."

Relief flooded her. She grasped his shoulders to steady herself. "Okay. Let's do it."

Ensign "Call me Robyn" Lees brought her boyfriend, a hybrid wolf shifter. "We fight like cats and dogs," she'd told Keira, with a teasing but adoring look at the tall, lanky man.

The men immediately gathered in the dining room, where the cheese fondue was set up on a side table. They began animated discussions while their wives and girl-friends shook their heads.

"Boys and their toys." Sienna, Lt. Parker's wife, shook her head. "I swear if Matt isn't blowing something up or shooting something or running as a wolf, he gets so restless."

Keira smiled stiffly. "You mean running with his wolf."

Six sets of eyes gazed at her.

"She doesn't know," Robyn told them.

"We're all paranorms. I'm a Fae," Sienna explained. "No need to watch yourself. Just worry about a sudden surge of magick or someone accidentally releasing a power bolt."

"Or Sully materializing in the bathroom when you're taking a bubble bath." This from Leona, a pretty blonde witch, who blushed when she realized what she'd revealed.

The women laughed and started talking about male faults.

Tightness in her muscles gradually faded as she listened. These women were ordinary, despite their origins.

Maybe I can fit in with Dale's world.

Leona sighed. "I get so tired of the guys all congregating together, and then we sit around and gab. For once, can we all get together? Any ideas, Keira?"

Inspiration seized her. "A few."

She went to the untouched Steinway and opened the lid, lovingly skimming a few keys. Dale had not played for her. But she sensed the music inside him, sensed his love for his art had been set aside, and had not died.

Keira sat at the bench and began banging on the keys. The women laughed and held their ears. But Dale entered the living room, dismay on his face.

"Sweetheart, I'm allergic to bad playing. Must you?"

"Only if you take my place."

Abandoning the piano bench, she looked at him. All attention riveted to Dale, who stared at the piano with the same avid longing he'd centered on her last night.

You can do it, she mouthed to him.

The cocky smile he flashed assured her he could.

Dale sat at the bench. The SEALs exchanged amused glances. "Cover your ears, wolf," Dallas joked to Dakota.

He began to play, fingers rippling over the keys, coaxing the music out with each skilled and swift stroke. Keira closed her eyes and enjoyed the music, her spirit singing with each note.

When he finished, a crashing crescendo, there was silence. Then Dakota clapped. Everyone else followed, the applause like thunder.

Gaze soft, Dale turned to her.

"Thank you, for giving me my music back."

He reached up, cupped her nape and kissed her. Keira closed her eyes, not caring they had an audience, not caring about anything.

She wanted to hold this moment in her hands, and cherish it forever.

"You'll thank me more if I don't burn dinner," she whispered, and kissed him again.

Scurrying into the kitchen, she focused on setting out the dishes. The other women drifted inside, helping, their chatter making her feel accepted and normal.

Now she was not a wolf held captive by demons all these years, but a woman with a man who cared deeply for her.

Maybe even loved her.

Like I love him.

The potato masher stopped in midair. Stricken she stared into the half-beaten potatoes. Love Dale? She couldn't love him, couldn't give her heart to a man accustomed to strict military procedure, who readily admitted his team meant more than any relationship.

A man grateful for her "woo-woo" methods, but who would never eagerly embrace her ideals of trying to find the good in people. Because he was too busy searching for the bad.

Keira ignored the bitter feeling as she continued preparing the meal.

Tonight would be a good night. No matter what. No demons, negative thoughts or sadness would dash her hopes for a successful dinner.

Keira pulled the dish of green beans from the oven as the doorbell rang.

Voices sounded in the hallway. A deep, assured male voice and a woman's voice that sent a chill rushing down her spine as she froze, holding the casserole dish.

"Sweetheart, look who's here!"

Turning, she peeped through the kitchen down the hallway.

And dropped the platter of green beans. It shattered on the floor, vegetables splashing at her feet, the walls.

Oh, please, no, not now, not now...

In through the door walked a fair-headed woman with a gentle smile and a tall, rugged SEAL. Chief Petty Officer Sam "Shay" Shaymore and his new bride, Kelly.

The only living people who could reveal her true identity.

Panic clogged her throat. Keira staggered back against the counter, staring from the kitchen at the happy reunion taking place in the hallway.

"We didn't know what to bring, so we brought it all. White, red and the bubbly stuff." Shay thrust three wine bottles at Dale.

"Champagne, Sam." Kelly kissed his cheek. "So good to see you again, Curt. You look well. Much better. There's color in your cheeks."

"All thanks to my girlfriend. Come on in, make yourselves comfortable. Need to get into the kitchen. I believe there's a crisis with green beans."

Crisis? More like a full-fledged emergency. *Break out the life vests, boys, I'm sinking.*

The other women fussed and helped her clean up the mess, efficient and effective, as she dropped to her knees. She focused on picking up the shards of broken dish.

Like the shards of her broken life.

Dale rushed into the kitchen and dropped beside her. "You okay?"

"The green beans jumped out of the oven and to the floor," she said lightly.

Concern etched his handsome face. "Forget it. I'm more worried about you."

A lump rose in her throat. *Soon, you won't be.* "I'm fine. Get everyone seated. Dinner's almost ready. I have more than enough veggies to make up for the dead green beans."

As the others gathered in the dining room, she bowed her head, fighting for control.

Shay would see her. And tell his commander. She expected nothing less. She was caught. Maybe she could plead a headache, go upstairs before Shay saw her...

If she bowed out now, she'd bring more attention to herself. Suddenly she just wanted the ruse to be over with, for Dale to know the truth.

He'd heard it from her, but did not believe her.

Maybe hearing it from someone else would convince him.

In the meantime, she'd do her damnedest to ensure everyone had a good time.

Dale deserved a nice night with his men and their significant others.

Pasting a wide smile on her face, she carried the first course into the dining room.

The man stared at her through dinner. Sweat poured down her back as she ducked behind the tall arrangement of fresh roses Dale had brought her. But there wasn't any escaping the scrutiny of Chief Petty Officer Shaymore.

Every dish was met with praise. Talk flowed easily, the women steering the conversation as surely as a captain guiding a destroyer out to sea, avoiding shoptalk. It was a lovely evening, or would have been, if not for the young SEAL studying her as if she were an enemy in their midst.

But I am.

When dessert was finished, she stood to clear the table. Shay stood, as well, and glanced at Dale. "Sir, I need to talk to you."

"Sounds official. This is a dinner party. Can't business wait until tomorrow?" he asked.

"Honey, he's right. Let's relax. No shoptalk," Kelly told her husband.

Shay sat, his narrowed gaze focused on her like a wolf's. Ignoring the panic curling in her stomach, she began to clear the table.

The others helped. She shooed the men from the kitchen.

"Dale, why don't you play some more? Entertain everyone. Try something modern that doesn't sound like a dirge."

He shot her an amused look. "Beethoven is not dirge music."

As everyone filed down the hallway to the living room, Kelly remained in the kitchen. "Keira."

Here it comes…

But the woman's voice was soft and her eyes were kind. "It's you, isn't it? The woman from the basement."

She started to deny it. Shoulders sagging she nodded.

"Sam and I didn't remember your name, some kind of memory block. But your face, I'll never forget it."

Hugging herself, she stared at the floor. "And you remember what I did to Dale."

"I remember how terrified you were, how you begged the demons not to make you hurt him anymore. You were forced against your will." Kelly glanced at the open doorway, where laughter drifted down the hallway, followed by the piano playing. "Have you told Curt?"

"I tried to tell him. He doesn't remember."

"A memory-blocking spell. Or perhaps he doesn't want to. You have to trigger his recollection of what happened."

"Don't ask that of me," she whispered. "I'd rather die."

"No one will blame you for what happened. You were a victim, as well."

Bitter laughter choked her throat. "Oh, right. Tell that

to them...." She jerked a thumb at the hallway. Paul and Robyn had already left with excuses. Only the SEALs remained, a close-knit gathering of men who'd die for their leader.

Or kill anyone who hurt him...

The woman clasped an odd silver pendant hanging from a chain around her neck. She rested a hand on her arm. "Then let me help you. Close your eyes."

Trusting this woman, trusting anyone who knew what she was, proved difficult. Keira shook her head.

"Please. I want to help."

Finally, she closed her eyes, relaxed. A warm tingle raced through her veins, and she felt a rush of connection, entwined with pure love. The love shook her to the core. Tears trickled from her eyes.

Then the warmth faded, and Kelly removed her hand.

She opened her eyes, wiping them with the corner of the frilly white apron. "What did you do?"

Kelly pointed to the pendant. "I used my triskele to link us. A slim link, but a psychic one. It will deflect Sam's fury because if he tries to hurt you, he'll sense me and all the love I have for him."

"Such a powerful love," she whispered. "You're blessed."

A sad smile touched Kelly's mouth. "I love him with all my heart, but he has faults, too. And one is struggling to forgive someone who's hurt him, or anyone close to him. Curt is more than his commanding officer. He worships him like an older brother and would do anything for him."

"I'll remember that."

When the last bottle of wine was polished off, their guests left. She joined Dale in the bedroom, collapsing onto the pretty window seat.

"You were terrific. Thanks." He kissed her, his mouth warm and firm. A tingle raced down her spine.

Dale started to tug his shirt over his head. Keira reached for the lamp.

"Leave it on." He stood before her, scars crisscrossing his muscled chest. "I want to make love to you in the light. "

Keira undressed and dived under the covers. Dale aimed her his crooked smile and tugged the covers back. Then he jumped onto the bed and pulled her to him, kissing her. His tongue traced the tight seam of her mouth. He tasted like cherries, wine and chocolate. Beneath the gentle, yet authoritative pressure of his mouth, she moaned for more.

He rolled over, opened the nightstand drawer and retrieved a condom. Dale ripped open the foil package and sheathed his erection. Then he applied a liberal amount of lubricant over his shaft.

"I'm sorry. I can't wait."

He mounted her and pushed his penis deep inside, past her tight muscles. Keira clutched at his wide shoulders, her fingers digging into the scars her claws had created. He began to move, his fierce gaze capturing hers. It proved too intense and she closed her eyes.

"Look at me, Keira. I want you to see who's making love with you," he told her.

He nuzzled her neck, blew into her ear. She shivered delicately, her nipples hardening into tight buds.

With exquisite smoothness, he pushed into her. Keira writhed a little, trying to find some ease as his thickness penetrated her fully. She sucked in a breath, and relaxed, opening to him. He pulled back, and began to stroke inside her, his penis rubbing against her sensitive tissues, the friction creating a delicious heat. His muscles contracted as he thrust, powerful shoulders flexing.

Slowly, he moved, giving her time to become accustomed to him. Tenderness shone in his darkened gaze. Something inside her eased, the demon blood receding to the furthest corners of her mind. Keira felt only pure goodness, and joy, none of the guilt always dogging her heels. It felt as if Dale's courage and goodness pushed away the evil darkness inside her with gentle, healing light, the strength the demons tried to steal from him now flowing freely into her as they joined their bodies. Silky chest hair rubbed against her aching breasts, his hard torso sliding against her soft abdomen. She arched to meet his rhythm.

Wonder came over her face as she watched him. His mouth parted on a gasp, lips trembling. The bed beneath her was as soft as down, the male pressing her backward onto it solid muscle. It felt as if he locked her spirit in his, a closeness she'd never experienced until now.

His thrusts became more urgent, harder, until his flesh slapped against hers. Wrapping her legs around his pistoning hips, she reached for it, the tension growing until she felt ready to explode.

Screaming his name on her lips, she climaxed, her core squeezing him as she shattered, her back arching. He growled in satisfaction, gave one last thrust and threw his head back with a hoarse shout. Dale collapsed atop her, his face pillowed beside her, his breathing ragged. She bore his weight, welcoming it, but then he eased out of her and rolled over, pulling her into his arms.

She lay in his arms, listening to his pounding heart, her fingers tracing the horrid scars lining his pectorals, the ridged muscles of his abdomen. But for once, she felt no guilt over them.

"Do you find my body repulsive?"

Startled, she raised her head. "No. Why are you asking?"

"I asked Dakota tonight for the name of a top plastic surgeon he knows. Man's an expert at removing scars."

"Why now?"

His expression shuttered. "Just thinking about options. My shirtsleeve rode up tonight. Leona, Sully's girlfriend, noticed my left arm. She cringed and turned away. A natural reaction. I'm used to it."

"A natural reaction for a woman whose worst day consists of a bad manicure, not tangling with demons. She's superficial. I'm not."

He smiled, but doubt remained in his eyes. *Fine. I'll show you....*

Keira leaned over and kissed his scars, one by one.

"These are badges of courage and sacrifice. You sacrificed yourself to save innocent children."

A sudden memory struck. "They can be removed by the one who placed them there, through a tremendous act of sacrifice and courage."

Such sacrifice was beyond her. *I'm a coward,* she thought, grief tightening her throat. *Can't do it.*

Because doing so would mean surrendering her life back to the Centurions. Only this imprisonment called for worse than a dark cell, and infrequent beatings and the terrible price her victims paid.

What the Centurions would do to her would make Dale's torture seem like a slap and a tickle....

Keira closed her eyes, resting her palm on Dale's chest. He pulled her down for a kiss. "No more talk of scars. I want to love you tonight, Keira. All night."

* * *

After, she lay cuddled against him. Soft and warm, sleeping like a contented puppy.

Dale stared at the ceiling, unable to sleep.

Sex had been explosive, exquisite and powerful. Filled with feelings he'd denied himself for years, he relished making love to this woman.

Keira had cracked open the cold shell and touched his heart.

He wanted to cherish her, protect her as a man did for a woman he intended to hold and keep. Keep her so awash in pleasure she'd never seek another's bed.

Not like Kathy. At that thought, the familiar ache returned, but this time, it was a distant throb instead of the wrenching pain from the past.

How could she fit into his world, with her unconventional gypsy lifestyle? The free-spirited attitude of a world outside the naval base called to her like a siren song.

Keira might remain content for now. But for how long? Would she pack up and move on like his ex, seeking a less structured life, filled with people like her who wanted to see only the good in others, instead of seeking out the bad?

Maybe she's right. There is a point to finding the good in others.

The thought startled him. With a rueful smile, he realized he had dropped his rigid black-and-white views and embraced the gray.

Just like she did.

"You're a witch," he whispered into her ear, kissing her cheek.

But one troubled thought remained, chasing away elusive sleep.

He'd opened his heart to this woman, shared his deepest emotions. Yet as sweet and open as she'd been, whispering her hopes and dreams to him in bed, Keira still held something back from him. And if it turned out to be something big, a betrayal as shattering as Kathy's, he must excise her from his life.

Dale couldn't forgive such deception from a woman again.

Ever.

Chapter 21

A steady rain fell the next morning as Keira trudged down the stairs, rubbing her eyes. In a crisp khaki uniform, Dale sat at the kitchen table, reading a thick report, an empty coffee cup before him. She opened the cabinet, took out a cup and poured herself coffee, added the creamer Dale had bought just for her, and then refilled his cup. They had settled into a routine of two people who intimately knew each other's needs.

When she set it before him, he glanced up, warmth in his gaze. "Thanks."

She leaned against the counter, sipping, feeling alive and happy for the first time in…when? Couldn't remember ever feeling like this, all the joy pushing back the darkness, making the past blur completely. He was dedicated to his job, focused on keeping the men and women of ST 21 safe. Little by little, she peeled back his layers, finding more of the man beneath.

The more she discovered about Dale Curtis, the more she liked. A tentative friendship had deepened to something more, her feelings growing stronger each day until Keira knew she cared deeply about this Mage. And yet beneath the effervescent joy and serenity, was a tiny blipping light. A lighthouse beacon winking through all the sparkling giddiness.

He's going to find out who you truly are. And then what?

Keira refused to consider. *I just want to be happy for once. I'll take whatever he's willing to give and worry about the consequences later.*

Still reading his report, he pushed back his chair and got up, sipping his coffee. His concentration remained absolute until he reached the counter, and set the cup and paper down.

Curiosity overcame her. "What are you reading? It looks utterly fascinating."

He spun around, grabbed her by the waist, papers spilling to the floor. "Not as fascinating as you."

He buried his face in her throat, delivering hot, nipping kisses. Squealing with laughter, she pushed at his chest. "Dale! I'm hungry."

"So am I," he muttered, sliding his hands down to her butt and squeezing. "I'm craving a Keira breakfast special. You, naked against the counter."

Pulling back, he looked at her, tenderness in his eyes. "Or are you too sore for this? I want you to feel nothing but pleasure this time."

A furious flush heated her cheeks at the intimate reminder of last night. In response, she pulled him down and kissed him, desperate to feel him close against her, keep the magic alive and dancing for a while longer.

Absorbed in his mouth nibbling at hers, his hands

stroking the small of her back, she dimly realized they were being watched. Dale pulled away, his eyes narrowing as he turned around.

Dressed in camouflage rain gear as if prepared for attack, Chief Petty Officer Samuel Shaymore stood on the deck outside. Even in the pouring rain, he could not disguise his cold fury.

Wriggling free of Dale's grip, she became uncomfortably aware of the thin cotton sleep shirt riding up her thighs, her nipples standing in hard points against the fabric. Far worse was the fear snaking down her spine like the stroke of a cold finger.

She knew why Shay was here....

She went to dart away, but Dale shook his head.

"I'm not letting one of my men chase you away." He tapped her nose, his gaze soft. "Stay here."

Dale slid the door open. "Shay. You've got lousy timing."

The SEAL's gaze slid to Keira. "Sorry, sir. I have to talk to you. Alone. It's very important."

Panic squeezed her chest. Keira fisted her trembling hands.

"Whatever you have to say can wait for my office. Fifteen minutes…" He glanced down at his watch, then over to Keira, his expression intent. "Make it thirty-five."

But Shay stepped into the door, rain dripping off his cloak onto the floor as Dale started to close it. "I'm sorry, sir, but this can't wait. It's personal." He glanced at Keira again with that glacial look. "Not about me, but you."

Dale's jaw tightened. He flexed his hands, then nodded. "My study."

The young SEAL pushed past, not looking at Keira. Dale sighed and dropped a kiss on her lips, his mouth warm and firm. He looked at her with such a devoted expression, she felt tears rise in her throat.

Knowing after hearing what Shay said, he'd never look at her like this again.

"This won't take long. Don't go away."

He playfully touched her nose and went down the hall. The study door closed behind him.

For a moment she stood still, looking around the cheerful kitchen, memorizing every detail of Dale sitting at the table. A memory to tide her through the upcoming lonely nights.

Keira hurried down the hallway to gather her things.

"Spill it, Shay. I am a little busy."

Dale watched the SEAL pace back and forth in front of the fireplace. In all the years he'd known the Mage, he'd never acted this agitated.

Finally he turned and looked him straight in the eye.

"Your relationship with Keira… You're getting quite close to her."

Dale narrowed his gaze. "And what concern of it is yours? It's my private life."

"She's not who she pretends to be."

He frowned, then relaxed. "You're a little late. I found out exactly who she is."

Shock slackened Shay's jaw. "You know?"

Dale steepled his fingertips, rested them against his mouth. "At the base before you arrived, I had Thad check her out. She's a Celestial Hunter wolf with demon blood, not only a Luminaire. She saved Sully's life from a demon in my basement."

"Maybe her motivation wasn't so altruistic."

He went absolutely still. "Say what you mean, damn it, and make your point."

Shay hesitated. "I don't trust her, sir. And I don't want to see you in a position where she can hurt you. Again."

Now this conversation had taken a peculiar twist. "I'm a big boy, chief. I can take care of myself."

An odd shadow of grief crossed the Mage's face. "Do you remember anything about that time in the basement, Curt? When Kelly and I rescued you?"

Dale's mind raced. Memories still fogged, only a shrill screech of pain, talons over his flesh. And deep, deep sorrowful sounds of someone weeping. Him?

As time passed, the memories became more clouded. Thankfully. But pulsing beneath was a blinking red light, a warning he knew he should not ignore.

But hell, it had been so long since he'd felt this peaceful, this damn happy. Why spoil a good thing with trying to recall a horrific nightmare?

"Keira is the wolf who hurt you in the basement. Kelly thinks she was forced into it, but I had to tell you to watch your six."

A horrific pain slammed into his skull. Dale held his head and bit back a moan. "The woman who tortured me had blond hair."

Shay stared. "Curt, she did not..."

"She did. I know she did." Dale stood. "If that's all, I'll see you on base. I don't want to discuss this any more with you or anyone else."

Shay nodded. But as he went to leave, Shay grabbed his arm. "Mage to Mage, Curt, I'm here for you. If you ever need me, no matter what, or when, call me. You're more than my commander, and more to Kelly, too. If we didn't care, I wouldn't be so worried."

Dale smiled briefly, touched the other Mage's finger, watching their auras spark pure gold. "You're a good man, Shay."

"You, too, Curt." Emotion pulled his face tight. "That's why I'd hate to lose you. Watch your six, Commander. Never let your guard down. Not even for a woman who loves you. Or one who pretends to."

He slipped down the hallway, leaving Dale to puzzle over his cryptic warning.

Fleeing to the garage, Keira found her bike, kick-started it and roared away.

Driving endlessly, tears streaming down her face, not caring where she headed, just running, running. Running from her pain, from reality.

Rain fell into her eyes, mingling with the salty tears. Little traffic on this side street this early. A black pickup truck approached from behind, the driver blaring the horn.

Dale.

Keira pulled over and stopped the bike and dismounted, barely able to see through her tears and the rain. The truck pulled up behind her, the motor shutting off. Dale jumped out, leaving the door open. He ran to her and clasped her arms.

"You okay?" he asked.

When she nodded, he cursed low and pulled her roughly into his arms. "Don't ever do that to me again. You scared the hell out of me, racing away like that in this rain where you could take a bad spill. Damn, Keira, if I hadn't seen you take off, and followed… Why did you do it?"

Her mouth wobbled. "Shay didn't tell you? What I am?"

Dale lowered his forehead to hers. "Shay warned me against you. I told him I know about your demon blood and I can take care of myself."

"Dale…" she began.

And then he kissed her, cutting off her next sentence, his mouth warm against her frozen lips, his arms solid and sure, anchoring her to him.

When they both broke apart, gasping for breath, Dale lifted her into his arms. He jogged to the truck and lifted her into the shotgun seat. He climbed in beside her and closed the door, chafing her hands. And then he stopped, made another low sound and pulled her into his arms again, his fingers fumbling with her leather jacket. She managed to remove it and his hands slid upward, cupping her wet, unbound breasts. He squeezed and kneaded, so warm, so good. Keira gasped for breath and hitched up her skirt. With a rough grunt, he ripped her panties, tossing the shreds aside as she fumbled with the zipper on his jeans. His penis sprang out, hard and ready.

"Condom. Glove box," he gasped.

She found it, ripped off the foil wrapping and he rolled it over his erection. Dale lifted her up and she slid down, half-afraid he wouldn't fit; she was too dry, but her body was ready for him, and they slid together like all her dreams, as if they truly belonged. He groaned and lifted her hips as she gripped his wide shoulders and began moving up and down, his thrusts becoming wilder and faster. "Come on, sweetheart, come with me," he urged and as he threw back his head and stiffened, she orgasmed.

Dale shouted her name in the truck, the symphony of the rain drumming against the truck, as the cymbals of thunder crashed around them. Keira clung limply to him as he finally slowed and held her against him, her wet body shaking with bliss now, the cold chased away by his heat.

She never wanted to leave.

She must leave, for she didn't belong with him.

He buried his face against her shoulder and gave a low curse again, kissing her throat. Slowly he lifted her, disengaging them, and then he ripped off the condom and tossed it onto the floor. Her breathing ragged, her heart knocking against her chest, she looked at him.

"And here I thought you never let anyone litter in your truck."

He kissed her again, his mouth tender and gentle this time. "Except with you. You throw all the rules out the window."

Dale zipped up his jeans as she put herself to rights, the space between her legs aching and pulsing and wet. He pulled his cell phone from his jacket pocket and dialed a number.

"Sully? Favor. Pick up Dallas. I need Dallas to drive Keira's bike back to my house. It's at…" He glanced at the street sign and gave the intersection. "Thanks."

He thumbed off the phone and started up the truck.

At his house, he hustled her into the shower, turned on the twin knobs to hot and undressed her. As she stood beneath the spray, shivering again, he soaped her body.

After, he toweled her off, helped her shrug into a terrycloth robe. Dale lifted her into his arms and placed her gently on the bed. For a moment she lay in silence. And then she turned to him, unable to bear the quiet anymore as she watched him stand at the window.

"You'll be late for work," she whispered.

"They can do without me for one morning." Lightning cracked, spearing the air with brilliant light. "Storm's getting worse."

"I used to be afraid of lightning, until my mother taught me it was a natural element of the earth, one that some Mages can harness for power." Keira slid out of the bed and joined him at the window, flattening her palm against the glass.

"I can," he said quietly. "But I haven't in a long time."

Keira clasped her robe tightly. He needed the power now. If he were to engage any more demons, he needed to draw his strength from the earth.

"Maybe it's time you recharged. It's the perfect opportunity." She clasped his hand. "Come with me, outside now."

Dale's brows wrinkled, but he followed her down the steps.

The rain slowed to a gentle patter, but lightning still crackled in the air. They went outside to the backyard to a clearing away from the trees. Wiping rain from her forehead, Keira took a deep breath.

"Stretch out your hands and focus all your powers as a Mage. You're going to be a lightning rod and pull power from the storm. You're more than 400 years old and you've done this before. You can do it and it's not going to be a direct hit. I'll help you."

Closing her eyes, Keira began the chant, coaxing the lightning to him. Dale extended his arms. His total trust in her squeezed her heart hard.

Creating a small ball of energy, she tossed it into the air. "Now, Dale! When the lightning hits the bolt, yank all the power into you!"

The bolt zigged and zagged across the sky and crashed into the energy bolt. Dale closed his eyes and yanked hard. Energy crackled and sang as it surrounded him in a white glowing light. He kept pulling and pulling, like a sailor towing a rope.

And then the skies grew quiet and the storm abated.

Dale opened his eyes. They were burning white, sizzling with power.

A little afraid, Keira stepped back. Never had she been close to this much power. Little sparks leaped off his body, crackling in the air.

Finally, the white glow died down and his eyes resumed their normal gray shade.

But Dale was not normal. She sensed it, knew it. He had gone from a strong, but frail Primary into a force of nature, a force equal to defeating the Centurions.

"You did it," she whispered.

He looked at her and his expression shifted, becoming hungry and intense. "I need…"

Dale took her hand and tugged her into the house, upstairs to the bedroom. Without words, he lifted her onto the bed, kissing her deeply.

Then he unzipped his trousers, his penis thick and straining toward her, and reached for a condom, then sheathed himself. Dale opened her thighs wide, his hands cupping her bottom, pressing his penis at her soaked cleft. He thrust deep.

Oh, gods, it was too much, too intense. Sensations overwhelmed her, his power singing to her, surrounding her, creating a friction between her legs, her breasts.

"I'm a demon," she gasped.

"You're a damn witch," he countered, thrusting harder.

They came together, shattering, their bodies shuddering, her shrill cries mingling with his hoarse shouts. After, trembling, she rested against his broad shoulder. "I have something to confess. I am the one who hurt you in the dark."

Dale kissed her temple. "Shhh. It's all right. Nothing you can do would hurt me."

"They made me do it. The Centurions…"

He kept kissing her, his mouth trailing kisses down

her neck. "I'll defeat those bastards. I could defeat ten thousand demons. They won't lay a hand on you."

Why wouldn't he listen to her? Keira moaned as he fastened his mouth on her breast and began to suckle her.

Tomorrow, maybe, when he wasn't so drunk on power and love.

Then he kissed her and began making love to her again and she forgot about being the demon who had tortured him, forgot everything except the erotic bliss he coaxed out of her with every powerful push of his hips.

Her man was headed down range.

Dale gathered a team together for an operation that would take him away for a week, maybe longer. And he put himself on the team, as well.

Standing on the tarmac with the other SEAL families, Keira placed her palm flat on Dale's chest, feeling his beating heart. Clutched in her left hand was her Celestial amulet. The amulet would help keep him safe.

But she risked his memories returning if he touched it, for it had been sewn into his flesh as protection against her wolf fangs.

"Can't tell you where we're headed. Hang tight, get together with the other wives and girlfriends."

Dale kissed her.

Thinking of the love Kelly held for Sam, she clung to hope. Dale was her lover, and he cared for her, had begun sharing his heart. Surely reason would overcome anger if he discovered her deception.

She tucked the amulet into the deep chest pocket of his shirt. "For good luck. It will keep you safe."

He kissed her, his gaze warm and tender. "Miss you. Don't worry, I'm going to kick ass. And don't stay up all night, eating all the popcorn when you watch your sentimental chick flicks."

She wrapped her arms around his lean waist, the rough fabric of his BDUs abrading her cheek, and hugged him tight.

Then she pasted on a brave smile and waved as he walked onto the tarmac toward the plane, trailed by the other soldiers. Always out front. Always the leader.

The briefing took place at a U.S. naval base in Kuwait. Adrenaline pumped through Dale's veins. He itched for action, but centered his breathing, as Keira taught, and listened to the platoon leader. He'd spent the past two weeks honing his training with VBSS: visit, board, search and seizure.

This was a night op, floating out to the enemy craft, sneaking the team on board before the bad guys could crack open an eyelid and say, "Huh?"

Night op with a twist. Interdiction of noncompliant vessel, a merchant ship intel said carried a shitload of weapons. Including chemical weaponry. Sarin gas, used to kill innocent children in their sleep in countries torn asunder by civil war.

The op began flawlessly, speeding out to the international shipping lane on a Mark V boat with his team on board.

Then, in a rigid-hulled inflatable, they pulled alongside the vessel, against the hull.

Dressed in black, wearing black balaclavas and masks showing only their eyes, they silently aligned their boat with the craft, the choppy waves bouncing them like rubber dolls, hooked on and boarded, climbing up the narrow ladder and over the ship's rails, quiet as mist.

Accuracy and stealth.

Dakota, the point man, signaled on his radio. Deck was deserted.

They fanned out, slipping open doors, tossing flash-bangs inside each cabin, then seizing stunned prisoners. Pow, pow, pow, precision and accuracy.

Dakota approached, sweat streaking the black grease-paint on his face.

"Report," Dale ordered.

"All clear. Shitload of illegal weapons in the cargo hold. Including enough dynamite to blow this bastard to hell."

A chill raced down his spine. "Get the prisoners to the aft deck and load them ASAP. I'm going for one last recheck."

"Curt."

"Do it."

Something about that last cabin niggled at him. They'd cleared all the cabins, but in the last one, something tinged his nostrils.

Weapon trained on the door, Dale entered the cabin. Empty. Bunk beds, a small desk, cramped quarters. Closet cleared, nothing in the head.

But his Mage senses tingled. He poked at the lower bunk with the barrel of his weapon, and flung it back. Nothing.

The tingle grew stronger.

Senses on high alert, Dale backed away, his gaze trained on the bunk. Never turn your back, he'd always drilled into his men. Not even when a room's cleared of ordinary human threats, because when the average terrorist was hauled away, something nasty and paranormal could remain....

The sheets on the lower bunk rustled and began to rise into the air. Shaping itself into the form of a six-foot-tall creature, with red, beady eyes, a slit of a mouth and gray, jellied skin. The stench of kerosene filled the room.

Hell!

Rolling away, he fired at the creature. Bullets pierced the gray jellied hide, and grayish goo leaked out.

Igninus demon. Not as powerful as the pyrokinetic demons that took down Adam, but lethal.

The demon advanced, holding out its hands. Bastard packed not bullets, but a different arsenal.

Demon fire.

It sprayed from the creature's hands, sweeping over the deck. An arc of fire shot toward Dale and missed. Tongues of flame danced closer, heat licking Dale's face. Needed more room to maneuver.

He darted for the door, rolled, dodging flames shooting his way, his mind keenly assessing the threat. If that fire reached the hold…

Dale slammed the door shut, feeling the heat pour through the steel frame. In moments, the demon would be freed and fry his ass.

Worse, fry his team and blow the ship.

Training in the firestorm chamber smoothly kicked in. *Hit 'em hard, at their weak point, and extinguish the fires. Can't fight the flames, can't carry enough CO2. Find the enemy's soft spots and attack.*

His mind raced over options. Igninus demons' true forms were comprised of a thickening gel acting as an incendiary device, like napalm. If he tossed an energy bolt, the demon would simply explode like napalm, spreading the fire. Bullets proved useless.

Fire was fire. Triangle of fire, heat, fuel, oxygen.

Remove the heat.

Evil versus good. Cold versus heat.

All this flowed through his mind in seconds, like a

fast-moving film. Dale took a deep breath, summoned all his energy directed by Keira into him through the lightning storm.

"One, two...three!"

Flinging open the door, he dive-rolled, sending streams of ice-cold white energy directly into the stream of fire. The Igninus roared and staggered back. Dale kept up the power surge, fighting the flames, surrounding the demon with white, cold energy.

Footsteps sounded, running fast. The demon began to solidify into ice, its glowing red body turning frosty.

Dropping his hands, he turned. Dakota, Dallas and Sully stood in the doorway, staring at the twisted lump of ice.

"Find all the foam fire extinguishers you can and hose down every single cabin. More could be lurking inside," he ordered, slumping against the doorway, suddenly weary, his powers diminished.

On the transport back to the States, he sat with his men. Good op. They'd not only taken down a vessel filled with weapons destined for terrorist use, but a cargo of demons, as well. Dakota and Dallas, using their Draicon wolf senses, flushed out two more Igninus demons hiding in the hold, ready to torch the dynamite, sending a foul cloud of sarin gas into the atmosphere.

Inside the C-130, it was noisy as hell, the vibration making his jaw shake. Dale leaned forward on the webbed bench.

"Those shit-kickers waited until the ship was close to NATO waters," Dakota said suddenly. "With the wind shifting, that gas would have hit our ships."

"They failed." Dale rubbed a hand over his face.

"Good job, Curt. You froze its ass. Glad to have you

back with us." A grin stretched over Dallas's face, sweat smearing the black greasepaint. "Knew that firestorm chamber training would come in handy."

"Except how do you explain it to D.C. brass?" Sully affected a high-pitched tone. "Excuse me, Senator, I know you're whining about budget expenses, but we need this chamber to protect civilians like you. Curt will do a little demo on your bony ass now with a blowtorch."

"Hooyah, Curt," J.T. called out. "That was some fine blow job you did."

"Frosty the blowman," Renegade added. "Kicking demon ass to the Artic. You're a mean son of a bitch, Curt."

Weary, but exhilarated, he grinned. Back on top again. Keegan was right. He needed time in the field with his men, needed to bond with them again. And this op proved it.

"Can't wait to get back to Kelly and some nice home cooking." Shay leaned back with a tired smile.

"You mean some home loving." Renegade poked him in the side. "Like Curt here. He's got a very pretty lady waiting for him. She even gave him a magick juju pendant for luck."

"More like protection." He wondered about that. At the least, the demon fire should have burned him. Not even his eyebrows were singed.

Keira had tucked the amulet into his pocket. He'd totally forgotten it....

Reaching into his pocket, he pulled out the small pendant. Two crescent moons interlaced. It felt warm in his palm.

Dale went still, staring at the amulet.

Flashes of memory surged, rolling through him like a slide show.

Panic squeezed his guts. Arms stretched above him, legs spread, sounds of whispering in the inky darkness. A slow stroke of a claw across his feet. Fighting, writhing, screaming in his mind, the delicate scent of flowers wrapping around his body, lacing through him, making his blood surge thick and hot, his cock stand stiff…

Blood, warm and viscous, seeping down his body, dripping on the concrete floor…

Drip, drip, drip…

Anguish surged, bright and hot as the white-hot agony of claws gouging out his flesh.

"Keira," he whispered, cupping the amulet.

"Curt? You okay? You're looking a little pale." Shay climbed over the men and knelt down, removing the amulet from his shaking hands. "Hey, buddy, take it easy.…"

Power exploded from him like a geyser, energy beams shooting from his outstretched palms, pinging off the airplane's interior. Men cried out, ducked down to avoid the bolts. The airplane tilted wildly. And then he was on the floor, strong arms holding him down, deep voices telling him to hold on, it would be fine, everything would be fine.

A long, deep scream sounded, an inhuman cry of pain.…

Dimly he wondered where it came from and realized it was him. The arms holding him down belonged to his SEALs.

"It's cool, Curt," Shay soothed. "It's all right. Everything's going to be all right."

Dale closed his eyes. Shay lied.

Nothing would ever be all right again.

Keira finished arranging roses in a crystal vase and set them upon the polished Steinway. Her man was headed home and everything had to be perfect.

Checking her appearance in the hall mirror, she smoothed down the pink-and-blue-flowered dress. Dale had teased that it made her look like a garden. A soft smile touched her mouth as she remembered how eager he'd been to remove it from her....

A truck pulled into the driveway. Bursting with anticipation, she ran to the windows and stepped back in confusion.

Not one truck. Four.

Men clad in green battle dress uniforms stepped out. Dale's SEALs. Dread twisted her stomach. Oh, gods, something had happened and they were here to tell her....

And then a tall, rugged man stepped out of the backseat of the last truck and stood. Dale. Weak with relief, she leaned against the window.

Relief turned to real fear as the SEALs marched up to the doorway, their faces grim. Her pulse spiked as she began to tremble. *He knows.*

The front door opened. Waiting in the living room, she watched the men file inside. Weapons holstered at their sides, they formed a deadly phalanx, stiff and solemn, refusing to meet her gaze.

At last Dale walked inside and quietly shut the door behind him. Heavy combat boots trudged over the wood floor. He came into the living room, face ashen and drawn, gray eyes hard as bullets.

"It was you," he said in a low voice.

Keira wrapped her arms around her waist. His expression seemed dead and empty. "I told you, but your memories... They put a block on your mind." Quivering, she bit her lip. "Please, let me explain...."

"Nothing to explain. You're the damn wolf who tortured me, turned me into a shredded mess. Keira."

Dale looked shattered. "Keira, the Luminaire who

believes good can be found in people. The woman who heals those who are broken…after her wolf claws break them. How many other men have you done this to?"

She could not answer, only wrapped her arms around her waist.

"All this time I talked to you of fighting evil, of battling dark forces, and you…did…that?"

Her heart squeezed tight. She managed a brief nod. "I never wanted to hurt you. I was forced."

His voice dropped to a bare whisper. "How could you make me believe in your goodness, in light and hope? What kind of sick game is this?"

"The Centurions forced me to torture you!" she cried out.

Please believe me.

"Did they force you to come here and destroy my trust in you?" He spoke in a whisper, as if every word wrung from him was too painful to voice aloud.

His voice became louder, more strident. "Break my heart all over again after I started to care for you, believe that we had a chance together? You betrayed me. I placed my life in your hands, my spirit! In the hands of the demon wolf responsible for this!"

He tore open his shirt and lifted the sweat-stained T-shirt below it, exposing the network of jagged scars bisecting his muscled torso.

Shay swore quietly and glared at her. Sully muttered under his breath.

"Dale, please. I'd take back every single one of them if I could. Don't let what I did in the past destroy what you have now." Tears blurred her vision. She wiped them away. "You care for me…I care for you. Reach beyond the pain and see what we have together. Just trust me a little…."

"Trust you?"

"I've shared with you my devotion. My heart. Give me a chance...trust me again and I promise I'll do anything for you."

Her voice dropped to a broken whisper. "Anything."

"The only trust and loyalty I'll give is to my team." He glanced at the SEALs. "They never caused me to question their loyalty. Not like you."

He took a deep breath, closed his eyes. "Keira Solomon, I renounce you. I renounce our agreement."

"No," she cried out.

The slave armband popped off her biceps, tumbling to the floor. Through her tears she saw the brilliant sapphire wink at her, as if mocking her protests.

Emotions in a lather, she felt her wolf give a rumbling growl. Without the protection of the armband, Dale was now vulnerable to attack. Keira squeezed her fists, desperate to control the beast. Must not turn on him, must not...

She looked up at Dale's face and saw the anguish shadowing his eyes, saw the tightened jaw and the grief. And felt a dim flare of hope.

"Keira," he said thickly. "Why did you do it? Why did you torture me in the dark? You've done nothing but help me since you got here."

Sensing his utter confusion and torment, she took a tentative step forward. "Because I was forced. They forced my wolf..."

A derisive snort from Shay. "Right. Don't listen to her B.S., Curt. Get this demon out of your life. I swear, after I saw what she did to you in the basement, how could you let her stay here?"

The wolf inside her snapped. Without the armband's protection, she found herself surrendering to the beast's emotions. Bones lengthened and fur rippled along her arms. Keira shape-shifted.

And faced Dale, emotions a red haze in her wolf mind, only wanting to get rid of this insidious pain, find relief with her claws. Growling, she advanced, stalking toward him. Face paling, he backed up, as his men withdrew their weapons.

"No," he said sharply. "Don't hurt her."

Dale dived for the carpet and picked up the Celestial amulet, holding it out like a weapon. Then he tossed it at her. The amulet hit her nose. Soon as contact was made, she shifted back into human form. Naked, trembling and vulnerable, she clothed herself by magick and stood.

"Told you, Curt," Shay said in a low voice. "How the hell can you trust her when she can turn on you in a heartbeat?"

I'm sorry, she wanted to say, but could not find her voice. It didn't matter. She saw the condemnation in his eyes, in the eyes of his men.

His team, the only ones he trusted.

"Get out," he said tightly. "Out of my house and out of my life. Sully, go upstairs, help her pack her things. I want you gone in twenty minutes. I've given you enough cash to tide you over a while."

Biting her lip to suppress her tears, she started to leave and saw him throw the slave armband at the piano. It hit the vase of roses, sending them spilling to the carpet. Water poured over the pristine, polished cabinet of the Steinway, dripping to the carpet. Like his blood had dripped in the basement.

Sullivan accompanied her to the bedroom where Dale moved her belongings. Packing didn't take long. She took the saddlebags and trudged downstairs, the ache in her chest turning into a stabbing agony.

Sullivan held the door open. She went through it. She did not look back.

Money presented a slight problem. She had left the 3,000 dollars in cash Dale had given her on his dresser. She had enough cash to select a nice hotel on the beach for two weeks, but Keira didn't worry about conserving her funds.

Without the armband's protection, it would not take long for demons to capture her.

For two days, she took a towel and chair to the beach, sitting on the sand, staring at the lacy waves crashing upon the shore.

Remembering how Dale rescued her from the churning surf.

Remembering how they'd made love.

And then the memories became so thick and rich with grief, she wanted to bat them away, but did not. Soon enough, they'd become wisps, cobwebs torn in the wind.

All she had to sustain her through the long nights were memories of Dale.

On the second night, Keira walked outside into the warm Virginia Beach air. A restaurant a short walk away promised good seafood and an oceanfront view while dining.

Sandals dangling from one hand, she strolled along the sand, shuffling her feet in the warm grains, avoiding the crush of pedestrians on the boardwalk. A short set of steps led to the boardwalk and the restaurant. Keira trudged up the stairs and gazed at the diners eating outside, separated from the boardwalk by a low wall. It looked like a fun place, crowded, with lots of laughter and good times.

Perhaps here, she would not feel quite so alone.

A strong, masculine scent filtered through the briny air, drawing her short. Lifting her nose like a wolf to the wind, she gazed around. Pedestrians squeezed past, talking and laughing. She saw no handsome navy commander with piercing gray eyes.

But the spicy scent of his cologne, twined with the richness of his scent of crisp pine and cold snow, tantalized her senses like steak to a starving man. Keira stopped, panic and longing crashing together.

At a corner outdoor booth, Shay and Kelly sat with Dale and a blonde woman she did not recognize. The blonde's hair was long and luxurious, and the tight black sheath she wore, along with a slim string of pearls, hinted of money.

Dale said something and the blonde laughed, squeezing his hand and leaning close to whisper into his ear.

A date, she thought, stricken. *I haven't been out of his life more than two days and he's dating.*

Keira swallowed hard. Yearning filled her, to draw close one more time, feel the warmth of his wide mouth pressed against hers, the strength in his arms entwined around her waist, sheltering her. Hear his whisper that nothing would tear them apart.

But it did.

She did not deserve happiness for her crimes. But this honorable Mage had done nothing wrong, except finally believe she was not evil.

He deserved joy, to find someone special who would cherish him.

As I did.

A sob wrenched from her throat. Two men in sailor uniforms glanced her way. Keira turned and scurried back to the hotel, her appetite gone.

* * *

They caught her the next day.

Keira struggled hard as the demon minions grabbed her arms in her hotel room. She tossed a white energy bolt at one, killing him. But then more materialized, dozens of them holding her down.

Flat nostrils twitching, they clapped a restraining collar around her neck.

They materialized inside a large, empty warehouse. The stench of old blood and death tinged her nostrils.

Seated at a card table was Antony, the oldest Centurion. Ghostly specters floated around him, the others still unable to take form, but freed from the bolt-hole. The minions threw her down to the cold concrete floor. The collar bit into her throat, making her gag.

"Nice to see you again, Antony. I see you're still a glutton. Ever think about a diet and exercise?"

"Leave us," Antony ordered. He thumbed a small device, the size of a cell phone.

When the minions dematerialized, he depressed a button on the device. Muscles spasming, she jerked and twisted on the floor. When the convulsions ended, she got to her knees and glared at the demon.

"I expected you to find me sooner. What's wrong? Your GPS malfunction?"

"A slight delay in Nicaragua, opening the bolt-hole to allow my brothers to escape." He studied his fingernails. "We had to wait until the armies under our control widened the doorway."

If only she'd found the bolt-hole and the book of ancient spells that originally summoned the Centurions from hell. But Keira did not know where it was hidden.

Antony, the only Centurion to keep form since the

demons were summoned by the soldiers fighting in the Contra war, hid the book well and kept moving it.

He gave a cold smile as she rubbed her neck. "Unfortunately, your new restraint does not work as effectively as the armband, but it will suffice. The Tasers Jimali stole for us make a poor substitute for controlling you."

Hope surged. Without the armband and the proper spell to compel her to shift into wolf, Antony couldn't force her to torture more victims.

"I can take whatever you dish out. I won't torture any more men for you, no matter what you do to me. Go to hell," she snapped.

"We know where your brave navy SEAL commander is. Tonight, I will take him captive."

"He'll fight you. He's no longer defenseless, and no longer able to be lured into a trap. All his powers have been restored."

He turned to a ghostly specter hovering nearby. "He will fight us. The base is secure. We cannot enter, even with Thad's identification card."

Panic tightened her chest. He'd already tested accessing the base. "Where is Thad?"

"He escaped when Jimali captured him. Unfortunately." Antony seemed confident. "But we have the means to take out your navy SEAL commander. We know his weakness for his men, and will lure him into a trap once more."

Antony seemed overly confident. He leaned forward, his belly spilling over the studded belt.

"Dale can't be touched. He's far too powerful."

Antony gave a mocking grin. "Yes. And with his death, I shall live forever, and seize his team for my brothers to torture."

Horror pulsed through her. "I won't torment him anymore. You have no power to force me to do so. You'll have to torture him yourself."

"Ah, but my methods are so inconsequential compared to the lure of your demon wolf, who can make him scream with pain and pant with lust. You are the reason why I have remained alive these past decades."

She was why the demon lived as a human. He had killed the one who summoned him twenty-three years ago, seized the Book of Spells used in the summoning and then tore through the fighting armies like a buzz saw, stealing the bravery they used to fight. But the energy infusion never lasted more than a few days. And then Antony had chanced upon her pack, and realized the riches of having someone else do his dirty work.

All those men she'd been forced to torment. Keira's heart clenched. She must atone for her misdeeds.

"Only you can save your navy commander. What will you do to save him?" Antony asked. "Will you die for him?"

Keira squeezed her eyes closed. His men were strong and might rescue Dale, but until they did, he would suffer more torment, and the haunted, empty look would return to his eyes. She wanted him to live, be happy....

There was a slim chance Dale and his team would track the demons. Thad was alive and the team would find the Centurions before other innocent men died. But they would probably not be in time to save her....

Fierce resolve filled her. She opened her eyes.

"I will. Spare him, and take me in his place. Leave him alone."

"Such a rich prize, freely offered." His thin, wispy laugh sounded like teeth chewing on tin foil. "Who needs a navy SEAL when we have you, Keira?"

Antony stood and reached into a small bag, withdrawing something. Horror pulsed through her as she spotted what he held.

The spiked whip from Dale's compound.

"A lovely little decoration. I had the pleasure of removing it from Thad when he used it against Jimali as she attacked him. Unfortunately, I was too late to save her."

He shrugged. "A pity. She served us well. But the whip is a good exchange for her life. How I have longed to test it on bare flesh."

Don't think of what will happen, she told herself. *Think of Dale, his courage, his wide smile as he played the piano.*

His happiness.

At the first strike upon her back, she arched and did not cry out, holding fast to the image of a brave navy SEAL commander.

You will not scream.

But a while later, she did…

Chapter 22

To try to cheer him up, Shay and Kelly held a small dinner party that week. Most of the SEALs from the Phoenix Force crowded around the table with their wives and girlfriends.

Kelly cooked a delicious repast, tender London broil with new potatoes and a delicate tomato basil soup.

Every bite of steak congealed like old grease in Dale's stomach. No fault of Shay's bride. Hell, a gourmet meal or an MRE tasted the same.

Ever since Keira had left, he found little enjoyment.

Shay had dragged him to a blind date with an acquaintance of Kelly's, a pretty blonde from her aerobics class. Deidre was fun, he supposed. Her loud, horsey laugh grated on his nerves and the thick, cloying perfume made him gag.

Unfortunately, he'd told a small white lie, assuring her

he'd had a great time…. Yeah, swell. And Kelly insisted Deidre join them tonight at their dinner party.

Seated around the long dining table, members of his team ate and laughed. No laughter rose in Dale's throat.

I've lost her. For good.

Once again, his impulsive temper kicked in. His damnable, rigid code of honor had booted her straight out of his life. The same code of honor that refused to listen to his wife when she'd pleaded for him to listen for explanations about why she left.

I can never forgive such betrayal.

But had Keira betrayed him? The woman risked all to heal him, and opened her heart to him.

What hurts more, he thought. *My pride at being a gullible fool, allowing myself to be lured into a demon trap, or my heart?*

Bitterness rose in his throat like acid. But pride and stubbornness made for bad companions.

"You look so lost in thought. Anything I can do?" Deidre tossed her hair like a mane, and preened, displaying ample cleavage.

He thought about palming Keira's much smaller breasts, her tiny, excited cries as he'd suckled her nipples and made her explode with pleasure. Unabashed and unrestrained, honest in every sensual reaction. He thought about the warmth of her smile, and how she'd trembled with passion in his arms, and how damn good she'd made him feel, how he wanted nothing more than to return the passion.

Hell, he thought. *I have to find her.* He thought of her alone, lost, wandering the world with demons searching for her.

Dale threw down his napkin and pushed back his chair and stood. "I screwed up, badly. I'm going after Keira, going to find her and bring her back. It's not safe out there for her. Who's with me?"

His men looked at him steadily, and one by one, they stood. Then Kelly whispered into Shay's ear and, scowling, he stood, as well. The depths of their loyalty squeezed his heart. They'd follow him to hell and back.

Kelly smiled and touched her husband's hand and Dale knew she'd talked Shay into it.

Suddenly her smile faded. A horrified look came over her. She arched, pushed back from the table and screamed.

Shay pushed back his chair so fast, it toppled backward. "Kel! What is it?"

But she kept screaming, horrible, anguished sobs of such pain, his heart dropped to his stomach. A person made those terrible sounds only for one reason.

He'd made such sounds in the dark, as his blood dripped off the platform in the basement....

Turning, Kelly stiffened, head thrown back, fingers digging into the table.

Streaks of blood dampened the back of her lemon-yellow blouse.

Bile rose in his throat. Shay's desperate gaze snapped to him. "Curt, please, you're a Primary, do something!"

Running to the screaming Kelly, he saw the silver triskele pendant around her neck glow with white light. Dale yanked the chain, pulling the triskele free. The pendant sizzled in his palm. Yelping, he dropped it.

And then a horrific pain lashed his back, a thousand burning knives sinking into his skin.

Just as quickly, the pain faded. Deeply shaken, he looked at Kelly slumped in her seat, chest heaving with each ragged breath.

The blood vanished from her blouse. An illusion.

Shay dropped to his knees beside her, chafing her hand. "Honey, what is it? What happened?"

Kelly lifted her gaze, no longer glazed with pain. "It's her. Keira. She's in horrible, horrible pain. I formed a psychic bond with her. It's as if someone is…torturing her. I felt every single lash."

Dale went still, his pulse racing. A terrible suspicion seized him.

The scars can be removed if the one who placed them there makes an enormous sacrifice.

Fingers unfastening his dress shirt, he opened it and looked down.

The scars were gone.

"Curt, whoa, what happened?" Dakota asked.

Not answering, he rushed to the large mirror over the sofa and stared. He tore off his shirt and examined his torso, the underside of his arms.

Clean, smooth flesh.

"Oh, gods," he whispered. "Please, it can't be so…she couldn't have done it."

He put his shirt back on, leaving it untucked and hanging open. When he returned to the dining room, everyone looked worried. All but Deidre, who looked totally confused.

"What's going on? Is this performance art? Are you guys practicing for a flash mob?" she asked.

Dale waved a hand. "Dakota, wipe her memories, put her in a taxi and send her home."

As the Draicon werewolf scrambled to comply, he turned to the other SEALs. "I want a fifty-mile perimeter psi search, using electromagnetic sweeps for demon energy sigs. Call in Thad."

"He's on leave for ten days," Dallas said.

"It's canceled." He quietly regarded Shay's still shaken

wife. "Kelly, I'm afraid I'll need your help to track down Keira, using your link to her."

Shay fisted his hands. "You have me, Curt. But no way, no damn way are you using my wife to find that wolf who tortured you."

Calm settled over him. Dale turned and regarded his SEAL. "Stand down, soldier."

"The hell I will! You nearly died on that table."

"I said, stand down." Steel threaded through his quiet voice.

Raising a hand, he flicked a finger and drew the chair upright, and forced Shay to sit. "Calm down. You'll be with her the entire time."

Glowering, Shay shook his head. "She nearly killed you, man."

"She also saved my life, and I was too stupid and arrogant to admit it." Such intense sorrow pulsed through him, he nearly reeled from it. Dale kept a grip on his emotions.

He only hoped he wasn't too late.

Twenty-four hours passed. Forty-eight. All his team's finest minds, equipment and scanners resulted in dead ends.

Thad had been found, clinging to consciousness, badly beaten but alive. He'd awoken in the hospital, murmuring about demons and whips.

Ordering security tightened on the ST 21 compound, Dale had a very bad feeling something nasty would soon unfold.

In his office he paced, ignored the phone messages, the stacks of papers requiring his attention. A knock sounded.

"Come."

Shay entered, concern tightening his face. "Someone called 911 the other night, reported a woman screaming from a warehouse near the waterfront. Kel checked it out…we drove by. She felt something…but very, very faint. We think it's Keira."

Dale checked his SIG holstered at his waist.

"Guns and bullets won't stop these bastards, Curt."

"I know. But we're going in with everything we've got. Get the team together. We leave in ten minutes."

Tension coiled his stomach as their Humvees pulled up before a deserted warehouse at the wharf. Rust coated the aluminum-frame building. The entire area reeked of the stench of fish, brine and something foul, like raw sewage. And a far more ominous scent.

The metallic stench of blood.

Dale slid out from the driver's seat. He checked his weapon and gathered his powers as they all crept toward the warehouse.

Holding up a fist, Dale signaled. *Wait.*

He sensed their tension, their eagerness to storm the warehouse and free her, but they were SEALs and knew to tread with stealth.

No telling what the hell lay beyond those doors, or if whatever held Keira would simply cut her throat and be done with it.

Hell of a chance, doing this in bright sunshine, risking not just some concerned Joe Citizen dialing 911, but without the cover of darkness.

Keira couldn't wait until nightfall. All his senses warned him that by then she might be gone.

He pulled down on his fist and they rounded the door. Dakota, point man, shifted into a wolf as Dallas opened the door.

Anyone inside would think a large stray simply wandered in.

Dakota released a low howl, the signal for finding something.

They stole inside, into a small antechamber. Still in wolf form, Dakota growled, pawing at the ground.

Sitting at a wood table, guarding the door to the warehouse entrance was a corpulent man. Plates of half-finished food and empty wine bottles sat before him. He blinked sleepily at the SEALs.

"Ah, visitors. You're late. We expected you a day ago."

"Keira," Dale snapped, training his weapon on the Centurion, recognizing that sniveling voice from the basement.

"Yes, the famous Lieutenant Commander Curtis. Pleasure to meet you again." The demon belched and scratched its groin. "Thank you for removing the slave bracelet so we could send out minions to find her. Tremendous favor you did us. Much better to torture her. All these years we held her captive, she never offered herself in place of another. Selfish little bitch. We searched far and wide for a brave warrior to torture, but the bravest of all was within our grasp. A woman. They always sacrifice themselves. Because of Keira, we are now flesh."

Fury coiled in his guts. Dale held on to his control by a thread. "Where are the others? There are six of you."

"Out, having a night of it. They left me here to guard the girl. What's left of her."

Control snapped. He lowered his weapon. "You fucking son of a bitch…"

Springing forward, he snapped the demon's neck. Surprise flared on its face, then it dropped down, head clattering onto a greasy plate filled with bones. Shay stepped forward and chanted a vanquishing spell.

The demon's body vanished, going straight back to the netherworld.

"Fan out. Comb every inch of this damn place," he ordered.

He had barely taken a step toward the door when he heard a low, strangled whisper. Dakota, in human form, at the door. His eyes wide and expression stricken. "Curt…"

Dale kicked open the door and rushed into the warehouse.

A figure hung, arms outstretched and tied to an overhead beam, the legs spread wide and attached to two supporting poles. Blood slicked the concrete floor below.

She was naked, coated in crimson. Blood, dear gods, so much blood. On the floor near her bare feet was a long whip studded with small silver spikes.

Gorge rose in his throat. Stricken, he stood, immobilized, staring at his former lover.

Unconscious. Thankfully.

Dragging a table over to the column, Dale climbed onto it. He reached for his KA-BAR knife and sawed through her bonds. When one wrist was freed, he tossed the knife to Shay, watching with huge, horrified eyes.

"Cut her down. I'll catch her."

The SEAL did, and Keira slumped in his arms. Warm blood oozed onto his BDUs. Dale's stomach clenched as he buried his nose into her tangled, mussed hair.

Please live.

Low, mocking laughter, burning agony lacing her flesh. The torment stopped, then continued. Moaning, she tried clawing at the air, but her wrists were bound. The demon holding the whip snickered, its round face sneering.

And then the face changed. Clean, defined cheekbones, a wide mouth and intense steel-gray eyes.

Dale laughed as he drew his wrist back to flick the whip once more....

Crying out, she bolted upright.

"It's okay. You're safe now. You're safe," a deep voice crooned.

Squeezing her eyes shut, afraid to open them to find the empty warehouse and the stench of her own blood, she flexed her back muscles.

Skin stretched and pulled, but the searing pain had fled.

Afraid she dreamed, or had died, Keira opened her eyes.

Bedroom, plain white walls, a blue-striped window seat beneath a tall window, shelves lined with books, heavy masculine furniture.

The powerful scent of male and power...

Her gaze swung right. Perched on the bed's edge, Dale quietly regarded her.

"How do you feel?"

Closing her eyes, she fell back against the pillows.

This was a nightmare. Dale had returned to torment her.

A warm palm settled over her forehead. Always so warm, chasing away the iciness inside her.

"No fever. My physician personally took care of you in the hospital. Dakota called in a favor of his people and brought in Maggie, an empath healer. You were very badly hurt, but everything's all right now, Keira."

Keira remained silent.

Worry shaded his gray eyes. "It took all her energy to heal you. Unfortunately, the scars will remain. But your body is healed."

Healed? Physical injuries would lessen, though the cruel scars would remain. But her heart had shattered and she wasn't certain if she could ever mend it.

"Water." Her voice cracked. Dry, her throat felt like sand.

Dale rose and lifted a glass of water to her lips. Hands wrapping around his, ignoring the sudden surge of heat flaring between them, she drank deeply, then licked her cracked lips.

Her throat felt sore. When she spoke, her voice came out as a thin whisper.

"Why can't I talk?"

"Temporary laryngitis." His expression darkened as he set the glass down. "From screaming. Dr. Mitchell says with a few days rest, you'll be back to normal."

"How long have I been out?"

"We rescued you from the warehouse seven days ago."

A full week for the demons to roam through Virginia Beach or even leave the country.

"Too damn close. We cut it too damn close, and almost lost you." His voice broke. "When I saw you there, in the warehouse…"

He cursed and looked away, squeezing her hand. She didn't respond.

Cold, her hands were so icy. It felt as if she'd never be warm again. Dale slid his strong, warm palm over hers. "You're safe now. I won't let anything happen to you. Go back to sleep. You need your rest. Do you need anything? Anything at all?"

She nodded. "Leave me alone. Now."

Turning over, she presented her back to him and closed her eyes, the agony in her heart far greater than the pull and stretch of healing tissue.

* * *

Dale returned at noon with broth and coaxed her to eat. Too weak to take the spoon in hand, she allowed him to feed her, only because she needed to recover her strength.

He remained at her side after, as she fell back asleep.

And he returned at dinner. He told her of his team's efforts to track the Centurions, using every method.

"They got to Thad, one of my men, first. Jimali started beating him, but he took the whip and killed her and managed to escape. Unfortunately, Jimali tortured Thad enough to cause one Centurion to become corporeal."

Dale's nearness made her ache. Once they shared intimate times in bed. Now he had become a stranger, a stranger who'd kicked her out of his house and protection.

He removed the tray from the bedside and sat down, stroking her hair. "Keira, why did you do it? One of the Centurions told me you sacrificed yourself."

She shrugged and plucked at the bedcovers.

"You did it for me. Why? After I kicked you out…" His face tightened. "After the way I treated you."

"Doesn't matter now. It's in the past, and I'm not about to make any more mistakes." She looked at him, the hurt and anger grinding through her like a freshly opened wound. "Especially with you. I'm here until I can walk out on my own, and then I'm gone. Whatever we had between us is over."

"Keira." He sighed. "Damn it, I want to tell you I'm sorry, but it seems so…"

"Lame?"

"Inadequate."

"Fine." The knot in her stomach grew. "Then let's focus on the business at hand. The demons."

He became stiff and formal, dropping his hand, the

commander assuming control, the man who'd loved her in the dark of night vanished.

"They're out there, roaming the streets, free. We need your help to stop them. You're the only living person with access to their secrets. If those damn things grab innocent sailors…"

She cleared her throat, feeling a little stronger.

"They won't. Ordinary humans lack sufficient strength. Now that they've tormented you, they will only pursue paranormal victims with powerful magick."

"Help us find them."

Bitterness washed through her. "I'll help you find them, because it's the only way I'll free myself. But once the demons are caught and vanquished, I'm gone."

For a moment, a shadow crossed his expression.

"Stephen narrowed the search area for the bolt-hole. The dark pulses of energy radiate close to the Honduran-Nicaraguan border."

"That's where I lived with my pack…when the Centurions attacked and tried to enslave all of us."

"We will get them. *Disperdere malum hoc.*"

"'Destroy this evil,'" she murmured.

Dale cocked his head. "You know Latin?"

"Spent many years locked in a cell with the Centurions speaking Latin when they didn't speak English or Spanish. It helped pass the time."

He stood, a determined look on his face. "I can't make up for those years, Keira. But I'm doing everything in my power to ensure it doesn't happen again. My team is focusing all effort on this. In the meanwhile, Sully's sister is here. Cassandra wants to perform a white-light ritual for you. It will help restore your energy balance." He looked intently at her. "Will you allow her to do this?"

Keira hesitated and then nodded.

* * *

Orders for deployment came for ST 21, seven months on a mission in the Middle East. Curt sent an entire platoon and the Alpha Squad. They were more than ready.

He needed the Phoenix Force on base to combat the greater threat. In the basement, his team had set up shop, hauling in equipment and taking turns sleeping in shifts.

They desperately needed Keira's help to find the demons. She trusted Sully's sister.

If only she trusted him.

Sitting at the kitchen table the next morning, Cassandra stirred a spoon in her teacup. With her long corn-silk blond hair, large blue eyes and slender figure, Sully's sister was a true beauty. But he only had eyes for Keira.

"The ritual went well. Her inner light was diminished, but it's stronger now."

Dale squeezed and flexed his fingers.

The witch gave him a knowing look. "You're wondering if you can ever make amends."

His jaw turned to rock. "I want to…. There is too much between us now."

"The distance is your pride."

"She betrayed me, in my own house."

"Only your pride was hurt. You threw her out of your house, out of your protection, because of your pride. Nothing more."

He thought of the laughing, vivacious Keira who had brought new life into his house, reenergized him. Was that woman gone forever?

"She won't respond to me." Dale buried his head into his hands.

Cassandra touched his arm.

"Never have I encountered such pain and sorrow. Keira has suffered a tremendous trauma. Her body has healed, but her spirit is damaged. Badly." Cassandra shook her head. "Such a sweet, brave soul. Her white light was but a flicker, surrounded by darkness. She has survived much evil by clinging to the light inside her."

Dale lifted his head, suddenly filled with fierce resolve. "I don't give a damn if I have to lie, steal, cheat or damn my soul, I'll see her recover."

Keira had embraced life with arms open wide. She was the strongest survivor he knew. Dale slammed a fist on the table, making the empty vase rattle.

Roses, he'd always bought her fresh roses.

Sudden insight struck. She'd appreciated the flowers, but he'd never asked her what her favorites were. Never asked. Simply bought what he thought would please her.

"You are beginning to understand the depths of such a heart." No condemnation in Cassandra's voice, only gentleness.

"She was the vision you saw for me in your crystal."

"Yes. Your redemption. You can be hers, if you will allow it."

"How?" He dealt with weapons and enemies, and bad guys and military bureaucracy. Not anything as elusive and esoteric as inner light and soul healing.

"Open yourself to possibilities, to believing it can happen. Open your heart to her and release your inner light." Cassandra gave her gentle smile. "You are a courageous and noble warrior leader, but you've been deeply wounded, Dale. You must find it within yourself to release the bitterness, anger and pain, and forgive. Only by letting go do we gain."

Despite his massive powers, at heart, he was too grounded and pragmatic for this. He believed in the physical, not the metaphysical.

For Keira, he would do anything, and set aside his

belief systems. He wanted her back, wanted to see the spark ignite her now dull eyes. Hear her laughter, sharp and clear as a silver bell.

A shuffling noise sounded in the hallway. Keira trudged into the kitchen in a warm fleece robe Cassandra had bought for her.

The coffeepot was bubbling in the kitchen. She poured herself a cup and stood at the counter, sipping. Dale quietly watched her.

His heart ached. If only she'd open up, and reach out to him. But she was listless and lifeless, an automaton.

The man in him wanted to hold her close, whisper apologies and soothe her heart.

The navy commander had demons to find and a populace to keep safe.

Dale took a deep breath. Could he ever reconcile the two? He hadn't done it in his first marriage. The navy came before all else, even his own family.

It's why Kathy left you. But Keira meant much more to him, had burrowed deep into his heart.

I'm not going to lose her, as well. Not again.

When three of his men came upstairs from the basement, Keira stiffened. She moved away from the counter, went into a corner, like a hurt animal, trying to avoid them.

Shay glanced at Keira. "Sorry to interrupt, Curt. Ran out of coffee."

He opened a door and withdrew an unopened package of hazelnut coffee. Shay stood awkwardly at the counter. Dakota and Dallas shuffled their feet.

He cleared his throat. "Glad to see you upright and vertical, Miss Solomon."

Keira ignored him and stared out the sliding glass doors at the pool.

"Report," Dale said.

"We've narrowed the range to Virginia Beach. Bastards haven't left the area."

Keira set down her mug. "Sooner or later, they'll find me."

She opened the sliders and stepped onto the deck. Alarm pulsed through him. Dale followed, leaving the door open.

Stunned, he watched her shrug off the robe. Beneath it she wore a one-piece red swimsuit. He saw a flash of horrific scar tissue bisecting her back, and then she jumped in the pool. Swimming with strong, sure strokes, she kicked up a small froth.

Dale squatted by the pool's edge. "Get out before you collapse."

"Go to hell. If I don't get stronger, they'll turn me into mincemeat again. This time, I'm fighting with all I've got."

"We'll protect you." He scowled. "I'll protect you. I promise I won't let anything happen to you."

She stopped, and treaded water, fury tightening her face. "Oh? Like you did when you booted me out? Nice protection, Commander. No, thanks, I'll take care of myself."

"Get out of the pool now. We need to talk."

"Screw you. You're not my employer any longer."

Frustration and anger coiled inside him. Dale stood and called on his powers.

Stretching out his arms, he concentrated and pulled her from the water. Shrieks of rage followed as Keira floated in the air to his side. Very gently, he set her on her feet.

"You bastard! You think you can control me? When it suits you, snap your fingers and I'll come running? How dare you manipulate your powers against me! Use all the power you've got but you'll never break me."

Something inside him snapped. He got in her face. "I never wanted you broken, damn it. And if you'd stop being so damn stubborn and proud, you'd see I'm trying to help you, not hurt you."

"Change of heart, because you already hurt me enough when you tossed me out without even allowing me to explain?"

"I overreacted," he admitted, gritting his teeth. "All I could think of was how you nearly killed me and made me vulnerable. And I endangered my team by letting you into my life."

"Because your team is more important than anything else. Even me. You never gave me a chance. Your job comes first, your almighty team."

He didn't like the truth slapping him in the face. Keira's shoulders slumped, her energy expelled, her face pale.

Trembling, she wrapped her arms around her waist. Dale took a shuddering breath and clasped her elbow, leading her to a chair. She collapsed in it, looking as miserable as he felt.

All the anger left, like air escaping a balloon replaced by a growing sense of urgency. Dale put a hand on the armrest.

"Keira. We have to work together on this. I'm sorry… so damn sorry. I can't undo what I did. All I can do is press on and fight these bastards who did this to you with all I've got. Everything my men have. We're a team. I want you to come to the base this afternoon with me and brief my men."

Despair clouded her expression. She shook her head.

"All right. I will. But you're part of a team. Not me. I'm all alone."

She pushed up from the chair and shrugged into the robe. "And I'm better off that way. You can never convince me to join a team, Dale. Because all teamwork's done in the past is chewed me up and spit me out."

That afternoon, she and Dale's SEALs gathered in the team's ready room, the men seated at long tables before her. Dale stood off to the side against a wall, arms folded.

Keira stood at the head of the table after Dale introduced her to all the SEALs. These men had formed an alliance against her when Dale threw her out. Mistrust flared. She'd work with them for a common goal. And once that goal was achieved, she'd be gone.

"Centurions were Roman soldiers," Keira told them. "Executed and condemned by a powerful Mage who fought with them, and then vanquished them to the netherworld for their cowardice. He cursed them to never walk the earth in flesh unless they finally acquired the courage they lacked in battle."

"We need to know everything you know. Even the smallest bit of information can help destroy them," Dale said.

"I know a lot." Keira grimaced and set down the pointer. "The only good thing about being stuck in a dark cell next to Jimali was she liked to talk, and she gave me a lot of information. She was with the Centurions since the time when they inhabited a small village in Nicaragua."

"Why were they in Nicaragua?" Shay asked.

"They were summoned during the Contra war in 1988. The fighting was pretty fierce and Miguel, leader of a small faction of Contra guerillas, was desperate. He had a last resort, a dark book of spells found in a Mayan temple in Honduras. So Miguel selected six of his most loyal and strongest fighters for a ritual to summon the spirit of ancient Roman warriors. He called upon the Centurions to come forth from the afterlife and possess his men with the strength to kill the enemy."

Keira took a deep breath. "The blood rite, combined with the violence from the fighting, opened a bolt-hole into the netherworld and conjured the spirits of the Centurion demons, who possessed Miguel's men. When they discovered they were human, they fled to the village where they began drinking and womanizing. Miguel discovered they deserted the guerilla camp and came after them with a spell to force the demons out. Antony, the strongest Centurion, killed Miguel and confiscated the Book of Spells.

"But the Mage's curse affected them and they began to grow weaker. One by one, they were forced out of their owner's bodies. Before it happened to Antony, he read through the book for a dark spell to become corporeal. By stealing the courage and strength of warriors, they could manifest their original human forms. The demons killed the people they had possessed and stole their courage. They became corporeal for only a few days. But they had more sources."

"An entire army of fighters to sustain them," Dale said.

"They went through both the Contra and Sandinista factions fighting in that area like a buzz saw, stealing their courage and strength until the men started dropping dead. But it still wasn't enough. The bolt-hole into the netherworld began to close, shutting out their opportunity to release more demons and use them to become more powerful. They killed a faction of both Contra and

Sandinistas, cursing them to fight forever, the ensuing violence leaving enough of a crack in the bolt-hole for the Centurions to summon other demons from hell. Once the violence builds to a certain level, it becomes a window for the Centurions to use. Only the Centurions can control the bolt-hole."

"But they still needed to be corporeal," Renegade said. "So did they start on the villagers?"

"The weary villagers had no fighting spirit left to siphon. And the war ended. The Centurions were becoming ghosts when my pack came to the village to help the village recover, to plant crops with methods we used from bonding with the earth to replenish soil bloodied by violence. Antony used a slave armband given to him by his lover and empowered it with dark magick to compel me to fight for him, to torture and terrorize brave souls so he and the others could steal their strength."

Dale rubbed a hand over his strong jaw, his gray eyes intense. "Let me take a wild guess. This Jimali was his lover in the village, who teamed with him to do his dirty work."

"In exchange for power and money." Keira sighed. "Antony is the strongest, the commander of the Centurions. He is the first to regenerate and the one who forces me to do his dirty work. He endowed Jimali with special powers to do physical tasks they could not perform when they were not in flesh."

"We know they can be killed in flesh. But how do we kill them as ghosts?" asked Jammer, the SEAL with close-cropped brown hair.

"In spirit form, they can be weakened by siphoning their dark energy." Keira glanced at Dale. "Someone can absorb their essence into their body with the right spell, and hold them captive. And then the demons can be expunged with the right spell and sent straight back to hell. The bolt-hole must be sealed with light energy and white light."

"I'd hate to think what happens to the person who absorbs those demons," Dakota said.

"That's what makes the spell so dangerous. It causes great harm to the person casting it. They become filled with darkness and devoid of white light. Right now they're gathering forces, letting out other demons in exchange for favors. They've formed an effective and lethal alliance."

She glanced at Dale. "This is why I'm not so hot on teamwork. I've seen the results of what they can do."

"You haven't seen the result of what my team can do." Quiet, deadly, lethal force radiating from him, he nodded at his men.

"The bolt-hole is a doorway from this world to the netherworld, controlled by the Centurions. Just like a toll-gate, they demand a price from demons who use it to access this world. The longer the Centurions remain flesh, the more power they'll crave. They will return there to open the bolt-hole and allow more demons to infest this world, in exchange for power."

Keira's gaze swept over the men sitting before her. "The worst kind of evil. Including pyrokinetic demons. They'll do what they did to your friend Adam multiplied times ten thousand. No training in your firestorm chamber can stop them."

Blood drained from Dakota's face. He quietly swore.

"We'll find a way to stop them," Dale assured his men.

"You don't know the methods they'll use to get their way." Keira stared at the distant wall.

Dale spoke. "I promise you, we will find and vanquish them. You'll be free, Keira."

Oh, she wanted to believe him, wanted to trust again. She knew the only way to do this was using her.

I don't want to die. But I haven't really been living, either.

Not until she found Dale. And even with all that stood between him, he'd taught her the power of courage and strength.

She didn't know if she could trust him again. But he insisted his team could defeat them, and she had to try.

"You won't find them. Not without me. You need to use me as bait to lure them in."

Silence hovered for a moment. Then Dallas nodded. "Excellent idea. She knows what they look like…."

"No fucking way." Dale's voice sliced the air.

Her stomach twisted in knots. "The only way you'll find those demons is by using me. Either you let me do this or I work alone."

"No."

"Their blood runs through my veins. Until they are destroyed, it will remain."

"We have defenses you can't even match."

"I have my defenses, as well," she said softly. "And mine overpower yours. My wolf is stronger and more powerful."

Dale studied her calmly. "I know. But we're a team that can overcome you."

She hadn't shifted into a wolf since the day he'd thrown her out. The change came upon her swiftly as bones lengthened and fur rippled along her spine. Keira snarled and leaped onto the desk at the room's front, growling, her wolf barely controllable, itching to prove she was far more powerful.

Dale said nothing. Between one breath and another,

he shifted as well, into a large gray timber wolf, about half her size.

Keira leaped at him, but in midair, collided with two other wolves as Dallas and Dakota both shifted at the same time. The two Draicon wolves pinned her down as she struggled.

Then Dale, in wolf form, loped over to her. Opening her massive jaws, she struggled to keep her wolf in line, the demon blood surging through her with the compulsion to attack and hurt. But the large gray timber wolf that was Dale did not attack. He growled at the other two wolves, who climbed off her and withdrew.

Dale the wolf tenderly nuzzled her throat, and licked her muzzle.

It's okay, he seemed to say. *It's me.*

Instinctively, her wolf recognized his touch and scent and submitted. She lay quiet and still, the beast at last no longer howling in anguished, emotional pain. This was a good man, a man who did not wish to hurt her.

He eased away, shifted back and clothed himself as she lay panting on the floor. The two other SEALs did, as well.

Suddenly overcome, she shifted into human form, lying naked on the floor. Dale looked at his men and snapped an order for them to leave the room.

When they did, he pushed a hand through her long hair.

"Teamwork has advantages. They were ready to protect me, but I would never let them hurt you. Ever," he told her gently. "Now can you trust me? Just a little?"

She nodded. "You keep telling me how important teamwork is, Dale. Now it's time for you to show me exactly how important."

* * *

For the rest of the afternoon, Keira stayed in Dale's office, going over reports he'd compiled to search for any suspected Centurion activity. Dale had grimly informed her he wasn't about to let her out of his sight. She was too important.

Important. Worth protecting because she was the link in a chain they'd use to bring in the demons. But was she important to his life, his heart?

Two hours later, Dale returned to the office with Renegade in tow. The younger SEAL held up the slave armband. Keira recoiled. Seeing it was like glimpsing a live cobra; she didn't want it to bite her again.

Dale's steady gaze regarded her. "Keira, I need your permission to put this on you. It's your choice."

Renegade held up the jewelry, the sparkling sapphire replaced with clear quartz. "I've analyzed the jewel, the source of the spell that controlled you, and removed it, replacing it with a clear quartz crystal. It's embedded with a microchip that picks up negative psi impulses from up to ten klicks away. Acts like sonar. When the waves bounce off you, the transmitter picks up the beam and traces it back to the point of origin."

Dale's expression shuttered.

"And it also works in reverse," she replied. "I'll give out energy waves as well, positive ones the demons can pick up. It will help you find the demons, but first, they will find me."

Dale nodded tersely. "But someone will be watching over you at all times. You're not going to be alone."

The armband pulsed with faint white light. Still, she felt uneasy. "It's safe? It won't compel me to commit evil acts?"

"No, but with the quartz, it might compel you to do

something noble and totally reckless, like suction demon souls. You're fine as long as you don't chant any incantations," Renegade said.

"Do it," she told Dale.

Holding out her arm to have her former lover slip on the armband took all her strength. Dale's warm fingers brushed over her chilled skin as he slipped it into place, the metal settling against her skin like a handcuff.

Would she ever be free of it?

"How long will this take?" she asked.

"Depends on how desperate they are to find you. If they're running out of power, it'll be sooner than we expect."

Dale parked a lean hip on the polished desktop. "Safest place for you right now is here. My men are warding the compound so the Centurions can't get in."

Renegade left, closing the door behind him. Unease spiked her pulse, making her heart pound harder. "Guess I'm a sitting duck until then. How effective is this warding?"

"It acts like a filter and will keep out the strongest demon." He frowned. "But there's a small chance minor demons can slip past."

"Like gnats slipping past mosquito netting?"

"Sort of. I've stationed men around the compound, just in case. Food will be here soon." He glanced at her empty water bottle. "You want anything else to drink?"

"A shot of ginger ale, with a bottle of whiskey and a straw."

Heat licked through her at his slow, sexy grin—it was the Dale who'd loved her long into the night and held her close. "Afraid all I have is the ginger ale."

"Some bartender you are. I'll take it."

At her nod, he left the desk and went to a cube-size refrigerator and bent down.

Whoa, what a view. She craned her neck, admiring the way his trousers stretched over his oh-so-fine taut ass.

Right, Keira. The man is off-limits. Then again, I'm not dead. Not yet.

Dale fished out two ginger ales. He popped the tops on both and sat on the sofa, placing the cans on the table.

Suspicion filled her. She joined him on the sofa, and took a long drink.

"I talked with the admiral. Asked him, again, to tell me exactly what he'd seen in your mind that day when he melded with you. He said the images were a blur, but I should ask you about the family you lost in Nicaragua and the U.S. soldier you met in the jungle."

Stomach knotted tight, she set down her soda on the table. Talk about her family, the family she'd forced herself to forget? But if it helped Dale's team find the bastard demons, then she'd do it. Keira cleared her throat.

"We can shift when we're a month old. My pack leader betrayed us to the Centurions for his life. Didn't work. They killed him after finding our people. The Centurions began killing us…taking the young away from their mothers, who died bravely, defending them."

Keira's throat closed. "Their courage gave the demons energy to become corporeal…. They siphoned off the white light in their auras, sucking it up like damn vacuum cleaners. I tried protecting Simon, my little brother. And I made a bargain with them… If they would let Simon live, I'd become their slave and do their bidding. Because I knew they would not stay in that form for long."

He said nothing, only moved closer, taking a drink from his soda before setting it back down. Condensation rolled off the aluminum can like teardrops. Then she felt the warmth of his palm settle over her clenched hands. Soothing and comforting.

"What happened to your brother?" he asked, his voice gentle.

Fingers clenched tight, she shook her head. "They found another demon to forge an ancient armband to enslave me…and then they killed Simon. I'm the only survivor."

Muscles contorted with the effort to keep grief at bay, she stared at the sodas, fighting the tears. No more. But he came closer, and then pulled her against his broad chest, holding her there, stroking her hair.

Holding her tight, as if he wished to soothe away all her pain.

"All this time, you've had no one to help you, no one to rescue you," he murmured.

A stray tear trickled out of her squeezed eyelids.

"It helps to cry it out. Go on," he whispered.

How many times had she longed to feel the comfort of another while in her dark cell, grieving for the family she'd lost? How many nights had she cried, counting down the days and weeks and vowing not to let the darkness drag her under?

Until she'd met Dale, no one else had held her like this. No one else had urged her to release the emotions she'd held at bay for years.

The tears came in a torrent as she fisted her hands in his shirt and sobbed for all she'd lost. After a while, she finally raised her head and wiped at her face as he fetched a box of tissues from his private bathroom.

"I made a mess of your shirt. Sorry. Didn't mean to bawl on you." Keira took a wad of tissues and blew her nose.

"You had no one to help you, and you fought the demons on your own. How old were you? Eleven?"

"There was a man, that soldier. My memories of him are a little fuzzy, probably because the Centurions messed with my mind. I'd gone mad with grief when I realized Simon was dead, shifted into wolf and went to attack the man. But he refused to hurt me."

He went very still.

"Odd," she mused. "It was as if we shared a moment of connection. He said he refused to return evil for the evil that had been done to me. There was something good and courageous and noble about him. I let him escape, and went back to charge the demons. But they caught me and forced me to wear the slave armband."

Dale quietly regarded her, but this time, his gaze sharpened. "Tell me about your brother. What did he look like in wolf form?"

"About the size of a golden-retriever puppy, with a white streak down his muzzle."

He cupped her face with his large, square hands. "Keira, he's alive. And safe. Etienne, one of my SEALs, and a Draicon, snuck him back into the States."

Hope flared, then vanished like an extinguished candle. "No. It can't be him, I saw him lying in the ditch with the others...."

"He was playing dead, hiding, when we found him. I ordered Etienne to find him a new home." Gaze steady, Dale looked at her. "Keira, I was that U.S. soldier you attacked that day in the jungle. My memory of that moment was fuzzy, until you mentioned it. I think the demons' memory spell erased my recollection of first meeting you in wolf form."

She could not speak, for the rapid beating of her heart

and the hope surging inside her. Keira stared at Dale as he caressed her still-damp cheeks with his thumbs.

"Your little brother is alive. Etienne made sure to place him with a Draicon family. He checks up on him once a year and reports back to me how he's doing." Dale dropped a gentle kiss on the corner of her mouth. "He's living with a large Cajun family near New Orleans, and he's in college now, studying to be a physician."

If not for Dale, her brother would have died alone in the jungle. But his team had rescued Simon, who lived somewhere, safe, in the States.

Teamwork did have advantages.

"Thank you," she whispered.

Very gently, he pressed his mouth against hers. Then Dale drew back, his expression solemn. "I know you can't forgive me now, for throwing you out of my house and my protection. I hope one day, perhaps, you can."

He sighed deeply. "I accused you of breaking my trust, but in truth, I broke yours. You trusted that I'd understand and I would be there for you. I wasn't."

An odd pulling tingled in her stomach. She stared at him as he cupped her cheek, trailing a thumb lazily over her skin.

"Dale?"

"Hmm?"

"Something's wrong. I feel…"

Jerking away, she stood up.

Panic filled her as the tingling grew stronger. Suddenly an invisible hand lifted her into the air, leaving her feet dangling.

"Help me," she whispered.

Then the invisible hand picked her up, shook her like a rag doll and slammed her against the opposite wall.

Just as quickly, the violence ended. "It's gone," she

said as he raced over to where she lay. "I felt them, but now I don't." She closed her eyes and reached out to search for the demons.

"They're gone. Back to the bolt-hole, thousands of miles from here. I sense it. But there's a presence, an evil that's like a cloud…it's very strong now."

"They can't access the base."

Screams and shouts echoed down the hallway. Dale drew his weapon. "Stay here."

He left, slamming the door behind him.

Icy cold snaked down her spine. A perimeter of safeguards ringed the compound to keep out the strongest demons.

But many more lesser demons could slip beneath the invisible cloak of protection like gnats worming through mosquito netting.

Keira bolted out of the office and ran down the hallway, following the screams, running straight into the gymnasium.

Carnage greeted her.

She ran outside to the firestorm chamber and yanked the door open. Dale, in the antechamber, wrestled with a two-headed demon on the floor.

Rage boiled through her, pure fury. The demon drew back and hissed, its red slit of a mouth showing jagged teeth.

She drew on all her anger, all her fury at the years of imprisonment, losing her family…and pressed the button to release the streams of fire.

"Dale," she screamed. "Throw him toward the chamber. Let's burn the bastard."

As he did, a tongue of orange flame hit the demon. It looked startled, trying to beat the flames out with long, taloned fingers. The fire seared the creature, singeing it, the disgusting stench of burning meat filling the air as the demon writhed and screamed.

Finally it fell over into a smoking pile of muck.

Dale clasped her arms. "Are you okay?"

She nodded.

They went outside and surveyed the damage. Dallas jogged up to them, an ugly bruise on his left cheek and deep scratches on his arm.

"Bastards snuck in through security. We got 'em all. But we lost Rodriguez." Dallas's mouth thinned.

Shay and Dakota joined them. "Curt, there're a few MPs at the gate, wondering what the hell is going on and who let off the fireworks," Dakota said.

Dale's expression shuttered. "Get the wounded all treated. You two deal with the MPs, delay them until we get this cleaned up. If necessary, alter their memories, but only as a last resort."

As he bandaged her burn in the infirmary, Keira felt the weight of Dale's grief and guilt, as well as her own, over the loss of his staff.

"I believed the base was safe from a demon attack." Dale's jaw tensed. "Until we find and seal that demon bolt-hole, there will be more attacks."

"I did this," she whispered as he finished wrapping her arm in gauze. "If not for me, all of your staff would still be safe."

"It's the price we pay to keep civilians safe, Keira. We all know the risks we take."

But his words offered no comfort. People died because of her. How many more lives would it take until this all ended?

Hours later, exhausted and worn-out, she and Dale went home, accompanied by his men. The SEALs went downstairs to the basement to spend the night and discuss their next course of action. No one was returning home tonight, not until they had an extensive debriefing with Keira.

Dale sent Ensign Lees home, and opened the cartons of Chinese food Dallas had picked up on the way over. His SEAL team and Keira sat around the basement's dining table and ate, discussing their options.

"The demons who infiltrated the navy base knew exactly where they were going because of me." Keira's pretty mouth wobbled precariously. "The Centurions have released more demons from the bolt-hole. They're gathering tremendous power. Soon, they won't need to be corporeal. They'll have enough demons to command their own army."

"If that happens we're fucked."

Trust Dallas to cut to the chase.

Dale wanted to keep Keira safe and protected from the world. But for years, she'd been exposed to evil, and knew nuances of that evil. Even their best intel couldn't come close to the knowledge she possessed.

"Keira, you're the only one who can pinpoint the bolt-hole. Stephen found an approximate area, but only you were there when they came from the earth."

He hated forcing her to remember things she'd wanted to keep buried.

Gaze dull, she glanced up at him. "I only remember as a wolf. Scents, sounds, not sights. The memories in human form are too clouded. You can't pull them free. They're buried deep."

"Then she'll come with us. As wolf." Dakota folded his muscled arms.

Dale's protectiveness cranked to overdrive. "No. Too dangerous."

She sat up, face alight with interest. "He's right. In my human form, I'm useless, but my wolf can track the scents. The bolt-hole will carry the scent of the Centurions, and my wolf knows the scent of them instinctively. I could track them through a blinding sandstorm."

His guts knotted. "Keira, we're going to do a HALO drop from 30,000 feet at night and cut through the jungle. We're SEALs, trained to do this. You're not. And you're a civilian. Brass would find out, and cut the op before it even got started."

"She can jump as wolf. Strap a chute on her, let her track 'em," Shay advised.

His men looked at him expectantly. Waiting on his word. He was commander of the best damn team in the U.S. military and always bisected his personal life from his career. Now his personal life stared him in the face and collided with the mission's objective.

They needed her on this op. And every single bone in his body screamed against it, wanted to lock her in a room and keep anything from ever hurting her again.

He hated this. It made perfect sense to take her along as a wolf. Hell, how many drops had Dakota or Dallas done in wolf form? SEALs from other units and other soldiers thought they were highly trained dogs.

But Keira wasn't a SEAL. She'd never trained for a covert op, never even held a weapon.

She rested her hand on his tensed arm. "Dale, please. Let me do this. It's our only chance of catching them." Green gaze pleading, she looked desperate. "It's my only chance of being free, and finally atoning for the bad things my wolf was forced to do."

Dale clenched his fists. Nodded. "You need a crash course first on drops. You'll be with me, double jump, the whole way."

Chapter 23

She'd never jumped from an airplane at 30,000 feet before.

Especially not in wolf form.

Keira had tucked the slave armband into Dale's pack. It would act as a transmitter, honing in on the frequency of the Centurions if they were present. But nothing could pinpoint the bolt-hole.

Except her.

In wolf form, she sat quietly by Dale's feet while the soldiers, non-SEAL members who were unaware that this was a paranorm mission, accompanying them cast uneasy looks her way. She'd shifted, making her wolf form smaller, possible now that the demons weren't there to trigger the slave armband and command the beast. Still, she imagined the sight of a 150-pound black wolf, all fangs and claws, unnerved some.

This jump was HALO—high altitude, low opening—

to avoid radar detection and anyone who might look up and see the parachutes opening. They needed stealth for an insert.

With Dale, she'd free-fall for a long period before he deployed his chute.

With Dale, she needed to trust.

Dale reached down and caressed her fur. Green and black greasepaint streaked his face. In his camouflage and military gear, he looked dark and dangerous, someone she'd never want to tussle with in human form.

"Easy, girl. We'll be there soon."

"Big dog," one pimple-faced private remarked. "Sure hope she don't piss all over the equipment."

"She's a soldier, not a dog," Dale snapped. "Respect her as you would respect me."

Keira looked at the solider, her tail thumping against the floor as the private bent down and scratched behind her ears. Dale looked daggers at him. "Hands. Off. Her. Now."

Gulping, the private scurried back to the plane's front.

"Possessive much, eh, Curt," Shay teased.

"Curt's taste in ladies has gone to the dogs," Sully joked.

"The wolves, Sully. Don't insult the lady." Dallas grinned at her. "You just ignore him, Keira. Sully doesn't know a wolf from a squirrel."

The buzzer sounded. Dale signaled the men to don their O_2 masks and then put his own on, slipping a custom-fitting mask over her muzzle, along with goggles.

He strapped Keira on a special harness tied to him, ran a reassuring hand along her hindquarters. She wore goggles and body armor, specially fitted for her.

"I trust you," she'd told him before shifting. "I know you won't drop me."

"Never," he'd replied.

The SEALs lined up as the back hatch opened and the light turned yellow. Outfitted in helmet, oxygen mask and combat gear, she scarcely recognized the men, but all turned and gave her a big thumbs-up. Then the light buzzed green, and they all fell into the sky.

Wind whistled past her. Cold cut through her fur. But she was free, flying! Dale held her securely, then the snap of the chute yanked them upright.

In the starlit night, they floated to earth. Keira gazed down as Dale guided their chute. Never had she seen anything more beautiful.

If she died here tonight, she'd be grateful for this moment. Floating through the sky, secure against the man she loved.

After they landed and buried the parachutes, they set off through the forest. All the SEALs carried weapons, pointed outward as they slipped through the thick jungle. A sliver of moonlight spilled through the branches. With her large paws padding through the undergrowth, she worried about making a sound.

Behind her, the SEALs moved in silence. Once in a while, she felt the reassuring hand of Dale touching her flank.

Sealing the bolt-hole came first. They had to prevent more demons from escaping.

Ribbons of scent assaulted her nostrils, but none associated with nature and freshness. The smell was putrid, the stench of mold and staleness. Evil. The wind shifted east, and the smell grew stronger, along with a thin thread she knew well.

Old wine turned to vinegar and sulfur. The Centurions.

Ears back, she loped toward the smell, approaching a narrow, mud-strewn path dipping sharply down the mountain. Keira followed it and heard the sound of gurgling water.

The path opened up to a wide ravine, where a creek moved in sluggish ripples over rocks, flowing downward. Keira shifted back and clothed herself, the stench too terrible to bear in wolf form.

She squatted, peering at the thin ribbon of creek wending down the mountaintop. The SEALs gathered around.

Dark energy pulsed from granite boulders tumbling down the narrow ravine. Water trickled sluggishly over the boulders, forming a small gray pool below. The stench assaulted her nostrils; decay and rotting flesh, and a blackness no light could ever erase.

As Sully went to examine it, she grabbed his arm.

"Don't touch it. It's poison."

The SEAL tossed her a questioning look. Keira glanced around, found a small stick and tossed it into the pool.

Upon hitting the water, the dry wood shriveled and then dissolved.

"I believe we found the bolt-hole," she told Dale. "See that small black pulsing in the water? That's the entrance to the netherworld."

He gestured to Shay. "Seal it."

Shay shrugged out of his pack. A white glow surrounded him as he gathered his powers. Throwing out his hands, he directed currents of white light at the rock formation. But the oval of blackness remained as he continued the onslaught. Shay dropped his hands and gasped.

"Sorry, Curt. It's too much."

"I'll help you." Dale started to gather his powers.

"No." Keira shook her head, sensing a dark presence

close by. "If you drain your white energy, you'll have nothing left to fight the demons. They're nearby."

His mouth twisted, eyes luminous in the moonlight. "If I don't seal it now, more demons will leave. Can't risk it. Stand back."

Shay began the chant, a low, melodious sound as Dale stood and a white glow surrounded him, silver sparks leaping into the air. A cool wind whipped strands of his silky hair as he closed his eyes. Dale stretched out his arms and directed currents of pure blue-white energy at the bolt-hole, his chants joining Shay's.

Water sizzled as the power stream hit the boulders, drying up, the oval of blackness finally shrinking and then disappearing all together. Gasping, Dale dropped his arms, the glow surrounding him vanishing.

He bent over, dragging in deep breaths. "Give me a minute," he muttered.

Sounds of gunfire cut through the night. Dale straightened. "Head for the hillside. High ground. Safer there, until we can assess what the hell is going on."

They climbed the hillside to a tree-lined plateau and sat on the rocky ground in a tall clump of grasses. Intermittent sounds of small arms being fired continued, the acrid stench of sulfur accompanying each volley of gunfire.

"I'm not taking chances with you," Dale said to her.

Keira didn't answer. She dug into his pack and withdrew a granola bar. Moonlight glinted off the slave bracelet as she fished one out for him, as well.

Palming the bracelet, she began to eat the granola bar in tiny bites. "Coming back here brings back a flood of memories."

Dale checked his weapon. "Was the fighting happening while you were living here?"

"We lived further south, closer to the village. There were stories of a haunted forest, of ghosts...."

She broke off in midsentence, staring at the two men approaching each other a few yards away. Dale shoved her downward and pointed his weapon.

But the newcomers showed no interest in anything but each other. The two soldiers raised their rifles and pointed them at each other. Moonlight rippled along their bent, slumped bodies.

Here, the war had not ended. Here, it continued, a curtain into a bloodied past. Dale watched as the two soldiers fired.

The crackle of gunfire split the air. Yet it sounded muffled, as if both men fired with suppressors.

Bullets met their targets. Both men dropped down, their weapons clattering to the rocks.

Dale held up a hand for his men to wait.

A minute later, the two soldiers stood, retrieved their weapons and retreated back down the hillside on opposite sides.

He stared at the dark stains on the ground, blood black beneath the full moon. "They're fighting a war that's been long over."

"Those men are dead," Keira said quietly. "They died a long time ago, and now they're condemned to repeat the same violence, again and again. They're victims to the Centurions, just like I was."

Dale turned to his men. "Sully, I need recon. Now. Find out what you can, what we're up against."

A few minutes later, Sully returned with a dark-haired prisoner dressed in a tattered and bloodstained olive-green uniform. The man had strong features, his well-defined cheekbones hinting of a Mayan ancestry, but his dark eyes were empty.

A zombie, compelled to do the Centurions' bidding.

Sully lowered his weapon and looked at Dale. "This is Juan. He approached me while I was doing recon on the hillside and begged to come with me."

"Who are you?" Dale asked.

"Tell them what you told me," Sully ordered.

The man sat down on the ground and began to share his story.

Juan had once he fought for the Contras. Now, he fought under compulsion of the demons.

"The Centurions killed us and our spirits became trapped, condemned to do their bidding. When the Centurions return and command us to fight, we must pick up arms again and repeat the battle. We're condemned to fight and keep fighting, without purpose or cause, only because we are slaves to the demons. We can never rest. We can never cease. And soon, there will be more of us."

"More of you?" Dale questioned.

"The Centurions have brought Necromancers from the netherworld, to summon the dead to walk the earth."

Keira's breath hitched.

Panic entered Juan's gaze. "I must go. They are calling me."

Moving as if in enthralled, the man returned down the hillside.

"We have to get out of here, find the demons." Dale scanned the area and then signaled to his men. "Get ready to move out. Sully, you remain here with her. First sign of trouble, teleport her out of here."

"No," Keira said slowly.

"The hell you say." He released a deep sigh. "One thing for you to find the source as a wolf, another to remain in this hellhole."

"It's too late." She pointed at the far side of the plateau, where a line of creatures faced them.

They didn't have to worry about finding the demons. Because the demons had found them first.

Chapter 24

Fanged creatures, with claws as sharp as dinner knives, advanced toward their group. Around them floated spectral beings—the Centurions. Keira realized they had allowed themselves to become ghosts, knowing the SEALs were out to kill them.

Dale pushed her down.

"Stay here and stay down," he snapped, then gestured to his men to advance.

Partly hidden by the brush, she watched the ensuing fight.

Skulls and crossbones. The images flooded her mind as Dale fought, throwing bolt after bolt of power. The Centurions danced away, taunting him. Ghosts flew over, around, insubstantial as mist.

One bolt sailed through a demon and slammed into a tree, incinerating it.

Dale was weakening, expending all his energy.

As he and his team fought, their courage unwavering, she knew what would happen. The Centurions had an army of demons to command, an army Dale would never allow beyond these borders. He would die first.

Dale continued to send bolts of white energy at the Centurions, but deprived of form, they laughed as they dodged the blows.

And then the three forms of mist took shape near the cluster of trees.

Necromancers. Demons who could summon the spirits of the dead and control them. With slits for eyes, flat nostrils and ugly slashes for mouths, their smooth, bald heads sported sharp spikes and they stood more than seven feet tall. Three of them, all waving wands of pure wormwood.

This was the pact the Centurions had made—to summon the dead and force them to do their bidding.

Dry-mouthed, Keira stared at the evil ones. On a par with pyro demons, they could raise armies of living corpses, commanding them to kill, threatening all in their path.

Dale and his SEALs could not fight them. Clouds of evil clung to them, their darkness too great to fight with magick powers.

But the team could kill the Centurions once those demons took form. Her blood, mixed with theirs, might do it. Keira remembered the spell she'd heard them chanting back in the warehouse.

"Sully, give me your blade!" she screamed.

The SEAL tossed her his KA-BAR knife. She slashed her wrist and ran into the fray, targeting the Centurions, spraying droplets of her demon-laced blood at the Centurions. As the blood hit the ghost shapes, she chanted the spell. Suddenly the Centurions materialized into their human forms.

Dale stopped his attack. "They're human. Kill them," he ordered.

Sully dematerialized near one Centurion, the demon's corpulent form quivering in real fear. Keira winced and turned her head as Sully reached out and wrapped his hands around the Centurion's neck. A sickening crack sounded.

As each demon dropped down, Dale and Shay chanted a vanquishing spell. One by one the demons died under the hands of the SEALs. But for Antony, the largest and strongest. Dale ran after him, his knife at the ready. But Antony raised his hands and chanted in a loud voice ringing over the glade.

Horror pulsed through her as the Necromancers emerged from the trees. Dale glanced their way, and that small pause was enough to give Antony time to slip the blade in his hands and thrust it at Dale. Dale dodged, but the blade sank into his shoulder. He grimaced and aimed his knife at Antony, and did not miss. Black blood spurted.

He dug Antony's knife out from his shoulder and cupped the wound. "Report," he said wearily.

"All dead, sir. The Contra and Sandinista armies are gone, as well."

"Keira!" Dale turned, worry riddling his face. Blood streamed from his wounded shoulder. "You okay?"

"They're coming," she whispered. "Oh, gods, they're coming. You can't kill them, they're too strong. There's too much darkness inside them."

The Necromancers advanced, creeping toward Dale. He had no white light left to fight them, expending it all to seal the bolt-hole and in the fight against the Centurions. With wild hope, she glanced upward, but the night sky was clear, no storm clouds near for him to draw more power.

He would die here. And then become a living slave of the Necromancers, a slave as she had been to the Centurions.

She touched the slave armband on her right arm. It glowed with light, a beacon in the inky blackness. Never use it around evil, Renegade had warned. *It might compel you to do something noble and totally reckless, like suction demon souls.*

Incantations… She knew the exact one. The Necromancers advanced. Shay directed beams of power, but the stream was too thin, too weak.

"Get out of here," Dale ordered. "Take Keira and go."

"Curt," Dakota said, his expression tight. "We won't leave you."

"That's an order." Dale drew his blade, stained with blood blackened in the moonlight. "I'm a Primary Mage. I'll handle them."

Her eyes wet, Keira tossed off Renegade's grip and tore off, facing the Necromancers. *"Malorum, malorum, malorum,"* she began to chant.

Dale turned. "No," he screamed. "Keira, don't do it."

"Veniat in me," she continued.

The white quartz on the slave armband began to glow. Keira drew in a deep breath and began to siphon the darkness inside the Necromancers, drawing on their evil power, taking it inside her. Filling her soul with their blackness, watching as a thick black mist streamed out of the Necromancers, floating in the air toward her. The dark power gathered until it became a large, whirling ball.

Her terrified gaze met Dale's. "I'm sorry. I love you."

And then with a tremendous breath, she inhaled the

darkness, feeling it whoosh inside her. The foulness of dark power, the stench of evil, filled her spirit, dimming the last bit of white light inside her, extinguishing it until it went out.

And then she felt nothing.

Summoning all his remaining strength, Dale killed the Necromancers with a last bit of white energy. They burst apart, showering the ground with black dust.

Burst apart, because there was nothing left inside them. No power. Keira had siphoned it all.

Sully wiped his forehead with a sleeve. "Last of them, sir. Bolt-hole's sealed."

Renegade shifted back into human form and tore into his pack, ripping open packets of gauze. He ripped open Dale's sleeve and began dressing the wound. But Dale's sight centered on Keira, weaving listlessly on her feet like one of the armies of the dead.

Light had vanished from her beautiful eyes. She said nothing, only stared ahead.

As if she were dead to the world...

One week after their return from Nicaragua, Dale paced his kitchen. Cassandra sat at the table, her gaze sympathetic. Catatonic, Keira sat at the table, as well. The deep scars on her back had healed the moment the Centurions died.

But she seemed dead as well, her empty eyes staring into space. He dropped beside her, chafing her icy hands.

She did not move.

"I called Etienne, and he tracked down your brother. He's on his way, Keira. Your little brother, the one you sacrificed yourself to save."

Still, she remained motionless, staring ahead.

Nothing worked. He'd hired a nurse to care for her, but though Keira remained obedient, performing all the normal functions, such as eating, she did not talk.

"Help her," he begged Cassandra. "Please. She's been like this since taking the darkness inside her."

"I can perform a white-light ritual, but the darkness will remain. The only solution is white-light cleansing and erasure of all her memories of this time." The Mystic Witch looked at him. "It will erase all her memories of all that happened before she met you. She will not remember you."

Stricken, he stared at Keira. "Nothing of me? I'll be a stranger."

"Nothing of you or your time together."

"What if I see her again? Will that trigger memories?"

"She may not react favorably, and avoid you," Cassandra warned.

Dale's insides squeezed. He stroked a gentle finger over Keira's cold, cold hands. "But she will be healed?"

"Yes. And she will remember her little brother. She needs time, Dale, time to heal from her terrible experiences."

Closing his eyes, he remembered all the good times they'd shared, the tender lovemaking, how he felt when he'd found his missing half.

And now, he would lose her.

Too late he'd realized how he'd been married more to the navy than his first wife. He'd expected her to make sacrifices and understand his rigid code of honor. And now he faced an even greater loss.

Kathy had been his wife, but Keira was his heart. He must let her go.

"Do it." Dale raised Keira's hand to his lips and kissed

it, barely able to speak for the thick lump clogging his throat.

"I will see to her welfare. She will be safe," Cassandra promised.

Dale stood and dropped a kiss on Keira's unmoving mouth, feeling her lips cold and unresponsive beneath the subtle pressure of his.

He bid goodbye at the door a few moments later, watching them back Cassandra's car out of his long driveway.

Then he watched them drive away. As the tears finally sprang to his eyes and rolled down his cheeks, he did not wipe them away.

Chapter 25

Six months later

After locking Runes and Tunes for the night, Keira got into her little car and headed for the beach.

Working at Cassandra Sullivan's store had been the best thing that ever happened to her, she thought. The kind Mystic Witch had given her a job when Keira's brother arrived, had helped her find an apartment.

Still, something felt missing.

Lately, she'd been compelled to walk the sands, shoes in hand, and gaze up at the stars. And more often, she'd been visiting the beach frequented by navy personnel. Each time she saw a man in uniform, her heart gave an absurd twist.

She was happy. Simon was in grad school at Virginia Tech and doing well. Her salary paid for a small two-bedroom apartment. After years of slavery to the Centurions, she was finally freed. She had no memory of being freed by the demons, only recalled seeing Simon when he arrived. Her little brother was alive and doing well.

When she asked Cassandra what happened, the Mystic Witch hesitated and told her that a courageous Mage had vanquished the evil.

Cassandra said eventually she'd get her memories back. Perhaps.

Keira sat on the sand and watched the surf lick the shore, listening to the crash of waves. Nearby, a tall man walked a large gray dog. The dog resembled a wolf. Silly. No wolves were on Virginia Beach.

Suddenly the dog broke free of the leash and bounded toward her. It knocked her over, licking her face. Laughing, she fended it off and then scratched the beast behind its ears. The dog grinned at her.

"Shay! Stop it. Get off the lady, now!"

The owner jogged up and grabbed the dog's collar, pulling him away.

"I'm sorry," the man apologized. "He's a good dog, but seldom listens to orders."

The wolf/dog seemed to give the man a wounded look.

"It's all right. I like dogs." She gave the dog a final pat.

"I hope he didn't scare you. I was jogging on the beach and he managed to get away from me." The man grinned, and it softened his severe features. "Though you don't look like the type to scare easily. Mind if I sit down?"

Keira considered. "Only if you promise you won't try licking me to death like Cujo here."

An odd look entered his gaze and then he gave a small smile. "Not until we're good friends."

She stole a look. He had short, dark hair, silvered at the temples, and incredible gray eyes. His body was toned with hard muscle. He looked like a man who made a living doing physical work.

"You work at the base," she said suddenly. "I've seen you on this beach before, and once when you were in uniform. You're a lieutenant commander, right?"

Keira didn't know how she knew that, but deep inside, she did.

"Commander. I received a promotion last month." Gray eyes twinkled as he tilted his head. "And you are...?"

She stuck out a palm, and he took it, his hand large and square and warm. An odd jolt of familiarity hit her. "Keira Solomon. I live not far from here."

"Dale Curtis."

He released her hand, slowly, though she had the feeling he wanted to keep holding it. Why did this man seem so...familiar? She didn't know any navy officers.

Compelled to touch him, she placed a hand over his heart. "You wear something. Here. A badge of honor, a pin... It scarred you when they pounded it into your chest during an initiation...."

Where did that come from?

"Yes. We call it a Budweiser. I'm a navy SEAL." His gray gaze held hers captive, searing, penetrating.

Keira dropped her hand, feeling embarrassed. "I apologize. I'm precognitive...and it slips away from me. I work in a New Age shop and Cassandra, my boss, says I'm very aware of others and their pain."

But he looked interested and began asking questions about her visions and her work, and he seemed so easy and comfortable to talk with, she lost track of the time. The sun began setting over the ocean, streaking the blue sky with rose and gold.

He glanced at his watch. "Getting late. I'm starved.

Say, I was going to grab some dinner before heading home. Want to join me?"

"What about your dog?"

Dale glanced at the dog, its ears pricked forward.

"There's a place on the boardwalk where we can eat outside. They won't mind him."

"Sure. I'd like that. Only if it's steak, and we split the bill."

He grinned. "Deal."

Dinner turned out to be a fun night, spent talking for two hours. He asked her out for the next night. And the next.

Every night for the next two weeks, Commander Dale Curtis arrived at her apartment and took her out. They ate at various restaurants or sometimes had a picnic on the beach. Keira discovered he was divorced, no children, and liked to play the piano.

"Once I made no time for it, but someone I knew convinced me I needed balance in my life," he told her.

One Sunday he took her to a spot on the boardwalk and treated her to a special thermos of hazelnut coffee he'd brought along in the truck.

"My favorite." Keira sighed with pleasure as she sipped the brew. "How did you know?"

A wry smile touched his full mouth. "Educated guess."

She liked this man with his quiet manner, assurance and confidence. He treated her like a lady, yet at times, she saw a sadness in his eyes and wished she could erase it.

And then he'd kiss her, and make her forget all else.

After a month, when he still hadn't done more, she began to wonder if there were something wrong with her. Or him.

So when he came to pick her up to take her out for dancing, she bluntly asked him. "What's wrong with me?"

Dressed in a dark gray suit, looking distinguished and handsome, he gave her a quizzical look. "Nothing. You look lovely in that dress."

"I'm not asking if I look too fat," she blurted out. "I want to know why you haven't done anything more than kiss me. We've been seeing each other for almost two months. I've met a couple of your friends, been to your house, even. But you…don't seem interested in me that way."

Heat suffused her. "You know. Why haven't we had sex?"

Dale pushed a lock of hair behind her ear. The tender gesture echoed in her mind and seemed oddly familiar. "Making love. With you, Keira, it would be making love. And I don't want to pressure you. I cherish our time together, cherish you too much to rush you into anything."

For an answer, she reached up and kissed him. "Guess what? I'm ready for a little pressure, big guy."

Something dark and sensual flickered in his gaze. "Tonight, then. After the club."

Much as she loved to dance, and the club he brought her to was a favorite, where they played lots of slow dances, Keira itched with impatience.

He drove to his house and parked in the driveway. As the ticking engine cooled, his hands tightened on the steering wheel.

"I want to hoist you over my shoulder, carry you inside and go all caveman on you," he said quietly. "But you deserve more than that. I can't promise I won't lose control, Keira, because I want you so badly it's taking all my strength not to take you right here. But I will promise I'll try to make tonight special."

When they got inside and he locked the door, she did not hesitate, but slid her arms around his waist and kissed him deeply.

They barely made it upstairs to his bedroom. Stripping off their clothing, kicking off their shoes. Arms entwined around each other, they fell on the bed, kissing. His tongue stroked, deep and sure, sparking a distant tug of remembrance. The man kissed as if he knew exactly how she liked it.

Heat flared in his eyes as he lifted his head. "So long," he said thickly. "I've waited and watched and wanted you for so long."

Dale's intensity frightened her a little, but then he began to kiss her softly, showering her with tiny, hot kisses that made her squirm and ache to draw closer. She clung to him, arching as he entered her in a hard thrust.

"Look at me, Keira," he said softly. "See only me."

Her gaze met his and she saw passion, tenderness, mixed with stark male possessiveness. And something else. Keira looked up into her lover's face and saw a reflection of herself.

He made love to her with exquisite tenderness, as they wrapped around each other in a desperate attempt to become one. Dale held nothing back. Every raw emotion was clearly expressed, from awed wonder to heated desire.

They came together in a blinding explosion of heat. For a long moment he lay atop her, gasping as she pulled him closer, then he rolled off. Keira lay on the bed, staring at the ceiling, feeling oddly shattered and yet overjoyed, as if he'd made love not just with his body, but with his heart. The intimacy they shared left her sated at last, filling the empty spot always inside her these past few months.

Dale drew his hands down her body, as if enjoying the feel of silky, supple flesh beneath the roughness of his calloused palms. Keira turned over and gazed into his eyes, heavy-lidded with satisfaction.

Suddenly memories rushed back in a flood, the wave cresting over her and crashing down. Dale Curtis. The courageous navy SEAL commander who'd given her back her life, had sacrificed everything to save her.

"Dale," she whispered. "Oh gods, Dale, it's you. I remember. Everything."

His expression eased into pure relief. "Good."

"You're here," she said, beginning to cry.

He smiled and stroked her hair, then kissed away her tears. "I never went away, sweetheart. Ever."

"There she is, sir."

The helo pilot spoke into his mouthpiece. Ears covered in soft gel headphones, Dale nodded and gazed at the sand. They'd swept this perimeter twice, but even hovering, it was hard to pinpoint a dark-haired woman with a jaunt to her step strolling on the sand.

She always enjoyed an afternoon stroll on the beach. After last night, he wasted no time. Keira remembered.

She remembered everything. And he wasn't risking losing her again.

"I'll circle around, give the guys a chance to clear an area for landing."

Dale clapped a hand on his shoulder. "Thanks. Owe you one."

"No, sir, we owe you. Least we can do."

He stared at the beach, and felt in his pocket for the

small box he'd kept waiting in a top chest drawer for seven long months. Pulse spiking, he waited as the pilot circled around, searching for a clear space to land.

Keira walked barefoot on the sand, absorbed in thought. Dale Curtis was honorable, brave and a good man. Making love with him last night had brought all her memories soaring to the surface.

Along with them, incredible joy.

She wanted this man in her life, and despaired of ever losing him again. But she wasn't certain if he wanted her equally. So much had passed between them.

I'm the demon wolf who tortured him.

And you're the demon wolf who saved him, the same little voice reminded her. *He's the best thing that ever happened to you.*

A couple playing in the surf stopped and pointed overhead. She glanced at the sky.

A helicopter whirled overhead. Several uniformed navy personnel were roping off the beach, waylaying bystanders. An MP jogged up to her, his expression serious.

"What's going on?" she asked.

"Official navy business, miss. Please wait here."

Awe filled her. The uniformed men, expressions serious, functioned like a unit. The power of navy teamwork, she thought, her heart beating faster.

She watched the helo hover and descend. Keira removed her sunglasses and peered at the chopper's window. A man clad in a navy's officer's uniform sat in the copilot's seat.

"Who is he?" she asked the hovering MP.

"Some VIP. Highly decorated naval officer."

"He must be very important for all this fuss."

The chubby-faced MP grinned. "Oh, he is. His men, they'd do anything for him."

Sand stirred at the chopper's blades, sweeping in a wide arc, as the helicopter landed several yards away. The side door slid open and a uniformed naval officer leaped out, jogging on the sand straight toward her.

He wore a dress uniform, with gold bars wreathing the long blue sleeves. A SEAL pendant on his breast winked in the sunlight.

Her heart beat faster.

And then suddenly the serious-looking MP's cheeks became hollowed, his bone structure changed…shifted.

Into the grinning, handsome face of Chief Petty Officer Sam "Shay" Shaymore.

"Please stay here. Like I said, very important navy business."

A few feet away, the uniformed officer stopped and fished something out of a trouser pocket. Lt. Commander Dale Curtis dropped to one knee on the wet sand and held out a small blue velvet box. Sunlight sparkled off the diamond ring resting inside.

"Keira Solomon, will you do me the extreme honor of becoming my wife?"

Tears blurred her vision. Keira nodded. Dale stood, slid the ring on her finger. His mouth was warm and firm as he kissed her. When he drew back, he gently thumbed a tear off one cheek.

She glanced around and heard cheers and several shouts of "Hooyah!" and saw Dale's entire SEAL Phoenix Force standing guard, grins splitting their faces.

"You arranged all this?" she asked him, sliding her arms around his neck.

"They volunteered. It's a team effort," he murmured. "From this moment on, you're the cocommander of the most important team in my life. Us."

* * * * *

HARLEQUIN®

NOCTURNE™

Bree Meadows is on the run. After witnessing the murder of her boss and friend, she flees with her young son. But the bad guys are in hot pursuit. Dropped in the middle of nowhere amid a torrential thunderstorm, things look pretty grim. To make matters worse, her son is in desperate need of medical attention.

Mark Winspear has been alone for too long. When the vampire senses a gorgeous female nearby, his instinct is to attack. Luckily his urge to protect is stronger. The doctor has history with the same men who are after Bree—and he's ready to avenge. As they set off to save the boy, they discover an attraction that might save them both—if they're lucky.

POSSESSED BY AN IMMORTAL

by

SHARON ASHWOOD

**Available June 2014,
wherever Harlequin® Nocturne™
books and ebooks are sold.**

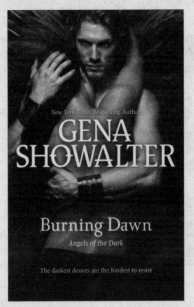

New York Times Bestselling Author

HEATHER GRAHAM

Enter a place of history, secrets... and witchcraft, with the next chapter in the *Krewe of Hunters* series.

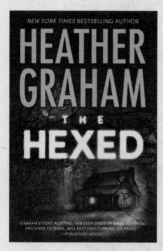

Devin Lyle has returned to the Salem area, but her timing couldn't be worse. Soon after moving into the eighteenth-century cabin she inherited from her "crazy" great-aunt Mina—who spoke to the dead—a woman was murdered nearby.

Craig "Rocky" Rockwell is new to the Krewe of Hunters, the FBI's team of paranormal investigators. He never got over finding a friend dead in the woods. Now another body's been found there, not far from Devin's home. And she's been led to a third body—by…a ghost?

Devin's discovery draws them both into Salem's rich and disturbing history. And as the danger mounts, she and Rocky begin to fall for each other. But the two of them need to learn the truth, and quickly—or Devin's might be the next body in the woods….

Available July 29, wherever books are sold!

Be sure to connect with us at:

Harlequin.com/Newsletters
Facebook.com/HarlequinBooks
Twitter.com/HarlequinBooks

MHG1637